IRELAND'S DESPAIR

1847

Rob Collins

BookLocker

Copyright © 2019 Rob Collins

ISBN: 978-1-64438-510-4

Published by BookLocker.com, Inc., St. Petersburg, Florida.

Printed on acid-free paper.

The characters and events in this book are fictitious. Any similarity to real persons, living or dead, is coincidental and not intended by the author.

BookLocker.com, Inc.
2019

First Edition

Library of Congress Cataloging in Publication Data
Collins, Rob
Ireland's Despair by Rob Collins
YOUNG ADULT FICTION / Historical / General | YOUNG
ADULT FICTION / General | YOUNG ADULT
NONFICTION / History / General
Library of Congress Control Number: 2019900457

DEDICATION

Dedicated to all aspiring writers. Don't give up, discover the passion. George Bernard Shaw failed many times before his talent was recognized.

Nassau Senior, English lawyer and economist is reported to have remarked about the Irish Famine: It would not kill more than one million people and that would scarcely be enough to do any good. (Gallagher, Thomas, Paddy's Lament, Harcourt Brace and Co., New York, London)

THE CLAN O' BRANIGAN

Flat granite polished smooth from hundreds of years of rain served the women of the village for more than one purpose. When the harvest was good and rent paid, granite slabs the size of a large table top became the "dancing stones" where the clan would gather in the evening. Near nightfall, at the edge of the fast -flowing stream they listened to tall tales, embellished of course, to the delight of all who listened, causing laughter and drawing a wink and a grin from the storyteller. They danced, and they drank. Dirty children splashed in the water saving their mothers the effort. They played games and just before the sandman caused small fists to rub their eye's they gathered around the clan storyteller to become captivated by the magical mysteries he told. On this day, the clan woman's aching knees would not allow her a bit of pleasure that evening, nor' a moment free to speak to the other women she paused to watch nearby. Like her, they toiled, bent over, scrubbing and rinsing. Tonight, there would be no dancing to the tin whistle and the bodhran for the clan woman Noreen. Now an O' Branigan, the lines on her face and forehead told of her regret, having married a man of the clan at an age of ten and five, or so her age she was told. Now, she was only 25. Gray streaks began to appear in her hair. Her man had turned away from being a loving husband, and she blamed the drink he laughingly referred to as the "water of life." Thoughts of her mistakes in life interrupted her task at hand. She pulled the wicker basket close, and with a sigh returned to the toil of reality to wet the children's clothing in the stream. Rubbing the cloth with the bar of soap and then a rinse, she stretched them with hands that hurried out the water. The sun would dry the clothing on the smooth expanse of level granite nearby. Tedious, was the English word for the work as described to her by the clan scholar. He encouraged and tried to teach the strange language with little success. She shook her hands. The stream's cold water turned them the color of the red sky in the morning. Weekly washing was necessary but took her away from her children who frolicked with the neighboring clan children, and they were unsupervised. She was not sure her husband, who was twice her age, would watch them or even be in the village when she returned. Two other married men of the clan, Willy Knock was the main instigator often coerced him to visit the new settlement and the pub hastily constructed at the crossroads a short mile away. Little money remained, but they always seemed to have the price of a pint, or two, or three. The O' Branigan men were out of work, but the potatoes had been planted, and then they waited.

Idleness led to heated discussions about religion, politics, and women. Fights broke out. Wives of the combatants would not speak to each other for days. Incidents of hair pulling and finger pointing took place much to the delight of the men observing the altercations. With arms around each-other's shoulders, two men of the clan watched their wives push, shove, point, and scream expletives. They laughingly cheered the combatants on until one of the women was pushed into the water. The victorious one did not escape unscathed her torn dress revealed an ample breast as she ran for the safety of her cottage. Later in the evening with all trespasses cast aside, they gathered around the fire next to the water gurgling over the stones, and the drum sounded. The dancing began. A bottle or two, hidden until found by a clan woman, was reluctantly produced to celebrate the warmth of the evening, and later when Mulcahy winked at Declan Murphy's wife, another fight ended the evening.

Food shortages were sure to occur before the next crop was ready. Potatoes, their main food source, would run out during the "meal months" when grain was made available at a high price. It became imperative that work programs be reinstated before the "anxious time" when potato fields were inspected daily. On their knees they prayed the vileness that destroyed past crops would not return. Anxious men waited for word the hiring had resumed, but others had given up hope. Road construction projects were the butt of many jokes as some roads ended at the edge of a cliff. The Irish men didn't care because it put them to work in return for food for the family and in some cases, a pittance, but those work details had been cancelled at the beginning of the month. Almost finished with her weekly drudgery, she would return to retrieve the dried clothing at the end of the day. The back of her hand cleared away drops of moisture from her forehead as

the faint sound of a broken rat-a-tat drum beat drew
her eyes to the hills in the far distance. Her knees and
back ached, but she was happy to be able to get to her
feet unaided, to stand upright with her hands on her
hips. She bent backwards, twisting and stretching while
her eyes caught the movement of two columns of men
side by side in the far distance. Mounted riders were
on either side of the militia who were on foot. They
marched the down slope, soon to disappear behind the
next knock (hill). Moments later the columns
reappeared flanked by the mounted riders who often
turned their steed to monitor the progress of the men
on foot. The wind brought faint sounds to her ears
reminding her of a parade she once observed when the
British, in a show of strength, marched through Carlow
town. The riders and those walking were headed in her
direction, and behind her, the clan O' Branigan, her
village. She immediately recognized the need for haste,
hurrying to spread the remainder of the washed
clothing on the flat rocks. Finished, she turned for one
last look before picking up her skirts and heading back
up the winding boreen (path) between the brambles
and blackthorn. If the marchers had not been noticed,
the cottagers would be urged to hide the children. She
was fearful. Her anxious return to the settlement
turned into a stumbling half run-walk until she reached
the outskirts of the village. What activity she observed
made her realize the marchers had been spotted.
Several of the families were in the process of moving
their children to areas remote from the huts and
cottages. Frantic mothers carried naked babies in their

arms. Others, she noted, did not attempt to hide the children.

"Surely, they would not harm the children," Mulcahy said to her as she passed him by on the way to her own humble abode. "True or not, you have heard the stories," she said in passing, not wanting to dally in the company of a polemic arguer who liked to pontificate after downing too many pints. "Aye, I have heard the stories wife of Danny O," he said as she paused, turning to look back at him. "You have no faith in our God," he continued. The woman Noreen continued to walk, she thought for a moment, but said nothing before she turned around and broke into a skirt-lifting run to her hut.

EVICTION

With a "whoosh," and then a snapping crack, the whip whistled through the air. The horse whinnied in protest when the sting of the lash raked his hindquarters. The chestnut strained against the harness to escape more pain from the lash. His teeth were bared in anger and hurt. Forelegs were raised pawing. His attempt to escape the stinging snake tore holes in the stagnant air. The rope snapped taunt. The uniformed man with the shiny, but muddy black boots, rewound the whip. Protesting groans were heard from the beam tightly tied by the rope stretched taunt to tear the thatched roof from the first of the village cottages. The militia workers, some of them reluctant, were urged on by the proper British officer who shouted orders. He wielded the whip repeatedly in the direction of the terrified horse. The snap of the whip was enough incentive for the chestnut. He lunged forward again and again. A wife and children knelt before the Brit pleading with him not to destroy their home. They might have thought had the devil himself come up from the depths of hell to wreak this horrible injustice? To no avail, their pleading laments went unheard by the demon, resplendent in his red tunic. The children cried clinging to their mother. Two militiamen held the arms of the man forced to watch his home being destroyed. With a cracking sound, followed by a protesting groan, and then another scream from the horse, the roof of the cottage collapsed into the interior of the stone walled cottage. The woman screamed, and her children cried as brother hugged sister. Enraged, the owner of the cottage used his fists, elbows and knees to fight his way from the grip of his captors. He rushed toward the British officer with his fists clenched screaming his outrage, but never had the chance to reach him. A shot rang out. The cottier father of five dropped to the ground as his wife and children fought their way from the clutches of those who tried to restrain them. With tears in their eyes, his family squeezed his hands, but his hands relaxed their grip, and they watched as he took his last smoke-filled breath, and then he died. Acrid clouds from the fired thatch caused the children to cough as they knelt sobbing over their murdered father. The militia had moved on to the next cottage, but they were confronted by the owner who stood defiantly at the half door with a pitchfork in his hands. The militiamen who approached were forced to back off while two of them who carried lit torches walked to the back of the cottage. Seeing the danger, the man with the pitchfork knew what it meant. He left his defense of the half door while he shouted his objection. His scream of rage was heard by the torch bearers who saw him, his pitchfork pointed in their direction. They both turned away, dropping their torches that sizzled in the damp grass. Frantically, they ran to avoid being impaled on the tines of a contaminated barnyard tool. Faced without resistance, entrance to the cottage was now available as other militia entered. Sounds of a struggle ensued. A woman's screams were heard. The newly enlisted Irish were numb to what they saw and heard.

The militia men emerged dragging a protesting woman out of the cottage. She fought unsuccessfully as two hands pulled her out by her hair. She stumbled and fell into the grass and was dragged some distance from the cottage. Not gently, a rope was tied around her neck. Her hands were bound behind her back, and the shiny black boot of the British commander pressed the breasts of the Irish woman into the wet of the green. Her husband, the man with the pitchfork, was relieved of his weapon, restrained and forced to watch. Whispered comments began among the militia who were not involved in the destruction. An exordium of protest hung like an ominous storm cloud about to burst over the village. Sour faces who watched the inhumane treatment of the woman were downtrodden Irish. Formerly, they all were paupers, hungry and poor cottier farmers and fishermen. Most of them joined the militia to survive. They were without work, and the food they depended on had been destroyed. Their allegiance did not change. They were Irishmen, and half of them had never experienced an enforced eviction. They watched as a ladder was propped against the roof. One militiaman climbed to the apex of the roof with an axe and a rope wrapped around his waist. Straddling the main beam, he lifted the axe to clear a foot of thatch away from each side of the beam. Minutes later, he could see into the dimly lit interior of the cottage. The glow of the turf fire brought the pleasant aroma to his nostrils as he bent down to wrap the rope around the beam. Light from the oil lamps attracted his eyes to reveal a sparsely furnished interior with a thick mat covering the smooth dirt floor. A double knot finished his work as he made his way down to the ladder and then to the ground. The rope snapped to taunt. Groans were heard from the protesting beam being dislodged. Militia who were Irish watched as the home of what might have been a neighbor, a friend or a brother was collapsed into the interior of the cottage. The end of the beam smashed the rough-hewn plank table and destroyed a section of the stone wall. A cloud of smoke rose almost immediately as the dry thatch contacted the smoldering turf fire in the hearth. Shockwaves resulted in murmurs and arm-waving discussion between several Irish militiamen. Animosity did exist between the Irish and the minority English of the militia who raised a hand, swearing allegiance to the Queen. However, the Irish were compensated, and forced to divorce themselves from their Irish neighbors and friends. Activity increased along the row of cottages placed close together, to the chagrin of many landlords who preferred the Irish build their huts or cottages yards and yards away from each other. Landlords accused the Irish of being unproductive when they stopped to greet the next-door neighbor rather than working their farm.

A second cottage was partially destroyed with a battering ram device, and a third had the rope tied to the roof beam. When finished, he climbed down removing the ladder as they now waited for the lash to be applied to the hindquarters of the horse. Families pleaded, but their pleas went unheard, and children cried. Cottage owners, men of the clan were restrained. But often, the husband was away, working the docks or the factories in Belfast or London. The uniformed Brit raised the whip. The Irish who were part of the militia took a step toward him then paused as he looked their way with a frown of disdain on his face. He applied the whip. The chestnut whinnied and lurched against the leather harness. The support groaned its objection. For the second time the cruel lash stung the hide of the horse. The tortured animal bared his teeth. A red streak appeared. Again, the lash was applied, and the beam twisted. The thatch began to sag and finally collapsed into the interior of the cottage. The chestnut stallion unsuccessfully bent his head back to clean his wounds. He performed only as the cruel lash commanded, and with his nose to the grass, followed his handler to the fourth cottage in the row of houses.

"How will we hang you, Irish wench?" His loud and sarcastic question was asked of the woman who was pinned to the ground by his shiny black boot. To obtain a response, he lifted his foot from her back to kick her in the ribs. "There is no tree on this desolate, rock strewn piece of realty. "Worthy it is, only for the likes of you and your offensive children and friends!" He kicked again. "Where did you hide your dirty faced little brats?" he asked. The woman remained silent except for her sobs heard by those close by. His outrageous conduct was seen by all, including a few of the turncoat Irish militia who were interrupted in their work and witnessed his brutal kick. Intentionally, his comment was loud enough for the uninvolved Irish in the militia who gathered together to hear. Anger and disgust appeared on their shocked faces. Quietly, they conversed among themselves, and a decision was made. They would prevent any further harm to the woman. Fists were clenched, and sticks slapped the free hand of some as five of them started toward him. Two more unoccupied Irish militia men approached the militia man who they knew as Fogarty, the one who killed the cottier named Callaghan. He raised his weapon and the two dodged laterally as the trigger was pulled, but the gun misfired. Fogarty was relieved of his weapon and received the butt end in his mid-section from Johnny Jackson, one of the new Irish recruits. Fogarty clutched his stomach and fell to the ground gasping for air assuming a fetal position. Meanwhile, the spokesman for the five who surrounded the British officer pushed him away from the cruelty he inflicted to the woman under his foot. Reaching down he picked her up from the ground. Her husband untied the rope from her chaffed neck and released her hands. Tear tracks were visible on both while they held each other. He wiped her face with his finger before they parted. She stood wobbly at first, pulling grass out of her hair and using her apron to dry what his finger did not do. The spokesman looked her over and what he saw was apparent on closer examination. His eyes sought out her husband who nodded to confirm her condition.

"She is with child, don't you know? An injustice it is to treat the woman as you have! You have exceeded the limits imposed by decency!" The spokesman, red faced, his nose inches from the Brit, jabbed his forefinger in the officer's face. The Brit's eyes were wide, forced by the tirade to step back, amazed at the turn of events already fearing for his own safety. "'Tis one thing to destroy a cottage, but 'tis another to hang an innocent pregnant woman, a cowardly act it is," he said. Murmurs of agreement followed as heads nodded. Their feet moved them closer to the speaker. He turned to face them. "No longer will this Paddy be part of a militia forced to destroy the homes of neighbors and fellow Irishmen." He pounded his chest with his fist. "Sure it is, I would not be part of his hatred, nor should you! What say you? Speak up!" He raised a clenched fist, his passionate plea an unqualified order.

"Hang the coward," an unconvincing voice came from the rear. The voice belonged to a man at the back of the group. Patrick O' Brien looked toward the sound. He spotted him at the back of the group that gave up the guilty one who wished he could disappear in the face of the spokesman's accusations and questions. All were silent as they watched and listened to the orator's fiery demand. He looked them all in the eye and there was quiet and foot shuffling.

"Only one of you? And you, Tommy Murphy would lower yourself to his level of cowardly conduct? We are better. Are we not?" His passionate, red-faced condemning plea was given with clenched fists involuntarily trembling in reaction to his anger. "It should be determined if the landlord agreed with this action, and if proved, a call from the Mollies would be an appropriate retaliation don't you know!" One clenched fist was raised, and a finger pointed accusingly. "Free him! Let him return to his comfort, but without his boots and with his hands tied behind his back. Convey our message attached to his tunic about the murder of Michael Callaghan and of his attempt to kill an innocent woman." His fiery speech ended as he turned his back on the cowering militia commander.

It did not matter the scribbled indictment attached to the back of the Brit's uniform would never reach his superiors. Notices of what took place that day were bound to appear in the most unlikely places, not there one day, tacked almost magically the next, posted to walls and posts, in pubs and privies from one side of the village to the other. Harassment of British rule would be the work of the Molly Maguire's who already were considered a disruptive organization by the English.

The work stopped. English sympathizers gathered around without comment, being neither in agreement or objecting to what transpired. Only a few took no heed standing apart, conversing while they smoked their Woodbines or those large bowled pipes with the curved stems. Two of the Irish militia, Morrison and O' Steen, likely thought nothing positive would result from the insurrection as they both chose to disappear into the Blackthorn and brambles. Others were sure to follow as the English magistrate in charge would not dismiss the revolt of more than half of the militia company. The murder of Michael Callaghan was secondary to the insurrection and the degradation of a British officer who was relieved of his boots and leather belt. (Irishmen knew the history of the English courts where a man accused of murder was freed because the victim was only an Irishman.) The men who remained loyal would follow until out of sight. The Officer's hands would be untied. Michael Callaghan, an Irishman was insignificant. Many of the Irish militia, including Patrick O' Brien were forced to go on the run moving constantly from place to place to escape British justice. They hoped to find, and usually did find refuge in country cottages, in the homes of freedom seeking Nationalists where a meal would be provided if the family had the food, they were bound to share. Captain Rock and his band of pitchfork carrying farmers had no problem obtaining recruits for their mischievous irritants directed at the English landlords. Recruitments into the Mollies, still a fledgling organization, were increasing, but no one truly knew how many Catholic Irish belonged. And, if you were to find the pub where they gathered, your talents as a recruit would be utilized as a message runner, or, trained to become a bomb maker who if caught risked an immediate trip up the thirteen steps. All would be welcomed into their fold scrutinized for a time to assure their allegiance to the cause of freedom from British domination.

EMBARRASSED RETURN

A ragtag militia reached the outskirts of Ennis. Two of their horses had been stolen along with the only weapon they possessed. Entrusted to an abashed English loyalist named Fogarty who shot the Irishman Callaghan faced severe punishment for the loss of the weapon. The grim- faced British officer long ago gave up his attempt to remain a commanding, authoritative voice to the eleven loyalists who returned with him. He was without his boots and he had to use one hand to hold up his pants. Of the 40 original militia marchers, the Irish were gone as well as eight English loyalists. The English attempt to organize the Irish into a force used to quell revolts, landlord tenant disputes, and to ensure evictions were carried out was failing miserably in many counties.

ROSSA

A crooked finger pulled aside the opaque curtain as Donovan Rossa casually leaned against the wall next to the window. He watched the former militia shuffle their way into the village. Their direction would take them toward the office of the magistrate. His eyes searched while his fingers played with a Woodbine which eventually ended up behind his ear. Rossa watched for one individual who was not there. Patrick O' Brien recently joined the militia, coming in from his farm because he faced eventual eviction. The notice was tacked to his cottage door by someone fearful of retaliation if served face to face. He could not pay, he had no money or food or work, and as a last resort, he joined the militia to put boots on his feet and a meal in his belly. Rossa knew Patrick would be hard to find once on the run, but he knew where he likely could be found, and he intended to enlist the man into the Molly Maguires. Rossa was remarkably successful in establishing safe houses for Nationalist fugitives in Knocknagree, Sneem, and Killarney, just recently adding Martha and Neil Howe, the operators of the Howe Livery and Blacksmith Shop in Killarney, and before, he was able to convince Margaret, and Flynn O' Connell to do the same. Their remote location on a plateau at the foothills of the "Reeks" was a perfect hiding place for a man running away from a meeting with the hangman. The last man in the disgraced troop left his sight as Rossa turned away from the window to feed fire to the Woodbine.

"I watched them leave on their mission and sure you have heard of what the mission was? Surely you must have heard?" Rossa repeated. His words were mumbled caused by the Woodbine bouncing up and down between his lips as he spoke to the bystanders who stood behind him. All watched militia men return, Muldoon and Danny Kissane were there watching the disgraced with their heads hung, not in total shame, but perhaps with a combination to include their first eye-opening participation in something distasteful to some and revolting to others. "Aye, sure I heard of it," Muldoon said as he turned away shaking his head in apparent disgust.

"You, Danny Kissane, should find out what took place at the village of the clan O' Branigan today." Rossa took two steps before grabbing Kissane at his shoulders, shaking him. "Go to the places where the English gather, and sure they will, to lick their wounds. Come back to tell us of the work they did today. The word must be printed and will be posted," Rossa said, as his unblinking eyes focused on a wide eyed and sober faced Kissane who nodded in agreement. In a remote location hidden in the hills, was a country pub ran by a nationalist sympathizer who printed the notices in the back room of the Red Lion Tavern.

"Sure it is, we will soon know Rossa," he said. They all watched him turn away to leave, but not before he made himself ready to play the part. His back was to them while he prepared. On his knee, they saw elbows move, and hands appeared at the collar of his coat. He bent down as his fingers reached for his boot. With a final shrug of his shoulders, he rose to his feet turning toward Rossa and his companions. Danny's transformation caused astonished looks to appear. His eyes appeared to be crossed and a silly, slobbering grin covered his face, leaving a wet spot on his unbuttoned shirt. A wink came as he turned to leave, one hand on his cap covering his curly locks. Danny Kissane used an effective ruse, casting himself as a slow, mentally challenged man who was not a threat to anyone or in league with any political persuasion.

If one looked close, the whiskers on his face were here and there. He was young in years, not yet 20, still the Irish who sought freedom from Britain's stranglehold looked to Rossa as a leader, and he was. He dispelled the myth of some dubious Irish who said the Irish 'may not lead and were known not to follow'. Some of the English knew him by name but not by face. He was a dedicated Nationalist, an organizer who had escaped more than one attempt to lock him in jail. Rossa had experienced being on the run escaping identification allowing him to move about without being detained on suspicion of being an Irish Nationalist which carried a greater English penalty than just being an Irishman, although being an Irishman did not in all cases avoid a trip to visit the man holding the noose.

DANNY KISSANE

Danny Kissane stopped to weed out any potential question to his subterfuge from the activity on the streets before him. Satisfied, he allowed the pub doors of the "Devil Duck" to bang shut behind him. Inside, heads raised to the sound, then returned to what was before. It did not matter what pub name was chosen, and in many cases the more outrageous was the painted sign, the more laughing visitors would be attracted to enter. The elaborate sign above him was an aspiring artist's work of questionable "art" depicting a fowl with wings spread, red eyes and ivory teeth more desired of an alley cat who roamed the brick back streets of the village. By nature, Irishmen were a gullible, superstitious people who passed down the tales of the banshee and the raven. He stepped to the street squatting down to where his fingers and palm rubbed the dirty bricks. While his eyes searched the streetscape and the boardwalks opposite, his hand to a cheek felt the grit of the street. If seen, onlookers would realize the man possessed limited mental capacity. The afternoon hour was a quiet time for pubs and restaurants. A brief closure allowed preparation for late afternoon and evening visitors. Activity on the street was limited to only a wagon with two riders that turned the corner and headed his way. Danny Kissane was spotted but by someone he knew.

"Yo, Danny Kissane, me' boyo," a good-humored voice shouted as a hand waved. Brendan Foley possessed the boisterous voice, seated in a one-horse wagon driven by his brother Donal, the quiet fisherman. Danny had yet to reveal his real self, unsure of the allegiance of the two hard working fishers of the lakes. To continue his ruse, he sat on the street rubbing both hands on the brick as the wagon passed by. They still thought of him as a ten-year old in the body of a 23-year old. The wagon squeaked and rumbled by as Danny watched the smiling faces of the Foley boys who were headed back to the Lakes of Killarney. Once a week the brothers delivered seafood to the Ennis pubs and restaurants. Cruise's Pub at the end of O' Connell Street was their best customer. When the wagon left his sight, he rose to his feet and ambled with his arms outstretched, weaving back and forth in the direction of the magistrate's office. To anyone who witnessed his performance, and it was, they would be convinced "the poor lad" deserved the assistance provided to a "simpleton" orphan child.

"A smile on a happy face can always be seen on Danny boy," Brendan Foley said to his brother. "A child is trapped in an adult body."

"Not sure I am brother," Donal replied. "He is always around, and sometimes I notice a difference from what we just witnessed. Have you?" Donal flicked the reins as the level road had been reached and the hour would be evening when they reached the shore cottage. Brendan was noticeably silent, his face a map of disconnected lines as if trying to remember similar occurrences in prior visits. Their Killarney business had diminished in the early spring of 1847 due in part to the decline in tourists, and the devastating winter. Fortunately, interest from a group of Ennis merchants banded together to sign a contract for seafood deliveries on Wednesday of each week. Optimism abounded for a return to a year without the potato scourge in the southwest counties of Ireland. Spring planting was in progress, but the abundance of seed potatoes from foreign sources was slow to arrive. Simple people continued to suffer, and they starved, and they died. British parliament continued to argue about the "Irish problem."

"Look over there, brother," Donal elbowed his brother who may have been nodding off, his chin slowly lifted from his chest. Donal's pointed urging alerted Brendan's sleepy eyes to a group of people between the buildings. They appeared to be foraging, searching through the garbage cans for something to eat. Both brothers leaned back to see, but the wagon's forward progress and a building blocked their view. Their eyes met. "The hunger continues," Donal said while Brendan nodded. "Aye brother, 'tis a third year and still it is told they still squabble among themselves, blaming one and then the other while the people starve." Donal and Brendan Foley were often witness to similar occurrences of extreme desperation.

Danny Kissane, to anyone who may have been watching, in his theatrical way, collapsed to a sitting position at the bench on the porch of the magistrate's office. He hummed to himself contentedly while his own conductor's finger waved in the air. His head bounced back and forth in time to his pseudo performance. Behind him, the remains of the militia shuffled their way out the door. Hands were in their pockets, their heads down having just experienced a thorough tongue lashing by a superior. In groups of three and four, they gathered together. Pipes appeared, and Woodbines were jabbed between silent lips, soon to be lit by matches vehemently scratched in unspoken anger at what had transpired on an eye-opening day. What Danny hoped for soon occurred as the day's events were reconstructed. Boldly, he rose to join one of the groups, his hand to his head to quiet his unruly hair, working himself in between two of the group who made room. After several weeks of training in the militia, they knew him. Danny Kissane would follow them imitating how they marched. Some of them acknowledged his presence.

"Aye, Danny, how are ya' lad," as their conversation continued, and Danny was able to continue his subterfuge, humming a tune known only to himself. Their conversation finally evolved to details of what took place on the hillside of clan O' Branigan that unpleasant afternoon. They paid no attention to the imbecile beside them. They knew the "town clown" the "man child" would have no memory of their conversations. Danny continued to hum while he listened, intent on capturing every scrap of information about what took place. There was no humor in any of the comments made regarding recent events in the

Irish hamlet on the hillside. They exchanged remembrances quietly, heads were bowed, and feet scraped the boardwalk. After several minutes, one man in the company took exception to Danny's presence.

"Sure Danny, would you leave us now, your humming is driving me bats, please us lad, go now, your tune is embedded in me' brain and sure I will hum it to the children." Danny said nothing while he stared at his feet with his hands in his pockets. He shuffled his feet, and when he looked up his eyes were wet with tears. "Sure you don't like my tune, sorry I am sir, I will go," he said. He turned away, head down as he shuffled his way down the boardwalk, retracing his steps back to the Devil Duck pub.

"What you have done Ellis? You hurt the poor lad's feelings," the man standing next to Ellis chided. Ellis shrugged his shoulders. "He will get over it, he tends to forget his own name," Ellis said. Danny turned back to look more than once, feigning his displeasure at being told to leave. His act would have won awards on the Dublin stage. Once out of their sight he relaxed a bit when the distance between he and the Devil Duck saloon was reduced to only a few footsteps. When he shut the door behind him, he was in the haven of his nationalist sympathizer friends, and his masquerade ended. He was constantly on the alert, and many a time he had to change from a man fully in possession of all his faculties to a bumbling simpleton in a matter of seconds. Before he relaxed, he scanned the barroom for unfamiliar faces. His search ended when his eyes fell on the face of Donovan Rossa who stood before him.

"You have no fear being here, Danny," as Rossa put his arm around Danny's shoulders urging him to walk to a corner of the room unoccupied by anyone in proximity, but Danny shrugged away, stopping to look at his friend. Their eyes met the others, and for a brief instant there was quiet.

"Sure it is, you can speak to me man to man and not man to simpleton," Danny said, "and I don't need to be led to the trough like an animal or the sorry child I portray," he said in a tone just above a whisper, but with a serious demand, a request, a pleading that bordered on a threat. "Sorry I am, Danny boy, your forgiveness please, your acting ability carries over to your true self and sometimes makes it hard to adjust to the change. Do my words bear any weight?" Rossa questioned. "I meant no harm, friend." Again, no words escaped the mouth of either, but just for an instant.

"'Tis difficult at times to revert to my true self, Donovan, I may be too sensitive, sorry I am, and the news I have brought to you caused sorrow for the Callaghan family. Michael was killed by the militia, they destroyed two cottages and the Brit threatened to hang the woman in the second cottage, I don't know her name. His cruelty started the rebellion that day, but surely you have heard of the other times...? The gun misfired preventing another Irishman from having to speak to St. Peter. O' Brien led the revolt. He and four others released the woman who was with child. Some of the English deserted as well as several Irish." Danny's hasty recount of what he heard was filled with nervous glances toward the door fearing discovery. "Who is the landlord of the village, did you hear?" Rossa asked, but already suspected what Danny Kissane would relate. "You, Rossa should know the name of George Bingham, am I right?" Rossa nodded and motioned to the barman. Two pints were promptly delivered to the table for two in the corner of the Devil Duck pub. "I pity the poor Irish in Mayo," Rossa said. "They know him as ruthless and call him the "exterminator!" His "estate" is held in demesne, I believe is the word. Irish land taken from them and given to him!" Rossa pounded the table top with his fist causing a reaction from barstool occupants. "I know not the word learned friend," Kissane responded to Rossa's sudden outpouring of emotion. "While your memory is fresh will you take your recollections to our printer friend for posters? What you have told me and with whatever you may have omitted from your memory should be included, Danny boy," Rossa instructed. Their experience in past months and years, led to belief instructions such as relayed by Rossa to Danny Kissane often could result in embellishments to the actual events, although sometimes unintentionally. The details of British actions appeared suddenly, posted before the dawn of the next day. Reports were destined to be relegated to minute coverage buried deep inside the leading English newspapers a week or two later. The next morning Ennis was a flutter with white sheets of paper. The breeze from the south gave children and dogs an opportunity to play games with the disturbing word embedded indelibly in ink on forbidden paper. Laughing and giggling, young children chased after the paper before it was carried away from their grasp by sudden gusts raising dust from dry parts of the street. Contests developed. One notice that flapped in the salty air was tacked to the magistrate's office door. Shop owners and helpers could be seen outside their shop reading the substance of what transpired at the village of the clan O' Branigan. The Irish residents and shop-owners of Ennis were outraged at the death of Michael Callaghan and the inhumane treatment of the clan woman by the British officer. Tommy O' Keefe led a group of townsmen to the door of the magistrate. He stepped forward to pound on the locked door. The others backed up waiting with anticipation, their gaze on the locked door impervious to the noise created by Tommy's bare knuckles. Donovan Rossa made it a point to be seen reading the notice tacked to the door of the Purple Unicorn pub across the street from the office of the magistrate. He glanced once or twice at the murmuring crowd behind him.

Danny Kissane helped the children capture some of the loose paper notices blowing around in the breeze. He, at times was surrounded by jubilant children who clutched handfuls of paper. His ruse was solidified when he chased a notice blowing down the street. He feigned losing interest in the chase to sit cross legged in the street, waving at people on the boardwalk. Muldoon, a friend of Donovan Rossa, and a sympathizer with the Irish desire to be free of political and religious domination, went home to his wife and three children.

THE FISHERMAN BROTHERS

Donal and Brendan Foley stretched arms and legs to get the blood flowing after they climbed down from the wagon seat. Their tireless horse was provided a respite from an unbroken pace half way to the cottage on the lake shore. After Brendan's knee bends restored circulation to his limbs, he watched Donal who made sure the horse was rewarded and given water.

"How many weeks will we make this trip, brother?" Donal asked while he held the pail of water for the horse quickly drained. "Sure it is brother, me' backside speaks to me, telling me not to make the trip more than once each week. It takes all day and then comes an early morning... but sure 'tis only one day." "We work too hard for too few coins in our pockets," Donal replied, "and if not for Flynn's contribution me' bones would feel more pain." As we do, Flynn works as hard as he ever did, but have you noticed how quiet he became over the past few weeks?" Brendan asked. "Aye, brother, I have noticed, and I will inquire of him his trouble," Donal replied while he checked the horse's hooves using a small hammer to free dirt from the shoes. Finished, he stood looking forward with his hands on his hips, moving left and right, stretching out the kinks from bending over. "See what is ahead of us, Brendan?" He motioned with his head to a group of walkers who suddenly appeared in the roadway. Two of them used sticks to help them make their way, a third, apparently stronger than the others walked without assistance at the front. The one in the lead carried a bundle on a stick over a shoulder. The weight of the bundle bent the stick requiring the use of both hands. Brendan, as if in thought watched without a word, his face an empty plate reflecting the unwavering gaze of his brother.

"Our offer of a ride should be welcomed," Brendan said, but his troubled expression said something else was on his mind. "Flynn is an honest, hard-working, compassionate man, don't you know, and he is deeply troubled by the scene presented to him all too often, the disease, sickness and suffering with little effort made to alleviate the famine. His words I remember." "Sure! It was not just the loss of their son and Margaret's depression? It must wear on him." Donal offered an obvious question not considered until just now. Brendan was silent. Donal felt Flynn hid the true reason for his withdrawal from the camaraderie they had apparently lost. "Take the leathers, brother," Donal said. "When we catch up, offer them assistance. We have some of Flynn's smoked salmon left. We will share." "Will Flynn be there when we arrive?" Brendan asked. "Aye, brother, he will. I left orders for him to prepare for delivery on the morrow. He will be smoking salmon, as well. You will be saved from skinning fish again."

FLYNN O'CONNELL

Flynn arrived at the shore an hour after first light after the Foley brothers had left for Ennis. It would be late afternoon before he would welcome their return with hot tea and warm biscuits slathered with butter and honey. Orders for the next day's delivery he packed were cooling in the lake water. Aromatic smells drifted from the smoking shed containing four dozen good sized salmon steaks he positioned on the cooking grid. Each week Flynn and the brothers saw the demand increase as the calendar marched toward the start of the tourist season. Deserving a break at mid-morning, he sat before the fire heating the tea water. No doubt he was worried about his son Devon, always the adventurer, who was upset he could not go with his father to the shore. Flynn sat sipping tea. His eyes moved from the mesmerizing view of the shimmering lake surface, to the smoking shed, and then to the knives he honed one by one on the stone. Flynn had become a source for a moment of entertainment to the Foley brothers, a break from their daily routine, amazed at his knife throwing ability. A year past they presented him with a leather sheaved set of throwing knives he could belt around his waist allowing him the ability to throw seven knives without having to retrieve them one at a time. Brendan Foley issued a challenge Flynn readily accepted. Being right-handed, would he be able to hit the target with his left hand? Flynn smiled and threw the knife. When it cut through the air missing the target, Flynn turned to Brendan and shook his head no. He continued to practice, only when he was free of duties for a few moments, or when the brothers demanded an exhibition. He won an additional week's wages from the unbelieving brothers when he said he was able to 'hit the target two out of three times while blindfolded.'

"You can't do it with your left hand while you are blindfolded," Donal challenged. "Next year," Flynn said, with his Irish grin covering his face. Their conversation took place before the death of his new son and the effect it had on his wife Margaret, who experienced months of depression. Flynn was not sure she was fully recovered from a devastating, mind altering tragedy.

MARGARET

In her own mind, she had recovered from the loss of Kevin, but, not from the isolation of the last four months spending much time alone with only Mary Margaret, the chickens and the Guernsey for company. During the freezing cold the chickens died, leaving her daughter and the Guernsey to keep her occupied in the most miserable winter she had ever experienced. Devon's company was limited by his studies, and he often accompanied his father to the lake or the pasture. Confined she was, like a prisoner in a 16 by 24-foot cottage. In late March, her painful, excruciating winter had thankfully come to an end. The O' Connell farm had suffered through the devastating weather delaying planting of the early potato crop. One by one the hens died in unreasonable cold. Biting winds made life outside the cottage wretchedly uncomfortable, an unwelcome and uncommon hardship from a frozen wilderness land to the northeast. Flynn was constantly in the sheep pasture. He and Devon made frantic attempts to protect the ewes and sheep from the bitterness they must endure or die from lack of fully matured coats. Dried wood was gathered to feed fires near the cliff face. The small amount of wood they recovered did not have much of an impact on the severe cold. Flynn looked more than once at the dwindling pile of turf at the side of the cottage. Eleven ewes were lost in December and January including four of them pregnant. The constant cold did enable storage of meat Flynn was able to save by butchering lambs on the brink of freezing to death.

Margaret sat at the spinning wheel sorting through items she had not looked at for years. Not knowing why, she suddenly remembered the basket. She climbed to the loft and recovered the dust covered reed container. When she returned to the ladder, the intelligent decision was to drop it to the floor. She held in over the edge of the loft and let go. The basket was large enough for her to set it at the side of the chair while she rummaged through. At the bottom of the basket she found knitting projects started years ago, some she recalled began when she was a girl of fifteen or sixteen, but then came the university years. Each item she retrieved brought flashbacks as she watched Devon and Mary Margaret work on their studies assigned to them. Memories flooded her mind with each project she pulled out, whether complete or not. Lovingly, she spread them on her lap. Her hands caressed each item. Smiles or sometimes frowns appeared on her face as incidents and recollections were resurrected from lost time and place. Her hand reached again and out came something forgotten from a childhood when she first became familiar with a sewing needle. A sigh escaped her and her whispered "Mother of God" made the children look up from their studies. She stared at a white muslin cloth mitten with a cross sewn into the back of the right hand. Her mind raced backwards to her childhood when she was first told Daniel would cover his right hand with a handkerchief before he would enter a Catholic church. Margaret remembered her words. "Why father, would he do such a thing? Who is Daniel?" Her father responded to her questions.

"Daniel was fearful of offending God and wanted to hide the hand that killed a man from God's sight." After her father had fully explained to her the mystery of Daniel O' Connell who had provoked the hierarchy of Dublin Castle by referring to them as "beggerly," a man named D' Esterre challenged him to a duel. Though dueling was illegal at the time, nothing was done to prevent the activity from taking place. London looked the other way. D' Esterre died after two days in agony having taken a shot to the stomach from O' Connell's first volley. How disappointing it was to all those who cast their lot with a dueling master. Dublin Castle lamented. Their hope to rid the Crown of a throbbing toothache was foiled. Margaret decided to sew a mitten he could use instead of a handkerchief, but never did an opportunity come to deliver her creation. Her thoughts returned to the present having received copies of *The Nation*, and *Punch* the English newspaper, from Martha Howe in Killarney. Reports indicated Daniel O'Connell, the Liberator, was in ill health. Physicians recommended a warmer climate to help his condition, and Italy was their choice.

"Time passes so swiftly," she said, causing the children to again glance up from their studies. She had to ready herself for Flynn's return from the shore. He had promised to take her to Killarney for a visit with

Martha Howe, who again offered to lodge her and Mary Margaret. She missed visiting with other women including Fiona Farrell, having been marooned by the wrath of the weather gods for months. Margaret was anxious to go and would not let her husband forget his promise. Moving the whale oil lamp to the chest with the mirror she peered at her face before running a comb through her hair several times. A new wrinkle had appeared, one she had not noticed before. She picked up the bottle of flowery scented water. Essence of Paris was printed on the label. Just a bit was tipped to her fingertip. Flynn said he liked the scent on her neck. She used it often, desperate for his attention. He brought it home after calling on the shop run by the Frenchman LaVigne and his wife. He occasionally stopped apparently enjoying his conversations in French with the owners.

It was one of those miserably cold, snowy and windy days in the horrible winter of '47 when Flynn took the time to talk with his wife about his past life and his experiences in France and in South and Central America while a member of the French Foreign Legion. Devon sat wide eyed, enthralled at what his father revealed, talking to his son in French. Margaret knew his secret (he talked in his sleep, in French), and gave her husband the key he had misplaced. His forgotten key would open the locked box containing memories from his past life, some of which he did not care to reveal while the children were present. Mary Margaret had a hundred questions, but she laughed when she looked in the mirror with the Kepi (hat) on her head. Today was Wednesday, the day the Foley brothers traveled to Ennis to make their weekly deliveries. They left before Flynn arrived at the lake shortly after dawn. He would have little time before darkness to share with her. Bessie the Guernsey would be begging for relief before Flynn devoured a quick candlelit meal of cabbage and lamb. Margaret took one last look at herself in the mirror. Unsatisfied, but it made her think out loud, "That will have to do for now, little time is there." She had to ready tonight's meal.

DISCOVERY

They came from four directions. Before dawn they came, others arrived in the early morning when the mist still clung to the hollows in the knocks. They walked to the meeting at the tavern, a converted cottage hidden from casual view in the valley of the knocks south and east of Ennis. The country pub was known to Republicans as the Red Lion Tavern. On this day and time, there was no need to hang the signage to indicate its function. Its true purpose was to offer a meeting place or a refuge for the night and a meal in the morning. Donovan Rossa was the first to arrive in the wee hours finding his way across a shallow stream on moss covered rocks. He was followed by Danny Kissane an hour or so later. The word had been issued by word of mouth from one Republican to another. Their mission was to recruit and offer encouragement to those being hunted by the Brits who relished the opportunity to send an Irishman up the thirteen steps with a bayonet urging him along, his hands tied behind him. All who were to attend the meeting took care to make sure they were not followed even though no roads or boreens (paths) led to the meeting place. All were secretly sympathetic to the cause of the Molly Maguire's, and several were active participants. By eleven in the morning, sixteen staunch seekers of freedom had gathered. All desired to be freed from under the thumb of the British. One of the later arrivals was Patrick O' Brien, the revolt leader from the O' Branigan clan village. Tommy O' Keefe, who drew the short straw, was the lookout in the event troops discovered the purpose of a non-descript building nestled in the valley of the knocks. Hugh Harrell, the Republican who printed notices of British atrocities sorted through what food was brought to the meeting. Some of it would be wrapped into bundles for those who might not get a warm meal for days. The smoked ham he sliced was gone in moments to those who had families in need. Donovan Rossa introduced himself to O'Brien. They talked quietly at a corner table.

"All of us here can be trusted, and you have not a worry at being discovered by traitorous, self-serving lips. All here believe the same, Patrick, and are you are one of them?" Rossa and O' Brien stared unflinchingly for a moment, at the other. "Not a family do I have Rossa. All I have was the result of what I witnessed at the village of the O' Branigan clan. I came here after the word was delivered, and you know we have their weapon and two of their horses were hidden and boarded. Fine animals they are, and I can ride with or without their English saddles. I would fire their barracks with flaming torches and escape into the night if given the chance!" "The Mollies would welcome your allegiance, Patrick," Rossa offered. "You have it," O' Brien replied. "Sure a field piece would aid us to wreak havoc while they sleep?" Donovan Rossa smiled while he nodded, in complete acceptance of his question. Their interaction ceased when the door of the Red Lion was pushed open by Tommy O' Keefe.

He was followed by eight others who had been out on the porch enjoying a pint.

"Aye, me' fellows, we have trouble coming our way. Best we all leave this place with haste. The brigands bring a weapon on wheels with them and who do you think might have alerted the bastards? I say." Immediately a rush to the window occurred, but nothing could be seen behind a far knock, but heard was the faint sound of a drum. Frantic activity began. All hurried to clear tables and to remove evidence of being there. Bundles of food for hungry families were tied to belts before they rushed out the door. A chair hit the floor in their frenzied effort to scramble out of danger. Hugh Harrell picked up the sign to be hung outside announcing to anyone who approached, the Red Lion Tavern was open for business. After storing the ladder, he ran inside to ready for the invasion, locking the door to the room containing the printing press. The tavern suddenly was quiet as the dispossessed and hunted quickly departed, hopefully unseen by those approaching. He knew few coins would come his way from the British troops. All the Irishmen were gone except Danny Kissane who remained behind. With his ear to the door Hugh Harrell heard the sound, the rat-a-tat-tat of a drum.

"Danny boy, you should go," he said. "Draw me a pint of the black stuff to draw their attention to me," he said. The barman Harrell hesitated before he reluctantly complied, spilling part of it on the bar as he hurried toward the window. What he saw made him gasp. The British platoon had reached the crest of the knock closest to the vale hiding the tavern. Three soldiers hastily prepared the field gun to fire. He watched one man ramming wadding down the barrel. "They are going to fire on us Danny, we must go quickly." A drum sounded again as the two of them stumbled their way to the rear door. Their exit was just in time as a cannonball tore a massive hole in the corner of the building. *"Boom,"* the sound came, delayed by the wind and distance. Shards of wood and stone exploded from the impact, falling to the grass around them. Slivers of glass peppered their clothing. "Run into the smoke," Harrell said as Danny Kissane raced for the shelter of brambles ahead of them. He looked back. The cannon was being prepared for a second salvo, and Hugh Harrell was yards behind him, a clear target.

"We must make haste Hugh Harrell," Danny shouted. Not being a young man, Harrell struggled, winded from the effort. Just then a shot ricocheted off a chunk of granite close by. Again, another report was heard. Puffs of smoke rose in the air from the gunfire as the soldier applied flame to the wick. The cannon lurched back on its wheels after being fired. A massive hole appeared in the rear wall of the tavern, the shot entered through the window, destroying the bar leaving rubble and smoke in its place. Hugh Harrell turned to watch his life being destroyed before his eyes. He stood in clear sight of the British guns as Danny Kissane rushed back toward the Nationalist printer who collapsed suddenly, clutching his chest. Breathing heavily, Danny reached him dropping to his knees to peer into Hugh Harrell's lifeless eyes that stared unseeing into the heavens. Another ricochet shot pieces of rock toward him. A sudden sting made him reach to his ear and blood appeared on his fingers. He had to escape. Bent down, he dodged first to the left and then to the right. Stumbling, he scrambled up at times on all fours as the whistle of gunfire sought him out.

From the relative safety of a brush covered high steppe, Donovan Rossa, Patrick O' Brien and Tommy O' Keefe watched the British cannon turn the Red Lion Tavern into a pile of smoking rubble. What remained was damaged but intact. The lock was still on the door to the closet at the rear corner of the building. Even though out of range of British guns, everyone else scattered, returning by a different route to their cottages or to the safety of a Republican sympathizer. Rossa's anxious eyes searched the landscape for the two missing patriots, rewarded minutes later when an out-of-breath Danny Kissane fought his way through tall berry bushes. Breathing hard with his head down, he sagged to the ground. Blood found a path down his neck.

"Worried I was Danny Kissane, you are wounded and why are you alone? Tell me," Rossa asked as Danny took another breath and raised his head. His red rimmed eyes looked at Rossa. "Sure, if we had not come here, our friend Hugh would still be alive. Sadly,

I watched him fall to the ground, felled by a British bullet. Our printer friend has gone away from us Donovan." "Unfortunately, they will look for him and take him away," Rossa said, handing a cloth to Danny as he stood up to peer over the tops of blackberry and brambles. He watched as the troops milled about the ruins of the tavern before a drum roll sounded, evidently to call them back to the crest of the knock where the cannon did its duty. "They are leaving, Tommy," he said as Tommy rose to his feet to look at the remains of the tavern with the press inside. 'Tis safe there until we locate a hiding place for it. Under the stars of the night, we could rescue and transport it." "Aye Donovan, Tommy O' Keefe is with you."

DANIEL O'CONNELL

The Republic of Ireland mourned. Word had been received from Rome regarding Daniel O' Connell. The Liberator had passed away in Genoa while on his way to Rome. Church bells tolled the news while women wept. Husbands went to the pub. He fought for their interests, both religious and political, and they would raise a glass often. The Brits said nothing, secretly pleased a thorn in their side had been removed. Martha Howe had her copy of the paper printed in green ink spread out on her dining room table. She read Duffy's account of his passing, often passages were read out loud for the benefit of her son Neil and his bride to be Silé (Shee-la) who stood behind her. Neil had his hands on her shoulders because his mother had been crying, shocked at the news of the passing. Martha Howe's hopes for Ireland's future were dashed as previous reports indicated O' Connell's health had improved. The London Daily Mail reported he was soon to resume his work and she was encouraged. She cried when she read of the death of someone who had provided personal help to the Howe family in a time of horrific loss, the murder of her husband at the hands of an English landlord. Gavan Duffy's editorial and eulogy in the "Nation" covered more than two pages and was a biography of the life of the "Liberator" who fought so valiantly, however, unsuccessfully, for the Catholic cause of equal treatment in the political arena, and to pray their own religion freely. Duffy wrote: 'Throughout his career he had been the subject of extravagant reproach and extravagant panegyric.' The latter praise heaped on him by his Catholic supporters overwhelmed the English denial of his agenda. The day the bells started their toll in mourning, the Foley brothers and Flynn O' Connell were making their rounds delivering smoked and fresh seafood, lamb chops and pork to buyers in the hotels, restaurants and pubs. Word spread rapidly around Killarney about Daniel's demise. When word was received, people dropped to their knees in prayer in the middle of the street. Flynn O' Connell was not one of them. People were seen blessing themselves with heads bowed. Flynn's final delivery was to the mercantile owned by Fiona Farrell. He wandered over to the Howe livery, not being bothered about the news of the death of a man who might have been his own father. Leaning on the fence rail, Flynn was carving letters into a discarded piece of wood he found on the street, when Malachy found him. "Aye, Flynn 'me boyo, a lovely day it is except for the news. Surely you have heard?" he asked. "Agreed, a fine day it is Malachy," as he continued to carve on the board. He had finished the letter O and said nothing in response to the "news." "Your expertise with the knife precedes you if you would allow me to use such a fancy word. The word gets around, don't you know," Malachy said as Neil Howe wandered over.

"How are you getting along, Flynn?" Neil asked. Flynn responded with a shrug of his shoulders and a nod of his head. Neil now recognized what his mother had said about how withdrawn Flynn seemed to be at least according to Donal Foley. Everyone knew he lost his new son. It was an awkward moment for them as Flynn seemed to be quietly contemplating his evident torment.

"Would you care to demonstrate your accuracy for us?" Malachy asked. "Do you have the time? I will prop a board against the rail for a target." He turned away to find the target, returning a minute later to prop the board against the rail fence. Malachy recognized Flynn's moodiness. "Sure this is not the throwing knife I use," Flynn said, "'tis the one I started using to fillet fish. Please step away from the target. I would hate to lose a friend to an errant throw." Laughter came from all, including a nattily dressed man passing by who stopped to watch the attempt. Laughter resulted from Flynn's comment, and appeared to chase away the clouds hiding Flynn's usually sunny disposition. He counted ten paces away from the board, turning with the knife in hand. His arm retreated, the knife held almost behind his ear. Released, the knife whistled through the air, end over end, hitting the board dead center, its point protruded on the other side of the board. Malachy worked it free, handing it to Flynn.

"Do that again Flynn," Neil said as another spectator joined the first, waiting expectantly as Flynn returned to the same spot. From around the corner, Donal and Brendan Foley appeared, finished with their day's deliveries. Flynn eyed the target and threw with the same result and near the spot of the first throw. A shout was heard from Malachy."That is all for today,"

Flynn said, knowing the brothers would be anxious to return to the lake. Donal saw the well-dressed tourists on their way to lunch, pause to see what would happen. "Just one more Flynn, please us with a throw blindfolded," Donal said. He had thought seriously about a knife throwing exhibition where money could be charged to watch. He pulled a folded handkerchief from his inside coat pocket. Cheers emanated, and hands applauded when Flynn nodded his acceptance, smiling briefly. He certainly had no choice as Donal urged him to the same spot and tied the cloth around his eyes. Donal, directed him with his hands placed on Flynn's shoulders to face the target and stepped away. Flynn readied himself to throw, moving his feet until he felt assured of his comfort. He paused, and with a deep breath his arm drew back, and the knife cut through the air turning end over end. It ended up several inches from the original throws as shouts of approval were heard from the small crowd gathered. Hearing the knife make contact, Flynn tore off the blindfold, wide eyed, to see the result. A massive smile covered his face as he raised his arms in celebration. Back slaps and plaudits were applied and offered from all who watched the impromptu demonstration. Brendan Foley, his arm around Flynn's shoulders laughed uproariously when he uttered a comment promoting laughter from those who remained nearby.

"Surely, we must catch more fish for this lad to clean!" Brendan roared. "Aye, Brendan, a lad who has too much free time to become so proficient with the blade!" Donal responded. The nattily dressed spectator approached Donal and introduced himself as David Ronan O'Neill, the Killarney Playhouse resident poet-playwright. He happened to wander by at the time, hearing Neil Howe's spontaneous reaction to Flynn's excellent throw when he exclaimed 'do that again, Flynn.'

"Pleased I would be to be introduced to the man," Ronan-O' Neill said to Donal, who looked for Flynn who was being congratulated. "If he is as talented as you say, and from what I just witnessed, the playhouse would be filled!" he continued. "How does...?" he started to question, his voice trailing down, his head shaking in disbelief.

"Flynn O' Connell is a private individual, a quiet man who reveals little about himself," Donal said, motioning to Flynn and Brendan. "To answer your question, he practices every chance he gets." "What he did blind-folded is astounding! Surely, he is not related to the "Liberator" although the name is the same," Ronan-O' Neill speculated almost to himself but out loud as Flynn and Brendan left Neil and Malachy at the fence. Ronan-O' Neill walked toward Flynn with his hand extended as Flynn walked toward him. He introduced himself. Flynn hesitated but took the offered hand with an inquiring look on his face. Donal and Brendan started back to the horse and wagon as Flynn and Ronan-O' Neill followed. An arm waving, head nodding discussion ensued with both parties using the same descriptive body language. The four of them arrived to where the horse was tied to a post in the alley at the side of the Rose of Erin pub. A handshake occurred between them as they parted company. The wagon pulled away. Donal and Flynn watched the departing back of the man who had expressed such interest in the knife throwing ability of a tall, black haired Irishman, who appeared to be carved out of granite. It was not long before Donal could not restrain himself from asking the obvious question. "Tell me, Flynn. Tell us about your discussion with Ronan-O' Neill. "He wants to observe my knife throwing at the playhouse before he can make a decision on scheduling a performance during the tourist season," Flynn replied. "He did not ask if I was willing." "Surely, we can provide an hour for you to show him your skill," Donal said. "Three days each week you assist us in Killarney. Brendan and I will be there to offer our encouragement." Flynn was silent, although he smiled when he looked Donal in the eye.

The well-traveled route back to the lake was again heavily populated. A long arduous walk to the outskirts of Killarney ended to where the "Castle of Hope," the cathedral under construction offered a respite. It was heard, and the word spread rapidly that food was available, but not all the time. Killarney town was one of their last stops for the poor and destitute before they arrived at Tralee or Cork where the ships waited to be filled with human cargo. Their decision was a dangerous gamble to survive an ocean voyage exposing them to weeks and weeks of misery below crowded decks in the most inhospitable of conditions. Words could not come from the three who faced British citizens who decided to flee from what was then and what was now. They watched as a disheveled group leading dirty faced children approached. The man carried a trunk on his back. His back was bent, his hands reached behind him over his shoulders from the weight of the trunk secured by rope, likely carried all their meager possessions. His feet were unshod. The three children had clothing barely offering protection from the cool nights.

DISPAIR

"Look would you," Donal whispered to Flynn while they watched aghast at what passed them by. Silently, they shuffled their way, downcast eyes void of emotion. Occasional blank stares to what lie ahead of them shocked Flynn, Donal and Brendan into recognition of the resignation and hopelessness those poor destitute Irish exhibited. More than one gut twisting instance was faced on their way to the turnoff taking them to the winding downward route to the lake.

"Remember don't you, that cold, cold day in February when we slipped and slid our way to Killarney? And you remember what we encountered along the way?" The heads of Flynn and Brendan nodded. "The woman, barely clothed, her feet raw and bloody, with ribs you could count, and nearby her children lay frozen as well by the cruel Gods of this evil winter," Donal concluded. "Well told, an ugly scene Donal, but sure 'tis evil Gods and a cruel winter, what say you?" Flynn offered. He approved of this day the weather Gods had provided when his eyes took in the blue of the sky, the fluffy white clouds to the right, left, and behind. His thoughts reverted to his brief conversation with Martha Howe who was anxious to see Margaret and Mary Margaret the next day. His daughter would be happy to see what he brought her in the cage. Pullets hens, not yet egg layers, eventually would provide her a daily activity she missed when the chickens died during the winter. Next to the cage was the burlap bag of grain to feed the birds for several weeks.

"What a contradiction in the treatment of humanity," he thought to himself, "when the Brits allow merchants to sell grain for the chickens, the pigs and horses, yet had little to provide their own starving citizens who died on the roadways on their way to a workhouse location where meager food was the payment for work." Donal noticed Flynn deep in thought, nodding his head from time to time, and took advantage of the opportunity, Flynn's moodiness and silence still on his mind.

"Flynn, my friend, so quiet you have been, what troubles do you have, and I know the loss you have suffered, what is it the Foley boys can do to change you to the man we knew?" Flynn was silent. He turned his head away from the friend who was trying to help. Donal knew to continue prying was futile. He left the wagon to walk alongside. Minutes later they were alongside the fence, now repaired, the site of the beginning of a sad and tragic episode resulting in the hanging death of an innocent sister and brother at the hands of British troops. As the wagon bumped and swayed its way they paused before a sign reading, "TRESPASS IRISH AND YOU WILL BE SHOT." Scrawled underneath the message were the words, 'or hung.' Flynn appeared to recognize the flat terrain the wagon now traveled as his head lifted. Donal watched his stare, fixed on the message as they passed and did not waver until its words could not be read. After, he saw Flynn's head again drop to his chest, accompanied by a momentary picture of despair on Flynn's face. A message flashed to Donal's brain. Hidden deep in Flynn O'Connell was the same compassion exhibited by the man who bore the title, The Liberator, Daniel O'Connell. *Was Daniel O'Connell Flynn's father?*

CONSPIRATORS

Danny Kissane's absence from the brick streets of Ennis would not be noticed. What would be noticed was the absence of suspected nationalists who were thought to be engaged in treasonous activities such as demanding Irish representation as members of parliament or spreading excrement on Lord Huffington's carriage seat. Donovan Rossa's absence, particularly during the time of the assault by British troops on the Red Lion Tavern, was sure to be noticed. Before he left for Killarney, a meeting was held to plan for the rescue of the printing press from the remains of Hugh Harrell's pub. Rossa stood by the window watching shadowy figures approach in the dark, one after another. In the starlit night, they came from different directions, always watchful before their knuckles were applied two times and then a pause, and two more, to the door in the alley. Muldoon, Patrick O' Brien and Tommy O' Keefe attended the meeting in the back room of the Purple Unicorn Pub.

"Why do you go to Killarney, Rossa?" Tommy asked, worried someone else would need to fill the leadership void, and he hoped he would not be the one asked. "I hope to meet with D'Arcy McGee and a former French Foreign Legionnaire who could aid our cause immensely. Today, no one knows the date McGee is to speak in Killarney, and he could be arrested. His talk will be in the next few days. That is what I know. Additionally, the question of who might have tipped off the Brits needs to be resolved, and when he or she is found, a lesson will come their way." "Find the traitor in our midst," were Rossa's final words before his meeting broke up at the time the sun started to peek over the hills. Patrick O' Brien was a wanted man and had to make sure he had left Ennis before someone recognized him. He had to sneak into Ennis under cover of darkness and would leave before the sun was fully awake for the village of Kildysart, where a safe place to rest his head would be his for a week. "Shameful it is for a man with the name O' Brien who is required to hide himself in Ennis," Rossa said to him when he entered. At which time, Patrick looked at him, inquiringly while he hung his coat on the rack. "Hundreds of years have passed since the kings who bore the name O' Brien established a settlement on the Inis Fergus with the help of the Franciscans. When I return from Killarney, I will inquire of the Friars. Helpful it would be to tie you as a descendent of the great Kings of Thomond," Rossa said. "The Brits could not touch you, without riots ensuing." Rossa remained a fervent student of Irish history.

Patrick longed to return to his cottage a half mile from the huts and hovels of the clan O' Branigan but was told by Rossa, "it would be watched" and likely had been destroyed and burned. Muldoon and Tommy O' Keefe were to seek out a location for the press. Once a secure location was found, the move would be made in the dark of night by the light of the moon. With the stick over his shoulder and the bundle with slices of ham, a loaf of bread, carrots and half a cabbage, tied to the end of the blackthorn, Patrick secured his cap and made his escape into the cool of the awakening of day. A chance meeting with anyone on the street would force him to change directions, however, at this early time he witnessed little activity other than the "knocker-up" who was seen several storefronts down the street making his rounds. Tommy O' Keefe left to go to the Cathedral where he had employment honoring the wishes of several of the Franciscans in residence. Muldoon, an adroit fisherman had a boat rental business near the popular fishing grounds on the river. He was able to walk freely around the town.

+

Flynn finally broke his silence when the aromatic smells emanating from the smoke house reached their nostrils. "What is ahead of us has become a part of me," Flynn said, "the smells of the sea and the smoke tend to wipe depressing thoughts from my mind. There is much to think about lads. I worry much and hear me when I say I need to practice with the knives. On the morrow, I will take my wife and daughter to Killarney. I will miss them after a day, and they will be gone a week. I don't want to embarrass myself at the playhouse when I demonstrate for David Ronan-O' Neill. Since Margaret and my daughter will watch, I must practice!"

"So soon, Flynn 'me boy, and sure you would welcome the Foley boys to watch would you not?" Donal asked. "We need to call on the vicar. Surely he could use fresh fish." Donal always tried to accomplish more than one thing.

As it was with Cork, Tralee and Waterford, the larger cities and towns were the destination of the country people who did not have food or employment or money. They were destitute, sick and starving, and they did starve and die. If not for people like Patrick Kincade, the vicar of St. Mary's Cathedral, more of the poor and desperate Irish would have died.

+

"Early afternoon is the time scheduled for the demonstration Donal, and you and Brendan are welcome," Flynn said while he moved the cage with the pullets off the wagon. The trip to the cottage with the birds and the feed bag over his shoulder would be taxing. Brendan was busy caring for the horse, his attention shifted to Flynn who was seen belting the knives around his waist. "I worry as well and sorry I am not to have told you we, Margaret and I, have agreed to provide safe quarters for 'runners.' We grieve almost daily for the poor we helped to keep alive, and during the winter we grieved daily. Our beautiful land is in danger Donal." Flynn's spewing of pent up emotion did not end even though he was ready to make his first throw at the target.

"The Foley boys feel the same about our land Flynn, and for the people who suffer unnecessarily." Flynn's throw hit the target with such force it split the board nearly in half, his emotive power transferred from his voice to his arm. "A young militant we met last year desires to meet with me. I received a message from a man who admitted he was a nationalist and a member of 'Young Ireland.'" Flynn's next throw was dead center as was the next, and the next. "Margaret said O' Connell's death would mean more activity from the militant factions. Negotiation has failed." "The Americans fought the oppressors and won in a relatively short time. How is it Ireland's people have been without freedom for so long?" Donal asked. "There are not enough like-minded individuals in Ireland. Many are satisfied with the status-quo. The Irish peasant desires only to be left alone to live their lives," Flynn answered. "Their lot could be improved if the Brits cared a bit for their own citizens, but they don't." Flynn threw again and missed the target entirely. The knife went flying into the brambles. He shrugged his shoulders. "My thoughts were elsewhere," he said. Late afternoon found all three relaxing around the fire. A blessed sun had gone into hiding behind a threatening cloud bank. The tea water was hot, and tin cups reached out expectantly. Brendan took the time to work out kinks from his arms and legs before he sat to apply flame to his pipe. Evidently, he was not interested in bringing out the board for a game of draughts (checkers). The air was still, the sea birds called to each other, and contentment enveloped the scene. Moments later, the tea was cooling, and Flynn was ready to leave for the cottage. Time was fleeting. Brendan and Donal Foley started their day two or three hours before the stars began to disappear. Flynn drained the last of the Assam tea from the tin cup. With the throwing knives still belted to his waist, he rose to his feet bidding the Foley brothers a good evening.

"The O' Connell's will find you in Killarney town," he said in parting. The wicker basket was in his left hand, the bag of feed over his right shoulder as he started for the cottage. The Foley boys watched him walk away, amused by the pullet that stuck its head through the lattice and pecked at Flynn's pants.

HUNGER

Donovan Rossa left for Killarney the day after D' Arcy McGee left Dublin for Killarney. Both would be there when Flynn and the family arrived at the home of Martha and Neil Howe, the owners of the Howe Livery and Blacksmith Shop. Patrick O' Brien walked for three hours without a break. Fortunately, he caught a ride for another hour before he had to resume his walk. Mid-afternoon found him beside a fast-moving stream. He took the time to quench his thirst and splash cold water on his face. Hungry, he decided to investigate the contents of the bundle he carried over his shoulder. The warm sun beat down causing him to pull his cap down over his sleep deprived eyes which grew heavy after he ate some of the ham and a raw carrot he washed off in the stream. He fell asleep, the result of a short night, an early morn, and then six or more hours walking up one hill and down another. He was elated, a cause for celebration, when a level stretch of green fell before his eyes. He carried a note Rossa had written to introduce him to the proprietor of the establishment he would call a refuge for the next week. The note would remain in his pocket.

They saw him sleeping, with his back against a grassy mound. A cap covered most of his face. A bearded man, two children, one of them a head taller than the other, looked for a sign of movement. Both children were skin and bones, ribs prominent when their clothing flapped in the slightest breeze. The man leaned down to whisper in the ear of the taller boy, pointing to where the bundle lay, inches from the man's fingers. The boy looked at his father who nodded emphatically, pointing, in an unspoken order to his son. He began to pull himself along using his bony elbows and knees to wind his way between tall clumps of green, toward the sleeping man and the white bundle tied to the stick. His progress was slow, the effort taxing what little strength remained in his frail body. The man and the younger boy watched anxiously, waiting expectantly to see what their desperation hoped to capture.

The tweet of a bird and the flutter of its wings brought him guiltily awake, his cap slipped to the grass. His fingers reached for the stick which was near his hand before he drifted off. When he didn't touch it, he raised up, his eyes frantically searched to his left and right. Nearby, in the grass, he spotted the white cloth. He crawled over to it, realizing his nap caused him to lose his provisions to someone who had a hunger that required theft of food. Remnants of cabbage leaves and stem which bore evidence of being chewed were all that remained. The stick was found and was retained as a remembrance each time his stomach growled when the stick he now used as a cane contacted the grass.

SANCTUARY

Tommy O' Keefe scraped his boots on the mat inside the cathedral. Reaching behind him he pulled the massive door shut and secured the latch. He heard the murmur, a low chanting of voices. The Friars were at morning prayers. Their day always started at first light ended hours after nightfall. Tommy made his way through the catacomb of rooms which led to the cavernous main hall from where the hour-long benediction was ending in a platitude of anticipation, lighting each lamp and candle he encountered along the way. His mission for the day was unknown until he was able to speak to Friar Jonathan. His passage through several empty spaces gave him an idea he would present to the Franciscan who assigned his duties each day. One of those candle-lit, empty rooms would be a perfect hiding place for the printing press. He arrived at the doors leading to the main sanctuary to find the cup empty of matches needed to light the oil lamps on each side of the door. He retraced his steps to find matches, returning to hear a higher chant of voices signaling the end of the prayer vigil and a hurried exit by the Friars to the room where a meager breakfast would be served. Should a Friar arrive late and end up near the end of the line, his "Spartan" breakfast, a biscuit, a small paddy of blood sausage and tea, might be missing, resulting in a fast until lunch was served? He lit the lamps, adjusting the flame as the latch on the door moved downward. The squeaky door was pushed open by the wrinkled hand of Friar Jonathan.

"Blessings to you, Tommy lad, a full day is ahead of you. I sense you are anxious about something." "Aye brother, anxious I am for our country. Our pursuit of a free Ireland has suffered a setback. Our meeting was discovered by the Brits, who shelled our friend's tavern in the knocks and shot him dead. He printed notices for Rossa and the Young Ireland group. The press is there to be recovered. We need a secure location, and I thought..." Friar Jonathan stared at Tommy without speaking, the silence was deafening. Tommy waited, respectful of the need for the Friar to consider what was offered.

"We have a press, Tommy. We are unable to use it for lack of working parts. We have a use for it as well and could assist you in the recovery of the press. Tell me the full story and I will contact Bishop Kennedy. You will lead four of our young men with our wagon to the site. No need is there to go under the moon, the Brits will not bother, and you must go soon before the site is plundered by scavengers." Friar Jonathan, a full head taller than Tommy, had his hands squeezing Tommy's shoulders while he gave him instructions. Tommy nodded.

MULDOON

An early spring morning, too early to attract the novice, the wide expanse of the Inis Fergus attracted Muldoon to cast his own line. His boat drifted ever so slowly on a mirror like surface. With little movement downstream, he flicked his wrist sending the invitation to rest on the calm waters. Over the years, Vincent Muldoon became captivated by the idyllic setting, a tree lined shore on one side and a grassy green bank on the other. Three seasons brought picnickers and children who fished from the shore or enjoyed a lunch at the tables Muldoon and his older brother Padraig had built and placed on the level expanse of the approach to the river. One boat became two, then three and later canoes were added. A building was constructed to enable them to conduct business. Later, after expansion, it became a year-round residence. In 1844, Padraig died, and then came a recurring tragedy, compounded by the actions of unscrupulous landlords against their renters. The rent could not be paid resulting in the cottier and his family being evicted, in many instances without notice. The famine caused by a disease which destroyed the potato crop resulted in the poor and hungry flooding into the town where a workhouse was being constructed. 1845 and '46 saw an increase in British troops marching through the town, holding drills near the barracks previously occupied by only two or three Brits. Gunfire was often heard to disturb the quiet of a sunny afternoon. Objections were murmured around the town to the brutal treatment of the poor and destitute country people who wandered into town. Often, they were met with the butt end of a British long gun. Pubs soon were emptied of the locals when the Queen's troops entered. The hungry poor who could speak English told shocking stories of the atrocities committed by militia and British soldiers alike under the approval and direction of the landlord who had no opposition. Defenseless people who saw and heard first hand of their tyrannical behavior cared little for the fight by some for political freedom. Loyal subjects of the Queen slowly recognized the ineffective government for what it was, and they changed their allegiance. However, one instance of British brutality was not enough, and many Irish closed their eyes. Vincent Muldoon changed his political views soon after he watched troops and militia return from an operation prodding an Irish farmer. The graybeard had his hands tied behind him and a rope around his neck. On bare feet, the man stumbled when his captor used the barrel of an Enfield rifle musket to hurry the offender along. Similar instances were repeated. Vincent began to hate the British invasion. One morning he discovered a returning contingent of troops took out their dislike of the Irish on his boats in the dead of night. One was missing, the remaining had holes in the hull made by British bayonets, confirmed when a broken bayonet blade was found underneath one of his craft. In the pubs, he hinted of his displeasure to people he trusted, and was given names and dates and places. He began to attend secret meetings and expressed a desire to become active in Nationalist interests to friends already active in the "Mollies."

REUNION

Devon directed the coal black horse named Jumper around the wagon to ride beside his father when the crest of the hill was reached overlooking the resort town of Killarney. Flynn's thoughts were directed toward the afternoon but reverted to the morning when he watched his son with pride. "My son is becoming a young man," he mumbled as Devon led the mare to the front of the wagon to be hitched. Margaret and her daughter were already seated in anticipation of the trip to Killarney. "Sure, pleased I am to see the smiles," he thought as Mary Margaret bounced up and down on the wagon seat, ready to begin the trip. Although the early morning was deluged by a heavy but brief assault from the heavens, the clouds were starting to feel the effects of the sun promising a rain free trip, and a week-long vacation for Margaret and Mary Margaret. As they passed the depot, Flynn spotted Tom Steele, the potato merchant, loading bags of disease-free seed.

"Aye, Flynn O' Connell 'tis a good day for my last trip to the countryside, and 'tis good to see you and the family and who might be the young man on that beautiful steed?" Tom Steele, the former bodyguard of Daniel O' Connell mourned the loss of his former employer but relished the opportunity to return to travel the countryside in Kerry, Cork and Clare. "A good day to ya' Tom Steele, proud I am of my son Devon who rides with us." Flynn looked back, waving a hand as they passed without stopping. Ahead of him was the town proper with wide brick streets being installed using some of the able-bodied from the workhouse near the St. Marys' cathedral under construction, and once known as "the church of the bishop." Margaret was the first to see a woman waving her hand before she picked up her skirts to run back down the boardwalk. Margaret recognized her as Silé Dooley. She waved, but what she assumed was a lookout had vanished down the street. Margaret smiled, knowing now her visit was not an intrusion, but a reunion with friends she had not seen for months. Off to the left Flynn could see the byre (barn) of the Howe Livery set away from the main part of the town. The fence was visible, but the blacksmith shop was hidden from sight. A left turn followed by a right took the wagon toward the Martha Howe residence. Margaret was thrilled to see her on the porch standing next to her son Neil and his future bride, Silé Dooley. Mary Margaret bounced up to wave at her friend Silé who waved back. Further down the boardwalk a lady approached preceded by two little girls who held unfamiliar skirts while they made their way to the porch with the sign "HOWE" over the door. Margaret recognized Fiona Farrell, the "aproneer" of the Farrell Mercantile. The two little girls, who had both grown an inch or so, were Sissy and Heather, both rescued by Fiona from the work house. They once were orphans and the older child did not have a name until she came under the wing of Fiona Farrell. At one time, she was called "girl." Margaret remembered them as frail and sickly. Now, the hollow cheeks were rosy, their hair shone beneath flowery bonnets and they both smiled their happiness at seeing Mary Margaret being lifted from the wagon by Neil Howe. Smiles were abundant, greeting and hugs were exchanged as Flynn removed luggage and Devon stood by his horse Jumper, reins in hand.

"Would you look at that young man ride!" Martha Howe exclaimed when she saw Devon ride up alongside the wagon. "Sure it is, you have grown a bit Devon O' Connell," she continued. "Come in please, all of you come in, Margaret O' Connell, so good it is to see you again." Mary Margaret was already renewing her friendship with the two Farrell girls, Sissy and Heather. Neil Howe led Flynn and Devon to the livery where Malachy Brandon, the blacksmith was opening the gate to the corral as they approached. Standing nearby was D'Arcy McGee, Neil Howe's friend from Dublin, an activist and Nationalist supporter. Inside the Howe dining room Silé was preparing the table as mid-day was fast approaching and the smells from the stove and hearth were caressing the nostrils of everyone. Neil was surprised to find his university friend standing there, although word was circulating of an impending visit. Greetings were followed up with hugs. Flynn shook hands with Darcy. "Can we talk later?" McGee asked. "I spoke with Ronan-O' Neill at the playhouse. He told me of your appointment this afternoon. May I join your party?" Flynn nodded. "You are welcome, and we will talk after the demonstration," Flynn replied. Neil and Devon returned from caring for the mare and her son.

"Good it is to see you D'Arcy and, please join us for a bite of lunch," Neil said. "'Tis appreciated Neil Howe, but I have a pub appearance shortly or I would be pleased. Will you be joining us at the playhouse? The man's skill is astounding, according to Ronan-O' Neill." "The livery calls to me this time D'Arcy. No doubt I will need to pay to see this man's skill." Flynn listened but said nothing until McGee was ready to leave. "With family and friends watching, I will miss the targets completely." Devon laughed with the others as Flynn rubbed his son's head. They parted company, D'Arcy headed for the Rose of Erin Pub, the others were ushered by Neil to the table readied by his mother and his future bride Silé.

EXHIBITION

A bench outside the Killarney Playhouse was occupied by two men, one with his hat pulled down over his face. Brendan Foley's snores told Donal his brother had fallen asleep on this sunny afternoon. His sumptuous lunch served by the flirtatious waitress Sally may have contributed to his need for a nap. Ronan-O' Neill paced, turning to retrace his steps as he pulled a pocket watch from a patchwork vest. First, he looked at the time indicated, before squinting at the sun. Impatient eyes searched the street again. His anxiety was relaxed as a small crowd, led by Flynn O' Connell marched their way toward him. The children did not mimic the adult's purposeful stride, playing keep-away from Devon in the street, hiding behind skirts, laughing. Everyone entered the shadowy cool of the playhouse through the door being held open by the man with the colorful vest. Donal shook his brother awake.

"Up with you brother, Flynn is here." Brendan had to gather himself to realize where he was. Though windows were open, and a breeze was felt sunlight could not penetrate thick walls. The women adjusted wraps around their shoulders before finding places facing the concave stage, on which, a variety of targets were arranged in a semi-circle. One of the targets was a life size cutout of a man with a red heart painted on the chest. Margaret and Martha Howe sat side by side. "I cannot forget our last trip here," Martha said to

Margaret. "It must be a good sign not to have the playhouse used as a hospital and mortuary." Although they looked at the targets, a moment longer on the man target with the heart on its chest, no comment came from either. "I shiver at the remembrance," Margaret said, the sick, the dying and death we witnessed will stay with me." The children were huddled together all of them appeared to be talking at once. Devon was the quiet one, his eyes on his father who was talking with Ronan-O' Neill. "Were you aware of Flynn's knife throwing talent, Margaret?" Martha asked. "We will wait to see that talent, Martha, and no, Flynn never talked to me about it at the cottage. He was always too busy to be involved in such an unproductive activity," Margaret said, with just a hint of scorn in her voice. "The Flax field awaits planting, and soon the sheep shearing will tire us to the point of exhaustion."

Flynn was on the stage with Ronan-O' Neill who had his hand on the edge of one of the targets. There were four animals painted on the target which moved when the circle target was spun. Devon watched his father shake his head or nod as they stood in front of each of the five targets. Fiona Farrell who was attending to her adopted daughters leaned over to whisper, "Flynn is ready to begin," her head turned to the children, "Quiet please! Watch him throw." Flynn paced off steps and turned to face the target. "Sure, not the distance, he threw from at the lake," Brendan said to his brother. "Not quite," Donal said as they watched the knife whistle through the air. Brendan's mouth dropped open as his wide-eyed look focused on his brother. Donal was just as stunned by the result of Flynn's effort. The audience was amazed, except for Mary Margaret who was playing with the little rag doll she brought with her. The force of his attempt moved the target mounted on an easel to its apex before slowly returning to rest on the floor. Flynn's knife was buried half way to the hilt in the center of the target. A buzz of amazed whispered comment circulated before Flynn increased the distance for his next attempt. Occupied with her rag doll, Mary Margaret jumped up and clapped her hands even though she missed her father's first attempt. She looked for approval from her mother.

"Now he is near the distance he was...," Donal mused. Again, the knife flew as if attracted by a magnet attached to the target. The knife joined the first, ending up alongside. The audience applauded. Flynn's audition continued to the fifth target. His success was greater than his inaccurate throws, and when he was asked to throw blindfolded, he was able to hit the target, the cutout with the heart, only two of five times. Margaret looked at Martha, who looked back.

"I don't like that target," Margaret said. "I don't either," Martha Howe said, nodding her head emphatically. On their way back, Flynn talked to Margaret about his conversation with Ronan-O' Neill who would present a proposal to Flynn for a performance in late August or September. He qualified his remarks to Flynn, citing last year when the playhouse was turned into a hospital, a mortuary for starving and dying Irish country people.

"He told me to continue practicing, and I would need to wear a costume and learn how to become a showman. I'm not sure I would agree to what he proposed." "I'm not in favor of using a man-sized target with a red heart," Margaret said. "'Tis getting late Flynn, you and Devon should be on your way shortly." "Missing you, I will my wife. In three days or even earlier if there is a need, I will be with the brothers. Is there anything you have forgotten that I can deliver when I return?" "Just bring yourself to me," she said, pressing herself into him with her arms around his neck in unabashed sight of all who remained in front of the Howe residence. Donal and Brendan Foley left quickly, being mid-afternoon with little time to pass at Brendan's favorite pub and a visit with Sally. Flynn left after thanking all for attending and asking Fiona Farrell if she had any additional needs to be delivered in three days. Devon had already left for the livery with Neil Howe who missed the exhibition and when the livery came into view Neil was talking with D'Arcy McGee outside the corral. Devon worked diligently, using a brush which brought out the oil and the shine on his best friend's coal black coat. Flynn looked inquiringly at the face of McGee, a young man, ten years or more, younger than he, who at his age had become a target of scrutiny due to his fiery condemnation of the atrocities committed by English landlords on their own lessees.

"I need the help of you and Devon in the coming days, Flynn. We have a man in hiding now who led an uprising near Ennis. He is now lodged in Kildysart but needs to be moved to avoid discovery. Can you assist us at least until Margaret returns to you?" "Help we can provide, but, not after Margaret returns," Flynn said. "Understood, it is O' Connell. Patrick O' Brien will be delivered on the morrow by Rossa who was here but already gone. I spoke with him so briefly at the Rose of Erin. Your location is so remote a sign must be left, or your guidance from the main pathway would be appreciated," McGee said. "What am I? A fugitive Nationalist patriot or a knife throwing showman? I think not!" Flynn bantered in jest, drawing grins from McGee and Neil Howe. "We will leave a sign for Rossa in the brambles. If he is to arrive using the valley of the cottager's we might watch for them from our location near the cliffs above," Flynn said. "Aye, a valley that must be crossed," McGee said.

THE VICAR

"It will be an adventure father," Devon said in Gaelic, overhearing the conversation after caring for his mount Jumper. The mare was hitched. Devon's feet were in the stirrups while his horse pranced, anxious to have his human friend relax the reins to let him run. Their next stop would be the domain of the vicar, Patrick Kincade. At the edge of town, the O' Connell wagon caught up to the Foley brothers on their way back to the lake. "Will you be calling on the vicar?" Donal shouted back at Flynn "Aye, Donal, the poor man suffers through 1845, the winter, and this spring of 1847 has continued to cause him grief." The wagons rumbled along making conversation difficult. Devon galloped on ahead, letting Jumper run for quite a distance before he halted his horse to wait for the wagons to catch up. The cathedral loomed before them but, the workhouse was hidden behind the tall trees. As they approached, all could see several workers at the edge of the trees where the burial ground was being prepared to receive bodies laid alongside partially completed graves. The smell of death was in the air. Patrick Kincade was nowhere to be seen. Flynn directed the mare to pull the wagon alongside the Foley wagon. Both were some distance from the fire under the black kettle as they watched the activity at the graveyard. Brendan pointed to the incomplete cathedral where work had resumed after a lengthy absence. Workers were not being paid causing work to cease for two years.

"Should we look for Patrick inside?" Brendan asked. All three of them looked first at one then the other, and all of them knew what anyone would be exposed to when entering the halls of death and dying commoners. One doctor, a visiting priest and two volunteers had perished from exposure to the sicknesses contained inside. No answer came, and they stared at their feet. "I fear for Patrick," Donal Foley said. Heads nodded as their eyes came up to search what was before them without finding what they sought.

"I will inquire of the workers," Flynn said as he climbed down from the wagon. Devon rode alongside as his father strode purposely toward the grave diggers. *Sure! I remember Neil Howe telling of his mother Martha aiding the sick and dying inside, and how he advised her to stay out of the cathedral,* he thought to himself. No doubt there was concern for Flynn about Margaret who was now living in the Howe residence, having daily contact with Martha Howe, and Silé Dooley who also volunteered to help before Neil talked to her. The first man Flynn approached paused in his digging using his sleeve to wipe the sweat from a glistening forehead. He leaned on his shovel as Flynn stepped to the edge of the hole where he stood."The vicar, Patrick, his whereabouts we do not see. Is he here?" Flynn asked the man who leaned on the shovel and turned his face away from his inquiry to gaze at his feet. Flynn waited, and with each second, without an answer the more fearful he became. "Aye, Patrick is very sick, he is cloistered at a nearby cottage under the care of a Killarney lady who volunteered to help him recover," he said. "His illness came upon him suddenly. He asked to be allowed to recover or die without visitors who could contract his malady, a fever and coughing." "A dedicated and compassionate man he surely is." Flynn said. "Our prayers, he motioned toward Donal and Brendan, who sat waiting expectantly for Flynn to return. Is anyone acting in his place?" Flynn asked. "We are," a strong voice came from behind. The men who were digging had gathered to hear the conversation between Flynn and the man, who elaborated. "We are the able-bodied from the workhouse, but the work is slow to be assigned, and Patrick, poor Patrick, you could see the illness overtake him so quickly. We know little but to work and we see what needs to be done, to plant the poor souls who lie here in the ground." "A few of us can band together to try to equal Patrick's loss," another man who stood behind said.

"In two or three days the three of us will stop with additions to the soup kettle. Patrick always found a use for what we provided." Flynn returned to the wagon where the Foleys waited expectantly. "Patrick Kincade has a sickness, Foley boys, he has been housed to recover and regain his strength, at an unknown location. Pray for the man we must." Flynn boarded the wagon and took the reins. "Soon it is Devon and I will go our way and you boys another. Will I see you in three days or two?""Disheartening words you brought to us Flynn. We will expect you to have hot biscuits, smoked salmon and tea ready when our eyes find the lamp lights on the shore in three days, my friend," Donal said. "Sure! We will pray for the man."

"Sorry news to hear," Brendan said as he urged their horse forward. Flynn flicked the reins and the mare pressed the leather. Their trip to the cottage was met by one sobering incident when half way home Flynn had to pull off to the side of the road. A four-horse team approached pulling a long wagon found to be loaded with the partially covered remains of deceased country peasants. The driver and his assistant wore handkerchiefs over their noses. When they passed Flynn, he turned his head away from the smell of sickness and death. Devon was speechless, but questions were sure to come. And the questions came while father and son sat across from each other at the lamp lit table. It was a long day, and night had fallen after Bessie, the chickens and pigs had been readied for the night. Heated water was used to clean the bowls of the remnants of hearty lamb stew not caught by fingers scraping tidbits from the sides of the dish. "Where was the wagon going, father," Devon asked, "what will happen to them if they did not receive the words of the priest?" Margaret's teaching included what she knew of the faith they followed. "Where will they be buried, in Killarney, at the graveyard, by the cathedral?" Devon's questions continued, one after another, he even forgot about the chess board and Flynn tried to answer each one as best he knew until the Sessions clock bonged nine times. The next day would be filled with new challenges.

Word had been received by Friar Jonathan. Bishop Kennedy had given his approval to the use of the printing press. Friar Jonathan was elated. He left before morning prayers were over to stand near the back door at a small iron barred window. He anticipated the arrival of Tommy O'Keefe and anxiously paced, waiting. His plan to send four brothers to recover the press and transport it to the cathedral made the Friar smile. Tommy would be relieved at the news. Assisted by a handwritten document, recovery of the press gave ownership to the Franciscans in the event of the death of Hugh Harrell. Friar Jonathan had authored the paper he used to authenticate the origin of the document torn and yellowed from age. It bore his signature and the signature of Bishop Kennedy. Should a question arise from anyone who objected, when the signature of the bishop was noted, free passage would be allowed? After many attempts, and after he had renewed the point on the quill with his pen knife, Friar Jonathan had satisfied himself with the likeness of his forged signature to that of the Bishop. The sound and movement of the latch drew the Friar's eyes to the creaking of the rough-hewn door. Tommy O' Keefe had arrived.

Donovan Rossa caught a cart ride for the last two miles to Kildysart. He thanked his host before jumping off prior to his arrival at the edge of the little village. He took the time to reset his cap to shade his eyes while he surveyed what made up the town's main business district. Four storefronts were decorated in multi-hued shades, blue, red, yellow and green. On one side of the street one of the buildings appeared to be a pub. Wooden benches framed each side of the door. Rossa noted that they were occupied by pipe smoking elders who appeared to enjoy the warming rays of the sun. On the other side of the street, two other storefronts were divided by an alleyway that led to a path with cottages facing the rear of the building across the way. From his angle of view, Rossa was able to see the rear of the two storefronts. One of the cottages on the end of the row had a fence surrounding a byre where Rossa hoped to find Patrick O' Brien quartered. A few cottages surrounded the village marked by short stone fences, promoting a picturesque sense of tranquility. Outside one of the cottages, a woman hung clothing on a line to be dried. He took notice of the lack of activity on the street between the buildings facing each other, allowing him to approach his objective with little chance of being noticed. He was not worried about being observed. He left the impression that he was just another country Irishman seeking a taste at the pub. He re-positioned his knapsack over an aching shoulder and headed for the rear of the byre. It was crucial to make sure hunted patriots were protected, hidden from eyes that would earn favors for Irishmen who were English loyalists who had to hide their traitorous deeds from neighbors and friends. Nearly out of sight of the main street, his eye caught movement at the door of the suspected pub. His fugitive guest and Parias

Connelly who furnished the hiding place walked arm in arm toward him. They were singing a rather bawdy ballad called "Hairy Mary" laughing when they came to a funny line. Clearly, they had spent considerable time in the pub known as The Ram's Horn Pub & Hostel.

"Tell me Patrick O' Brien why I should not worry you might have been discovered," Rossa said. Before he could reply Connelly offered an excuse. "Tis my doing Rossa, Patrick was introduced as my visiting nephew," he said. "There are no English collaborators in our village." Stoic, Rossa stared at the protector and then shifted his dubious look to O'Brien. "For your health Patrick, I hope Connelly is right, get what gear you have, we must be on our way. You will be the guest of Flynn O' Connell and his son Devon for the next few days." "Aye Patrick, I will miss your hard work and company while you were here," Connelly said.

A FUGITIVE GUEST

High noon found Flynn and Devon outside the low stone perimeter fence surrounding the sheep pasture. Two hours had passed and still there was no sign. They continued to search the valley where they hoped to see Donovan Rossa and the fugitive Patrick O' Brien make their way toward them. Flynn had built a small turf fire that hissed when sporadic raindrops found the flame. Hopefully, the smoke would attract the eyes of Rossa and their future guest. Shelter from the elements was provided by the tarp Flynn propped up with sticks to fashion a lean-to which offered some protection from the threatening weather gods. Devon concentrated on the cubes of pork impaled on the end of the stick he held to the heat and flame. The meat began to emit sensory hints to the nostrils of both the father and son who watched patiently for the arrival of two, one on the run, the other a protector of an asset available for a future rising. Flynn's addition of some of Margaret's spice had added to Devon's desire for a taste before the meat was fully cooked. Flynn had watched Devon salivating before his eyes shifted attention from a search of the valley to the progress made by the fingers of fire reaching for the morsels on the end of Devon's stick. For a moment, he was mesmerized by the tongues of fire fed by the dripped fat from the pork. The flames flared, and the fire's fuel sizzled on the coals of the turf. Two specks of movement in the valley below released Flynn from his momentary trance. He shook Devon's shoulder and pointed to the valley below. The two specks came into view and then disappeared behind brambles or rocks to re-appear as Devon caught sight of them. "Now I see them father." Devon turned his attention back to the fire where Flynn had propped the branch holding the meat over the fire. His eyes gave only a fleeting glance at the smoldering turf before into his line of sight appeared another movement from the other end of the valley. "Look father," Devon jabbed his finger excitedly. "A horseman behind a line of soldiers, do you see? They will see our fire, father!"

"I do see them Devon. They are crossing the valley toward Rossa and away from us." Flynn felt helpless being so far away. He hoped the two would see the troops before they were discovered. Both watched the distance between become smaller and smaller, but still a mile, at least, between what could become a confrontation between a fugitive and the hunter. The cooking meat forgotten for the moment, the piece nearest the fire now was charred to a blackened coal-like lump. Frustrated, Flynn stood with his fists clenched, unable to help as the distance narrowed. He recalled a similar instance years ago in Vera Cruz when he laid wounded on the docks, unable to prevent the horror he watched develop before his eyes, the flames, the heat, and the cries of the children. The nightmares had declined now, after ten years. He watched the rider move his mount to the front of the line, picking his way around and through blackthorn and bramble, around hazards partially hidden in the tall grasses. *Who would be first to discover the other,* he thought as most of their attention was to their feet to avoid being bloodied by thorns, or hobbled by twisting an ankle. Rossa and Patrick O'Brien fought their way, still unaware of the danger ahead of them. "What will the soldiers do, father? Fearful I am," Devon said as he held a piece of meat, hardly nibbled while he stood at his father's side. Flynn was silent until he felt a tug at his pocket. Devon wanted an answer, his own face a cloud of anxiety. He had recognized the contingent of Britain's finest all shouldered long guns. "If someone watches over Rossa and Patrick, both would be alerted and 'tis possible the troop is not looking for Patrick but only on a training march." Flynn reached for the stick holding a chunk of well-done pork. "Say a prayer to God for their safety, son of mine," Flynn said while he continued to think of a way. "Devon son gather any wood to add to the fire. Damp grass we will add to make more smoke. They will see it and change direction away from the soldiers." He broke the sticks with the meat over his knee and added them to the fire. Dry wood was scarce, but in an ever-widening circle both were able to collect a few pieces to add to the turf. Damp grasses were added to the top and acrid gray smoke billowed into the stillness of the day.

+

Rossa and his fugitive charge walked from Kildysart to the outskirts of Ennis where they caught a freight wagon headed to Killarney. They hopped off near the far end of the valley and started walking toward the foothills on the other side of the valley. Their attention was not on what was in front of them but rather to the foothills watching for the smoke signal Flynn had promised to light. Suddenly in the distance a gray cloud spread wide and high behind the shrubbery and berry bushes.

"Look there, Patrick, see the smoke," Rossa said as he turned his charge to the direction of the billowing cloud."Aye and my ears have heard a shouted word ahead of us," Patrick said as both became cautious, bent over and creeping to the cover provided to their left. Using any available shield, they scampered from shrub to tall grass, their route now a gradual incline. Again, out of breath they stopped and went to their knees hoping to hear what Patrick heard. Silence reigned until the call of the sea birds overhead drew their attention. Without any warning, the sound of musket fire startled both Rossa and Patrick O'Brien. "We must leave here quickly, Patrick," Rossa whispered. "Trouble is near." What they didn't know was one of Flynn O'Connell's sheep had wandered away from the pasture over a mile away and now lay dead, the victim of a British musket ball.

The report of the musket echoed to the ears of Devon and Flynn as smoke rose from the long gun's barrel. They could see images gathered around whatever was found to warrant firing a weapon. "I fear we have lost one of our sheep," Flynn said. "Sure it is, their attention was distracted. Rossa should be able to take advantage and run to safety." He longed this day for a return to his cottage that had become the haven for a suspected traitor to the Crown. His former life may have become interrupted by his hidden allegiance to an effort, however, unadvised to duplicate what transpired nearly 70 years ago on another continent.

There were times when no cover was available, and they crawled on hands and knees across a clearing to the relative safety of the next clump of bushes. Rossa often walked backwards, bent over, his eyes searched the direction of the musket fire fearful they would be seen and chased. Sweat beaded his brow on a brisk but sunlit spring day. A pause for a breath caused him to consider the scratches on his arms and hands from the thorns of the berry bushes they were unfortunate to encounter. *I will bleed to death before we reach safety,* he thought.

"Stay quiet Patrick, your shirt and back are bloody." A thorny branch was still attached to O'Brien's shirt. Rossa carefully freed it without suffering a bite from a thorn. He stood up on his toes, his arms separating the bushes to allow unimpeded sight back toward where the gunshot was heard. He went to his knee again, whispering to Patrick although they were far enough away not to be heard. He pointed, making a circular motion with his hand. "Careful we must be not to lead them to the O'Connell farm. We will go that way watching all the time to make sure we are not followed." O'Brien started out followed by Rossa who looked behind him and walked backwards so often he lagged behind O' Brien. The fugitive Patrick had to wait for him to catch up.

Minutes later they had arrived at a point high enough for them to see what was below. Half a mile away the British contingent was gathered around a fire.

"Father, I see them," an excited Devon jumped up and down as he pointed to a spot below them that was not in their original line of sight. The roundabout route took longer but assured Rossa they would not interest the British in the smoke from Flynn's signal fire. Flynn's eyes found where Devon had pointed. "Time it is to put out the fire Devon," as he moved clumps of turf to the side where damp grass eventually would extinguish the coals. Steam and smoke rose but why would anyone be attracted to Irishmen heating water for tea over a mile away. Flynn watched the fugitive Patrick and Donovan Rossa scramble up the slope, dodging in and out from behind berry bushes and blackthorn, using that shield between them and possible pursuers who were currently occupied on the valley floor. At times, they used both hands and feet to make their way toward Flynn and his son who knelt watching their progress. Their panting arrival leaning over with hands on their hips required a few deep breaths before Rossa spoke.

"I thought we were dead men when I heard the musket fire, Flynn." "What did they shoot at?" O' Brien asked while leaning over with hands on his knees. He stood up, turning toward the pasture beyond the low perimeter fence and the sheep, some of which were curious about the activity and approached anticipating the grain they occasionally received. "Aye,

Patrick, what you see was surely the target. Some of them tend to leave the pasture to wander, but always return to the safety of the cliff and the rocks," Flynn replied. "'Tis sad for the O' Connell who lost a number of them to the winter and one more to starving country people." After providing water to the thirsty pair, Devon capped the water bottle and their walk back to the cottage began. On the far side of the pasture, they walked past the flax field already beginning to reveal new plants bursting through the soil. "A daunting task you have undertaken O' Connell," Patrick said as he surveyed the field and the surrounding area, "I speak of the field of flax. I know of the toil necessary to prepare the field, plant and harvest the crop. You must believe the rewards are greater than the effort." "Aye, 'tis tiring for all the O' Connells,' but provides Margaret a less taxing day by using the linen wheel," Flynn replied. Nearing the corral, Devon ran ahead mounting the rail with a hand extended to scratch the ears of the black horse that rotted over to the fence. "Please sit yourself inside while the water heats," Flynn told them. "I have crusty bread and butter, honey and leftover smoked salmon." Devon pushed through the half door. "I will get the butter, father," he said overhearing what Flynn said. Devon returned outside to the north side of the cottage where the dugout cellar was used to keep perishables fresh. He had the tin of butter in hand when a shot rang out, echoing off the face of the cliff, and then another. He burst through the half doors. "Father, did you hear?" The thick stone walls of the cottage muffled the sound to the ears of the three that sat at the table. "Gunfire father, two shots I heard. The soldiers are on the path near us." Flynn and Rossa scrambled out the door, followed by Patrick. The wind carried the sounds made by more than one person. The British company was less than a quarter mile away from the plateau where the O'Connell cottage hid behind the thorny shield of blackberry and bramble.

"Did they follow us, Flynn?" Rossa asked while a worried look covered his face. Flynn did not respond immediately. "If they followed us Patrick and I must leave," Rossa continued. A void of silence occurred while they all listened for the sounds of movement. "They are going away from us, toward Killarney," Flynn said. "What caused the rifle fire?" Patrick asked. "We will investigate after we all refresh ourselves inside," Flynn said, turning toward the half door. Devon followed Rossa and Patrick O'Brien inside where a jar of honey sat next to a loaf of bread and a plate of smoked salmon. The water for the tea steamed in the pot hung in the hearth. All were tired and hungry. Devon had collected the eggs Flynn scrambled with a bit of milk and butter. The loaf of bread and half the smoked salmon were quickly devoured. A few minutes to stretch and loosen boot laces followed. The mid-point of the afternoon had passed as the Sessions clock bonged the half hour beyond four o'clock, prompting Flynn to bend over to retie his boot laces. He rose, stomping his feet, a signal to the others who although tired, they were as well interested in what had transpired on the path to Killarney. Rossa stretched and twisted while O'Brien bent over to grab the toes of his boots, rising to windmill his arms, all of them needed to get the blood flowing again. No words were spoken outside the cottage. All of them would revel in hearing only the calls of the sea birds and the wind rustling the tall grass. Flynn looked at Rossa who looked at Patrick. "They are gone," Devon said. The walk to the path began, with Flynn leading the way through the bramble and blackthorn. Ahead was the hazardous rocky slope that George Brewster cursed repeatedly on his return to Killarney after a visit two years ago.

British soldiers lounged in the grass around the fire that roasted the ewe they happened upon during their march. The shooter continued to receive pats on the back for his good eye, saving all the need to open the pack they carried. The officer in charge had only one order. "Gather wood and dry grass." Others took charge of the butchering. Within minutes, a fire was started, and the troop took turns turning the carcass on an improvised spit. Flame from the fire kissed the fatty parts causing an eruption of sounds as the meat seared. Time did not allow for the roasting process necessary to cook the lamb completely, the meat close to the bone barely warm and raw. Much was wasted since they faced a three-hour trip back to the barracks on the outskirts of Killarney. The march began, following a path used by indigent cottiers from the country hamlets and farms in search of their next meal. An hour into their return through the valley their path merged into another, obviously heavily traveled, with wheel tracks and bare earth peeking out of beaten down grass. From a different direction, another trail merged into the more heavily traveled route. On their left, the cliff protected the sheep pasture of the O'Connell family, out of sight to them, and near the beginning of the foothills of MacGillycuddy's Reeks, a low mountain range, the most prominent outcropping in Ireland. Their route had changed to an increasingly difficult climb up the slope having departed the flat valley recently traversed. Some of them grumbled, forgetting the earlier part of the day when their march was down a gently sloping entrance to the valley, but they trudged ahead, avoiding chunks of granite and bramble thorns that raked across unprotected hands and cheeks when their attention wavered. Undisciplined yelps in pain and curses permeated the air, quieted when the mounted officer turned his mount and fixed his steely eyed stare on the offending soldier. Their mumbling protests continued even though the route had leveled. A wide path sloped down on their right and on their left was an almost vertical wall, overgrown with bramble above that hid whatever was behind. Unnoticed by the company was the partially hidden entrance that eventually led to the humble abode of Flynn O'Connell and his family. Without a modicum of warning, a screeching, screaming sound was heard. The Banshee-like screams came from the mouth of a naked man who rushed toward the mounted officer with his arms raised. His horse reared in fright, throwing the Brit to the ground. The naked man ran screaming down the line of troops and was immediately followed by another man who attacked one of the troops attempting to wrest his weapon from him. A struggle ensued. The second shirtless man was no match for the soldier who threw him to the path. It was at that time a shot rang out, and the naked fellow fell to the ground. The echo barely silenced when a second round was heard, and the shirtless fellow who attempted to resume his attack joined his partner. Chaos reigned as armed troops spread their feet with arms at the ready watching for any further intrusion. A few soldiers struggled to fix bayonets. The horse ran for a distance before tiring, stopping to nibble on vegetation growing from the side of the rocky wall on the left of the pathway. The horse heard the shrill whistle and started back toward the grounded rider holding the carrot in his hand. Two of the soldiers pulled the bodies off the path to a hollow in the side of the rocky wall. "Look at them would you! The blokes are skin and bones! Count their ribs," he said, "no doubt remains on what drove them mad. It was their hunger." "Leave them as they are," the officer said, a message to others who come this way. Leave the Union Jack, one of the small ones. Mount our flag between them." Their march resumed, an hour away from the Killarney barracks. Bayonets remained fixed, and eyes alertly shifted, searching to the left and right as they walked.

+

Flynn led the group in a hurried walk to the *boreen* as time was on the wane and attention to the farm had yet to take place this day, the first he experienced in what might be called political insurrection. It was not to his liking. The four gathered together on the path. Flynn took charge. "Rossa, you and Patrick head to the left until you determine that nothing is amiss ahead of you. Devon and I will go to the right, and we will meet back here. Give a shout if something is found. 'Tis possible the shots were fired at the birds or for practice." They parted company and not a hundred paces later a shout was heard from Rossa and then another from Patrick O'Brien. Flynn and Devon ran back to see Rossa and O'Brien standing in the middle of the path with their hands on their hips. As Flynn approached, Rossa pointed down toward the base of the rocky hollow in the side of the wall. "Were they the reasons for the gunfire Devon heard?" He said. "I cannot find nary a hint of a reason for the fellow's nakedness." "'Tis the place Devon and I used to feed the passersby twice a week during our winter months," Flynn said. "We won't know the reason for such extreme action on the part of the Brits, but musket balls ended their hunger."

"Late it is Flynn," Rossa said, "I will take my leave now to arrive in Ennis at dark is well advised. While Patrick is here, put him to work and I will no doubt see you and the fishermen in a week or two. Our runners will leave a message with Neil Howe for either you or Patrick," he said waving as he started walking back retracing the route through the valley. "Rescue that flag, Patrick, it may come in handy for Flynn," Rossa said while walking backwards before turning back toward the rocky slope that would take him past the O'Connell cottage and pasture leading to the valley. "'Tis late Patrick. On the 'morrow is time enough to cover the lads." Flynn was thinking of the Guernsey, the sheep, the pigs and the horses. All needed attention. Patrick stepped carefully between the bodies and pulled the Union Jack from between the bodies.

+

Rossa alternated between running and walking, twice passing people who were headed in the opposite direction. Their next meal or possibly only a morsel waited for them at the site of the cathedral that was partially hidden behind some of the oldest trees in the county. His mind raced, anxious to find what had happened in his absence. *The printing press; was a location found? Had the hunt for Patrick O'Brien quieted, as they sometimes did? Were Muldoon and Tommy safe and avoiding scrutiny? So much was needed in Ennis, Killarney, and in the country hovels and hamlets of the beleaguered Irish commoner. We need to be able to live without fear.*

+

In the early evening before Rossa's arrival in Ennis, Muldoon and Tommy O'Keefe walked on either side of the wagon, trying their best to sneak out of Ennis during the supper hour. Headed for rubble that once was the Red Lion Tavern, they, and four friars were dressed in the brown hooded robes and the open toed sandals so common among the Franciscan's. Muldoon and Tommy O'Keefe prayed to become invisible. Darkness would hide them but not until their arrival to retrieve the printing press that miraculously survived the bombardment of the British cannon. In the wagon were the tools they would need. Levers and rope, heavy sledges and pry bars would be necessary to clear debris and knock down a wall. Fortunately, there was little movement on the streets at the edge of town and the cathedral would act as a shield to their escape. Little comfort came from the sun below the horizon and the hood of the garment. Two imposters hoped they were inconspicuous, afraid to talk, afraid to look to the left or right, fearful of discovery.

THE APRONEER

Fiona Farrell had a new challenge, and she was determined to meet the sudden change in her life. Two little homeless, parentless urchins were now a part of her. Sissy and her older sister, Heather Anne would be a part of her life, every day, every night. Unmarried and childless, she realized how difficult her task had become since that rainy day at the realm of Patrick Kincade who was a Godsend to many starving and homeless Irish people. Her two adopted girls had no knowledge, other than the hardships they faced each day and their relationship with others in the clan. After days of conversation, her questions convinced her, their world consisted of a clan encampment or a country cottage. Now that the miserable winter had gone away, Margaret O'Connell will be spending more time in Killarney ending a lonely three months since her last visit to Killarney. Fiona wanted to talk with her about tutoring the children as she did with her son and daughter who made remarkable progress. Devon O'Connell was fluent in Gaelic and helped his father with the language, Flynn's third, as he was comfortable speaking in French. Fiona was hesitant to bring up the idea the day Margaret arrived, allowing her and her daughter the time to get settled in and comfortable in Martha Howe's spare bedroom. This morning will see her visit the Howe residence to bring up the idea to Margaret O'Connell.

"Thump, thump, thump, thump," the sound she heard was her adopted family making their presence known as they pounded their way down the stairs. Fiona stood waiting for their hugs as her girls yawned and stretched at the bottom of the stairs. Sissy rubbed her eyes with the back of her hand. "Good morning, my children. Come here to me." Fiona held out her arms, wrapping still sleepy orphans, who hugged her back. "Did you sleep well, Heather Anne?" Fiona asked. "Were you warm enough?" Heather Anne nodded, and Sissy broke their silence. "We sleep in a real bed, ma'am, with warm covers. Before, I shivered. Now, I don't shiver at all." Heather Anne nodded again and tightened her hold around Fiona's waist. A dreamy smile covered her face.

"Two young ladies need to make ready for the day before we breakfast," Fiona said, pointing toward the door where the bowl, water pitcher and drying towels hung on the rack behind it. "Yes ma'am, Heather Anne said. The girls relinquished their hold and ran for the door. After the table was cleared, and the dishes were washed and dried, Fiona gave her new family their school assignments for the next hours. She hoped that, by repetition, the girls would learn the English alphabet. Fiona realized that her efforts were insufficient, and her teaching skills were minimal, not at all adequate. The National school could not place the girls until next September. Although the mercantile had been open for two hours, only three customers had visited. Shortly after, an unexpected visitor made the bell sound over the door. A smiling Mary Margaret O'Connell was followed inside by her mother, Margaret.

"So pleased am I to see both of you," Fiona said, walking toward them with arms extended, "have you settled yourselves after such an eye-opening exhibition by your husband?"

"Fiona, I have been asked repeatedly by my daughter to visit. I had little time to get us settled," she motioned to her daughter whose eyes were searching until she found her friends who were partially hidden by a cabinet full of merchandise. Mary Margaret made herself right at home, pulling a chair back from the table to kneel on, her elbows on the table top while she watched Heather Anne and Sissy practice printing the letters of the alphabet. "Let us watch them for a moment, Margaret," Fiona said, with her hand on Margaret's back to direct her toward the cabinet where they could observe the three at the table. Mary Margaret was being a little pest by displaying her knowledge of the alphabet's letters, pointing to each as she identified the letter while she giggled. She stopped when she looked up to see her mother shaking her head, a frown covering her face. "I have tried to blend teaching them without taking away from the new pressure I faced during the winter...very few customers...two hungry children, all new to me, Margaret," Fiona lamented, likely hoping that Margaret would recognize her dilemma and offer her help. "Would you like tea?" Fiona asked. Margaret smiled and nodded acceptance. Both looked up at the sound of the bell over the door to announce the arrival of the apothecary, Prescott Piggerman.

"'Tis a good day, ladies, I have medicines for the sick and hungry. Has Kincade returned?" "He was not seen two days ago, Mr. Pigg." The country poor still come daily. Some of them are starving, many are sick, and they die on the way," Fiona said. "I will deliver your offering to whoever is in charge later today." The apothecary tipped his hat and turned to leave. "Brave you are Miss Farrell to mingle among the sick and dying. Your place among the angels is assured." The bell sounded, and the door closed behind him. A sigh of resignation escaped Fiona as she turned back to the stove. "Now, where were we?" Fiona retrieved the porcelain pot with the water from the stove top. Margaret turned over the cups and spooned the tea into both cups while she listened to Fiona's indirect appeal. "I am limited to what I can do to teach them, so inadequate I feel," she said so quietly Margaret barely heard her comment. Fiona filled the cups, returning the pot to the stove, and reached for the china sugar bowl. She dropped two lumps into her cup and pushed the container toward Margaret. "I know what you have yet to ask me Fiona, and I do appreciate your dilemma. Unfortunately for me, like you, it's a matter of time. My exodus will see me back at the cottage, the sheep and the Guernsey. What I could do for you is to prepare a plan for you to follow until you are able to secure a nanny or to enroll the children in the National school." Her hand reached for the hand of Fiona and their eyes met.

RECOVERY

The crest of the last hill had been reached. Below them, the ruins of the Red Lion Tavern were barely visible in the hollow of the knocks. Dusk was turning to dark as eyes searched to determine if their safety would be compromised by proceeding any farther. Ears listened to the lack of sound in the night, the huff of the horse the only break in the stillness. A flick of the reins released the watchers from their vigilance. Wagon wheels began a creaking roll down the slope. As they approached the ruins, their feet and horse's hooves encountered scattered debris blown up and around by British cannon fire. The driver directed the horses to the undamaged corner of the building, pulling the team to a stop between a pile of suspect stones. Just beyond was the miraculously undamaged corner of the tavern and the location of the press. The eyes of the monks recognized the out of place debris for what it was. They left the wagon and gathered around the makeshift grave of Hugh Harrell. Tommy O'Keefe stood next to Muldoon, his head bowed, his lips moved in silent prayer. Muldoon moved to the wagon reaching over the side feeling for the pry bar. A heavy lock was still engaged. It was bolted to the three-inch thick door and would need to be released before entry and removal of their objective could be accomplished. Three of the monks were busy clearing away debris from the front of the door, the fourth stood guard, a sentry, his hood lowered to his shoulders to assist as he scanned the countryside. The three moved out of the way when

Muldoon and Tommy made their way through the cleared path to face the formidable barrier protecting their ability to print the truth.

"Aye Tommy, both of us should be able to pry the lock free." Muldoon lifted the pry bar to the mechanism, bracing his foot against the door jam. His hands gripped the bar over his head, Tommy behind him adding his two hands to the effort. The monks watched the effort, hearing the grunts of the men and the protests of the iron being pried from the wood. The combination of their weight, strength and the bar prevailed as the heavy iron lock broke free from the massive oak door. A shout in triumph came from one of the monks, cut short when fearful eyes stared to demand his silence. His sheepish look advertised regret for an impromptu reaction. Although the corner of the building still stood protecting the space where the printing press was hidden, the shelling from the artillery attack knocked the storage closet out of plumb. The door would not open even though the lock was removed. A crowd of hooded monks acted as a shield to the two Irishmen in front of the door. Hands waved, and shoulders shrugged from those only familiar with another occupation.

"Pry the hinges from the door," one of the monks offered, but the hinges were recessed. "Beat the door down with the hammer," another suggested, but heads shook in refusal due to the sound that would resonate in the night's stillness. Fingers pointed as eyes examined every inch of the obstacle searching for a solution until Muldoon attempted to wedge the pry bar between the door and its jamb to no avail. Friar Alfred, the driver of the wagon suggested that since the bottom of the door rested on the bare earth, the bar should be forced under the door and lifted free of the ground. Boards could be forced underneath, the pry bar removed and used to pry the door away from the frame. A few moments of discussion resulted with no other potential solution offered, considered worthy enough to give the idea a try. Friar Alfred left the discussion and when he returned his hands carried a heavy sledge hammer.

"Position the bar at the bottom of the door. I will drive it underneath. Gather boards to slide under when the bar is lifted," he ordered as he positioned himself with the hammer in hand. In unison, working together, three monks and two political activists were able to free the door. At the precise moment the door was opened, the moon made its first appearance that evening, shining light over the landscape. All eyes glanced upwards. "A good sign or a bad omen, I know not which," Friar Alfred said as he replaced the tools in the wagon. The moving of the press went quickly with long boards positioned to slide the press to the bed of the wagon. Tarps were tied down to hide the press from view and the return trip began. Friar Alfred's head nodded as if in agreement to the disappearance of the moon behind a cloud bank. He hoped the clouds might furnish wetness needed to obliterate the wagon tracks leading to and from the cathedral. Press rescuers return trip began in a much more relaxed mood than when a few hours earlier they crept silently and guiltily away from the rear of the cathedral. In their mind, the trip had been successful. Recovery of the press was made without incident and the dark of the night would shield their return. Conversation resumed with an occasional hint of laughter being heard from the monks. Muldoon and Tommy O'Keefe were silent knowing their exposure to potential questioning by the Brits would not be relieved until they had the press safely secured in that unused space in the home of the monks. Recent events and increased scrutiny by loyalists brought Rossa's remark back to them about their need to reveal the informant in their midst. So far, their attempts were hindered by the increased diligence nationalist sympathizers practiced when in contact with individuals whose allegiance had yet to be determined. Muldoon had an opinion and made it clear on the person he suspected.

"My 30 pieces of silver would be paid to the one who reveals the allegiance of Johnny Byrne," he said, more than once. He often would cite the time the butcher visited the boat livery after Muldoon discovered the malicious action by British troops who damaged his rental craft. "He did nothing but chuckle, saying, 'you will be a busy Irishman repairing your leaky craft, won't you?'" Others disagreed with Muldoon's suspicions. They accused him of holding a grudge against the butcher who complained about the rental fee he paid. "You charge me a greater rental than you charge the Brits," he voiced in an accusatory tone. "I was pressured to lower my price," Muldoon responded. He told Burns he stood his ground with them one day resulting in a boycott of his business for a time, and then came the incident with the damaged boats. "The Brits don't come as often now, and that is just fine with me," he said. "The locals and the tourists have returned. The locals stayed away when the Brits came. No doubt it is the eyes of the Mollies should follow the butcher and confirm his meetings with the miserable Brits."

Their slow trek continued, up one knock, and when headed down the other side, the driver's foot rested on the brake. A respite for the horses came when they reached the valley before another leather straining trudge up the next knock, aided by two of the monks who decided to push. Moonlight emerged for the second time, drawing brief glances from all, except Friar Alfred who hoped for rain. He preferred it wet to hide the wagon tracks. "A penance it would be and a release from the abstinence on the 'morrow I would hope for but surely will not receive," he lamented. At the top of the hill with only one more to traverse, Friar Alfred brought the team to a halt, climbing down from the seat to stretch and view the nightscape. One of the monks made sure the horses received water. Night time saw no movement, human or animal, on the grassy mound barren of the low stone fences so common in Kerry and Clare. Flickering light, the faint glow of torches in the distance was seen by Friar Alfred and the rescuers on what was the level path from the north leading to Ennis.

"The poor and the hungry walk to the town," Tommy O'Keefe said, pointing to the glows in the distance. He was overheard by Friar Joseph. "Our resources are limited, and we are asked to make sacrifice after sacrifice. My stomach will growl until the morn with my only meal taken at mid-day. Two days of the week, we partake of food, twice. Two days we partake of food, once. Our strength wanes on those days and we pray. Our efforts are surely not enough," he lamented. "We join them in their suffering."

Friar Alfred climbed back to the wagon seat grabbing the reins. With a flick of his wrists, his foot resting on the brake, the wheels began to turn. Their return resumed as the moon hid again. Raindrops splashed on faces that looked to the heavens.

MEETING

A walk to the cathedral awaited Fiona. She decided to take Heather Anne with her, leaving Sissy in the care of Jasmine, the student Fiona enlisted to assist her at the mercantile. Jasmine volunteered to tutor Sissy in between customers which pleased Fiona, lifting some of the pressure from her. The basket she would carry with her was filled with the apothecary's medicines and a few items of clothing from the store inventory. On their way, they would pass the Howe residence. She hoped Margaret's second day would be one of rest and just a few thoughts on how she might direct the education of two little orphans.

"Are you ready Heather Anne?" Fiona stood at the bottom of the stairs waiting for her new daughter to come down. Sounds from the room above indicated a hurried preparation was complete, and then Fiona heard the bedroom door shut. Heather Anne appeared at the top of the stairs. "Ready I am," she said taking each step cautiously in shoes yet to be fully broken in. Fiona unfolded a banian (white wool) wrap, holding it out to drape over her new daughter's shoulders. All mercantile items that she offered for sale were of the highest quality. Fashioned in the Aran Islands, hand crafted sweaters and scarves were highly prized by tourists. Heather Anne smiled a happy smile as she twisted her hands in the soft wrap. Sissy was at the side of Jasmine who waited on a customer at the counter. They both waved as Fiona picked up the basket and turned to leave. Out on the street they were greeted by a fresh spring early morning where the sun peeked in and out from high mountainous clouds of white and gray. Still, it was too early in the morning for the tradesmen and deliveries to clog the streets. Gentlemen they met tipped their hats to the ladies as they passed by. On their way, they passed by restaurants and pubs, the hotels and hostels, on and off the boardwalk and past vacant lots. Forced into the dampness of the street, off the boardwalks and brick streets, Heather Anne was prompted to stop to clear mud mixed with offal from her shoes.

"Oh, yuk" "'Sure 'tis the first shoes I have ever had," she said, more than once to everyone, but still preferred to be barefoot around the mercantile. Fiona decided to alter the route, bypassing the Howe residence, cutting through a vacant lot next to a pub, the name of which she could not remember. Their route was two streets away from the Howe's and for a time the route was a brick street under construction that would merge onto Cottage Street. She regretted her decision to take the short cut when she and Heather Anne were confronted by a group of hungry Irish peasant women and their children who clutched the skirts of their mothers. Their hands were held out to them as they approached, their eyes focused on the basket carried by Fiona. Their pleadings in the Gaelic language were not understood by Fiona, but unnecessary because of the obvious emaciated condition of the women. Fiona's hurried walk detoured around the group when without warning a man approached from the rear and grabbed at the basket she held.

"Get away, please!" Fiona shouted and fought to retain the basket with both hands but lost her grip when the handle came free. The contents spilled out. Hungry people went to their knees looking for something to eat.

"Run to the street, Heather Anne, run!" Fiona shouted. Heather Anne ran into the street, stopping suddenly to look back as a four-horse freight wagon passed just missing the little girl. Glass bottles spilled contents, and tins were opened by the indigents. When no food was found the tins were discarded, contents of the containers scattered. Fiona picked up her skirts and ran to Heather Anne. They both escaped, running out into the busy street. When she looked back, one of the women held an article of clothing to judge the size for the child next to her. Fiona was shaken by the experience. She watched as a man came out of the side door of the pub to chase scavenging Irish cottagers away. A staring contest developed as the hungry people walked a few paces away, waiting for the man to leave. Another man tipped his hat and ushered Fiona by her elbow to the boardwalk on the other side of the street.

"Doyle Wentworth is at your service, ladies." He directed Fiona to a bench. "Please sit for a time. That was an unexpected way to start your trip. You are still as white as last winter's snowfall." Fiona sat, still shivering, with an arm around her adopted daughter. She looked up at Wentworth, a puzzled expression on her face. "Are you a tourist here Wentworth? Fiona asked. With his hat in hand, he made an expansive gesture, extending his arms outward that seemed to indicate a large area of consideration. "I, as you might surmise, am an Englishman, here to secure a location for a group of investors who desire to build a 40-room hotel and bar room in your lovely town. I may find it difficult, being what I am and because the current political upheaval here remains unchecked." "A disgrace, a travesty it is," Fiona replied. "I have recovered sufficiently, Mr. Wentworth. I want to check what might remain usable in the alley over there," Fiona said. She jabbed a finger in the direction. "It was meant to assist at the workhouse near the cathedral for the sick and dying." Fiona rose intending to proceed at once. "Had I possessed food in the basket, I would have given it to them," she said. "Medicines meant to ease suffering, was all that I had in the basket. We thank you, kind sir for your assistance. A gentleman you are. I am Fiona of the Farrell Mercantile. My daughter Heather Anne and I thank you again." "A moment please, allow me," Wentworth said, reaching into an inside jacket pocket. His hand reappeared with a leather wallet, from which he extracted several pound notes he folded between his fingers. "Purchase what you can." Replacing his wallet, he took Fiona's hand and made sure her other hand closed on the folded currency. "All my countrymen are not as some might expect," he said, as Fiona, without a verbal thank you, smiled faintly, turning to step into the street.

While Fiona and Heather Anne hoped to recover some of the apothecary's medicines, Flynn and Patrick O'Brien carried shovels over their shoulders as they headed slowly, and uninspired for the boreen, and their appointment to at least cover with rock, two unfortunate Irishmen. Devon remained behind to catch up on schoolwork after feeding the chickens and pigs.

"Never has there been such activity in the valley as we saw last evening when checking on the sheep," Flynn said. "Two years ago, stone fences changed the green into a chessboard. Smoke was seen from the cottages and huts. Now, the huts have been leveled, the stone fences removed, and the sod was turned for field crops. The British use the valley as a parade field, marching back and forth, causing birds to take flight when volleys of musket fire are heard. They are too close to us, and I fear for Margaret, my son and daughter when I am away at the lake shore." "What would be the cause for the increase in British activity?" Patrick asked. Flynn had an immediate thought. "Possibly, quite possibly they are looking for you." That reason appeared not to have entered Patrick's mind as Flynn stared at him quietly waiting for a revelation that did not come. He decided not to vocalize his thought. Instead, he furnished the more obvious reason. "Margaret feels that pressure from the landlords to quell the Molly Maguire's is the principle reason. I agree with her." Ahead was the rocky incline leading to the boreen. Flynn suddenly signaled with his left arm to bring their progress to a halt. Patrick looked at Flynn, questioning with his eyes. "Listen," Flynn said quietly. They both stood, leaning on the shovel handles, concentrating on the sounds heard, the rustle of the brambles in the breeze, and the cry of the sea birds above. Flynn was pleased because of the sounds he did not hear. He let his arm rest at his side.

"Now, I understand," Patrick said. With his left arm outstretched for balance, Flynn made his way down to the path. "Heed the loose rock Patrick," Flynn advised as he almost lost his balance and the shovel, his arm wind-milled to recover from his own foots' encounter with a loose piece of granite. They reached the well-traveled path without incident. Flynn looked first at the direction travelers from the countryside would come and then to the opposite where the bodies lay exposed. The shovels, held by two hands, rested on their shoulders as they slowly trudged toward the unpleasant task ahead.

+

While back in the town, Fiona and Heather Anne crossed the street, stopping once to allow a fancy carriage pulled by a high-stepping horse to pass them by. Fiona's search of the ground in the alleyway found nothing that could be salvaged. Tins were opened, contents blown by the breeze, the powders and liquids lost in the damp soil. Bottles were broken, and boxes of medicinal powders torn open and scattered. The few items of clothing disappeared to warm someone who may have had to sell all but the clothing they wore. She stood her hands on her hips in the center of the mayhem created by hungry people in their quest for something to eat.

"Come with me Heather Anne," she reached out her hand, "we will call on the apothecary to, this time, with funds to buy some of the medications he donated in the past." Fiona's fingers tapped on the shoulder of her adopted daughter, not to reinforce a parental order, but as a pardon for what she was thinking as they departed the alley. "The English was a kind man," Heather Anne observed looking up at her new mother's frowning face. Fiona nodded, hearing her daughter's words but, her eyes were shifting from one scene to another as they made their way. Activity on the streets had increased, some of that activity attributed to the number of country people flooding into Killarney. Those that were healthy but hungry were on their way to the ports of call at Tralee and Cobh or Waterford, exiting the land they loved forever, leaving because they sought to live their life free. Fiona increased her pace. Heather Anne lost her grip on Fiona's hand.

+

Rossa returned to Ennis in the darkness of a moonless night. He learned from informants at the

Devil Duck Pub to contact Friar Jonathan at the Friary as soon as possible. He left immediately but was too late to assist in the recovery of the printing press. Friar Jonathan's kindness provided food and drink to quiet the rumbling he heard from Rossa's belly. "Those sounds are ones of emptiness," he said to the Friar who smiled, then left to return with a plate. Rossa admitted he was famished after a long walk in the late afternoon and into the evening. The plate was licked clean. "A simple meal, so heavenly," he said approvingly. He thanked his benefactor while he waited for the four Friars, Muldoon and O'Keefe to arrive. Impatient, he left the room with the iron barred window to pace back and forth before his anxiety won out. To anyone who may have watched, they would see only the glow of the Woodbine and the drift of its smoke rising as Rossa walked into a night void of the stars and the moon hoping to meet the wagon. The glow of the Woodbine would disappear quickly before anyone who watched could catch a fleeting glimpse. As the crow would fly, Rossa was one mile from the cathedral. He followed the route taken by the wagon toward the knocks often looking behind him always fearful of those Irish whose loyalist eyes watched and reported suspicious activity. Those traitors to the nationalist cause for freedom were always rewarded but treated with contempt or given the silent treatment by their neighbors. He hoped his late at night excursion was not seen and did not arouse anyone's suspicion if he were spotted leaving the back door.

+

Friar Alfred, the driver, was aware of the concern exhibited by two of his "Friars" and thought it best to approach them with his plan. Even though dressed as a monk, further assurance would help ease their fears. He brought the wagon to a halt. He then turned to address two Irishmen. "I feel it best for Friar Jonathan's benefactors if you would remain behind and take a different path back to Ennis. I counted on us not being noticed when we departed. To leave the cathedral with six and return hours later with four could prove troublesome if we were seen by the same person, however remote," he said. "Divest yourself of your garments before we reach the crest of the next knock. We will part at that time. Make your way back to us when you feel confident." The two conspirators looked at each other. "Aye, that we will do, Friar, to cast me' line on the 'morrow would cause me great pleasure," Muldoon said. O'Keefe punched Muldoon on the shoulder, grinning as he did. Friar Alfred turned away and flicked the reins. The wagon wheels creaked in protest.

+

Fiona and Heather Anne left the apothecary who displayed a huge smile on his face. "Thank you and come again," he said from the porch, more in jest Fiona recognized, but he was obviously pleased to be able to sell what he had given for free in the past to a very attractive and convincing woman. Not a religious man, he still could be seen looking skyward, questioning, as his lips moved in mumbled thanks? His business had suffered through a long cruel winter, but he had not the burden of a wife to support. He watched her walk away. A cacophony of sounds reverberated against the eardrums of Fiona as she and Heather Anne exited the mercantile. Fiona shut the door emblazoned with the old English letter F behind them and headed up the boardwalk toward the outskirts of town. The clatter of iron-shod hooves and steel-clad wagon wheels on the brick was followed by quieted pounding when the horses reached the dirt portion of the unfinished road. Shouts were heard from one person to another across the street. Heather Anne stopped to watch an altercation when doors to a saloon swung open to spew two loudly argumentative individuals who pushed, shouted and shoved each other with straight-armed, unkind anger. "Why do they fight, ma'am?" Heather Anne asked. "There is so much here to thank." She looked up at Fiona who was silent, shaking her head unable to provide an answer to her daughter's question.

Horses snorted, children laughed while they played a dangerous tag with teams of horses delivering goods to waiting hotels and restaurants. A black dog chased and cornered a scruffy tabby that suddenly turned arching its back hissing with bared teeth at the dog. His tail suddenly stopped wagging. The dog looked left and right to consider any alternatives to his attempt to escape his dangerous pursuer. On the street the only order was disorder that bordered on chaos. Bedlam and mayhem combined into one theater as every species imaginable fought for space to move forward on the crowded main. Sheep passed by, driven by their shepherd to an unknown location. The tinny sound of bells around their necks added to the myriad of sensory stimulation. The grunts and snorts of always hungry pigs were heard attracting the attention of Heather Anne who excitedly pointed to the cart where a snout poked its way through the slats. Scruffy dogs followed the cart alongside, barking at the occupants that squealed, further infuriating the two mongrels. Further up the street the boardwalk ended, and Fiona's right arm protected her daughter from the mayhem on the dirt street at mid-morning. Oblivious to what was mass confusion, alarming tourists and locals alike, a fiddle player stood on the boardwalk on the other side of the chaos taking place on the street. His bow moved with confident precision over the strings. The violin, the source of his sensual music, reacted to the movement of the player as he tried to rise above the clamor. The sound emanated sporadically, only high notes could be heard over the din, a lament, and he smiled his love of the sweet music he played. He didn't care if other ears heard. His eyes were closed in total rapture, although they may have been helped by the smoke from the Woodbine between his lips. Without a doubt he was mesmerized, swaying to sublime notes meant to counter the noise, unencumbered by the activity on the street. Fiona was, for a moment transfixed, her ears strained to hear, piecing the missing

parts of his instrument's soliloquy together. The noise
irritated those who listened but could not hear. A lull in
the clamor allowed his music to be heard from the
musician's fiddle. His lament changed to a fast-paced
reel. Her foot began to tap, but her attention was
distracted when she caught glimpses of what went on
behind the buildings where the fiddler stood.
Scavengers entered her vision. They searched for food
in the alleyways between and behind the pubs and
hotels. Two of them were on their hands and knees,
searching. *Could it be?* Fiona thought, *do they search
for darkened circles of dirt contaminated with grease
drippings?* The Foley brothers claimed to have seen
instances of women and children eating dirt behind the
hotels and restaurants where the garbage was left to be
carted away. Heather Anne watched her new guardian's
eyes stare. Her adopter mother initially exposed to a
mind-altering event was obviously a little shocked by
the activity, her eyes wide, her mouth covered by her
hand.

"What do you see Fiona? Heather Anne
nonchalantly watched, still hesitant to address Fiona as
mother, preferring ma'am, but remained anxious when
she called her by her first name. Fiona appeared to
accept, nodding, causing the little girl to sigh in relief at
her choice, but she failed to answer her daughter's
question. Heather Anne appeared unconcerned with
the hunger those desperate women exhibited and did
not press Fiona to answer. She twice lost her attention
to activity on the street but continued to shift back to

follow Fiona's sight line as she continued to watch two
emaciated women grovel on the ground on their hands
and knees. With a shrug of her shoulders, she glanced
at the latest ruckus on the street. A disabled freight
wagon over-loaded with metal strapped barrels had lost
a wheel. Rather than fix the wheel, arms waved, and
shouted expletives were heard while children captured
a loose barrel. They proceeded to roll the barrel down
the street, laughing and scattering several sheep being
driven by an irate herder. The wheel lay on the ground,
avoided by pedestrians who gave sour looks to the
irritated people who jabbed fingers at each other.
Heather Anne looked up and pulled on Fiona's skirt.
"I was hungry and ate scraps from plates. I saw it often
when I was hungry, but I gave my food to Sissy," she
said as she turned away from her focus on Fiona to the
mayhem in front of her, "Sissy never, never-never had
to eat dirt!" she said, emphatically shaking her head, an
endorsement evident to Fiona when Heather Anne
turned back to project visual arrows impacting Fiona
like an unexpected thunderclap in the darkening sky of
summer. Heather Anne's tight-lipped facial expression
revealed the enormity of her unintended revelation.
Loud, boisterous shouts from the street turned Fiona's
head toward the summons to be noticed. The grinning
brothers Foley took mere seconds of time away from
their concentration to gain her acknowledgement when
they passed by. Donal Foley stood with his feet spread
for balance, waving his hat. Brendan stood for just and
instant to wave his hat while jockeying the horse down
the street. "On the 'morrow early we will call," he

shouted. She returned their wave. A shy Heather Anne kept her hands wrapped.

CONFRONTATION

Today was the second day of Margaret O'Connell's brief change in scenery meant to assist in clearing her mind of the despair she felt from the loss of Kevin her newborn son. Fiona thought it unusual to see Donal and Brendan as she expected to see them the following day with her orders, an indication of increased demand by early visitors to Killarney and its attractions. Flynn would be with them to make deliveries of his own, and to reunite with his wife who he hoped would begin to recover from the family tragedy.

Donal maneuvered the horse around a long car stopped to de-bark passengers and unload baggage in front of the Queen's Crown Hotel. "Absolute madness this is brother," Brendan said as they approached one of the main intersections in the town. "What do they do in London to create order on the street?" Brendan asked, as pedestrians, animals and wagons all converged, and all of them in a hurry, desired to cross or turn without regard for the other. Each driver or walker convinced themselves of their priority to the right of way. "Sure brother, I have read of attempts by the Peelers to regulate street traffic in London and not a doubt I have 'tis needed here." They made their way through without incident but were slowed by the funeral wagon of Finbar Roach, the undertaker, who was removing a pauper's body from the side of the street with the help of his young assistant. Brendan blessed himself as they passed the wagon, turning his head away from the smell of death that emanated from the funeral hearse. "From the looks of him he was not a local citizen or a tourist," Brendan said, a hint of sarcasm in his voice. He thought it best to change the subject. "Wise we would be to select a different day to make deliveries as merchants must prepare for the weekend choosing Thursday as their day," Brendan continued. "Or a later time, such as mid-afternoon," Donal countered. "You will NOT keep me from my luncheon with Sally!" Brendan replied. Sally, a wait-person 20 years younger than Brendan, possessed an attribute that Brendan loved to pat. Now, they were on a side street where drivers of wagons and traps escaped to quiet skittish horses, where traffic was not as hazardous to man or beast. "We have had a profitable day my brother, and time it is to call on the vicar's worthy helpers with our left overs to help fill empty bellies," Brendan said as he directed the horse to the main street and into the foray coming in as they were heading out of Killarney.

Fiona watched the Foley brothers maneuver their way through the traffic with Donal standing, one hand on the side of the wagon, the other waving a toothy smile, evident on a forehead covered by a mop of curly red hair, a curl of which hung to an eyebrow, and freckles that covered his face like the thousands of stars that twinkled in the night sky. Her thoughts returned to the present after she saw the Foley wagon turn the corner to disappear out of sight.

"Let's be on our way my daughter, the day is early and warming and I pray for the return of the vicar, Patrick Kincade."

"A kind man, full of love and compassion he was while Sissy and I were there for those lonely, hungry days," Heather Anne said. "He tried to feed us and keep us warm, but someone took my blanket on the second day, and we shivered. I held Sissy tight." Heather Anne who had been walking alongside Fiona suddenly stopped. Fiona looked back to see Heather Anne, arms at her side, her fists clenched. "She cried ma'am! I was afraid for her!" The little girl's lips trembled, even though tightly clasped, and wetness glazed her eyes before she took steps to Fiona wrapping her arms around her waist, her face buried in Fiona's clothing.

+

Before Fiona's trip to the cathedral, the wagon guided by monks and nervous would-be nationalists, faced a night of intermittent stars and rainy intervals. The Franciscan Friars had reached the point where two conspirators would leave to find a new way into the sleeping, un-seeing eyes in the town of Ennis. "We bid you Godspeed, you! You Irish seekers of freedom," were the parting words of Friar Alfred. "We will not be harmed if stopped and your safety is our concern." The wagon wheels lurched forward after the monks watched the backs of Muldoon and O'Keefe disappear into the darkness. Smoke rising from the buildings in the town caught Friar Alfred's eye only for an instant, as fast-moving clouds allowed the moon a brief appearance. A candle or lamp winked out as the Franciscans watched for activity still too far away to confirm what moved into their sight. They relaxed. Was it an inner fear of a confrontation with those opposed to religious and political freedom wished for by most British citizens in Ireland? Not for the monks who supported efforts for both purposes. They had no fear.

ADVICE DISCARDED

Dawn was breaking moments before Flynn left for the lake shore. His departure was delayed by Patrick O'Brien. With the pail of Bessie's milk in his hand, O'Brien voiced a determined need to go back to his former home. "'Tis a need I have to recover what might have been missed! Any small thing that remains I need. I have been told what they do. They destroy and burn, kill animals and dig up gardens." All were a probability in retaliation for his actions in leading an insurrection that saved the life of a pregnant Irish woman, and the humiliation of a British militia officer, according to Donovan Rossa. "Friend Flynn, I need to see for myself what might have been done. I have been tormented ever since and must go. With a bit of Irish luck, I will return to enjoy the hospitality of the O'Connell for at least a night. I respect Rossa's need to caution me about returning to my humble cottage. I will use stealth and care to avoid capture. Please relay that to him if your paths cross." "That is assured. Come inside Patrick, you cannot leave without provisions for what may be an extended absence." Flynn's hand on the back of O'Brien ushered him to the door and then inside where Flynn found a shoulder bag. He directed Devon, who had returned from the corral, to fill a container with water from the rain barrel. Flynn added biscuits, a small jar of honey and an ample portion of smoked salmon wrapped in cloth. Inside the ornate wooden chest Flynn removed the small British flag recovered from the site of the two dead Irishmen they covered with stone in the past days. "The Union Jack may help you to avoid capture should your stealth fail you Patrick! I have no need for it." "Kind you are, friend Flynn. I will take my leave." "Take this blanket, the night is cool, and a fire attracts," Flynn said. Flynn placed it over his shoulders and eye to eye, without words, Patrick O'Brien made his exit. The half door swung shut behind him. Flynn and Devon left the cottage for the bench outside to watch his departure. The sun's glow was prominent in the east. At the point he would leave their sight he turned and waved his good-bye. "Patrick yearns to return to his past life," Flynn mused as he watched. "He was a joy to watch as he relieved the Guernsey of her milk. 'Tis my hope we have not seen the last of the common man turned militant fugitive. He has suffered much," Flynn said, as Patrick O'Brien disappeared from their sight. "You are well Devon, to spend the day in charge of the pigs, the chickens?" "I am father, I will be here when you return," Devon said. "Jumper and I will visit the sheep and make the count for you." "I will bring news of your mother and sister when I return this afternoon," Flynn said. "Take smoked salmon with you," Devon said running toward the corral as Flynn got up to leave for the lake.

Later that same morning Fiona Farrell and her new daughter were making their way down the boardwalk and the brick streets leading to the edge of town. When the town was left behind a disturbing sight greeted their eyes.

The road out of Killarney leading to the cathedral reminded Fiona of a gauntlet. They were forced to run before reaching their destination. The grass and rocks on the roadside were populated by indigent country Irish with nowhere to go. They sat and stood leaning on sticks in groups watching Fiona and Heather Anne make their way down the road. Women who sat talked to them in Gaelic, hands outstretched, pleading for whatever their native language tried to convey. Fiona kept her arm around her daughter's shoulder, keeping her as close to her as she could, a fearful reaction remembering the incident in the alleyway in Killarney. Fiona was happy to have left the road behind them as they headed up the slope on the grass. She stopped to look behind her.

"No room at the inn," she muttered to herself. "Fiona?" Heather Anne asked not hearing her comment. "The building where you and Sissy were quartered must have reached its limits," Fiona explained. "The playhouse may become a place for the sick and dying," she mused. They reached the grove of centuries old oaks where 30 or more men, women and children sat or stood in the protection of the umbrella created by the tall trees. Several haggard, poorly clothed people stood in a circle and stared at the black kettle being attended by an unfamiliar face. Alongside him, leaning on a cane, was an easily recognized face even though the face had lost the full cheeks and ruddy completion Fiona pictured in her mind. The illness took a toll on his muscular body. He was obviously a stone or two thinner. The sight of him startled her to a stop.

"Patrick Kincade!" Fiona shouted. "Do you recognize him Heather Anne?" Fiona picked up her skirts and hurried toward him. The vicar waited with one arm held out, the other on the head of the cane waiting to greet her with his one arm. A weak smile covered his face, and dark circles under his eyes made it obvious to Fiona he was still not fully recovered from the sickness. "Patrick, Patrick, so well it is to have my eyes to your face this day," she said as Patrick pulled her toward him. "And well it is to be back here and to see you," he said. "This sight..., he motioned with his arm after he released her, was not what I wanted to see when I returned from more than a fortnight of ill health, but my strength is returning however slowly."

"Well it would be for you to continue on the mend before you release your helpers," Fiona said. "I have with me the captive child you released to my care," Fiona said. "Remember do you, of the child named Girl? She now has a name she likes as she does the flowers in the meadow. Heather Anne is her new name." Heather Anne, who had been glued to Fiona's side, stepped away and curtsied, something she learned from her little friend Mary Margaret O'Connell. A horrible winter was behind her and still Fiona hesitated to reveal to the vicar that Heather Anne had a sister. Many times, Fiona had assisted Patrick, often twice or three times a week with his mission and until now a fear, prevented her from revealing what she had done. "She had a sister, Patrick, and she is as well in my care. Her name is Sissy, and she now has a surname and that is Farrell. I could not find you on that day you released this young lady to my care after she told me the waif shivering outside the workhouse door was her sister, I had not a heart in me to break apart the younger from the older who cared for her and kept her alive." Patrick listened, his eyes fixed on hers. His face revealed a weak smile while he nodded his acceptance of her confession.

While Fiona did what she could to assist the vicar and his associates, Flynn O'Connell waited, hidden from sight to allow a company of British regulars to pass up the road toward the valley. When the sound of their drums vanished into the morning, he rose from a knee and crossed the path to Killarney, avoiding his regular route to the lake that had started to show signs of foot traffic, the grass beaten down in spots. After a few minutes, Flynn decided he would choose another location for his next trip. Loose rock, gravel combined with thorny brambles made traverse hazardous to life and limb. He stopped often to look back up to the road still void of travelers and freight wagons. The sudden caw of a raven broke the tranquility. Interrupted peace turned Flynn's head away from his search of the road to the shimmering lake surface in the morning sunlight. Donal and Brendan Foley already had returned from their early morning fishing trip. Flynn's eyes found the Meehan boat pulled onto the sliver of sand comprising the beach hidden between the rocks and the Aspen grove. Always referred to as the Meehan boat, it was a much better craft than what they had. The boat was purchased from Bobby Meehan who passed away a month after Donal assured him that he would have a decent funeral with a priest in attendance. Gray smoke drifted upwards in the still air from the cooking fire in what was called "the black house" used to smoke cook fish, fowl and pork. As Flynn made his way down to the water's edge, he could see the Foley boys moving containers of fish to the side of their cottage. The table under the overhang would soon be employed by Flynn to clean and filet. Distracted by a jumble of thoughts that sped past, Flynn was forced to grab thorny branches to steady him while sometimes stumbling toward the grass and sand of the level beach leading to the shore. He stopped to pull a painful thorn from his palm as visions of Margaret and Mary Margaret were followed by his mind's image of Patrick O'Brien walking away from the cottage. His image was followed by that of Donovan Rossa who appeared to replace Patrick O'Brien who had suddenly disintegrated from his mind's eye.

+

Flynn did not know it. On the previous night, Rossa knelt in the damp grass, his hands in pockets of the jacket with the collar turned up, and his cap pulled down tightly over his head. He waited expectantly, often turning to search the nightscape behind him. His eyes pierced the darkness, but his ears would be first to receive notice of the approach of the rescue wagon with the printing press, only if they returned on the same route as taken when they left the cathedral. He flicked the Woodbine into the damp grass as the rumble of wagon wheels and the huff of a straining horse turned his head to the sound. The moonlight reappeared as he got to his feet to see the team burst out of the darkness. "I see but four of you, and where might be five and six?" Rossa asked as Brother Alfred brought the team to a stop. Rossa grabbed the leather on the one horse scratching his ear as he questioned the Friar, who rose from the wagon seat, stretched and jumped to the ground to face Rossa. "The two you speak of were the ones in most danger. I sent them away by a different route to avoid detection. The Brits may question our motives for being out at this hour, but we will not be harmed. We have verification of the reason for our mission," he said, waving the forged letter in the air above his head. "I suggest you do the same before we reach the town. How well do you know your neighbor?" "I have none," Rossa replied. "If too late I will come to the back door," he shouted over his shoulder as he left the wagon in a route that would circle the town from behind. "The door will be unlatched," Brother Alfred shouted, releasing the brake and urging the team forward. He glanced once to see the receding image of Donovan Rossa disappear into the night.

O' BRIEN'S RETURN

Earlier in the day, Patrick O'Brien was nearly overcome with the shivering excitement and emotion of returning to the home he once knew, and it was not that long ago. His heart pounded, and it pounded only in part from his hours of running, and walking, and running some more. He rested, tired and hungry, at the top of a knock overlooking a shallow vale within a mile of what he hoped to see as he left it, untouched, a shuttered window and white smoke rising from the turf fire in the hearth. However, based on what he had been told by more than one Irishman, he knew his chances were nil, and his heart sank at the thought. He was told of what they would do to his animals, and they would laugh while they watched the ewes and the ram die a slow death. While he ran, and then walked, he gave little thought to what Flynn and Devon had stuffed into the shoulder bag. Now, after hours, he felt the pangs of hunger grip him and he opened the bag and sorted through suddenly realizing how thirsty he was. In his haste he had passed over two or more streams of fresh water and could have refilled the small corked jug Flynn had Devon fill from the rain barrel. A biscuit with honey chased away the sounds that made him pause in his quest. Re-corking the jug after two more swallows, he changed the bag to his left shoulder and resumed his hope for a resurrection of past happiness. In a very short time he would be at what he thought was a vantage point. The apex of the knock overlooking and offering him a chance to survey the site of the cottage without being detected. Again, he thought of the animals and his loyal friend who would wake him in the morning with a wet tongue when the sun rose from its sleep. Any witness would have seen the hurt and anger that was transmitted to his face from his mind's picture. His consuming fear, his stealthy approach to his own humble cottage, the result of his interference with an attempt to hang an innocent pregnant Irish woman. Mixed emotions pummeled his very soul. He ran, and stumbled, uncaring his own safety, discarding the fears he had before when he looked right and left, and behind fearful of being recognized as the guilty one who humiliated the British officer in front of his command. Out of breath, his lungs screamed in protest. Not knowing for sure where he was, he raised up from his hands on his knees, where he had been bent over and breathing hard. His shoulder bag slipped to the grass unnoticed as his eyes saw nothing but the brambles in front of him. He stood on tortured legs, up on his toes rubbing tears of happy/sadness to focus on what he hoped was there, what he had come to see. But what he had come to see was not there! Even though he feared the worst, he had hope. He was thunderstruck. Where his cottage stood was now a level blank rectangle of bare earth with shoots of new grass emerging, surrounded by a field of green. A second area of turned earth was his former garden. Not a trace remained to identify the area as a life-saving provider of potatoes and cabbage. The roots of cabbages had been removed. The stone, the thatch, his meager possessions were gone as if they tried to wipe away forever the existence of a man named Patrick O'Brien. He was devastated. Later, when asked, he would say that he felt like he had been hit with a sledgehammer! He collapsed to the ground, in shock at the unbelievable sight of what had been done to his past life. Tears filled his eyes, and sobs wracked his body. He lay in the grass with his tearful face wetting the sleeve of his shirt. And then, as if to further torture his mind, he heard a sound that was totally unexpected. He raised himself on an elbow and heard the unmistakable sound again, a whine, a yelp! When his eyes focused on the origin of the sound, he saw Corky his faithful companion, a black and white Scottish Colley. On his knees now, his dog limped toward him on three legs, yelping happily as he reached his master. Patrick's tears were licked away during the reunion. When the welcome had exhausted both, Patrick found the healing scabs on his dog's flank and removed the thorn that caused his pain resulting in a yelp and a "kee-yi kee-yi" from his wounded buddy. The dog soon realized he could use his foreleg and spent several minutes cleaning the wound area with his tongue. While the dog ministered, Patrick debated whether he should continue down the slope to the site of his former cottage. *I have come this far.* His decision was made. With the dog in his arms he struggled down the grassy knock hoping to find a memento missed in their dastardly cleansing, their punishment imposed in absentia until he was eventually captured. Memories flooded his mind, a dam creating a small lake breeched to release thoughts of the short time he had to live the life with his Kathleen who died of the consumption (tuberculosis) so early in their marriage. He kicked at the earth where the cottage once stood, glancing to the location of the grave, hesitant to visit in fear of what they might have done to desecrate the site. He could see the cross he had fashioned was missing prompting him to investigate further. Stones had been removed and scattered around leaving bare earth sure to attract animals. A miniature Union Jack faded from the sun and rain hung from a stick between two rocks. Underneath the flag, Patrick saw something of metal partially hidden in the dirt. Patrick carefully placed his dog friend on the ground, retrieving the remains of his meager supply of food from his shoulder bag. A chunk of smoked salmon was quickly wolfed down by a famished animal without food for several days while wandering around the site waiting for the return of his master. Patrick watched his dog devour the food, agonizing over the skin and bones condition of Corky, his ribs prominent. In his disgust, Patrick knocked over the Union Jack flag with the back of his hand. Scraping away dirt from what appeared to be metal, he uncovered a shiny tin box. He opened it to find a folded scrap of paper. Once opened it revealed only a hand-written message addressed to him. It read:

Patrick O'Brien
Feast your eyes on what not you see
For soothe foretells what you will be

The note was a warning to be watchful for those who would continue to look for him. Patrick tore the note into little pieces letting the wind do the rest. He replaced the rocks and circled the site hoping to find the cross with the name Kathleen with the date of 1844. The more he circled the more disheartened he became. Unsuccessful, and with a sigh of resignation he returned to the cottage site, observing the ground had been raked, likely to assure nothing was missed in their "cleansing." Corky wandered away, drawn toward a grassy depression with water quickly lapped up between looks back to reassure his master was still within eyesight. He did not want to lose his master again. Patrick refilled the water jug, corking it with the palm of his hand. He did a complete circle to search the surrounding knocks, recalling the threat contained in the message. With the shoulder bag adjusted, he picked up Corky in his arms. He, and his faithful friend, began the long trip back to the O'Connell cottage.

THE VISITOR

The return trip to the cathedral by the rescuers of the printing press proved uneventful for Friar Alfred and his three accomplices. That is, until they came into sight of the alleyway where they would turn toward the rear doors of the cathedral. What brought Friar Alfred to yank back on the reins to halt their progress was what appeared to be a nighttime arm-waving altercation between the butcher Johnny Byrne, Muldoon and Tommy O'Keefe. Fists were raised, and fingers pointed. Friar Alfred, after assessing the potential of the situation, flicked the reins and wheels began to turn. Friar Alfred had heard the whispers and speculations surrounding the rotund butcher who served both the Irish and English merchants with equal product and service. Suspicions were rumored in the Nationalist circle. Johnny Byrne was in league with the British as an informer! His mere presence, no matter the time of the day or night was in Friar Alfred's mind not at all a coincidence. He would need to be articulate, and he was, and convincing should any carelessness be exhibited by his two citizen helpers. He slowed the team and reined them in across from the back doors.

"I see our helpers have arrived," he said to no one in particular, leaving the wagon seat. He turned toward the silent monks. "Two of you may leave in time for benediction." Friar Alfred turned to address Muldoon. "A timely arrival and I see a muscular assistant with you! I was not made aware you had invited more help," he said.

"We did not!" Muldoon was obviously agitated by the appearance of the town butcher. "We awaited your arrival and not but minutes later we were approached by the butcher who indicated interest in what we were doing here at this hour."

"Johnny Byrne, a good evening to you. The pig's heads you offered were a savior for many families. No need do we have for your kind assistance, and we do thank you for your spirit of cooperation in our effort to spread the word of God to all sinners and miscreants. You may leave us to our task. The evening has been long, all are tired, and benediction waits on us," Friar Alfred concluded. "It is true then you have secured the press from the vale in the knocks, the Red Lion?" Byrne asked. "True it is Johnny Byrne, a need for repair parts to our own printing device may be obtained, though not assured until we assess the damage the British bombardment created." He waited for a response for just an instant before moving back to the wagon to begin untying the tarp. Johnny Byrne stuffed his hands in his pockets, turned and hurried away into the darkness. "Have we been compromised?" Friar Alfred quietly asked. "He was inquisitive, and we told him we were there to help unload the wagon for the Friary," O'Keefe said. "Did you tell him the wagon carried the press from the Red Lion?" the Friar asked. A guilty look appeared on the face of Tommy as he and Muldoon exchanged eye contact. "Yes... we did and so far, he only knows the press is for the use of the Friars," Tommy O' Keefe said. "True it is," Muldoon supported.

"We asked him what brought him to the cathedral at this late hour," Muldoon offered, but he did not answer the question. He said that he would stay and help, he was insistent." "Certain it is he will report our activity if he is the informant we suspect. You should be wary of a visit from the Magistrate," Friar Alfred concluded. "Late it is, let us empty the wagon." Rossa heard the tirade between the butcher and his two helpers from behind the iron barred window. He did not want to show himself to the man considered a traitor to the Irish cause. Byrne was considered an informant who ran to the English at every opportunity presented. Rossa watched Johnny Byrne fade into the darkness. He waited for several seconds to be sure he did not reappear. The heavy door creaked when he pushed it open causing work to move the press to stop while Rossa reacquainted himself with Tommy O' Keefe and Vincent Muldoon. Both of whom still felt guilty about telling Johnny Byrne about the press. Concerned they were as well about the reaction Rossa would have because he was near enough to overhear the conversation between the butcher and themselves. "You did well," Rossa said, after hugs were exchanged, "'Tis unfortunate to have Johnny Byrne show up. A coincidence or were you followed?" "Johnny said he was working late and just passing by when he heard the wagon approach. We have no reason to believe we were followed," Tommy said as Friar Alfred approached. "If you are questioned, I will speak in your defense and verify your presence was to aid the Franciscans. I have the paper as well," Friar Alfred reached into his robe to extract the folded sheet. "Once we move the press to its new home it would be wise not to be seen together. All of you must go your separate ways for at least a few weeks." "The boards are in place. One man on each end of the boards will help prevent a disaster," Muldoon said as the press was lifted to the edge of the wagon bed. The press was guided down the boards to the ground without incident. Four men carried the press through the door being held open by Friar Alfred.

+

Two hours of cleaning, filleting and packing orders was followed by on and off showers during the trip to Killarney for Flynn and the Foley brothers. Rain and a variety of delays caused a longer than usual trip. The road was blocked for a time by a shepherd and his flock of Kerry Hill sheep before they veered off to a different direction. Donal Foley brought the wagon to a halt when they caught up to a man with a round topped chest strapped to his back. He was bent over from the weight appearing to be on the brink of exhaustion. The woman with him was frail, her face and exposed skin were covered with blotches. A brief conversation took place between Flynn and the couple, and from what Flynn was able to discern, with his limited comfort of

Gaelic, they were on their way to Tralee. The man and woman were leaving Ireland. All their earthly possessions were in the trunk and though it had handles on each end, the woman was too weak to help carry it. "Can they ride?" Flynn asked. "Surely we can get them as far as the cathedral." "Aye Flynn. Tell them in their language. There is room for both to sit," Brendan said. Flynn was able to convey the message using the language of the hand and his limited use of Gaelic. The man nodded in understanding bending down to pick up one end of the trunk. With Flynn on the other end, who was surprised at the weight, wondered how the man was able to carry it, they placed the trunk on the wagon bed. The man talked to the woman and both boarded the wagon, one on each side of the trunk with their arms resting on it. "Patrick will do what he can for them," Donal said. "It pleases me to see that Patrick has recovered nearly all of what he lost during his illness." "Aye brother. Sorely missed he was," Brendan said as Donal flicked the reins. Brendan and Flynn walked side by side. "Me boyo, surely you must be anxious to visit your wife and daughter. Will they return with us?" Brendan asked.

"And sorely missed she and Mary Margaret are," Flynn said. "When Patrick O'Brien is gone, she will return. O'Brien left to see for himself what remains of his homestead and will call on Devon and me when he returns. I fear the Brits will lie in wait for him to return. The draw to one's home is at times irresistible, even in the face of danger." Ahead of them loomed the tall oaks and evergreens hiding much of St. Mary's cathedral under construction. A tall spire rose majestically over the oaks, reaching to the heavens. Flynn motioned to the man and pointed. Their heads turned. The number of trees concentrated in one area must have amazed the two passengers whose eyes were focused, unblinking at the sight. To them, trees were seldom seen, virtually non-existent. What they knew were the blackthorn, the whitethorn and the variety of fruit bearing shrubbery that provided a variance from their normal diet of potatoes, cabbage and potatoes. People from remote areas of the country with little exposure to the world that surrounded their village or cottage were not able to read their own language, but only speak it. The light breeze brought the aromatic smell of turf burning under the vicar's cooking pots under the protection of the canopy provided by the massive centuries-old oaks. Minutes later, Donal brought the horse to a halt at the point where they always stopped either on their way to Killarney or returning to their little cottage nestled on what was their miniscule beach on one of the Lakes of Killarney. Flynn spoke to the man, gesturing toward the people under the trees and near the fires smoldering. Patrick Kincade the vicar waved, his arm in the air motioning for them to come forward. Brendan assisted the woman who tried to prevent his help. She shook her head, showing herself, the blotches, and her sores before Brendan forcefully picked her off the wagon bed. Tugging and pulling, Flynn was able to tip one end of the chest to the ground safely before Brendan came to lend a hand.

"They," Flynn motioned to the passengers, "are on their way to Tralee, if my understanding of the dialect they used is correct," Flynn said to Kincade. "She has the smell and look of sickness, I fear," he continued. "Bless you O'Connell, a day or two of rest here and the food might aid them. A doctor is to arrive by long car on the 'morrow," Kincade said. "From the looks of them, the need of transport other than by their feet is a requirement I will investigate. Foley boys, will I see you on your return?" "Aye Patrick, early this afternoon we will return," Donal said. "We have deliveries to make and pounds to collect." Donal returned to the wagon where Brendan was already seated, reins in hand, indicating a desire to sit rather than walk. The fish merchants resumed their trip into town. As they reached the bottom of the hill their progress was halted by a uniformed British officer who stopped a covered carriage and appeared to be questioning the occupants. Another two-wheeled cart was behind the carriage in front of the Foley wagon. The soldier strode to the rear of the carriage where he watched the driver open the storage compartment. Apparently satisfied, on his inspection, the compartment door was closed by the driver. He was returned to his seat and allowed to proceed. The soldier reached the side of the next cart and could be overheard asking for the destination and purpose of the cart driver's visit. Again, the driver was released and allowed to proceed as Brendan moved the wagon forward to meet the soldier. "What is the purpose of your visit to Killarney today?" he asked without as much as a "good morn" out of an unsmiling countenance. "We are delivering orders to Killarney merchants. We have fresh and smoked fish for the hotel kitchens and several pubs and restaurants," Donal said. "Why are we being delayed?" Donal continued, as he uncovered one of the containers bearing live salmon. The officer motioned to the other containers that Donal uncovered.

Surely, you don't fish the sea off the rocky coast, the lakes?" Before Donal could reply he answered Donal's question. "Arms smuggling to militants is on the rise. We want to nip it before any blood is spilled," the officer said. "You may proceed," he directed. Brendan urged the horse forward. Within minutes they were in sight of the Howe Livery and Blacksmith Shop located on the edge of the business district near the Depot. Flynn departed, leaving Donal and Brendan to make the deliveries to the Farrell Mercantile, the Queen's Crown Hotel and three other pubs and restaurants. He headed for the Howe residence, anxious to see his wife and daughter after three days. Mary Margaret saw him approach and started to run toward him shouting; "Flynn! Father I miss you!" Flynn was ready as she ran toward him, picking her up, twirling her around in a "bear hug" embrace. "I missed you too, daughter of mine, is your mother inside?" "Yes Father, I will get her for you." Mary Margaret had been playing with the girl named Sissy on the Howe front porch. The girl disappeared inside and seconds later reappeared hand in hand with Margaret, who picked up her skirts and ran toward Flynn. A reunion commenced in the middle, and down the street from the house. Carts and pedestrians veered around them who were oblivious to anything but each other. Sissy and Heather Anne watched the reunion from the porch.

"You have left my son Devon in charge of the pigs and the sheep?" "Aye Margaret, he had schooling to attend to. He is well and misses you and his sister and will join me on our next trip here. He is becoming a young man, very responsible." "Each day and hour I miss you, my Devon, and my home, but I have not finished helping Fiona prepare a plan for the schooling of her new daughters, Sissy and Heather Anne. I will return with you at weeks end if Patrick O'Brien has departed. Well it has been for me... to be here with Martha and Fiona and Mary Margaret. My sorrow is eased," Margaret said. "If it were not for the increased British presence in the town, there would be peace and harmony, not tension and fearful watching," she continued. "The British soldiers are everywhere! Some of them are courteous. Others are disdainful. They look at you like you were vermin, like the sewer rats in London and Belfast, and I have seen the rats in London. The hunter dogs are victims! If they survive, they bear the scars!" "I have been to Paris and the same exists, my love," Flynn replied, his attention drawn to watch a man approach he didn't want to see.

He shook his head at Ronan O'Neill causing him to stop, knowing he was interrupting a reunion. "I see no purpose in discussing an infestation problem in some of Europe's largest cities," Margaret answered after watching the playhouse curator leave. "The rats have donned a red uniform and wave the Union Jack," Flynn said. "Patrick O'Brien would tell you of why he is on the run for his life." "I will be content in living and loving you and my children in the small world you have so magically created for me, Mr. O'Connell. I am blessed, and I have been blessed, and you love, are the reason, my husband." All this conversation took place while arm in arm Flynn and Margaret slowly made their way, stopping occasionally, to the less hazardous side of the street in front of the Howe residence. Other words were whispered by both. Lips touched cheeks. Martha Howe waited patiently as Silé Dooley poked her head out the door with a wave of her hand that was unseen by an occupied couple. Martha had a smile on her face while Mary Margaret and the girl named Sissy stood next to her holding the others hand, both in wait for the reunion to come to an end. Flynn filed away a thought. Margaret did not mention of Kevin. That gave him reason to be encouraged, hoping she was on the mend from a season long despair. Two hours later, after a lunch prepared by Martha Howe and Silé, it was time for Flynn to meet the Foley brothers at Clancy's for the return trip to the lake shore. Brendan was insistent their lunch be taken at Clancy's pub, because of his infatuation with Sally Donaghy, the young barmaid, although he would not admit it. Donal heard him say more than once that, 'it is all in good fun' but Donal was not so sure. Earlier, he cautioned his brother to limit his lunch time frolicking. He reminded his brother the heat of the day would quickly ruin any remaining fresh fish to be dropped into the hands of the vicar and his assistants. Even though Brendan took heed of his brother's advice, he still had the time and the appetite, and the thirst to consume a hearty lunch as well as three pints of the "black stuff" (Guinness) all necessary to a body weighing nearly 17 stone. When Donal pushed through the double doors of Clancy's to the boardwalk, he noticed a British soldier tacking notices to the posts and door fronts down the street. That made him turn back to look at the door to the pub to find a notice printed in bold print. The order was signed by the magistrate, Tim O'Rourke. Merchants and customers heard the pounding hammer on the doors and posts and left the pub or the hotel to investigate. Soon, the boardwalk was filled with people gathered around to read and discuss the notice posted to the door. Flynn stepped up to the porch as Donal exited. Brendan paid the bill and walked through the half door where he found Donal near the door pointing to the notice. Brendan's first glance outside when he left Clancy's was to the activity on the boardwalks across the street. With his hand leaning on the door jam, he read the notice while shaking his head. He had no comment. He just turned away with a shrug of his shoulders.

"I will walk Donal," Brendan said, when they reached the patient horse that turned to look at them approach. "I need to rid myself of the sumptuous lunch Sally prepared for me." As if in agreement, the horse's head bobbed up and down while her tail swished at the flies. "Hear my brother's words, do you hear them Flynn? "Sumptuous? An educated man is my brother! I am amazed Flynn," Donal said from his seat on the wagon. Brendan nodded in agreement, with a broad smile on his face. Flynn, with Brendan alongside, set a fast pace ahead of the horse on their way out of town. They passed the livery where Malachy Brandon was seen at the forge with a heavy hammer in his hand. Neil Howe was in the corral on his knee examining the hooves of one of the horses boarded for the day. He heard the Foley's shout and waved his greeting. "Has Margaret's sorrow been eased?" Brendan asked. "Aye, friend Brendan, she is on the mend and in three days I will have her back," Flynn said. "She found inspiration from Tennyson. She memorized one of his saying, "I must lose myself in action, lest I wither in despair," Flynn quoted. Her action, being her assistance provided to Miss Farrell of the Mercantile in the education of her two new daughters. My love said how disturbing it was to have so many British regulars in the town. Tension is high, and the Brits have few manners and look unfavorably at the Irish. Every citizen senses the eyes of the Brits who watch. The war between the landlords and the 'Mollies' must have reached new heights." "Sticks of cured and hardened Blackthorn, although formidable, have no chance against a musket ball," Brendan said. The edge of the town was now behind them and ahead, a new soldier had replaced the one that stopped them on their way into Killarney. He was occupied with the driver of a freight wagon and gave a squinty eyed look at Donal, the wagon, Brendan and Flynn. The driver, obviously irritated and frustrated by the delay was being forced to uncover the freight he carried to allow an inspection. Not 'nary a nod came in response to Donal's 'good day to ya' as they passed each other on the road from Ennis to Killarney. Flynn noticed the soldier's long gun, with the bayonet mounted, was within an arm's reach cocked and at the ready. Donal and Brendan Foley, and most certainly the driver of the freight wagon, did not miss its implication. They recalled the words of Flynn when he talked of Margaret's concern about the tension and fear created by the British troops in town. They now realized her same anxiety existed among shopkeepers, including Fiona Farrell of the Farrell Mercantile, along with dining room captains and barmen when they made their deliveries. Now however, they left the tension behind them and all took a needed deep breath. All eyes focused in the distance for the first glimpse of the tree tops swaying in the breeze at the rear of St. Mary's cathedral. "Visitors, both welcome and unwelcome seem to have declined, at least for the day," Brendan said from the wagon seat. "The British regulars are given basic courtesies without question, but I remember the vicious "uncle" of Silé Dooley who may still roam the countryside." A usually busy path from the cathedral into Killarney was noticeably void of the hungry country people who had given up or been evicted from their homes and decided to leave their homeland. "Aye brother, although unwelcome visitors I disagree. The British presence has dramatically increased. I thought the same of that gypsy Traveler, and the presence of the soldiers may be the reason, what do you say?" Brendan paused in thought, his head down, before he replied. "Not to dismiss your thought brother, but what if? ..." and then came that pregnant void, the only sound being heard was the clip-clop of the horse's hooves and the squeak of the wagon wheels.

"What if..., what is your thought brother?" Donal replied. "They die in droves, by the hundreds," Brendan said.

+

Though Patrick Kincade lost weight battling his illness, he was still an imposing figure, easy to pick out from a crowd. What was different to see as they approached was his volunteers doing the work while the vicar leaned on a cane. He saw the wagon coming his way and motioned, telling a volunteer, who nodded, to off-load what the Foleys had brought. Flynn's contribution was a pig's head, feet and meaty neck bones from a newly butchered pig. The smoked hams were sold to the Farrell Mercantile advertising the ham as "apple smoked" to provide a distinct flavor unlike any other available locally. Flynn's presence and contribution to the soup pot was acknowledged by the vicar who faced Flynn directly, eye to eye.

"I heard of the loss of your son and I prayed for him. Your wife is well? Some still believe the fate of unbaptized infants, the Tarans are to be relegated to a special place, not heaven, not purgatory, and if they do receive a final blessing, they are still buried in an area outside of holy ground. Assure Margaret, if she is one of those who adhere fervently to the myths and legends that your son received God's grace and has a place in the heavens above. There will be no visits by ghostly apparitions on All Hallows Eve. No visits from will-o'-the-wisps or howls of the werewolf will be heard." While he spoke so directly to Flynn, the vicar had his hand on Flynn's shoulder. The vicar turned away to acknowledge the Foley brothers.

"A good day it is Patrick. We have unsold trout for the stew pot," Donal told him. "Your color is returning since we saw you last." "My strength returns slowly," Patrick said. One of the vicar's helpers was busy cutting up fish, while another added the pork to a second black kettle. Three able country cottiers whom Kincade said had been evicted, were digging graves in the area designated as the cemetery some distance away at the edge of the trees. Women with babies in their arms leaned against trees. "They will not visit Killarney because of the British soldiers." He pointed to two of the men. "Those two are "on the run," Tralee and Cork are their destinations. Being here, both have no fear of discovery. The Brits do not come here. I suspect the smell of death keeps them away. After two years I do not notice. Others are in the work house and a road building project is to start shortly," Patrick said.

The groan of the massive oak door at the rear of the cathedral drew eyes to a raven-haired girl who pushed it open. She had a soiled apron with what appeared to be blood stains tied around her waist. With an unpleasant task ahead of her, Silé Dooley walked toward them, her head down, her hands in the pockets of her skirt. She stopped in front of Kincade and raised her eyes to meet his. "The woman named Aideen, she was the one with the young boy, has died, sorry I am to tell you vicar Kincade." "She will not be the last," he said. "Is there someone caring for her child?" He looked toward the men digging the graves. "Maureen O' Donahue from the town took him away before she died. He is only three and of course, does not understand death," she said. "I as well, do not understand. Most of the children who arrive here have seen death at some point in their young lives. Please me to go to the grave diggers and ask them to remove her body," the vicar said with a sigh of resignation. Kincade bent his head and blessed himself as Silé turned to leave. The Foleys and Flynn returned to the wagon. "In three days, we will call on you again, Patrick," Donal said with a wave as he took the reins. "Wait Brother, my lunch was walked off and I now can direct the horse with skill and alertness," Brendan said as he reached to pull the reins from his brother's hands. A humorous smile covered his face. Donal was literally forced off the wagon seat by his bulky brother who climbed aboard and gave a hip shove to Donal. Flynn grinned at the horseplay between his two employers. He walked shoulder to shoulder next to Donal behind the wagon. "A comforting man is the vicar Patrick," Flynn said. "My Margaret's sorrow would be lessened if she could listen to his words." "Aye, that he is, and a smart young woman is the Dooley girl, Flynn. She overheard his comments to you and recognizes Margaret's sorrow. She is likely to relay his thoughts to her when she returns to the Howe residence."

"Hard it is for even educated, intelligent Irish like Margaret, to break away from the myths and legends of the past," Flynn said. "Mention of the Howe name reminds one that Martha Howe was prevented by her son from helping the vicar inside the cathedral where the deathly sick received a little comfort," Flynn continued. "Neil Howe should be doing the same for Silé Dooley," Donal said.

Brendan's skillful driving took them to the point where Flynn would leave the shore route to veer off in a slightly longer route to the cottage over-looking the Lakes of Killarney. He said his good-by, adjusted his bulging shoulder bag with the potatoes and disappeared into the flowering shrubbery at the side of the road. Six hours passed since he left Devon in charge of the horses, the Guernsey, chickens and pigs. The sheep took care of their own needs. Ample grass and water, an occasional taste of grain and the protection of the rocks and cliff all were recognized as a reason not to stray. He anticipated Patrick O'Brien's return. Somewhat fearful that harm would come to him from his trip to his former home. When Flynn's eyes caught sight of smoke rising from the turf fire, and then when the cottage came into view, it brought a smile to his face. His return did not go unnoticed. The mare with no name and her equally black son watched him approach. A loud head-shaking whinny came from the yearling colt named "Jumper" causing the half-doors of the cottage to burst open to reveal Devon. His eyes searched and found Flynn approaching through the berry and brambles.

"Father, Father, Patrick was here, but he left to go to Ennis! I gave him water and food," Devon shouted. "His cottage was gone! His garden was dug up! Not a trace remained. He was disheartened, Father!" Flynn relieved himself of the shoulder bag made heavy by the seed potatoes he purchased from Tom Steele. He went to a knee in front of his son. His arms pulled him close. "You did well son of mine. Your mother and sister miss you and will be coming home. Did you finish with your studies?"

"I have much to learn Father. I am learning about the moon, the stars and the planets named after the gods of mythology. 'Tis fascinating, Father! I will need a spyglass! Patrick rescued his dog, Father! They tried to hurt him, but he ran away and came back. Patrick found him! His name is Corky. He is black and white, and Patrick said he was a Colley from Scotland!" His excited son finally paused to take a breath. Flynn was pleased Devon showed interest in the dog, apparently, Flynn hoped, he forgot about the incident in the pasture in 1845, the year a hungry pack of dogs attacked them. "Come Father, would you like tea and a scone with honey?" Devon asked. He took his father by the hand and led him back toward the cottage.

"Will you help your father plant the late potatoes?" Flynn asked, seating himself at the table where a plate of scones covered by a cloth waited next to the honey jar. "I will father, and after, we should go to the pasture. I need to take Jumper for a ride!" Devon furnished another reason for Flynn to believe his son had recovered from the dog attack incident. Until just recently he was reluctant to go to the pasture, but that appeared to have changed as he did the count by himself when Flynn was away. *Or was it the idea of taking Jumper for a ride,* Flynn thought.

+

In his heart, Patrick O'Brien knew there was a risk in returning to Ennis, just as a risk was taken when he visited his former home. In a short time, culminated by his visit to his wife's grave site, he had been transformed. Politically complacent in the past, his focus was to provide for himself and his wife on a desirable spot of land in a fertile valley. Now, he wanted to right the wrongs he had witnessed and personally experienced. He wanted to do damage, to retaliate. All that he knew and loved had been taken away, erased, first his lovely bride only 23 years old, and then what remained of his life was wiped clean from the green grass of Ireland. He knew where to find Donovan Rossa, confident he could take refuge in the Friary as a last resort. His arms grew tired from carrying his faithful friend Corky. At times he allowed the dog to limp alongside until he stopped walking, his injured paw in the air, exhausted, to drop to his belly in the grass. The dog's strength was gone, not having eaten for several days prior to his tiring trek back to the O'Connell cottage where he and Devon mixed a concoction of meat, eggs cooked grain and cabbage the dog wolfed down in minutes. In a very short time, Corky and Devon O'Connell became enamored with each other. Patrick briefly considered leaving Corky with Devon. He quickly dismissed that thought, chastising himself for even thinking of abandoning his canine friend. When he came to the valley below the plateau his level of alertness increased dramatically, in remembrance of a previous escape from harm when he and Rossa barely avoided a contingent of troops on what was likely a training exercise. He stayed on the well-worn path, leaving only when others approached from the north. Three hours later, when the sun was past its zenith, he stopped to rest. His dog was at his side and lapped up the water his master poured for him. His tail pounded the grass. Patrick O'Brien, the fugitive, was an hour away from Ennis. He began to consider what he would do when he arrived. He had questions. Had enough time elapsed for the Brits and English collaborators to concern themselves with other endeavors? Instead, they chose to be on the lookout for a man no one really could identify. *I am from the countryside and rarely did I venture into Ennis,* he reasoned to himself. *I will change my name and appearance,* he thought. With that to consider, an image was recreated in his mind. The shadowy recall was the bent over figure of Danny Kissane who changed his looks to that of a bumbling man-child in an instant. He rubbed both cheeks feeling a three-day growth of beard, pulling his cap down low to his eyebrows. Kissane was a man to be contacted. He knew being in the company of the Friars would provide him safe-haven until he could meet with Rossa, Muldoon and O'Keefe. He felt it necessary to let them find him rather than frequenting a known Nationalist hangout such as the Devil Duck pub. Three times the wind brought the dull bong of the bell in the cathedral tower, first loud, but the wind blew part away, and then barely faint, but the breeze brought it back, loud again. Mid-afternoon had been reached. Patrick stood up and looked toward the sound. He started to question himself again. *Am I a fool for putting myself in harm's way?* He fervently wanted to do damage to that Brit, the one with the shiny boots, one of which rested on the back of that pregnant woman of the O' Branigan clan. Already, he had pledged his support to Donovan Rossa, telling him he would do anything including bombing the barracks of the British contingent outside of Ennis.

TRAVELER WOMAN

Silé Dooley untied the bloodstained apron. Holding it away from her with her forefinger and thumb she dropped it into the pile of clothing in the basket near the formidable rear doors. All of it to be boiled before anything could be used again. It was a day, the second this week in her commitment to volunteer when two residents died while she was working. Their passing was preceded by spewed vomit mixed with blood appearing on the clothing of anyone nearby. Silé was unfortunate to be leaning over the woman at the time, although she stepped back, but just a second too late. Starvation and disease took life from two women who passed on Silé' s second day this week. On her first day, a man and a woman, who may have been husband and wife, died while holding the others hand. They had not the strength to fight off the diseases brought on by lack of food, and in many cases what food available to them was given to their children. Once she was outside where the air was fresh, and the smell of disease and death behind her, she removed the cloth, the mask covering her nose and mouth. Back home, she still felt guilty about calling "living" with the Howe family home. She would wash the cloth before using it again. Days past, Neil prevented his mother from working inside where segregation of the deathly sick the only alternative available. Neil was not happy Silé continued to disregard his objections to her working in such dangerous conditions. He did not find one of her comments to his concern funny when she said;

"Gypsy women are immune to illness, but I love you for your caring." She walked away, looking back at the trees and the black kettles being tended by other caregivers recruited by the vicar. The priest and a doctor visited at least once a week. Her eyes found Patrick and she waved, but he was busy at a table, and did not acknowledge her good-bye. Silé recognized how distraught the vicar was to hear the news of the cancellation of the work program for Killarney. The curate of Dingle brought the news. A few hours later the magistrate asked Patrick for the key. He locked the work house door. Tim O'Rourke, the magistrate, said nothing. He walked away, his head down, not understanding the orders he had to enforce. The work house was closed. Her walk back to town was normally one when she and Fiona went over the events that occurred during their time at the cathedral. Today however, she was alone as Fiona and Margaret O'Connell were involved in preparing short term, and long-term plans for teaching the two new Farrell daughters, Heather Anne and Sissy. Martha Howe was committed to a meeting with Killarney business people, English and Irish alike. She asked to be excused. The height of the tourist season was near. Silé Dooley could see Killarney town becoming besieged with haughty English politicians in vests with gold chains, and mutton chop whiskers. Martha Howe told her they should be fearful of the Irish barbers who wielded a glinting straight razor in their hand. Politicians said they were here to see for themselves what needed to be done, but rarely left town. The potato disease affected the 1845 crop, and the 1846 crop. People starved and then they died. When they didn't die thousands packed up what they had and walked to the shores where the ships would take them away. The year was 1847, and Silé knew that an irritated Martha Howe expressed a damning question on how those politicians could view the problems in the countryside from a seat at the dining table. She saw them with a bib stuck in the shirt collar. She saw them seated in the local pub listening to the fiddle player play, his hat on the floor to catch the coins he hoped were flipped his way. When she asked the politician why a solution was not reached after nearly three years, she reported he said;

"A bloody, bloody shame, they squabble among themselves, the conservatives, Protectionists and the Peelites 'tis balderdash as well to allow the landlords to wield such power and control over the Whigs. They argue while the Irish Commoner who provided ship load after shipload of consumer goods to England, die on the roadside. I have not been notified, but Sir John Burgoyne, head of the relief commission, is rumored to pay a visit." When mention of the relief commission was overheard in the pub, hearty laughter broke out from the locals who listened intently to the conversation between the Englishman and Martha Howe. A visit by any English politician was considered a victory by the Irish. Few of the Queen's men ever paid a visit to their emerald green island. Potatoes were planted again by the eternally optimistic Irish. Those who could afford to buy the seed, at an inflated price, planted a crop. Potato merchants out of London were not in a negotiable position with the Irish. The screws of adherence to the politics of the time, and the warped ideology of Charles Edward Trevelyan made seed potatoes akin to gold. Silé heard second hand the priest was deluged with requests to take supper with a country family in return for his blessing of the potato field. Prayers were said daily by families on their knees in the fields. Silé crossed to the other side of the street to avoid a group of people who were rummaging through trash piled in the alley between two pubs. Instead of going directly to the house she turned left. Ahead of her was the Howe Livery. Neal and Malachy would be grooming horses and pounding iron until the sun began to sink below the roof of the Queen's Crown hotel. On the way, she noticed a British soldier opposite the alley where the people searched through the garbage. He watched. He did nothing. Silé's thought was, *if, he happened to be compassionate and understanding of the plight of the Irish commoner, he would allow their desperate attempt to find food in the trash to continue, if not, could he be derelict in his duty?* British occupation of the town continued to irritate merchants and publicans who lost regular customers when the Brits arrived. The boardwalk ended. She picked up her skirts. Her feet managed to find the dry part of the ground in an area near the edge of town. It was not a route that saw frequent foot traffic.

To anyone who watched, her attempts to avoid mud and water, an imitation of an Irish step dance. Back and forth, side to side, but always advancing. Blades of grass in the puddles sprouted upwards, reaching for the sun. The corral and the Howe livery and byre were ahead. Silé counted an unusual number of spirited horses being boarded, one of them a red, jumped, kicked and huffed as he trotted around the corral fence. She turned the corner heading for the blacksmith's forge. Red uniforms above shiny black boots greeted her eyes. Another red uniform was leading a limping horse away, but she spotted Malachy's muscular body behind the uniforms in animated conversation with the soldiers. His arms outstretched, the palms of his hands up indicating he was taking a defensive position to whatever point was being made by the Brits. Neal stood by quietly, as Malachy calmly reasoned with the three customers. Malachy's hands went to his side and the Brits turned away, shaking their heads, a disgruntled look on both faces.

"An unreasonable lot are the British, Neal Howe," Malachy said as Silé reached them. "But a fine day it is with the blue above. We are blessed," he said. "A troubling day you have had?" Silé asked after planting her lips on Neal's cheek. "Aye love, somewhat troubling," Neal replied, providing a welcoming squeeze and a friendly pat on her behind. "The early part of our day was a typically ordinary one," Malachy said. "Neil tended to the leathers and the saddles, I to the carriage and the iron work, however, when I was asked to board and treat a diseased animal, I would not. I told them the animal should be destroyed, and that made them angry. The horse dripped from the nose and trembled when standing." Neil nodded in agreement. "Like nothing we have seen before Silé, and I have doubt that you, so used to the horse as you are, would not have seen the same!" "Neil Howe, I have told you of the allegiance the Dooley's had, and still likely do, to the horse. The animals are treated with more regard, and I have told you, with more regard than the daughter of a father!" She turned her back in remembrance, not wanting Neil to see the tear that resulted from her sudden vehement outpouring of remembered emotions from past experiences. Neal reached out, encircling her waist with his arms whispering, he hoped, comforting words in her ear. Malachy returned to the forge. Silé turned in Neil's arms. "So many are sick and dying back there," Silé pointed in the direction of the cathedral. "Two women with children died today Neil, right in front of me, and it tortures my mind." With his hands on her shoulders Neal took a step back. His eyes examined every inch of her dress. "I see stains at the hem, is it blood?' Neal asked, resurrecting the fear he had for Silé' s safety while assisting Patrick Kincade, the vicar. "It is blood Neal my love. My only comfort comes from not being watched by the troops while I am there. Here, I feel like a bug about to be crushed by the sole of a shiny black boot!" Wetness appeared in her eyes, and she sighed, a trembling sigh. "'Tis blood for sure Neal, she gave her food to the children!" The wetness in her eyes became streams making their way down her cheeks. Neal held her tight as she dabbed away at her tears. Neal looked up to see Malachy at the forge looking his way. He appeared to be waiting.

"The livery calls to me, love, back to work I go," he pointed toward Malachy who waited patiently. "Silé my love, a visit with your little friend Mary Margaret might ease your troubles." His fingers trailed down her arms to her hands where he had applied a gentle squeeze before he backed away, a look of concern covered his face.

TINKER DAUGHTER

Silé Dooley, the abused escapee from a childhood trapped in a Traveler gypsy clan witnessed and endured her own challenge. Now, her heartache remained. Her pain the result of what she was part of, disease and death, least of all tending the soup pot of the vicar. She fought her original despair, determined. Many times, in her past life her fists would be clenched, she tried not to cry, but she did. She had the intelligence to teach herself, often she resorted to thievery, stealing books, one written by an Abcedarian that helped her to read and write English. She learned and understood the Gaelic language even though dialects changed from the northwest to the southeast. Always on the move, the Traveler wagon wheels rolled from one county to another, never in one place long enough to incur the wrath of someone who was cheated or robbed. Twice she ran away, the first when she was ten and three, or four, only to be recaptured by the clan led by her deranged uncle, a kidnapper of young women, and a suspected murderer. Adults in the clan needed someone to wash their clothing, fix their meals, and do whatever she was told to do. Few of the Dooley family strayed from the traditional tinker way of making a living. Those who wavered cast a cloud of distrust and suspicion over anyone who contacted any member of the Dooley clan. She was never asked, always told. She ran for the second time after she overheard plans made by her own father and uncle. Their plan? To make her part of a stable of young women for the pleasure of whoever would pay the price!

She watched Neal walk back to where Malachy stood with his hands on his hips. A deep trembling sigh made her turn away to face the present, and what was left of the reminder of the day. She realized how tired she was, her emotions ran the gamut from the joy of trying to make a difference in someone's life to the sorrow experienced when all her efforts and the efforts of others proved futile and the grim-reaper came calling. On the porch of Martha and Neal's home, Mary Margaret and Sissy played with rag dolls. The girls held each doll up to say hello to Silé, and then they laughed. Silé went inside and collapsed to the couch near the hearth.

THE BIRTH OF THOMAS O'BRIEN

With his fist raised, Patrick O'Brien looked one way then another ready to knock twice, then knock twice again. He waited at the rear door of the cathedral, anxious to hear sound of a lock being disengaged and then the grating sound of rusty hinges. He listened, waiting because he was told someone inside would be within hearing. He felt exposed, looking to his left and right wanting to avoid all kinds of contact, favorable or not, with friend or adversary. Without a response to his first knock, this time he applied his fist loudly. A knuckle broke skin from the effort. He wouldn't be able to hear any feet shuffling to the door on the other side. The oak slab doors were several inches thick. Fearful of discovery, he could do nothing but wait, and he knocked the knock again. He waited...and he waited, and he watched people a street away between buildings going about their business. They paid no heed, but that gave him little comfort. He was beginning to dislike being a fugitive. And then, in a near panic a man appeared hurrying his way, but at that moment the massive door creaked open.

"God save us! It's you Patrick O'Brien, hurry yourself in," Friar Jonathan said, pulling his weight with two hands to close the door behind him. "Rossa worried for your safety, as did I, and hungry you must be. Seat yourself and we will talk after I bring food." Not allowing Patrick the time to respond, he disappeared into the labyrinth of rooms and hallways

173

that made up the rear of the building. O'Brien breathed a sigh of relief and sat down. A minute or two later, still a fugitive he jumped to his feet to peer one way then another through the small iron barred window in the room. He stood there for minutes, one cheek creased by the iron, then the other as he tried to increase the angle of vision, watching, watching, but saw nothing. The sound of shuffling footsteps came to his ears.

"Not a fear you should have Patrick. You are in the Lord's house and you should not be afraid." Friar Jonathan returned holding a shiny metal tray with a mug, a bowl and a plate with food. "Come with me, a table is in the next room." He turned, motioning with his head, waiting for Patrick to follow. Ravenous, the little food Devon provided was not enough fuel for a six-hour walk. He followed the friar to the table where he sat across from him quietly while he watched Patrick devour what was in front of him. Patrick did not comment on the quality of the food, nor did he speculate on what else was contained in the bowl of thick soup other than the carrots and potato. A few minutes later, Patrick used his sleeve in satisfaction, and drained the mug of water dry. Finished, he placed the mug on the tray and pushed it away. For a few seconds, silence reigned as their eyes focused on the other. Friar Jonathan's face was a map of aggravation, irritation and questions. He spoke for the first time.

"Why did you come back, Patrick? You have presented an enormous problem for us, now that you are here. We cannot let you leave until we can assure ourselves of your safety in the town and I think I have a solution!" He raised his index finger upward, paused as if in thought, and he was. "You will become a student, studying to become a Franciscan, the twin brother of Patrick O'Brien!" You will become Thomas O'Brien and I doubt Thomas that any questions will arise after we flood the town with flyers to announce your arrival and your history. Friar Jonathan's grin was a complete reversal from the worried, questioning face seen earlier. His eyes sparkled, pleased at his own humor. Patrick sat without a word listening to Friar Jonathan's plans. "You will have the freedom you seek to walk freely in Ennis and to speak openly to your believers who argue for the need to be free from the oppression of the British." Now it was Patrick's turn for a change to occur in his facial features from one of acceptance to what the Friar offered, to one of concern and questioning. "While I accept what you have outlined so quickly, I do not want to become a prisoner in the Lord's house. I agree that a change in my appearance, a shaved head will aid me to freely move about."

"You will become a friar in training with the ability to move freely in the community. You will not be a cloistered monk relegated to a life of prayer and fasting inside the cathedral, Patrick. You will wear the hood of the habit in the color that designates you as a student. You will wear everyday clothing, and the hood can be lowered at any time," Friar Jonathan explained. "I have not had the time to thank you for the food," Patrick said. "I am overwhelmed by your quick-thinking solution. So grateful I am for your kindness." Friar Jonathan rose from the table. "You will be quartered here for the night and for possibly a few more days. Follow me to your room. I will show you around and introduce you, and then I must get busy. Friar Louis will cut your hair and shave your head tonight. I will be in the press room compiling notices to be posted. You will have a visitor or two on the morrow. Posted notices are sure to attract Rossa and Vincent Muldoon."

+

The newly named Thomas O'Brien's quarters consisted of a narrow bed with a straw mattress and a roughly woven blanket. There was a chair and table on which sat a bowl and a pitcher of water. Two thick candles with matches were nearby to provide any needed light to a windowless room without a door. A small towel was near the bowl. His head of hair was gone, a new experience for the new Thomas. His hand reached repeatedly to rub the stubble left by the hand wielding the razor. Friar Louis seemed to take extreme pleasure in cutting his hair and waving the razor in his face. He fell asleep as soon as his head hit the mattress. In the morning he was summoned by voices echoing throughout the caverns and caves of this stone walled edifice. A new day was just beginning. Thomas O'Brien found himself in a line with a bowl in his hand being helped by one hooded monk, or was he a friar he didn't know which, on what to do and where to go. All the time the directions were given gently, a pointed finger with a smile, a gentle grasp of his elbow and a nod of a head to point the way, and a smile, but no words came forth. The new Thomas appreciated the kindness they provided to someone they didn't know. More than once the new Thomas was about to respond with words of appreciation that did not come. The hooded figure did not wait for a thank you. He had already turned away, nodding with that seemingly ever-present smile. Friar Jonathan found Thomas O'Brien at the table surrounded by other Franciscans with their hooded head uncovered. All of them bowed their heads for the longest time, their lips moved in silent prayer words, before heads rose and spoons lifted. When Friar Jonathan sat down his presence was acknowledged by all at the table with a nod and smile. Friar Jonathan knew a question would come, and in anticipation he furnished the answer to the question the new Thomas O'Brien was about to ask. "The five monks at this table have taken the oath of silence, Thomas. They can speak but cannot, being sworn to silence with their hand on the bible. Some of the monks have adhered to their oath for more than ten years. In all the years I have been here, I have never heard any of them speak except for one." The monks overhearing Friar Jonathan's words nodded in agreement. "Is their nod not a form of speech?" the new Thomas asked, "and what happened to the one who spoke?" "A form of communication it is, but 'tis not the spoken word, Thomas," Friar Jonathan replied. "The monks learned to communicate without the spoken word. They use their other senses and talents as you yourself just experienced being directed by the monks by pointing, by a gentle nudge or a nod of the head. In answer to your second question I will not answer but will refer your attention to your company at the table." The new Thomas O'Brien shifted his eyes away from the friar to focus on the occupants at the table across from him. Their heads were lifted to the roof and each index finger drew a line across the throat in an unmistakable sign to indicate the demise of the monk who failed to honor his oath of silence. "The monks humor themselves Thomas, the offender is no longer a monk."

+

In the pre-dawn darkness, before the knocker-up made his rounds, shadowy figures tacked the message printed on white sheets of paper on doors of business places, pubs and restaurants up one street and down another. They appeared to be unconcerned that some of the notices escaped the grasp of messengers to drift to the street. They ran from place to place posting the news to the sides of pubs, on railings and porches, wanting to finish the job before the sun conquered the night, and to avoid being discovered as one of the messengers who were likely Nationalist sympathizers. However, this notice identified Thomas O'Brien as a recruit trainee to the Benedictine Friary. The notice asked that townspeople welcome him and gave a brief history of the friar in training. No mention was made that identified him as the twin brother of the fugitive Patrick O'Brien. The notice identified Friar Jonathan as the author originator of the notice. Thomas O'Brien did not participate in morning prayers but was summoned to the dining hall and was directed to where Friar Jonathan sat with one of the notices in his hand.

"Sit yourself Thomas and a good morn to you and a short night it was for your benefactor. There will be questions when you venture out to the streets. If asked about your name you should emphasize that your lineage can be traced back to the great kings who took the name O'Brien, the founders of the settlement that became Ennis. If you are asked about Patrick, you have not seen him for several years as you have been working and studying in Paris. In addition, you might say your relationship was strained before you left for Paris and he did not desire to be contacted by you. If, anyone remarks to you that your likeness is much like Patrick, you should then say that he is your twin brother." The new Thomas ate his Spartan breakfast while he listened and sipped his tea. "Someone that studies in Paris should be able to speak a bit of the language," Thomas said.

"You will be spending an hour each day with Friar Benjamin who will introduce you to the language. Soon you will be able to mix French words into your conversations to strengthen your history. Do not offer information, but answer inquiries when you can." Friar Jonathan paused and took a bite of his biscuit and drained half of his tea. Quietly, a hooded and robed figure approached. He held up a purple hood and that part of the garment that covered the upper shoulders and chest. Friar Jonathan nodded his approval, taking it from the speechless monk and handing it to the new Thomas. "Our day began at dawn's first light. Your day is beginning, Thomas." It was 6am. The bong of the cathedral clock echoed through the stone walls. Friar Jonathan took the new Thomas O'Brien through a maze of hallways lit by candles, and rooms some with doors, some without. He stopped abruptly at a closed door and knocked three times. They waited, and then the latch moved. The door creaked open, behind that door stood a robed man with a white beard. The top of his head reached the breast bone of Friar Jonathan or his soon to be subject yet to be introduced. The small room was dimly lighted by candles on the floor, attached to the wall and on a tiny chest. Although he never was incarcerated in Kilmainham jail, the room would equate to a prison cell in the mind of the newly named Thomas. "Enter please, both of you to my humble accommodations. I secured an extra chair for your comfort. Friar Jonathan, please tell me to whom I have borrowed the extra chair for? "Pleased I am, Friar Benjamin to introduce your new pupil, Thomas O'Brien, a descendent of the Great Kings of Thomond who the Franciscans aided in establishing, our town of Ennis." Friar Benjamin turned away, an attempt to hide his smile because he already knew who the real Thomas was, having heard from Friar Jonathan in the early morning hours. "Please sit yourself, and you, Thomas O'Brien, would you please take my time to explain why you have sought the protection of the monks and the Friars, here in this temple of our God, a risk we take in view of the ill will held by the minority to our belief?" Patrick, now bearing the name Thomas, looked inquiringly at Friar Jonathan.

"Is it necessary for me to respond to one who has been instructed by you, his superior, to recount my unfortunate past?" The new Thomas O'Brien asked. "He has the right to know, from the source, the truth of the matter as our God has made it clear that all men are created equally in his eyes," Friar Jonathan replied. "I have made him aware of your circumstances, and verification from you is what Friar Benjamin asked." An imaginary clock located in the cool damp room of the friar would have ticked for seconds that to anyone who was witness, and there were none but the three, would have seemed like minutes before the new Thomas began what must have seemed to him, a confession of guilt. During his recant of past events, the spectrum of emotions was on exhibit; shock, anger, sorrow, fear and relief were all expressed and recognized by his audience. At one-point tears came, and at another, clenched fists pounded the table, followed by a smile when he told of his joyful reunion with his dog, and the wellness he experienced from learning he was not alone in his effort to rebuild a life.

THE RUSE

An hour past the sun's first rays the brick streets and damp rutted paths and alleyways of Ennis were coming alive. Mongrel dogs chased feral cats until a cat would stop to challenge, hissing with bared teeth, and arching its back. Doors opened. Citizens stepped out on the street or boardwalk to stretch and yawn while pulling suspenders over shoulders. Sheets of white paper were plastered on buildings and blown around in the street by the lightest of a morning breeze to be trampled by horses and run over by wagon wheels. Laughing children ran past followed by a grinning Danny Kissane who winked as he passed by in feinted pursuit. Animated groups of men and women gathered in front of a posted notice, possibly talking with each other about Friar Jonathan's introduction of Thomas O'Brien that was tacked to a door. Donovan Rossa was one of the people reading the notice. When he finished reading, he hoped not to hear any speculation about the name of the new friar student. Nothing was garnered from the women gathered who whispered to each other, except for one loud comment about the heavenly dessert she enjoyed for lunch the previous day. Later in the day he would pay a visit and pound on the rear door of the cathedral. He wanted to reacquaint himself with the new friar in training, the man he recruited, a ruse he suspected from the moment he read the name O'Brien. *Why was he here?* he thought, *when he was supposed to be in hiding at the O'Connell farm in the foothills overlooking the Lakes of Killarney."*

Abandoning his feinted pursuit, Danny Kissane veered to his left down an alley between the hardware store and the Green Dolphin Pub and Hostel. His intent was to catch up with Rossa and tell him of his plan to assist the new Thomas O'Brien in avoiding discovery. Danny did not stop to read the flyer, part of his portrayal as a mentally challenged youth trapped in the body of an adult. He overheard all that he needed to know upon hearing the name O'Brien in conversations, not wanting to give anyone the impression he could read. He returned to where Rossa was standing, but on the next street parallel to Cottage Street. With his hands in his pockets he skipped and hopped over to Cottage Street. He spotted Rossa coming his way. With that foolish grin on his face he ran to meet him. He put his arm around Rossa's shoulders whispering to him.

"Patrick is here, I know as I'm sure you do, Rossa," he whispered. "Let us skip our way off this crowded street to that bench," Rossa pointed to the bench at the side of the dentist's office. Rossa tried his best to imitate Danny's skip, stumbling and causing Danny to laugh uproariously. Once they were seated on the bench, Danny continued with his arm around Rossa's shoulder. He played along with his ruse, nodding when Danny would whisper something then he would laugh, pounding his knee. He told Rossa he would become the new friar's pupil enabling Danny to relay messages about Republican activities, movements and plans of the Molly Maguires. Rossa removed Danny's arm from his shoulders and rose from the bench. Their plans were to leave in separate directions and meet later at the Devil Duck Pub for sausages, toast and jam. Those plans were interrupted briefly when up to them walked Johnny Byrne, the butcher. Danny Kissane patted Rossa on the head, and waving his arms, skipped away humming a tune. "You, Donovan Rossa are a friend of Dopey Danny?" Johnny Byrne asked without any other form of greeting. "'Tis not kind of you to call him Dopey Danny, he is a child in a man's body. Everyone should be the friend of Danny," Rossa replied, "he is a mere child who is full of love and caring, and you as well should treat the young man with kindness as he is hurt too often by those who do not understand."

"Compassionate words you speak, but for a moment a thought crossed that for other reasons you consort with he of the weak mind," Byrne said. "I appreciate your word compassionate, for truly I am, however I do not appreciate your word consort, and what makes you believe Johnny Byrne that I am an associate of Danny Kissane?" Rossa asked. Johnny Byrne, an educated man, realized his mistake. He shrugged his shoulders. "Surely, when I saw both of you on the bench, I sensed a caring friendship, my apology Rossa I used the wrong word." "You did, and I must be on my way. Good day to you Byrne." Rossa turned and walked away leaving Johnny Byrne to watch his departing back.

Rossa knew that regardless of what he said in defense of his chat with Danny Kissane, a mention would be made of the time he was seen with Danny on the bench outside the dentist's office, if the butcher Byrne was the spy for the British that they suspected him to be. He would recommend Danny take extreme care, to be watchful of those who would follow his movements when he was out and about.

SCHOOLING

That same day back in Killarney in the Farrell Mercantile, Margaret O'Connell reveled in her attempt to help Fiona Farrell with the education of her new adopted daughters. She and Fiona sat at the table discussing ideas and rules that should be followed. Quite often Fiona was interrupted by customers looking for help, and by the two daughters who would run inside to stand by Margaret's side answering questions with a nod, soon to run, and then return to see what was in store for their future. The children had their own ideas welcomed by Margaret who wrote furiously while they talked. Her mind compiled a cornucopia of recommendations based on the limited ability of Fiona Farrell to cope with a totally foreign profession. Heather Anne and Sissy were captivated by Margaret's writing, pointing to written letters of the alphabet they recognized in her cursive style. Heather Anne knew the alphabet and Margaret told Fiona that Heather Anne was quite intelligent, asking question after question, some of them not at all what was thought an unschooled young girl would ask.

"Why do you pay money to the church you don't go to," she asked Margaret when they were alone, and Fiona was waiting on customers. "'Tis unfair, and you should not have to do it," she continued. "I would not," she said stomping her foot to emphasize her thought. She sat down next to Margaret who was astounded at her question and opened her mouth to ask where she

186

had heard...but before she could complete her thought, Heather Anne continued.

"I learned a new game from Silé. She told me to write down words that used only the first five letters, a, b, c, d and e. I found eight of them, Margaret. One of the words I wrote down was cab. We have cabs and carts and cars in Killarney. Silé said it was short for the French word cabriolet. Why do people speak differently, Margaret? Silé said that I did very well, and she was proud of me. It made me happy Margaret! Will you teach me how to write the letters like you do?" Sissy was tugging on her skirt. Heather Anne gave an apologetic shrug and followed her sister, turning to wave with a smile with Sissy pulling her by the other hand through the door. Fiona returned, scissoring her hands together and taking her seat.

"Now, where were we at? I glanced over to see you held captive by Heather Anne. What transpired while I was tending to business?" "So little time I have Fiona," Margaret said, shaking her head while adding another thought to the list she compiled on the paper. "Flynn will be here today, and we will return to the cottage. What we have done here this morn is only a start, the basics in what is needed..." at that moment Fiona was summoned by the bell over the door, "to advance their interests," Margaret continued, watching the departing back of Fiona Farrell who received no response from her greeting to the two British soldiers who entered the mercantile.

CHANCE MEETING

When Rossa was out of sight of Johnny Byrne, he stopped to wipe his brow. He was still a young man made nervous by the sudden appearance of a suspected informer. He took a deep breath and looked behind him. The man he hoped was not in his vision was not. Donovan Rossa breathed another sigh, this time in relief. He gathered his thoughts, deciding to take a circular route to the Devil Duck Pub using the muddy back streets. Often, he could not and was met by politicians and pickpockets, one of whom he recognized as a scourge to merchants and out of town visitors whenever "Shifty Sam" arrived in their town. Rossa's route through the side streets was halted more than once by itinerant beggars from the formerly productive farms and fertile valleys. They contrasted sharply to his travel on a heavily populated street or boardwalk. He saw well-coiffed ladies in fine attire escorted by elegant gentlemen in top hats and tails. Just beyond the Queen's Crown Hotel, its covered porch with tables and chairs occupied by tenants was the Devil Duck Pub. Benches were placed on either side of the front door. Seated on one of the benches was none other than Johnny Byrne. Rossa did not hesitate as he reached for the door.

"'Tis a good time for 'bangers' Johnny Byrne," he said pushing the door open. "And a pot of tea to remove the chill," Byrne responded, a little sarcastically. Rossa ignored his sarcasm and moved

inside the pub that appeared to be taken over by
visitors and tourists, the Devil Duck sign had done the
work intended. He walked to the room with no door
off the main bar room. Inside, he paused to scan the
bar from one end to the other. Danny Kissane was
seated at a table with three others playing a card game
called Twenty-Five. One of the men was Tommy
O'Keefe. The other two were introduced as Walter
Duff and Liam McDougal, from Millstreet. They were
"on the run" and identified as two of the participants in
the action taken against a brutal landlord. They drove
off his cattle, knocked down fences and set ablaze a
building used to store crops. An informant turned
them in and was later found out. In the foggy early
dawn hours a few days later, the informant was visited
by the Molly Maguires. He suffered a leg wound in the
altercation that developed into the need to remove his
infected leg above the knee. Danny had assured the
two newcomers they had nothing to fear inside the
Devil Duck pub. "You do know who greeted me
outside when I entered?" Rossa asked. He received
inquiring looks. "Our friend Johnny Byrne was on the
bench when I arrived."

"He should spend more time butchering than
lounging around to see who comes and goes," Tommy
O'Keefe said. "We should watch the watcher, and if
our fears are confirmed, a message should be sent!"
"Agreed, it is Tommy. Will we be able to enlist the
help of our two friends who are not known in Ennis?"
Ever the recruiter and organizer, Rossa looked first at

the two newcomers and then at Tommy O'Keefe. All three of them squirmed at the question, looking back and forth at first one, then the other.

"Would a better watcher not be in the new monk in training, our friend Thomas whom we all know was Patrick?" O'Keefe questioned. A pause occurred while Rossa considered O'Keefe's proposal. Three sets of unblinking eyes waited for Rossa's answer. "Talk I will with Thomas later today. He may become a close friend of the butcher, Johnny Byrne," Rossa said.

While Donovan Rossa, Tommy O'Keefe and Danny Kissane met that day, Flynn, with Devon mounted aboard Jumper, walked to the pasture later in the afternoon to check on the flock. Shearing time arrived too quickly for Flynn, fearful of his limited ability to relieve 40 or more sheep of their heavy coats. After Devon came upon one of the ewes tangled up in thorny brambles, he released the animal uninjured mumbling to himself about his forgotten gloves and the two lines of red scratches on his hand. Father and son walked to the perimeter of the pasture overlooking the valley below. Their attention was drawn to line of specks seen coming their way followed by a second line. Growth on the valley floor made it impossible for the troops to proceed side by side. Flynn knelt on his knee watching while Devon tended to his horse friend hidden behind tall brush. Minutes passed. The marching soldiers drew close headed for the rutted path taking them nearer to the plateau and the O'Connell farm. While they waited, the sun continued to drift in and out of the clouds to the west. Devon grew impatient.

ACCUSATION

The day was hot and humid. The man with his hands tied behind his back could not ward off the flying irritants swarming to his sweat. His neck was red and chaffed from the rope and drops of liquid dripped from the tip of his nose. He had faith in his God sure the British authorities would find him innocent of the accusation made against him after a neighbor unwittingly told the magistrate he recognized the fugitive Scot who stayed the night at the cottage of Conor Kennedy. Declan O' Donagh, the neighbor, swore to Conor he didn't think his detainment would result. Conor Kennedy explained in a calm voice that he didn't even inquire of the man's name. He had to endure this penance for the sake of his sons who protested so vehemently that British guns were leveled at them. Young and brash were his sons who were taken in by the fiery speeches of D'Arcy McGee and the militant words of Donovan Rossa, the organizer and recruiter who already convinced their neighbor in the foothills to provide shelter to suspected collaborators of the Molly Maguires. They dreamed of what it would be like for them to leave for America, enthralled by the words written by the sons and daughters of friends and relatives who made the journey and were soon to send money in every letter. The written word urged them to do the same and leave to a land where they would be truly free. Their letters spoke of freedom in a country where the land was fertile and cheap, a land where one could work for a decent wage with money left over to send to the brother, the sister or the lover.

REVOLT

"Should not we return, Father? 'Tis getting late and I am hungry." As in agreement the head of Devon's mount moved up and down. Flynn returned his focus to the line of troops now near enough to see four men in a group with their hands tied behind them and with ropes around their necks. Now, they we within the length of the pasture near the cathedral and still they came. Flynn was shocked to see that one of the men bound so cruelly was Conor Kennedy whose sons helped in past years with the sheep shearing. The other two men and a woman were unknown to Flynn. His thoughts raced backwards to the time he spent as a Legionnaire while he surveyed the two lines of soldiers. He knew Conor Kennedy did not deserve the cruel bondage only meant for the most hardened of criminals. Kennedy was a gentle, hard-working, honest man who paid his rent and was in fear of his God. Flynn observed four of the soldiers were armed with long rifle-muskets. He counted 30 soldiers and he squirmed. His mind sorted and discarded one idea after another, debating how...and then Devon's hand tugged on the pocket of his jacket. They looked each other in the eyes silently, and Flynn O'Connell made the decision. There had to be another way and likely he thought of his wife and family. Playfully he knocked off Devon's cap and rubbed his head. He had to free Conor Kennedy. An attempt would begin the next day. Shoulder to shoulder they continued to watch until the second line of soldiers escaped from view. His final glance at the valley below revealed another group of people following hundreds of yards behind the British soldiers. Flynn waited, and when close enough to be identified, he recognized the faces of Liam and Paddy Kennedy, the sons of Conor. There were four others with them, two carried pitchforks and two of them had axe handles over their shoulders. He assumed them to be neighbors who had cottages next to and across from the Kennedy cottage. Flynn was on his feet waving and shouting to attract their attention. Liam Kennedy acknowledged, and the group changed direction heading up toward Flynn and Devon.

"Aye friend Flynn, they took our dear Father, unjustly accused of harboring a fugitive," Liam said, as the six men sat on the grass having walked for hours following the troop. "A neighbor recognized the Scot and got a message to the British barracks commandant. He did not think they would detain Father who did not know the man. He did what anyone would do for a Scot, Irish or even an Englishman in his moment of mindless compassion, by providing shelter for a night and a meal to fill an empty belly," Padraig said. "We intend to get him back! We will use force if necessary."

"Wise you would be Kennedy boys, to argue your case peaceably before waving a pitchfork at the Brit with the gun," Flynn said. "First of all, you should protest the treatment your father received on being only suspected of a crime. A rope around the neck with hands tied behind the back should be reserved for murderers of women and children. In the morn I will be in Killarney with the Foley brothers and will assist you. I have an idea that D'Arcy McGee also might assist to help free your father. He is supposedly in the town to speak." In addition to reuniting with the most influential woman in his life, he intended to speak with Fiona Farrell, the most influential Irish woman in Killarney. She intervened on behalf of Martha Howe and Neil when she arrived with the aide-de-camp of the Liberator, Daniel O'Connell who signed the document Upton Page, the aide to O'Connell, carried with him. The document pledged legal support to Martha Howe to thwart her landlords attempt to double rent payments in the middle of the contract. Fiona Farrell was an enterprising merchant who sold on tick (credit) to those she decided were worthy of her trust. Conor Kennedy was one of those. Devon had climbed aboard his horse friend Jumper, who wanted to run, jump over granite and clumps of tall green grasses. Flynn directed Liam and Paddy to the direction taking them to the path and then to the main road into Killarney. On the outskirts they would find the barracks between the cathedral and the Howe Livery on the edge of town. Although the Kennedy boys had visited Killarney in past years, the barracks was a new addition to the landscape surrounding Killarney. It was quickly constructed to house up to 50 troops due to the rise in complaints by landlords about the harassment they received from militants including the Molly Maguires and the Whiteboys. "Care you should take Kennedy boys. Don't do anything rash and get yourselves shot or scheduled for the gallows," Flynn said as they departed.

He did not mention "transportation" to the penal colonies in Australia, Tasmania or New Zealand, never to be allowed to return to the land they loved. For some, it was the fate worse than death, the ultimate in cruel and unusual punishment. Flynn remembered his talk with Neil Howe who said that his brother was in 'a bit of trouble' supposedly being accused of aiding escape attempts by transported Irish colonists. He was accused of providing safe passage on ships bound for Bordeaux, Lisbon and Cork.

"Time it is for us to go," Padraig said, his eyes squinting toward the East where the brightness of a dawning day was in its infancy. How quickly word was spread. Padraig, with Liam standing nearby, surveyed the gathering of pitchfork carrying farmers. Neighbors and supporters of Nationalist interests readied themselves to march on the office of the magistrate. An early morning mist mingled with hot breath of participants turning frosty white in the still air. The ground hugging fog spoke of the penetrating cold causing foot stomping and hands-in-the-pocket attempts to keep warm. Poorly dressed friends of the Kennedy family had prepared themselves too hastily and inadequately in their hurry to support a friend and neighbor. Conor Kennedy, an Irishman, was currently under arrest and unjustly accused of harboring a fugitive. Pipe smoke drifted in the stagnant air as 40 or 50 protestors walked silently down the center of the street in a still sleeping town. The "knocker-up" had yet to make an appearance. At the intersection of streets, the four corners were filled with establishments catering to the gregarious nature of the Irish to begin an end to the day with a pint in hand and a story to tell. At that intersection, the protestors were met by a group headed by D'Arcy McGee and Flynn O'Connell. Between them, the banner they carried read, FREE CONOR KENNEDY. They were followed by several townsmen and women including Neil Howe, and Malachy Brandon, the operator of the Howe Livery and Blacksmith Shop. Fiona Farrell, the Mercantile owner carried a ledger book with her. She was accompanied by Silé Dooley, the soon to be wife of Neil Howe. The mercantile owner was sure to have something to say in defense of Conor Kennedy. The Apothecary, Prescott Piggerman, fell behind when he tried to avoid puddles and muddy spots in the roadway. After he spent an hour previous day polishing, he didn't want to tarnish the shine on his favorite black boots. As the crowd moved from one side of town to the other, the numbers increased. Liam Kennedy elbowed his brother.

"Look, would you," motioning toward people exiting building on either side of the street. Behind him, a green flag emblazoned with the Irish harp waved back and forth. Signs sprouted up written in Gaelic sure to have a message that could not be written in the Queen's English. The crowd grew to over 100. McGee talked with Kennedy neighbors who agreed to speak on behalf of Kennedy who had no knowledge of his guest being a wanted fugitive. The crowd continued to grow, and a strong masculine voice in the rear began to sing. Very soon his voice was joined by others who were accompanied by a man with a bodhran. The sun was about to escape the horizon chasing away the mist hugging the bare brown earth. Hands came out of pockets and arms circled shoulders of a friend. Axe handles were raised in time to the singing and the beat of the drum. Liam Kennedy turned and walked backwards for a time.

Surely, we cannot be denied brother," as he waved an arm toward the crowd following behind. Padraig smiled broadly and nodded, his fist punctured the air above. On the other side of town, a runner notified the magistrate Tim O' Rourke of the approaching, in his words "mob." He chose not to make light of a situation that could escalate into a confrontation. His was an undermanned office even with 2 barracks regulars who would report to the magistrate later. He handed a rolled-up paper to the magistrate. Tim O' Rourke was a reasonable man who listened intently to the story told by the barracks Commandant who turned Conor Kennedy over to him to be held until he was charged. O' Rourke knew Kennedy to be an honest, hard-working Irishman who traded with town merchants and the last person you would suspect to knowingly harbor a convicted fugitive. He considered the report deciding he could do little but speak to the crowd when they arrived. He grabbed the ring of keys from the peg on the wall and opened the door to the cell area. He inserted the key into the first cell door containing the

Irishman George O' Leary who spent the night as the magistrate's guest. George had consumed too many pints the evening before and was refused service. In a drunken rage, he threw his mug breaking the mirror behind the bar of the Two Pence Saloon. He sobered up and was being released after agreeing to make restitution to the pub owner. His key turned the lock. The next cell contained Conor Kennedy.

"Your friends are about to arrive Conor Kennedy," the magistrate told him, motioning with the rolled paper in their direction. "Listen now. You can hear the beat of the drums and the singing." A hand was on the back of each of his guests as he directed both to the office telling

O' Leary to be wary of the drink. "You will be barred from the pubs, and you will be my prisoner for more than one night... if we meet again, George! Good day to ya'," he said. George O' Leary made a hasty exit.

A boisterous crowd waving flags and singing a bawdy ballad paid little attention to how near they were to their destination. Flynn O'Connell, D'Arcy McGee and the Kennedy sons saw the door to the magistrate's office open. Out stepped Tim O'Rourke followed by Conor Kennedy who was not shackled or bound in any way. Little by little, the crowd finally became aware of their mission and the singing quieted, along with the beating of the drum, only yards away from the stoop of the magistrate's office. Tim O'Rourke waited for their arrival and turned his attention to the paper, until now forgotten. Unrolled, he tried to smooth it out against the wall of the office building noting it was signed by the British Commandant. His eyes were distracted from the written word when D'Arcy McGee began to speak but returned his attention to the paper because one word caught his eye. The word was "release" and it made Tim O'Rourke raise his hand asking for time to read the words that brought a smile to his face. The crowd waited expectantly as the magistrate digested what was written. He raised his eyes to the crowd waving the paper above his head with one hand.

"The fugitive Scot has been captured and arrested. The Commandant has issued a release order for the man Conor Kennedy." It took a moment for the crowd to capture the meaning and then a roar came from those gathered. Conor Kennedy stepped off the stoop of the magistrate's office into the arms of his sons who had tears of happiness leaking from their eyes. Arm in arm, marchers began their version of the Irish jig in the street, fists pumped upwards as if a great military victory had been the precursor to their jubilance. Pubs would be opened early to take advantage of country and city folk that mingled together in a celebratory mood to welcome a fellow Irishman back to the British version of freedom. Flynn O' Connell and D'Arcy McGee waited for their turn to greet Conor Kennedy as neighbors and friends surrounded him.

SUSPICION

At a table inside the Two Pence Saloon, an unlikely pair sat facing each other with hands grasping pints of dark malt beverage. Animated conversation took place between the butcher Johnny Byrne and the Monk in training Thomas, ne Patrick O' Brien. A pseudo friendship developed by Thomas to offset his stratagem to uncover the thought to be traitorous truth behind the suspicious activities of the butcher, Johnny Byrne. The "new" Thomas was aided in the ruse by his new supporters, and the Franciscan monks. The town meat carver drew interest being nearly always within eye or ear shot of activities of a Nationalist nature. Not affiliated with any church or religion, Johnny Byrne was thought, and appeared to be, an atheist, a black sheep in the flock of white Kerry Hills, soon to be shorn. His lack of commitment was a reason for the majority to question his purpose, and raised suspicion among the Catholic majority whose allegiance, for most, was to the local priest and his message, and to country. Their country was Ireland.

"A Godless man like yourself should take heed of his advancing years and prepare, just in case mind you, of what lies beyond, the afterlife," Thomas said, reaching for the hand with fingers tapping incessantly on the table top. The hand with the tapping fingers pulled away. "You speak of God and life after death and where tell me are the one who passed before us?" Johnny Byrne argued. He had an exasperated, unbelieving look about him as he motioned to the barkeep pointing to his mug, then looked at Thomas questioning. Thomas shook his head rising from his chair not wanting to become involved in a lengthy discussion on religion that he knew little of.

"Leave I must Johnny Byrne, we will meet again without a doubt. I am off to prepare another soul for his eternal reward." Thomas smirked to himself at his choice of words as he pushed through the doors to face an afternoon sprinkle. He did not notice that Johnny Byrne left his table to watch him leave. He leaned against the window, watching until Thomas disappeared into an alley. Johnny Byrne fixed his cap and hurried out the door headed for the alley.

HORRIBLE DISCOVERY

Donal and Brendan watched Flynn until he disappeared behind the shrubbery. The remainder of their return trip back to the shore cottage was done to the sound of wagon wheels and the clip-clop of the horse's hooves. No doubt both brothers were reflecting on the events of the day. The Foley brothers missed the celebration after filling their orders and found Flynn at the Howe Livery on their way out of town. He relayed how the pubs became crowded with celebrants who moved from one tavern to another. Flynn was finally able to reach the side of Conor Kennedy to wish him well as their talk shifted to the sheep shearing to begin shortly. D'Arcy McGee, his fiery speech not needed, was introduced. The singing began in earnest after two or three pints. Mid-morning was left behind as a hazy threatening sky hid the sun soon to reach its zenith. The wagon's movement was halted for a time to provide right of way to the herder, his dog, and his flock. William Longford, the herder, stopped for a short visit with Donal and Brendan while the dog watched the sheep. Longford was on his way to a small settlement outside of Killarney to have his flock shorn of their wooly coats. Brendan watched the herder reward his dog as they parted company. A pleasant return resumed. The afternoon sun that sent a path of light shimmering down to the lake surface caused Brendan to squint. Near the shore the wide reflection was dotted by something noticed by the older brother who elbowed Donal.

"Do you see what I think I see there on the lake?" Donal shaded his eyes. "'Tis a log or a stump I hope to God it is," Donal replied, peering intently. "What do you think it is, my brother?" Donal asked, and waited, but no response came from Brendan. Moments later, three objects were visible drifting ever so slowly toward the beached watercraft and the minute patch of sand shaded by the overhang of water loving Aspens. At the bottom of the hill, Brendan was able to relieve his foot of the necessity to brake and brought the horse and wagon to a stop. Silently they watched the water lap bringing with it ever so slowly what both brothers feared to mention but knew. Grimly aware of what must be done, both began to perform the tasks needed each time they returned to the shore. Reports from other fishers of the lakes indicated they too had come upon emaciated bodies floating in the waters. Donal and Brendan Foley had yet to have their boat bumped by a floating corpse in the gray, fog filled precursor hours of night.

CHORES

Light from two whale oil lamps allowed Flynn to sort through the bag containing the sprouting seed potatoes he and Devon would plant later in the morning. The ideal planting time had already passed, but Margaret insisted that a late planting would act as insurance in case, in her words, "something dreadful strikes the early plantings." Finished with his examination, he poured the tea water again, and looked to the loft for signs of Devon's coming awake. Still very early, he shuffled his way to the window, wind milling his arms, and saw the hint of sunrise in the east. Once his feet left the carpet, the dirt floor sent a chill and a reminder of the woolens Margaret had knitted. He reached for the pipe and bag held in the wall where a stone was removed but pulled his hand away. "Bessie the Guernsey would be pleased to be relieved of her production earlier than usual," he thought. He reached for the empty turf bucket. One of Devon's duties was to keep the bucket filled and Mary Margaret always reminded him, but this dawning morn she was with Margaret in Killarney. Flynn imagined the guilty look that would appear on his son's face when he noticed the filled bucket. When he pushed on the plank door the breeze retaliated causing Flynn to grab his coat from the tree before he ventured outside. His glance was drawn to the smoldering turf fire. Cool morning air infiltrated inside to stir sparks and create new tongues of flame in the hearth. He remembered the cloth Margaret filled with thresh, sewn tightly together with needle and thread to block the breeze. With the bucket overflowing he returned inside to find Devon on the fourth rung of the ladder to the loft.

"Good morn Father," Devon said, his eyes immediately drawn to the filled turf bucket Flynn placed next to the hearth. Devon swallowed guiltily, "another cup of tea father...with the honey?" Devon jumped the remaining two rungs to the dirt floor. Flynn smiled, removing the thresh bag from the hook on the tree, stuffing it under the door. "Should not you collect our breakfast from the henhouse? I will visit our friend Bessie while you can toilet yourself for the day," Flynn replied, not wanting to compound the guilt his son felt for an omission Devon had made in the past. "Yes father, I forgot. A full day we will have, and ma'am and 'sis will come home today, won't they father?" Flynn paused to look back at his son who exhibited a look of anxious uncertainty. "You said she would stay longer to help the mercantile lady, and...and, Mary Margaret had the company of Heather Anne and Sissy...and...." "Not a fear do I have son of mine. Your mother and sister will be sad to depart Killarney, but happy to be re-united with you, Bessie, the chickens and pigs, and with your father," Flynn replied, turning up the collar on his coat. Flynn left the cottage for the byre as Devon busied himself pouring warmed water into the bowl to ready himself for a day just beginning.

+

Later that day Flynn was bent over, leaning on the short shovel. The late crop of potatoes was planted in the mucky, sod covered earth at the lower slope of the garden. His back was sore. Flynn stretched and twisted while he watched Devon visit with his best friend, the coal black horse named Jumper. "*Ah, youth,*" he thought as he watched his son unaffected by the morning of planting five long rows of potatoes. With the shovel over his shoulder, Flynn surveyed his own and his son's handiwork as he walked between the rows to the tool rack at the end of the garden. He called to Devon.

"Son of mine, time it is to prepare a bit of food before we leave for Killarney. You can ride Jumper." Flynn's statement brought an immediate smile to his son's face. "After a bite, lead the mare to the wagon. We will stop at the lake cottage of the brothers Foley to inquire if they are "in need" of my assistance on the morrow." Flynn turned away and headed for the cottage. Devon could be seen jumping up and down, arms in the air at the thought of riding his best friend into Killarney. Hot tea, liberally laced with honey, milk for Devon, brown bread with butter, and smoked salmon prepared Flynn and Devon for the afternoon trip to the lake, and then to Killarney to collect Margaret and Mary Margaret. Flynn wrapped the remains of the brown bread and chunks of smoked salmon in cloth in case they were to meet hungry Irish on their way, and he knew it to be a likely probability. The unfortunate country people continued to endure starvation, sickness and death on their way to a closed workhouse and a black kettle containing a thin soup. Flynn would miss the burials that took place the previous afternoon. The Foley brothers debated, if one were to witness, the debate bordered on the argumentative as two brothers tried to decide on how to dispose of the unwelcome visitation. In the water for only God knew how long, the bodies were decomposed so badly that bones barren of flesh were evident. The brothers finally agreed that a burial at sea would be the only method available to them. The rocky slope leading down to the location of the cottage and the minute stretch of sand that composed the beach was not an option. The bodies were wrapped in an unused net, secured and towed to the middle of the lake where Brendan tied a large piece of sandstone to the netting. The weight carried the poor souls to their eternal rest at the bottom of the lake.

On horseback, Devon arrived at the lake shore minutes before Flynn and the wagon. Devon could not resist letting his mount run when the opportunity of a clear uncluttered path was presented. He found the Foley brothers seated around the glowing turf. Each had a steaming tin cup in their hands. "Aye, young O'Connell, get down from your fine horse, seat yourself and have a cup of my fish soup," Brendan proudly offered. Devon dismounted, but had no comment on the offer. "Are you alone, or is Flynn following?" Brendan questioned. "Father brings the wagon Mr. Foley. We are going to Killarney to bring mother and sister back home today," Devon replied, as he led the horse to the tree line looping the reins over a branch. "An accomplished horseman you have become young Devon," Donal Foley complimented, "and a magnificent steed you ride," Brendan said, as heads turned to the raspy squeak of the wheel brake being applied. At the top of the slope, Flynn left the wagon seat and poured water for the mare with no name before he walked down to greet the Foley brothers. "Aye, Foley boys the O'Connell comes to offer relief from the drudgery of cleaning fish and scraping paint...but not today. An important mission we have this day."

"A welcome sight it is to see the smile on your face Flynn O'Connell," Donal Foley said. Brendan nodded in agreement. "A family united is reason to smile," Brendan added. Flynn turned his attention to Devon. "For sure a long sandy beach at Gweesala or in Galway where the races are held should be the place to race your black at breakneck speed. I watched you son and caution you. I saw you bounce in the saddle more than once. A shame it would be for your angelic face to be scratched and bloodied after you are thrown from the saddle!"

"Sorry I am father, I will heed your word although Jumper likes to run, and I choose good footing for him. Mary Margaret said my face is "devilish." Laughter erupted. Flynn grinned at Devon's revelation. Donal added more turf to the fire as all gathered around. Brendan was first to recount the happenings after Flynn left the path yesterday. "We have heard the stories from others who fish alongside us. Sad are the tales they tell of families without hope who hand in hand, fling themselves into the sea, a death to avoid the sufferings of disease and starvation." The potatoes rotted, and the Herring left. There was nothing for them. They sold the boat, the nets, and the poles." In a low tone of voice, Brendan continued to tell of the burial process and the suspicion of some of the fishermen who thought the lochs would become contaminated and destroy their livelihood." No one spoke. A void was created until a somber faced Flynn rose to his feet, looking at the heavens where dark clouds gathered. "We must hurry away brothers Foley. The sky threatens. Margaret waits for our return. Shall we see each other on the morrow? "There is a need for you on the second morn Flynn," Donal said. "The need for a reunion with wife and child for at least the night and a day is of most importance," Brendan said. "I support my brother, Flynn. We will see you on the morning after the morrow," Donal said as Flynn started up the slope waving his cap in the air. Devon walked the black horse alongside his father.

Margaret and Fiona Farrell were still formulating plans for the children's schooling when Devon arrived on horseback followed closely by Flynn with the wagon. A happy reunion took place in front of the Farrell Mercantile followed by a few tears because Mary Margaret and her mother were leaving. When they arrived at the home of Martha Howe, Neil was inspecting the little used carriage that waited for the horse with no name. "Sure as the rain will fall, you will take your family back with you in mother's carriage," Neil said as both hands pulled back and forth on the top of the wheel. Martha Howe insisted that the O'Connell women be transported in the carriage. Neil ushered everyone inside for tea before he led the mare and wagon to the corral. He unhitched the mare, leading her back to ready the carriage for the trip to the remote O'Connell cottage. Well it was for Martha Howe to furnish the elegant carriage. Neil was securing the roof of Peter Howe's gift to Martha when threatening skies opened to release a momentary pummeling of ice pellets, some the size of a half pence. "If there is a God in heaven, protect me," Neil shouted. He raced for the porch after adjusting the carriage roof. When he arrived under the protection of the overhang he turned back to look. As quick as it came, the assault from the war in the heavens had ceased. His eyes caught a glimpse as the sun peaked through a hazy white overcast. He immediately blessed himself.

INVESTIGATION

Johnny Byrne, the Ennis butcher, hurried his way as best he could on a balking leg to catch up with the monk or friar in training. He heard the terms used by others and by Thomas O' Brien, but he couldn't decide which one applied to him. He really didn't pay much attention to those secretive hooded men who walked with their hands hidden while they mumbled foreign words to themselves. The alley was empty, his quarry no longer in sight. Johnny Byrne had to decide whether to go left or right. Numerous pubs were on either side, but the friary, the habitat of the Franciscans was on the left. Something akin to a predator's instinct made him turn left toward the lair of the monks, a religious order he tried to avoid, but he could not escape what seemed to be the chance meetings with the newly cloaked man of God to be, who suddenly appeared out of nowhere. Several storefronts ahead of him, was the friary, and he chose to circle around and approach from another direction, hoping to run into an acquaintance to appear less interested in the goings-on around the cathedral. Johnny Byrne harbored a suspicion about his prize, and if proved right he would be amply rewarded as he was in the past. His desire to become occupied was granted when Andrew Timkins, the manager of a popular Ennis hotel, ran over to him breathing heavily.

"Aye ya, Johnny Byrne, pleased I am to catch up to you this fine day. Sad I am to say your delivery of yesterday morn was ruined by a foreign substance. The smell forced me to dispose of the order and cancel a dinner guest reservation for 8 people. The hotel will not be able to pay for that order I am sorry to say." Johnny Byrne was thunderstruck at the revelation, rendered speechless for a moment, unbelieving with his mouth open and head shaking the negative reaction to the information. "You still may be able to see for yourself, Johnny Byrne. At days end the maggots found your beef and lamb palatable." The message delivered was an immediate disruption to the butcher's original objective. He failed to notice the heavy back door of the cathedral friary open to release Thomas O' Brien, Donovan Rossa and Friar Alfred.

Word traveled quickly, the one not to hear until now was the butcher. Inside the cool stone walls, Rossa swore, with his hand on the bible that he had no part in the contamination of the meat delivery to the hotel. "As the green grass grows, we must have someone operating outside of our umbrella," Rossa said, as they exited to see Johnny Byrne in animated arm waving conversation with Timkins, the hotel manager. "Someone's dinner plans were foiled," Friar Alfred said. "Perhaps a message was left to indicate responsibility." Rossa looked at Thomas who without a word received the unspoken message. He turned away, his hands hidden in the robe and started walking toward the butcher's place of business on the river side of town. Remembering his instructions, his head was bowed, his lips moved as if in prayer as he walked.

Someone before Johnny Byrne knew the advantage of being near the river and its meandering currents where carrion and tripe could be easily disposed of. Today the wind was right to dispose of the scents and smells emanating from the rear of the building set close to the river bank. At the front, fresh meat could be purchased, and as Thomas crossed in front of the window, he could see movement inside. The butcher's assistant was on duty, but Thomas was more interested in what he might find at the rear of the building. Not being sure if he was noticed as he approached, he considered several reasons if questioned but decided no one would suspect a monk of any mischievous intent. When he reached the back of the building, he peeked around the corner to see a man holding a lighted torch. When Thomas stepped around the corner the man dropped the torch into a pile of wood scraps and paper at the base of the wall and ran. Flames from the torch licked hungrily at the piled accelerant. Thomas ran around the building pounding on the wall to alert the people inside. His shouts were heard up and down the street.

"Fire we have, fire...fire at the back," he shouted as he burst through the front door. Suddenly, the wind had changed. Smoke now drifted inside the shop as the assistant and Thomas frantically searched for pails to hold water. The butcher's assistant found tin buckets and raced for the back door, straight arming his way through followed by Thomas who was followed by a customer who was inside. Ever increasing flames crept up from the starter fire to the side of the building. Neighbors from down the street saw the smoke. Knowing the fire danger to wooden buildings they grabbed rakes and shovels before running to the smoke. Onlookers who raced over to assist formed a line. Bucket after bucket of river water was passed and splashed against the dry wood of the building. Rakes pulled flaming embers away. Shovels of moist earth helped to suffocate burning coals. After several frantic minutes the fire appeared to be out. Those who helped with rakes and shovels leaned on the handles and wiped dirt and sweat from their faces. The new Thomas poured one last bucket on the pile of wood and paper. A man with a rake turned the pile over to reveal any remaining scraps that might reignite the flames. Thomas watched the rake turn over burned paper. He bent down to retrieve a crumpled sheet with printing, charred and soaked. Most of the printed words were illegible, but what was seen were the partial words conspira..., and ...tain Rock. He carried the remnant to the interior of the butcher shop being inspected by the assistant who was joined by Johnny Byrne, the butcher who had just returned from near the cathedral where he heard of the contaminated meat. He was surveying the damage while thanking those who assisted.

"How did this happen and who is responsible?" he asked of those who gathered around. At that moment, the hooded Thomas entered. "I was alerted to the fire by that man," the assistant said, pointing a finger at

Thomas O'Brien who carried the soaked sheet of crumpled paper. "Smoke attracted my attention, Johnny Byrne. I happened to be on the way to visit a friend, and saw a man leaving in a rush after he ignited a pile of dry wood with a lighted torch. We were able to extinguish the flames with the help of neighbors and friends. I did not recognize the man but found this in the rubble." Those gathered around looked and pointed at the printed words.

"No doubt there is that you have made an enemy, Johnny Byrne. Captain Rock and his band have paid you a visit," said one of the onlookers who leaned over the shoulder of the new Thomas to view the words. The gathered stared at the silent Johnny Byrne, head down with his hands in his pockets. "A message has been delivered to you, Johnny Byrne, and you should take heed," Thomas O' Brien said, letting the soggy paper fall to the counter. "You have a new friend, and well it is to have such a man as a friend," the Englishman, Malcolm Whitten said, nodding toward the monk in training. The butcher took 3 strides toward Thomas, standing in front of him just inches from the face of the monk trainee. "You and I have met each other when you have told me of the afterlife and how I should prepare myself. Now you save me this horror, I am indebted to you Thomas O' Brien, if that is your name, for at least your action so promptly," he said, sincerity evident in his eyes before he turned away to look at the paper on the counter.

Thomas O' Brien left the butcher shop, but not before he silently accepted the plaudits, back slapping and verbal adulations and exaggerations of those who decided he was the main reason Byrne the butcher could remain in business. They walked alongside him, behind him and ahead of him. They told people they met of the heroism of Thomas to save the building that remained the butcher shop of Johnny Byrne. The new Thomas remembered who he was supposed to be, walking with his head down, his lips moving in pseudo prayer, allowing young children to clutch his robe as he walked down the street that led back to the friary.

GODSPEED

Parting words were said, and hugs exchanged. Margaret and her daughter stood next to the Peter Howe carriage. Neil had re-acquainted the mare to the carriage she had pulled only once before. The carriage was lighter and made more comfortable for passengers. Overstuffed seats were covered in fine leather. It offered travel somewhat protected from the weather by the skirted canopy above the heads of the occupants. "Now remember," Martha Howe said pointing a finger at Flynn who stood at Margaret's side, "you are to return Margaret to us in two weeks for at least a weekend." "Can I go too?" Mary Margaret questioned. She was pulling on her mother's skirts, anxiously looking from Martha Howe to her mother. Fiona Farrell said her good-by earlier and returned to the mercantile, but Sissy and her older sister remained. Sissy stood with tears in her eyes, but tears changed to smiles when Margaret and Martha both assured Mary Margaret she would be welcome. More hugs were applied. The bags were packed away, an anxious Flynn searched the skies often, reins in hand in the driver's seat. Devon was aboard his best friend who pranced and shook his mane in anticipation of the return to the remote farm in the foothills. Neil Howe stood next to the carriage at the driver's seat.

"When will you return with the Foley brothers, Flynn?" he asked. "The day after the morrow the Foley boys will need my services," he replied. "Fortunate I was to miss what they discovered on their return yesterday."

"The loch claimed three victims of the potato scourge. The Foley boys buried the poor souls at the bottom of the loch, a gruesome task to remove the bodies from the small strand between the granite," Flynn related. There was a brief silence as both men contemplated. "You will miss the public hanging in three days. The captured Scot is to be executed that morning," Neil said. "I hope to miss the event. Was he guilty? Or was it a Brits conviction?" Flynn asked. "All I know is from what Ma Howe said that British justice is swift when evidence is irrefutable," Neil replied. Flynn looked at the sky again.

"We must go Margaret. Hurry yourself into your seat," he said while extending his hand. "Late it is love of mine. The sheep, the pigs and the bovine wait for us," he grinned, but Margaret didn't smile, but took his offered hand. "How is it my husband that I am sad and happy at the same time," she said as she helped her daughter to her seat. "Pleased I am wife of mine that you are happy. We will be together again." "I am happy Mother," Devon said. His black mount huffed when he let him approach the mare to rekindle their mother-son relationship. Silé Dooley and Mary Margaret held each other for a moment before Margaret helped her daughter to board the carriage. With his left hand on the reins, Flynn waved his hat in the air as the mare leaned into the harness. Sissy and Heather Anne ran alongside the carriage until they arrived at the muddier part of the road but continued to shout and wave their hands at the departing O'Connell family.

"Your bum will not hurt when we arrive at the cottage, my daughter," Margaret said. "What a difference it is compared to travel with the wagon." "But mother, how can we sing the bumpity-bump song when there is no bumpity-bump?" The carriage reached the cemetery prompting Margaret to ask her daughter for quiet. "Shush, and bow your head my daughter," Margaret said. She held a finger to her lips as they passed by the graveyard of the Tarans, the unbaptized infants who were denied holy ground. The burial plot was followed by the monoliths erected to remember those who had passed on to their ultimate reward, whatever the reward. Killarney lay below them now, soon to be lost to their vision. They watched the picturesque tourist town slowly recede from their eyes. Spires of smoke climbed upwards from the chimneys to the heavens. No wind bothered to disturb the tranquil scene that captured their attention. Flynn cast a quick glance heavenward to the indecisive clouds above that spit an occasional droplet of water and ice. He flicked the reins again.

NEW LIFE

It happened again! The pain made Silé Dooley bend over. So intense was the attack she let go of the pail with the hot water. It dropped to the floor, splashing. She groaned, muttering to herself while clutching her middle. Her words, purposely uttered were in Shelta, the dialect of her clan. According to Neil and Martha Howe both acquainted with the words, if spoken in English would not be well received in a house of God. Self-educated, Silé spoke the language of the clan, the Irish Gaelic, mixed in with the Shelta and the English, a combination so confusing most on hearing a conversation would turn and walk away shaking their head. Her marriage to Neil Howe was more than a week away. According to Neil, and her future Mother-In-Law, it was important to be married in the faith of their church. The former Traveler run-away did not care. Martha Howe was consumed with the excitement of the marriage of her son and Silé Dooley, her wish granted after nearly two years of waiting. She busied herself. With a measuring tape in hand, Silé could picture how she stood with her hands on her hips, turning this way and that, and hearing her words.

"Silé Dooley where are you, I need to measure the length again to make sure, please. Are you hiding from me? Come out, come out child." Silé heard the women of the towns talk. She was told and now understood how important it was to them not to be with child prior

222

to the wedding. Gathering in groups of four or five they whispered, heads nodded in agreement among themselves glancing toward the Howe residence shaking their heads. Oh, how they knew the temptations of young people. They knew they lived in nearby rooms just down the hall from each other. Martha revealed much, in confidence of course, but soon trust failed. Perhaps some of them were as guilty in their own youth. There was an occasional smile, titter, or fingers to the mouth trying to prevent what was said in confidence.

Priests who did visit Killarney did so only occasionally, their ranks thinned by the pressures of the potato famine, and the accompanying starvation, sickness and death. When a Mass was said, it was an event conducted in the open air on the pasture field near the cathedral. Often, the site for Gaelic football when the sun came to dry the sod while grazing sheep and cattle trimmed the grass to ankle length. She bent to the wishes of Neil but found it hard to change from what she knew growing up in a godless Traveler clan where a wedding was virtually unknown. The night he came to her rescue she recalled her words to him; *please stay with me.* The rule understood in her father's rogue clan was "her man or his woman, and if there was to be a "wedding" it was a performance to mimic a union conducted by a legitimate cleric. The clan leader was not a man of God. She took a breath, the pain subsided. Leaning on the mop handle she waited a moment to steady herself before she picked up the pail, now with no hot water needed to splash on the floor to wash away the sickness and the blood. She tossed the pail toward the open door. The town volunteers, men and women, took turns cleaning away the disease and death remnants in the cathedral room known by many names. Today was her turn. She must be careful. Neil would be sure to examine her dress for signs of her activity when she returned. *I need more hot water!* Her thought was answered by another volunteer named Samuel Culhane who carried two more steaming pails saving her from heavy lifting. "Aye Missy, empty those will ya' and I will fetch two more," he said, seemingly hesitant to venture inside the room. He stood with one foot on the threshold and watched as Silé struggled with the heavy buckets. "'Tis I who you see in front of you, I, who would wear a mask or cloth over me face Missy, and you should do the same," Samuel said, wiping his hands on his pants as if he had contaminated them by touching the door jam. He hurried out without a word. Silé didn't answer because she was busy wiping her brow with her soiled apron. When she looked at the door Samuel and the buckets were gone to be replaced by the figure of Patrick Kincade. On this day she saw only glimpses of Patrick, the vicar, whose prior illness rendered him a shadow of his former self. He walked with a cane. Volunteers and others were directed to do what he formerly did. Today, he stood leaning on the blackthorn cane after he entered.

"The water should boil. I have moved the fire and the kettle as close to this door as possible. Heat is quickly lost," he said as he gestured with his hand pointing behind him to indicate the new location. "A strong back will bring you the buckets of water." From his pocket he pulled a white muslin cloth with ties. "Wash it after it is used. Use it each time you are here to assist," he said without further instruction he turned away, leaving to confront his next challenge. Silé watched him exit. He looked tired, on the edge of defeat, and that worried Silé Dooley. He never failed to thank her. Today he said nothing.

Ever since the day she left the wagons to escape from the clutches of her clan Traveler family she was continually exposed to the reality of the world outside of the camp. Locks were released, and doors were left open. Where there were doors, they faded away from an opportunity to move forward. She unlatched herself from the rogue Traveler camp. Now, away from the restrictions of a life always on the move she had at her disposal a ring of keys to unlock any door she confronted. On the rainy night she met Neil Howe, she left the Traveler camp to get away, and walked and ran to the cathedral. She looked for who might be in charge and settled on the muscular man at the black cauldron, a cooking pot.

After a conversation with Patrick Kincade, the man who held the ladle, she volunteered to help, uncaring and unconcerned about the potential danger that took the lives of doctors, caregivers and priests. She knew of the sickness and death in and about the cathedral. The odors that drifted to the noses of her uncle, her brother and herself who were yards and yards away in the Traveler wagons two years ago were unmistakable. Today, her sense of smell did not fail, and as she found, the crudely fashioned mask tied to cover her nose and mouth was meant for another reason.

ENCOUNTERS

One by one, Patrick O'Brien's followers dropped off and returned to the neighborhood near the butcher shop. The friary loomed large in the distance. He was half way there when the last child who walked alongside let go of his robe. They lost interest in the robed man who mumbled prayer words to himself and failed to answer their questions. Patrick breathed a sigh of relief refusing to accept the adulation afforded him. He reveled in what he thought was a small victory, interested in what Donovan Rossa, Friar Jonathan and Friar Alfred would think. Did his discovery of the wet, partially burned paper indicate action was taken by the band of agrarian activists led by a Captain Rock, his band referred to as the Rockites. *How could they be contacted to confirm their suspicions were true,* he thought as a myriad of possibilities raced across his brain. So deep was his concentration he carelessly bumped a delivery man and his packages to the ground.

"God save me," the delivery man shouted. "I have been assaulted by a man of the cloth!" He sat on the ground for a moment before he took the hand Patrick offered and got to his feet, grinning and checking for damage as he brushed away the damp earth that soiled his pants. "Seriously hurt I am not," he said still grinning. "Pleased I am to make your acquaintance, but under other circumstances I would have preferred,"

Patrick said bending down to retrieve the parcels on the street. "My attention waned, sorry I am."

"The expensive crystal goblets I carried I delivered earlier I am happy to say," he said as the new Thomas placed the last of the packages in his waiting arms. "Can you forgive my lack of attendance at Mass? My attention waned." "No, I cannot, but I will pray for you," Patrick said smirking as the delivery man walked away. The new Thomas, the pseudo trainee resumed his return to the new home recently provided, but now with a greater awareness of his surroundings, a street filled with wagons, carts, pedestrians, dogs and cats. Minutes later he was at the door of the friary. He reached for the handle, but the door opened to reveal the face of Donovan Rossa.

"A lovely, lovely day it is Patrick, come inside." It was obvious to the new Thomas that Rossa was in a jovial mood. As Patrick entered, Rossa did a few steps of the Irish Jig. "We have an ally who took action this morn against a now known informant! Stunned, Patrick stared at Rossa, unbelieving how what he learned earlier was also found so quickly by Rossa. "I came from the butcher's place of business...a fire was started, and I found what may be..." "Evidence of action taken by the Rockites," Rossa interrupted, adding emphasis as a fist punched the air above his head. "Yes! And how did you...?" he asked, still astounded by Rossa's knowledge. "Seat yourself Patrick, our friend Walter Duff is "on the run." He was discovered as one of the followers of Captain Rock. It was he or a confederate who set the fire you helped put out. Walter Duff has been in hiding here... he and I have talked several times. He told me of the mass grave outside of Millstreet where hundreds were buried. Duff was the one who saw the butcher and a British officer together. He saw the butcher hand a note to the Brit. It had a list of names of known Nationalists, not of any help to the Magistrate who already knew of the allegiance of those listed." "How did Duff see the names on the note?" Patrick asked. "A door was left unlocked," Rossa said. Walter's entry into the office was not noticed. He took a chance I would not have advised." "I should not have helped to put out the fire." Patrick said the disappointment evident in his voice. "On the contrary Patrick, the message was delivered. We will see if our butcher's politics have changed, if he has learned his lesson. If not..." "He will be visited again," Patrick finished Rossa's speculation. At that point, Friar Jonathan entered. "We will visit him again, and with a vengeance if his conspiring continues," Rossa said. "You have gained in obtaining his confidence with your action. He should be more receptive to your attempts to draw him out if he continues to run to the Brits." Friar Jonathan cleared his throat. "Pleased to take care, Rossa, the use of the new Thomas's given name should be discontinued. If you were to be overheard our deception could be compromised," Friar Jonathan cautioned.

THE HILL PEOPLE

The woman named Noreen stopped with one foot in mid-air when she spotted the white paper tacked to her door. She groaned, knowing immediately what it meant as her eyes traveled up one side of the rutted lane and down the other. The white papers tacked to each cottage or hut with a half door fluttered in the breeze. Wives who spoke the Gaelic stood outside staring at the paper. Some of her neighbors, their arms bent at the elbow, and their hands gesturing provided a clear message. They could not read the English words, but they all would know what it meant. Others, who could read cried, went to their knees or ran down the lane screaming in an arm-waving rejection of what they read. Evictions continued. And now they faced what others faced in the valley. Her neighbors in the lush valley, free of the countless conacre fences found in the north, were rendered homeless when landlords decided to seek higher profits from leased land where rent payments were always one year in arrears. Leases were written to make the first payment due before the harvest automatically placing the contract in default. Unsuspecting Irish who could not read and were not represented fell victim to unscrupulous landlords. Neat little white-washed cottages were torn down before the eyes of families forced to watch neighbor after neighbor lose everything they owned, confiscated by the landlord to be applied to unpaid rent. Those Irish who could read and had representation, did not escape. They, as well, had fallen victim. George Bingham was a cold, calculating, devious and ruthless sort who would use others to act on his behalf knowing the Irishman in question would not lease from George Bingham. The lease was then transferred to Bingham unbeknownst to the Irish renter. Tears welled in Noreen's eyes as she dropped to her knees, for just and instant, beseeching God in the heavens above her to intervene. She knew it would not come, but she prayed. Some of the clan O' Branigan thought the landlord's militia would never come again, the hill people would not be worth the effort after their failed first attempt. Her ears listened for the drums. The first time, when her neighbor Aideen Callaghan lost her husband, their only notice was the sound of the drums as the militia approached through the knocks toward their settlement. There was no time. *How much time do we have?* The woman named Noreen was frantic. *We must prepare ourselves. Bingham, I am told is our landlord. God have mercy.*

ROAD TRIP

Patrick O' Brien's ruse as a future religious raised serious doubts in his mind. His main purpose for his disguise was to shield him from the wrath of the British and potential imprisonment or worse. Secondly, he would gather information about activities detrimental to the Nationalist cause, to uncover those who conspired with the British. Today, the new Thomas was returning to Ennis after a monk-like tour of the countryside surrounding Ennis. Hard for him to accept were the words of Friar Jonathan prior to his departure, *you will be true to your habit. No food will accompany you. Your flask of water will last a day.* His visits were always received with a demand. He always provided his blessings over the food however meager it might have been.

However, there was one exception when he came upon an isolated mud hut with a thatched roof. No smoke rose to the heavens from the chimney. Only a hole at the peak of the roof served to let smoke escape. A cardinal sin it was to let the fire go out. The new Thomas grew more and more apprehensive as he approached. The garden was overgrown with weeds where blackened remains of what once were potato plants peaked through. Tools were strewn about, rusting. He heard no sound, curious he bent down to view the interior of the hut. The smell of death arrived before his eyes adjusted to the darkness to capture three lifeless forms inside. He turned, stumbling away, covering his face with his sleeve. To Patrick, the scene was an immediate reminder of what transpired in the remote farms and villages in the past two years. The bodies were mere skeletons partially covered with skin that bore evidence of disease. The potato scourge had claimed another family, but Patrick could not determine which was the man or the woman. He blessed himself. His training mission took him in and around brambles and blackthorn, up one knock and down another. He never became hungry or thirsty, but he missed his dog Corky who became a pet of the entire friary. He slept on straw mattresses in humble cottages of cottiers and families unaffected by the potato blight or the greed of unscrupulous landlords. His purpose had only one disheartening but important success. Even though his feet were sore after a week, he hurried his walk back to Ennis after visiting what was left of the hill people. He remembered well when the people of the clan O' Branigan were subjected to a previous attempt to evict and to destroy their cottages and huts. The eviction of the hill people failed when he, the neighbor Patrick O' Brien, intervened after a threat was made to hang a pregnant neighbor. A new threat now existed told by the woman Noreen O' Branigan, left with her children and the potato field while husband Danny sought work on the docks and on the bay of Galway. The new Thomas carried with him the lease agreement Noreen and Danny had signed years ago. He knew very little about legal documents, but on examination he did not see the name George Bingham. The peasant woman Noreen went to her knees in front of the new Thomas, crying and begging for relief from the threat. Potentially, it would leave her and her children homeless. He was forced into a scenario to that of a true monk, a man of God, who comforted, reassured and made promises he was not sure could be fulfilled. Patrick O' Brien willed his aching feet into a faster pace.

+

At a barracks located between Ennis and Killarney, two landlords stood before the barracks commander lamenting their reasons why the British should assist in the eviction of tenants who were delinquent in their Gale Day rent payments. "Your problem it is, not ours," he told the landlords, one of them being George Bingham. "Why don't you have a small amount of patience? Their potatoes wilt again, and they will die! Or, they will pack their belonging into a knapsack and leave! We are short-handed with the increased activities of those murderous Irish "patriots" who call themselves the "Rockites" or the "Whiteboys" or the "Mollies," I have no time to recruit, train and lead another ragtag group of Militia!" Bam! His fist shook the desktop. Red-faced, he glowered at both, his eyes shifting from one to the other. There was a pause while Bingham and Sir Henry Woodworth considered the lamentable outburst by the British commander. "You then would have no objection to my own recruitment of "helpers" to assist?" Bingham knew he would have no trouble recruiting English loyalists, Catholic haters and the Protestant yeomanry who had little love for the Irish peasant population. The Brit behind the desk tried to regain his composure. His finger pulled at his tight collar. "Do what you must do, but I don't want to hear about what you have done! Do you understand me?" Bingham turned and smiled at Woodworth. The officer's excuse was truthful as, in addition to providing protection to the estates of English landlords from the harassment of those Irish tormentors, many troops were assigned to protect exports bound for England. The food the Irish produced would not feed them. They were starved and died.

VISITATIONS

Patrick Kincade removed one hand from the knob of the blackthorn to wave as the elegant carriage receded into the afternoon. Two faces, a little girl with curly locks and a brilliant smile, waved her hand. The other, had a blank look indicating concern or confusion, he did not know which. He returned his hand to the knob of the stick. His attention shifted to movement beyond the trees. A freight wagon approached pulled by a team of mahogany horses. Its cargo was covered by a tarp and the vicar knew what was hidden underneath. Rumors of a mass gravesite near Millstreet did not stop wagons from coming, the third in the last month. Cloth covered the nose and mouth of the driver and the man seated next to him.

"He is not the same man Flynn," Margaret said after moving to the seat next to her husband. "I fear for him." She turned to watch for Devon who remained behind to finish a mission assigned to him by one of the volunteers, and as Margaret watched, he was now back in the saddle and headed their way. Mary Margaret was on her knees at the back of the carriage. "Catch up Devon!" she shouted, "catch up!" Devon was still too far away for her to see his gritty smile while he raced after the carriage at full gallop. "Take me to Kevin's grave when we return Flynn. I want to say a prayer for our little Taran," she said. Flynn turned to look at her with his steady gaze that asked questions.

"You remain captured by the legends of the past Margaret. Patrick told me our little Kevin is part of the peace of heaven with the other angels and saints." "I do jest when I use that term husband, legends and fables are the words of the seanchaí, the storyteller," she said. "Our son will not be looking for us on All Hallows Eve as the legends say. No matter how much one wished it were true. I will not dwell on the past and what cannot be changed, but what can be changed are the lives of two young orphans, Sissy and her older sister Heather Anne. Their lives have already been changed by the compassion of Fiona Farrell who has undertaken a daunting task. I will do what I can to assist."

Devon urged his black friend to the front, picking his way between the blackthorn and bramble to find the best route for the carriage on the way back to the cottage. The mare and her black son both sensed the nearness of the cottage and the corral as each huffed. "Jumper" tossed his mane and had to be restrained by Devon who allowed his mount to veer off toward the corral hiding the water trough. "Should we allow Devon to let Mary Margaret ride with him? Is Devon an accomplished horseman at such a young age?" Margaret asked. She watched Devon maneuver his horse through and around the brambles using his knees, the reins and his voice to direct his sure-footed mount. "She continues to pester me," Margaret shook her head, hoping for an answer that did not come immediately. "He is 11 Margaret, but older than his young years, don't you know? I hope she will be satisfied to ride with Devon while I have the reins in hand. The horse needs to become familiar with an extra body aboard," Flynn said. "A walk around the corral each day will get Jumper acquainted with a flighty five-year old. "And she with him," Margaret responded. "For both, it will be an awakening. Has Devon allowed you to ride "his" horse?" Devon dismounted, lifting the gate using his shoulder and led his mount through. "His possessiveness is cause to worry a bit, but yes, I have made friends with the horse and I "was allowed" to ride bareback on two occasions!" Flynn responded, grinning, as he guided the mare to the water trough inside the corral. "I remember how Mary Margaret cried when she found her favorite hen dead in the henhouse. How did she arrive at the name Olivia for the hen? She had a hard time pronouncing it," Flynn questioned, while he freed the mare from the carriage. "She wanted a name that began with O settling on Oscar or Olivia until she was told that Oscar was a man's name, resulting in a lengthy explanation as you might imagine," Margaret said. "I can't comprehend why my child's mind chose a letter of the alphabet, and you have heard her recite both English and Gaelic." "No doubt there is that Olivia was an English hen. An Irish name was not even considered?" Flynn asked, incredulous. Margaret smirked, but said nothing.

"I will check the fire in the hearth Father," Devon said after freeing Jumper from his saddle and bridle. He stopped to watch his black friend race at breakneck speed around the perimeter of the corral before coming to a turf tearing stop in front of his favorite rider. Devon gave him a pat on the neck. As soon as they arrived Mary Margaret disappeared into the cottage. When Devon pushed through the half door, she was sitting at the table talking to one of her rag dolls.

Quietly, hand in hand, Flynn and Margaret returned from "the altar stone" where baby Kevin was buried behind the flat granite. On more than one occasion they stopped to celebrate their reunion. At twilight, the summer moon peeked out from behind mountainous clouds. Chilly air came without warning forcing Margaret to adjust her wrap around her hands. Through the garden they walked, now near the corner of the corral where the shelter offered the animals a little protection other than the solitary tree at the far end of the enclosure. Suddenly, a whirring, buzzing sound caused Margaret to search the sky, turning a full circle, looking for the cause. "It appears bats have invaded the shelter roof," Flynn said. 'Tis a good thing they are here. Fewer mice and spiders in the thatch is a good thing, don't you know!" His face bore a toothy smile. "One of those creatures flew right over my head," Margaret said. She reached both hands to cover her head, her wrap falling to the ground. "A fine canopy over our bed puts me at ease my husband, but still, I will fashion a curtain to drape from the cover!" She shivered then picked up her dropped shawl wrapping it around her shoulders. "Wear a bonnet in the early evening lest I need to trim your locks to remove a denizen of the night," Flynn advised. Margaret shivered again at the thought. Flynn saw an opportunity to wrap his arms around her pulling her close to him.

"Never, will I let a creature of the God harm or frighten you," he whispered in her ear. His promise was his remembrance of the dog attack two years ago in the pasture. Devon was surrounded by a hungry pack, prompting Margaret to enter the fray to save her son even though she was pregnant at the time.

THE MESSENGER

Aching feet forced the new Thomas to sit for a time at the edge of a bubbling brook, a stream where he found a pool of water warmed by the sun. A brief rest and a soaking provided momentary relief. To combat the warmth of the sun, he removed of his hood, tunic and skirt. He bundled it together and slung it over a shoulder. Without the identifying habit he was now just an ordinary Irishman with an alias of Thomas O'Brien. And, without the habit cottiers would not be as inclined to offer food and a place to sleep. Hours ago, he left the hill people and the woman named Noreen who offered him more than just a grainy portion of hard bread. After dipping the bread in the water, he carefully chewed, fearing he might break a tooth. She watched him eat with her hand on his shoulder. The sun was past its zenith. Shadows were lengthening prompting the messenger to rise to his feet somewhat rested and revived. His return trip was just beginning, and he hoped he would arrive in Ennis in time to alert those who might prevent a second attempt to destroy the lives of the clan O' Branigan. But his thoughts and concerns took away part of his attention to his journey. Wary of slime covered rocks, he gingerly started across the stream using a staff to aid his slippery traverse. He was several feet from the opposite bank when his balance was lost. The new Thomas ended up seated in waist deep water. Out of the unappreciated bath, he hoped the afternoon sun would soon render him dry otherwise a night spent in wet clothing would not assist a restful sleep. His eyes swept the horizon hoping to see a spire of white smoke rising to the heavens in the stillness of a summer afternoon. Moving out of the shade near the stream made him long for the rolling grassy plain and pasture land he followed for five days. Here, the footing would be hazardous, but beyond lay an expanse of green and an occasional tree and shrubbery that promised wild berries. Carefully, he made his way thinking of the rocky expanse south of Galway known as the Boíreann (Burren), near the village of Kinvarra. While he stumbled on loose rock, his eyes cast always downward, he remembered an old parable; *the Burren had not enough water to drown a man, nary a tree to hang a man nor earth enough to bury a man, or near to those words.* Somehow his feet found sound footing on the first cousin of that barren piece of realty in north Clare. His hurry increased the chance he would never reach his objective. On a few occasions he did glance quickly toward the grassy meadow awaiting his feet, but not to the Ash tree that stood prominently in the forefront. As his footing improved, his attention shifted to the whitewashed cottage wall that stood out in contrast to the green shield in front. He stopped to shift his pack and his heart sank. On the far side of the tree partially hidden by the trunk and the canopy, his eyes identified two bodies that hung from a limb shading the front the small cottage. In a nearly automatic reaction, the sight shock diminished to the point he searched for the knife he didn't possess. Then, the most unexpected occurred causing his head to snap toward the sound he thought he heard from the interior of the cottage resulted in a tingling sensation on his arms. The new Thomas took one last look toward the tree and walked with a purpose toward the cottage door. When he looked at the tree, he wouldn't have seen the hand that pushed open the half door from the inside. The door closed, and the hand was withdrawn before Thomas turned away. He scraped his booted feet on the boards outside the half door and pushed. The sudden transfer from light to the dark interior of the cottage with no window required an adjustment, but before his eyes adjusted a voice shouted;

"Patrick O'Brien, I have you! You are mine Irishman." Patrick's eyes saw shadowy movement of arms lifting...and Patrick's eyes opened wide as the bayonet on the end of the rifle-musket pierced his chest, raising him up and backwards, falling, falling..., life ebbing away and then, a dark curtain was lowered over his consciousness. The new Thomas did not feel the sudden stop when his lifeless body hit the floor. The disgraced British militia man who was humiliated by Patrick O'Brien months earlier had found closure. Patrick O'Brien's killer was obsessed with a raging need to find and punish the low-life Irishman who turned his promising military career upside down. He became a trusted friend of the butcher in Ennis who was one of the queen's servants and a suspected informant on activities of a traitorous nature performed by nationalist and Catholic interests. Suspicious of the arrival of a new candidate at the Friary, he encouraged the butcher to meet with the new resident of the monastery. That day, in the Two Pence Saloon he saw the face of Patrick O'Brien and his hatred grew. Every waking moment was spent searching for an opportunity for retribution, and then duty called him away. But he returned to the barracks outside Ennis to support the same landlord and lead a second militia force to evict cottiers who could not pay the rent or the tithe. The event turned bloody when a pitchfork wielding cottier killed one of the militia men. Again, he lost control of his charges, although their actions did not concern him. He sharpened the blade of his bayonet while the militia hung the killer and his wife. His assignment bore fruit when a lookout reported that a man approached. He ordered the 11 militiamen to hide behind the cottage while from the interior darkness of the cottage he watched the man approach. Burned into his memory was the portrait of Patrick O'Brien. Astounded, he watched the come to life image walk unsuspecting toward the cottage.

DOUBTING THOMAS

"How many have volunteered?" Rossa asked as he watched Tommy O'Keefe wet his thumb and turn the page of the notebook. Tommy's fingers completed the count. He looked up at Rossa, his finger on the page of the hastily scribbled tally. "We have 23 and if we hear from McGee today, we will have a dozen more, but we still do not know of their destination." "What about the weaponry?" Rossa asked. O'Keefe shook his head as he turned the page. His finger traced its way down the sheet. "We have two long guns," he said, shaking his head. "Current enforcement parties bear more arms than in the past," Rossa said. "Aye, and now the Brits rely heavily on English sympathizers and Catholic haters," O'Keefe responded. "Danny Kissane overheard their plans. He found out how many would be in the raiding party, in addition to 10 or 11 Ulster men, most of them armed we need to surmise. Our 20 or 30 farmers with rocks and pitchforks, knives and axe handles asked to stand? However, surprise and ambush will be on our side," Rossa continued. "Our first order of business will be to take out the Brit in command, and the men who bear arms. With luck they will scatter, and we will collect the weaponry discarded. The hill people can again live until the next effort to eliminate them is made!" O'Keefe was skeptical. "What if...your plan fails us? We are not soldiers, we are farmers, laborers, Irishmen..." he shrugged, turning away with hands in his pockets, not waiting for an answer.

Two knocks...and then a third was heard. The latch was turned, and the door opened to admit the elusive Walter Duff of Millstreet. Finding sanctuary in the back alleys and back rooms of Ennis was his talent while on the run. Walter Duff was not known as a man of few words. "Aye, me boys, a lovely day we have to be on the right side of the muddy street! Rightly, you have chosen to eliminate foot traffic past this door," he said with a wide smile and a nodding head. Knowing eyes looking at each man present for their approval of his assumption the meeting was to be held at this out of the way location for that purpose. Back slapping greetings took place, and then for a stagnant interval a pause occurred.

"Word has not come to us on the whereabouts of Thomas O'Brien according to Friar Jonathan," Tommy O'Keefe commented. "'Tis 14 days past since he left with the expectation that he would be gone 10. I fear for him and the friar asked for prayer on his behalf." Another stagnant interval broken with the sound of a boot scraping the wood floor. Heads were bowed. Rossa cleared his throat. "I had limited contact with the new Thomas before he left. Does anyone have doubts that Thomas is truly committed to his new role? Is he too much a monk in training rather than a patriot for a free Ireland? I have not received any indication from Friar Jonathan his concern other than for his safe return, have any of you?" Another knock twice, then a pause before the third turned heads to the door as hinges squeaked to reveal the face of the man known by some as "Dopey Danny," Danny Kissane. He looked behind him, left and right, before pulling the door shut and facing the three conspirators. As a forgetful man might do in the house of God, Danny's quick hand pulled the cap from his head. He twisted it in his hands. "What brings you here today, Danny?" Rossa asked as Danny, head down, still twisting his cap looked up. "I regret the news I carry to you today. Our friend, the new Thomas O'Brien, is no longer with us. I overheard news of his demise while I was sweeping the porch at the Queen's Crown hotel. Four Brits were enjoying afternoon tea. Thomas was returning from a visit with the hill people. Don't you know he was murdered by the British soldier who led the original attempt to evict the clan O' Branigan?" "Sad news indeed," Rossa said. "Do you have any news of a lighter nature Danny Kissane?" "I fear not, but I overheard the eviction party is headed for the huts of the hill people," Danny said.

LEGIONNAIRE

Part of Flynn's early morning ended when he left the cottage to the sound of the Sessions clock that bonged five times. Boarding the Howe carriage, he urged the mare forward looking back at the cottage door where Devon stood waving. The farm was now in the capable hands of his son and wife who would soon share relieving the Guernsey of her production. Devon was to teach his mother the art of milking. Mary Margaret would be charged to collect the eggs and feed the chickens. In the carriage, Flynn packed milk, butter and three dozen eggs to be sold to the Farrell Mercantile. His plan to work for the Foley boys, drop off the carriage, call on Miss Farrell and meet with D'Arcy McGee. He would return with the brothers in the afternoon. All in one day limited the time he could spend with each task. No time would there be to socialize with the locals over a pint. Militancy was on the rise in the countryside where freight wagons loaded with pork, beef and lamb for export were attacked by hungry farmers. More often the freight wagons were escorted by armed British troops. He had a feeling he would be asked to become more involved in nationalist republican activities when he met with the activist McGee. He was told of Flynn's prior service in the French Foreign Legion by Neil Howe, a young man impressed with the knowledge, but confused about Flynn's life choice. Ahead of him was the slope leading down to the Foley cottage, the boats and the chopping block where the knives would be clean and sharpened, ready for his use. The tall aspens and the dense shrubbery hid the cottage and the boats below from view on the land side. Flynn had no fear of losing the mare and the carriage in the birth of the day, but caution prevailed as he led the mare behind three tall evergreens. He wrapped the reins around a tree branch then poured water for the mare. Being a patient animal, she would graze on the tall grass under her feet, content until Flynn returned. After he loaded the milk, butter and eggs into the small wheeled cart he and Devon built, he lowered the wick on the ornate brass oil lamps attached to the roof supports of the carriage. The little four-wheeled cart became a favorite toy for Mary Margaret. She would seat herself in the wagon and pout if she didn't get Devon to take her outside and pull her around the cottage. Devon usually relented. Today, she would look for it. Flynn started down the slope with one arm stiffened against the brake and the wagons surrender to gravity. The oil lamps on each side of the minute beach burned brightly, a beacon to the Foley brothers who fished the lake in the dark of night. Flynn pulled the wagon into the shallows and offloaded the containers of milk and butter to cool, glancing at the faint glow of the turf fire that required his immediate attention. He hurried to the stone wall of the cottage where the turf cuttings were stored and filled the pail. Shortly after, the turf burned brightly heating the tea water and warming Flynn's hands. Above his head the clouds disappeared to reveal the brilliance of the moon turning night into an imitation of day. He paused, about to pour the tea water when he heard the mournful cry of the loon, a harbinger of the dawn about to arrive? Or was it a call to a mate...or.... He poured the water.

DAWN MEETING

Flickering flames from oil lamps cast shadows on the faces of the fishermen and the boats gathered tightly together in the chill of the night turning slowly to gray. Brendan Foley's hand gripped the side of the O' Coughlin boat while he listened to the animated conversations taking place between the occupants of four fishing boats that came together to resolve a serious question. Jerry Steen was silent for the moment while he examined the long gun he retrieved from the bottom of his boat. "A fine weapon I hold in my hands. Seven more are hidden under the tarp at my feet," he said. "Nothing but a poor fisherman I am who agreed to get these arms to the other side of the lake. They need to be delivered to Killarney in support of nationalist Republicans and seekers of a free Ireland." His eyes searched the faces around him, but no one spoke until Donal Foley cleared his throat. "Long we have watched both sides from the relative safety of the lakes, uncommitted, while friends and acquaintances risk all working in the shadows of potential discovery. We have seen what is happening to our land and to our people and what we do is too little." There was no response until after the mournful lament of the loon was heard by all followed by a faint response in the far distance. "Here on the lake in the dark of night I have no fear of the Brits," Shamus Killian said. "Let them wage war between themselves and let me fish." "Filled with a hate am I," Sean Cullen, the youngest of the fishermen said: "When the bodies of poor Irish wash up against my hull in the night. Not a superstitious man am I, but I wake when I sleep in a cold sweat when I recall the faces in the water, the sunken cheeks, the bulging eyes." He leaned over the side of his craft searching the waters around him. Finn O' Coughlin who sat near to Brendan Foley in his boat leaned to Brendan's ear and whispered; "Would you deliver the guns to McGee?" Brendan looked at Donal, his brother, who nodded. Brennan did not overhear the request while he and Sean Cullen lamented in a demonstrative, arm-waving discussion ending in an outlandish comment. "Soon there will be no room for the fish!" Cormac Brennan said, "I jest of course, but in the pubs the talk is of the poison in the lake." The dark, turning to gray, drew heads and eyes to the east. Oil lamps on the bow and the stern of two of the boats flickered and went dark. "Follow us Jerry Steen. We have no room for the weapons in our boat. McGee will thank you for our delivery." Donal Foley directed. The boats began to drift apart, and oars were lifted to stab the lake waters headed for the other side of the lake. Brendan manned the oars of the Meehan boat, always called the "Meehan boat" after its former owner. Donal warmed his hands over his homemade turf furnace watching Steen follow behind. The nights catch flopped around in the containers, splashing water occasionally on the furnace causing steam to erupt. The sea birds were airborne, and the mournful call of the loon was heard again. The dark was soon to succumb to the power of Sol. Donal watched two oil lamps grow dimmer and finally wink out as the last boat moved to the other side of an island in the lake. Strong strokes from the muscular arms of Brendan pulled his craft four lengths ahead of Steen who struggled to keep the boat ahead in sight.

"Sure! You have no pity for my frailness," Steen shouted. "What to do if I become lost?" "Look to the east," Donal shouted because the sun's rays had arrived over the hills. Steen ceased his efforts to look and realized the boat ahead had lengthened the distance between them. He renewed his efforts. "No pity you have," Steen lamented. He rowed harder.

+

Flynn prepared himself, donning the heavy apron to protect his clothing from the surprises occurring in the cleaning and filleting process. One of the beacon lamps went out. He turned the wick up on the other expecting to see the Foley brothers in sight of the beacon at any moment. His eyes searched the water as far as he could see with the fog rising to hinder his vision. Patches of blue were visible above his head sure to render the fog a brief hindrance. He returned to the tripod to check on the biscuits in the kettle. He lifted the lid with the gaff hook and in the same instant heard a shout from Brendan Foley. His voice was as strong as his arms were to the oars. "Flynn 'me boy we are here!" At that very moment the bow of the Meehan boat burst through the fog. "More biscuits and butter you need Flynn, as company follows behind us if he has not become lost!" Brendan's loud comment was meant to be heard. Three pairs of eyes squinted into the fog to see nothing but the swirling mists rising ever so slowly over the lakes mirror-like calm. Seconds elapsed, a minute came and went. They continued to watch and listen for the sound of an oar breaking the surface. No sound fractured the silence.

"He was not that far behind Brendan," Donal said with a plea for consideration in his voice. Eyes strained, but each ear caught sounds of dry wood breaking under foot as a lone figure fought his way through the tangle of overgrown shrubbery and Aspen toward them. His arms were raised to fight off thorny branches as he fought his way. "Only for a moment did I lose my way. My craft is beached between two rocks," he pointed, and a thorny branch ripped the sleeve of his shirt. Moving into the shallows, Flynn and Donal looked in that direction and saw the stern of his vessel. The bow hidden between two gigantic granite boulders. "Are you wrecked? Do you leak?' Donal asked, a look of concern covered his face. "No, my boat is seaworthy. I lost sight of you for only a moment. I was following the light of your lamp when I entered fog so thick, I panicked." "Come sit with us over tea and a biscuit," Donal pointed to the tri-pod where Brendan was already seated with a steaming cup in hand. "Your cargo will be safe for the time we take for the tea, a biscuit with honey if you like. Did ammunition accompany the arms?" Flynn had little time to spare, offloading containers of live fish, but he did overhear Donal Foley's question. Jerry Steen shrugged his shoulders. "It would help the freedom fighters don't you know, he said apologetically." Flynn stood with the smaller of the two containers in hand looking at Steen, unbelieving the weapons came without ammunition. "Pitchforks and axe handles are as good as a rifle without ammunition," Brendan commented.

"What about the means to forge the musket balls and what caliber are the weapons," Flynn asked. Jerry Steen shrugged his shoulders again, looking very uncomfortable. "I fear I was just the means of transport," Steen said. He had his hands in his pockets and nervously shuffled his feet. "You should have asked Jerry Steen!" Flynn said, in a voice that took exception to the uninvolved attitude of the man, a trait seen of many Irish who were satisfied with the status-quo. Jerry Steen nodded in acceptance of his neutrality. Donal and Brendan Foley were surprised at Flynn's sudden outburst. Flynn though had second thoughts. "Sorry I am Steen, as I myself am as complacent. Not at all am I involved in any freedom movement but see around me the need for one, and the attempts by too few to change," Flynn said. "Allow me to inspect the weapons, later. I have fish to clean and fillet, what say you Donal. No doubt you have orders to fill." Brendan and Donal, surprised at Flynn's sudden interest looked at each other with questioning eyes. "'Tis the legionnaire soldier in him rising to the surface," Brendan whispered to Donal as they walked toward the cottage, Donal for the order sheet, Brendan for more smoked salmon and honey for the tea. "His own military training he has suppressed for years, it may soon be resurrected," he continued. "Aye brother but would be a shame to lose him to a challenge facing impossible odds." "And Brendan Foley would need to resume cleaning fish, until an adequate fellow can be found to relieve me from that disgusting task," Brendan lamented.

Adept with a knife to fillet as he was throwing at a target, Flynn worked feverishly for an hour before he left the table to check on the mare and the carriage. Satisfied that all was well, he resumed cleaning cutting steaks and disposing of the innards in holes he previously dug. Donal wrapped orders for delivery as fast as Flynn could cut, chop and fillet. In the very early morning while hurried preparations were being made for the trip into Killarney, Jerry Steen retrieved the weapons and fought his way through the tangled shore growth. With each trip he carried with him two of the long guns. He propped the guns against the cottage wall. "That will not assure our safety," Donal said shaking his head. "Until we devise a way to transport them undetected in the wagon, they go inside." Flynn dumped pails of water on the table top using a long-handled brush to clean off the carrion remaining. "What you could do is construct a false bottom under the cart bed, fill it with thresh, slide the weapons in and close the end," Flynn offered. "Thresh would keep the arms from bouncing around creating noise and attracting attention. Do you have any plank boards as long as the weapons?" "I think not Flynn. Available lumber was used at the table and the roof. I thought of tying the guns to the bottom of the cart, however, I prefer your idea if we can secure enough material," Donal replied. "I have several sources in mind. Don't be in a hurry to deliver the goods, remember the armed guard who inspects each trap or freight wagon on the main road," Flynn advised as he walked to the water's edge, squatting to rinse forearms and hands. Brendan was loading the last of the orders including the large container with fresh fish flopping around inside. Shaking water away Flynn dried his hands on his pants before he began to inspect the weapons taking hold of the first musket that stood against the wall. The outside of the barrel was pitted with rust. The inside of the barrel was the home of a web spinning creature familiar to Margaret and the children back at the cottage. He moved the suspect weapon to the side. Minutes later his inspection was complete. Three more unserviceable rifle muskets were stacked against the wall. After he retrieved the cart with the milk and eggs, Flynn started for the slope and the carriage. "I will look for you at Clancy's Pub for a bite before we start back. I will have the wagon and if I find lumber...be safe Foley boys," Flynn waved his departure. Jerry Steen was on the water after freeing his craft. He stood in the boat preparing to raise a sail as a wind from the east promised him a breezy return to the other side of the lake.

Flynn arrived at the Farrell Mercantile after being thoroughly questioned by a British guard on the road leading down to Killarney. He was suspicious of a man who smelled of the sea driving such an elegant carriage. Flynn was forced to open every compartment, furnish the order from the Farrell Mercantile for the milk and eggs, remove blankets, and explain the contents of a small tool box. He was finally released when traffic started to back up and drivers became impatient, letting the soldier know of their displeasure. He delivered Fiona's order and took another, before he left thanking her. He urged the mare down the street to the Howe Livery where he was met at the Byre gate by another inspector, Malachy Brandon, the blacksmith who was responsible for the maintenance of the Peter Howe carriage. Greetings were exchanged, but few words were uttered while Malachy did a thorough check of every inch of the carriage. Flynn smiled knowing Malachy's lengthy examination was a ruse to make him uncomfortable. "I tried to find a dry route," Flynn said, laughing to himself. "Dust, a wee bit of mud and a spatter of raindrops will require several hours of labor from me, and my able assistant Neil," Brandon said with a mischievous look on his face as he watched Neil Howe approach with a shoeing hammer in hand. Neil's riposte quieted Malachy's humorous barb. "You are in the employ of the Howe Livery Mr. Brandon and for sure you have forgotten you gave me the balance of the afternoon to myself! My day is finished!" Neil's satisfied look, he winked at Flynn, was too much for Malachy who hung his head. Neil put his arm around the blacksmith's wide shoulders and extended the hammer to him. "The horses have new feet," Neil said.

"A lovely afternoon you will enjoy." "Oh, the suffering I must endure," Malachy said. "Many tears I shed." Flynn laughed. "The two of you should go onstage at the playhouse! The audience would rise to their feet applauding your performance," Flynn laughed again. "Thank you, kind sir," Neil said sweeping his cap from his curly locks bowing majestically in the elegant theatrical manner. Hands loudly clapped from a spectator who happened to be none other than D'Arcy McGee.

"Agreed it is, a bit of humor in these distressing times is forever welcome and needed," McGee said. He continued to applaud one hand against the other held over his head. "So that you and Neil can work on your next performance, may I be excused? McGee and I have business to attend." Flynn asked the question with just a bit of sarcasm in his voice. "Aye friend, Malachy must get back to work," Neil said tipping his hat. "I will join you at closing for a pint Malachy," Neil said as he proceeded down the street. Malachy and Flynn pulled the carriage into the byre leaving one of the doors open to allow light inside. The mare with no name relished her momentary freedom, trotting around the inside of the enclosure, huffing and shaking her head. Flynn joined McGee at the corral fence. Both leaned elbows on the top rail. "You may have heard of the militia imported from the north to evict the hill people, the clan O' Branigan outside of Ennis?" McGee questioned. "I did not hear of it," Flynn answered. "You came to me to ask for my help and to a point I am already involved in the nationalist movement. Long guns are in the hands of the Foley brothers. My plan to get them here requires lumber to build a hidden compartment under the wagon floor." "As a last resort, the planks across the muddy street could suddenly turn up missing as they sometimes do at the time of the Fire Festival," McGee said. "Lumber is delivered each week to the site of the new hotel. Scrap lumber is piled for anyone's use at the end of the day. Usually it's gone the next morning. Before you leave, check the site. You may find what you need," McGee said. "'Tis likely you did not hear of the loss of Patrick O'Brien. He was killed outside of Ennis by a Brit militia commander."

"Sorry I am to hear. You could say his life ended much earlier," Flynn said. "A good honest man lost. Our prayers will be for him." The next few minutes were spent planning an attack on the militia. After going over the route they would take, and where would be the most advantageous spot to gather, they both agreed on a location. Cover of rocks on both sides would place the attackers above the marching platoon. "How many men will be involved and how many weapons will be available?" Flynn asked. "They say... they will show up, but the Irish are sometimes so unreliable, I hope 35 or 40. When was the last time you fired a weapon in anger?" McGee asked Flynn. "I have not since I left the Legion, now I am more adept at knife throwing and carving salmon. I loath to pick up a weapon except for a knife or in defense of my home and family," Flynn replied. "I have a suffering wife and two children who deserve my full attention." Suddenly he remembered. "Do you have a source for gunpowder and the means for creating .75 caliber musket balls?" Flynn asked. "Eight 'Brown Bess' muskets arrived without either powder or ammunition. Four of the weapons are clean and in working order, the other four could only be used with the bayonet fixed." "I have "mollies" I can call on. Would you lead the attack?" McGee didn't want to be so direct with his request, but had to, otherwise time to find another would mean the eviction of the clan O' Branigan if a leader could not be found. "We need someone with military experience. Confirmed volunteers are angry, have lost someone close to them, lost land owned or leased, but are willing to fight or just to express their displeasure at British presence on "their" land even though they rent land they, or their grandfather once owned until it was taken away." "Understood, it is. Margaret and I face a threat from the brother of George Brewster who intends to sell rather than renew our lease. Less than three years from this day we need to decide on what to do," Flynn revealed. As if it were cast in stone, Flynn remembered the words of Paxton Brewster and the date his lease would end on the first day of spring in 1850. "I would hope for answer from you by the end of the day, O'Connell...otherwise, I will need to pick from the lot who have committed, or cancel the attempt," McGee said. "Your answer would be no if needed that quickly," Flynn responded. "I would not commit until speaking with Margaret, and that would be later today.

Are the supporters of Captain Rock and the Molly Maguires aware of the militia's mission?" "Aware they are, but non-committal regarding any action. I know the "mollies" might wait until the last minute to intervene," McGee said. "There are very few well organized responses to Protestant injustices. Most are sporadic, a spur of the moment action taken by one, or two or sometimes a handful of desperate, pitchfork carrying farmers who see strength in numbers, and think they can evade a musket ball at 20 yards!" "Whatever you decide to do McGee, get word to me," Flynn said, looking up and down the street, anxious to be on his way. "I will prospect for lumber. The Foley brothers search as well." Although disappointed, McGee reached out for the older man, the embrace akin to brother to brother.

His account settled with the Howe Livery, Flynn pocketed the receipt Margaret was sure to ask about. He ended the relative freedom of the mare. She walked toward him when he entered the corral. Once hitched to the wagon Flynn directed the horse out to the street, headed in the direction of the new hotel under construction. The early morning mayhem of traps and carts, freight wagons and children were absent when the sun was an hour past its zenith. A mid-afternoon hiatus was soon to allow preparations for the return of the tourists in the late afternoon. Flynn urged the mare into a fast trot.

SALLY DONAGHY

The Foley wagon came to a stop in front of the Farrell Mercantile. This was to be their last customer of the day. Donal pulled the container with the live salmon to the end of the wagon waiting for Brendan to grab the handle on the other end. Once the water in the tank was changed and payment was received from Jasmine O' Barsky, Fiona's assistant, their day was complete. Jasmine handed Donal an envelope. "Please count it. An order for Friday is inside as well," she said while she used a towel to dry her forearms after adding fish to the glass tank. Brendan was already out the door, not waiting, in a hurry to get to Clancy's for lunch and a visit with the licentious waitress Sally who often would sit on Brendan's lap to take his lunch order. Earlier, Donal had cautioned his brother.

"You must know you are not the only fish in the sea, my brother," Donal said, after one lunch a month or more ago Sally wantonly displayed an ample amount of cleavage for his benefit. "Once you are gone, she will turn her attention to someone else." Brendan proclaimed his innocence at the time stating again how much he enjoyed the food she brought to the table. Although, Donal was not blind to the care Brendan took in his appearance. He washed, he shaved, trimmed his fingernails and used the scented water he purchased at the Farrell Mercantile. Today, the tavern tables were all occupied except for one in the far corner. Brendan entered unseen by his infatuation.

Sally had little time to display her penchant for infectious flirtations. Her smile, if she smiled, was forced, her brow and nose were shiny from her effort to satisfy all the demands of the patrons, some of whom were irritated at her lack of attention. Most of them were men, shopkeepers and laborers who came to enjoy lunch for the same reason as Brendan Foley falsely related to his brother. His answer was so blatantly obvious that Donal shook his head and walked away. Hands reached out toward her, but on this busy lunch day she deftly evaded the attempts usually allowed, providing only a wink in return. She strained from the weight of a tray of dirty dishes in hand, or mugs of dark stout dripping foam on her apron, and to the already hazardous footing of the slippery wood floor. Donal found his occupied brother, whose gaze focused on every movement of his fantasy, not acknowledging the presence of his brother when he bent to look around Donal as he stood at the table. Brendan Foley's eyes followed her. He transferred to his mind every perceived sensuous movement of the woman, his denied obsession.

Sally did see him walk in, his eyes on her, but she was too busy to acknowledge his presence. Her heart thumped in her chest. He was the man she loved, and he loved the attention she showered him with, but he thought her ministering to him was just an innocent flirtation. She was aware of her sexuality and used it to full advantage as a Clancy's Pub barkeep or server, and to attract his attention. Young men were at her door constantly, their hat in hand, the other holding a bouquet of wildflowers picked from the meadow. Two and three days each week she would look for Brendan Foley, the fisherman. Three years ago, she saw him occasionally. Over the last two years she saw him with regularity. His brother didn't know he always left money under his plate. The first time he did she pulled him aside and tried to give the money back, thinking the worst. He did not take it. Other male customers left money on the table, but they wanted her "favors" in return. Brendan did not. She was always gracious in her refusals, never wanting to lose a customer for Wiggins, the Pub owner. Up to the time she began working at age15 she survived as a street urchin, begging for food and coin of the realm. Sally Donaghy was a survivor of the potato famine of 1839 that took both parents and a brother. Now at age 22, an age considered by some to be "old" if unmarried, she was in love with a crusty fisherman, 20 years her senior. Countless times she could have left Killarney for London or Dublin in the coach of a playwright or performer on the stage, but she didn't survive to be 22 without recognizing, or just being suspicious of any offer made to her. She didn't want to become someone's mistress. And now, wiser than her years with only one exception, she was trapped in a one-sided relationship unsure if it would ever become two. With a lull in the clamor for her attention, she rushed to the hallway where the facilities were located, where the mirror was hung. Her fingers combed through her hair, her apron was lifted to her face to wipe away something she saw, but was it only the unlit hallway? She straightened her dress and ran back to take the order of Brendan Foley, her love, and Donal Foley, his brother. She hoped Brendan's affection for her was not as a father would have for a daughter. Composing herself with a hesitant smile that came and went, she hurried through the tables filled with diners who all wanted to talk, toward the corner table. Her nods and brief smiles as she made her way would have to suffice until she reached her destination. *What will I say? How to greet him today?* Sally Donaghy's thoughts raced through her mind, and then she was at the table, leaning over, her hands on the table top, her nose inches from the nose of the love of her life. Brendan's eyes shifted their focus to hers. "Brendan Foley...," her lips touched his forehead. "'Tis three days since you crossed the threshold into my world! You have been missed, but a pleasure it is to see you this day." The redness began to recede from Brendan's face. He remained speechless, but his eyes were unmistakable, they drank in every inch of her, his steady unwavering gaze caused Sally to step back but his hand reached out. Murmurs of speculation rushed their way around the room as Sally took his hand and stammered. "We have loin of pork, lamb shank, brown bread and butter with potatoes, all of them your favorites," Sally offered, pleased she had made such a dramatic impact. Out of breath, she turned to Donal who placed his order for salmon, brown bread with honey and tea. Donal excused himself sensing a moment of privacy might be needed. "And now Mr. Foley what would be your pleasure?" Brendan rose to his feet as Sally scanned the lunch crowd, some of whom were becoming impatient. His large fingered hand still hid hers. He pulled her close to him. "I, who have a yearning for one who could be my daughter. But he wants only for that daughter to be my wife. And that is, my sincere wish," Brendan said, regaining his ability to speak. Murmurs increased. Spoons tapped table tops.

"Well said," a man at an adjoining table overhearing responded. The table beyond that was tipped over as a young man rose to his feet in an obvious clenched fist rage spilling dishes, food and beverages into the laps of patrons who had joined him. "Old man! What do you speak of?" He shouted. With malice aforethought he walked menacingly toward Brendan. Hearing the words, Donal Foley stopped on his return from a visit with a fellow fisherman on the other side of the room.

"No business is it of yours," a strong voice from the pubs entrance came as the doors banged shut. The irate customer turned to see who had the nerve to interfere in a private confrontation. After clearing his boots of debris Flynn O'Connell walked seemingly unconcerned toward the corner table where Brendan, and the woman he had just promised himself to stood hand in hand. With intent Flynn spoke in a loud voice. "I remember the day you threw Foxworth out into the street Brendan Foley, and could it be I have the chance to return the favor?" He turned to look at the young man glowering two tables away. While this incident took place, Sally released her grip to help restore order and placate the fellows who had their lunch spilled to their laps. The jealous young fellow threw coins on the floor and stomped out of the pub after thinking better of the odds. Donal helped the publican to right the table. Flynn dragged an empty chair and sat down next to Brendan. "May I ask what caused his anger, Brendan?" Flynn's hand was on his employer's shoulder while Brendan stared at his boots. Donal sat down next to his brother.

"A cowardly man I am Flynn, to take six months to strengthen myself to ask the woman to be my wife, and I have yet to get an answer or my lunch!" At that moment Sally was winding her way through the tables with a tray. She stopped when she overheard his remark. "Your answer is yes Mr. Foley, and your food, late but hot is here!" Dining forks banged the table tops. A shout of "here, here" was heard and several patrons raised glasses. Brendan's brother Donal was speechless. He couldn't believe what his brother had done. Sally Donaghy set plates then leaned over planting a kiss on Brendan's cheek.

"Sure it is! you two brothers have a lot to discuss," Flynn said walking with the brothers back to the alley where the horses and wagons waited. "The new hotel site had scraps of wood pleased that I would take them away before fights broke out among those who would burn wood rather than buy turf." He poured water for the mare. "This day this Foley boy is a happy man," Brendan said. He did a little jig in the street. "Brother

Brendan hides his secrets from me, his own brother!"
Donal said incredulous, but with his arm around the
neck of his big brother in a playful head lock. Six-foot
lengths of lumber lay in the bed of Flynn's wagon.
Donal picked up one board, then another and again a
third, squinting down the length of each. "Yes, yes, and
this was the scrap they threw away?" He looked at
Flynn. "Aye Donal, the hotel is being built by an
Englishman who wants nothing, but the best material
used." "A fine cottage could be built by an Irishman
with scrap lumber such as we see here," Donal said.
"We should visit the site each day Brendan, stone is
plentiful, wood is not." "'Tis a small but fine cottage it
would be, if built by an Irishman," Brendan said with
his toothy Irish smile. "For her I will build a large
cottage with stone walls and wood floors, warm rugs
and..." prepared to leave, both wagons and horses were
suddenly surrounded by poorly clothed men, women
and children. They came from around the building
into the alley and on the encounter their hands were
extended, beseeching. Two of the women had infants
wrapped in blankets, another had her baby held out in
front of her with both hands while she lamented
sorrowfully in the Gaelic dialect Flynn could not
interpret. The baby appeared to be dead. Flynn flicked
the reins and the mare moved forward, one step, then
two, distressed by the crowd of people in front of her.
Her head went up, she huffed, and her forelegs came
off the dirt. Flynn tried to sooth the mare, heard his
voice over the clamor, shook her head again and
huffed as if to say, "I am fearful." She moved forward

again as hands grasped the sides of the wagon box, looking. The Foley wagon had much more success off to the side of the group that concentrated on Flynn's wagon. "Why don't I..." Donal uncovered the box with the smoked salmon and the crusty bread loaves they planned to drop off at the cathedral. "Aye, do it Donal, they are hungry," Brendan finished his brother's thought. Flynn pointed at the Foley wagon where Donal was standing with the box in his hands. Two of the men shuffled their way to Donal reaching up to take the box. The men were soon surrounded. Hands reached out for what they all envisioned, the only thought to occupy their minds. Both wagons were now able to proceed with Flynn in the lead. "In some counties the early potato crop failed," Donal said. "The blight is not as widespread as last year, but still, 'tis another heartbreak for the Irish people." "The poor babies," Brendan muttered, almost to himself. "Look at them would you, they are starving! The food in the box will do what? What will it do Donal...extend their suffering?" Donal did not reply. The woman with the baby Flynn thought was dead was on her knees waiting for her portion of whatever was in the box. Her dead infant was on the ground behind her, wrapped in a scrap of cloth that served as a blanket.

Flynn was the first to arrive at the lakeshore, the Foley brothers not far behind. His plan to unload the lumber and start for home was stymied for a time when he found the body of a man washed ashore wedged between the Foley fishing boats. He used a gaff hook to pull the body out of the water to the sand. About that time Donal and Brendan arrived. Flynn returned to the wagon and started to unload wide planks of lumber. He looked for help that didn't come. Minutes after Brendan saw to the needs of the horse, he and Donal stood in front of the boats their eyes on another casualty of the potato scourge. "Not a place do we have to bury the lad," Donal said. "A burial at sea is no longer an option for me," Brendan said. "Fearful I am about contaminating our fishing grounds!" "Aye brother, as am I. Shall we roll him onto the sled, pull the sled through the brambles to the granite rocks and cover him?" Donal questioned. "I thought of the cave Flynn discovered, but the cave is much too far away."

"I will do the deed if you would bring the sled while I get my coat and gloves. The brambles tear skin." Brendan said, as he headed for the cottage. Donal turned to see Flynn stack the last of the wood against the side of the cottage. "Your new wood contrasts with the old on the wagon bed, Donal. You must make the new to look old, otherwise questions will arise. Another way is to paint exposed surfaces on the wagon. The Brits continue to inspect freight entering Killarney, care must be taken. Have you decided on a resting place for your visitor?" Flynn had one foot on the wagon step ready to board with the reins in hand. "Not a burial at sea, but a resting place under the granite debris on the shore beyond the brambles is his destination," Donal replied. "Your thought has merit Flynn O'Connell.

Brendan and I will use it when a compartment for the weapons is constructed."

THE WEDDING

"Silé Dooley, you have a post!" Martha Howe shouted, with her skirt held up in one hand, waving the envelope in the other, she ran down the boardwalk to her front porch where Silé waited. Out of breath, she found Silé leaning on the broom handle. Even though work on the cathedral of St. Mary's ceased in 1845, Richard Pierce of Wexford was still in charge. His approval had to be obtained if someone wanted to use the cathedral for purposes other than its current use as a hospital site for the sick and dying. Silé tore open the envelope sealed with wax bearing the initials RP. Not exhibiting the excitement Martha Howe expected, she unfolded the paper. Her eyes raced across and down pen and ink script. "Well. What does it say?" Martha Howe was more anxious to know the content of the paper than her son's future bride. "Mr. Pierce talked to the priest. He will allow us to be married next Friday, five days from now, in the entrance, the outer lobby can be closed off from the main hall," Silé answered in a tone of voice that surprised Martha Howe thinking her insistence on the wedding location would garner a more positive reaction.

Silé Dooley, of course, grew up in a Godless environment, a clan of gypsy travelers with no religious affiliation. She would just as soon be married on the front porch of the Howe residence, but bowed to the wishes of her future Mother-In-Law.

"And, there is additional support," Martha Howe's revelations were held back until an opportunity presented itself. "According to the vicar, a priest will arrive in time to perform the wedding. He will say mass, hear confessions, visit the sick, and provide last rites. A wedding or two is likely his other duties," Martha said. Silé was confused. *Didn't Martha listen to what the paper indicated?* "Or two?" Silé looked inquiringly at Martha who sat down at the table with a two-week old edition of Punch, the English newspaper. "That foolish fisherman fellow who sells to Fiona and other hotels and pubs caused a scene at Clancy's from what I hear," Martha said, leafing through the newsprint. "Was it one of the Foley brothers!" Silé asked. "What happened?" "The older of the two asked that trollop Sally Donaghy to marry him! Why, he must be twice her age and daft as well. A table was tipped over spilling lunch soup and a young man, obviously jealous, was ready to challenge him," Martha said. "Flynn O'Connell intervened and saved the day I heard." "Love has no age limitations," Silé mumbled. "How do you know she is as you say, a trollop?" "Nor has lust no age limits," Martha countered. "You must have heard she flaunts herself shamelessly to any and every man who walks in to Clancy's Pub, and Maddy Polk who lunches there once a week told me, in confidence of course, how she conducted herself." Silé knew the true Sally Donaghy. She decided to leave before opposite viewpoints turned into a heated discussion and then to an argument. Madeline (Maddy) Polk was known by women in the community as the town "gossip" Martha Howe not one of the informed. In the community, Martha Howe was thought to be a bit "standoffish" and women avoided contact with her ever since the death of her husband Peter at the hands of George Brewster.

"Your son needs to know he is getting married in five days," Silé spun on her heel turning away with the post notification held above her head. Martha captured the first happy smile on Silé' s face as she shut the front door. Outside on the porch her nose was greeted by sweetly scented air from the hillsides full of yellow gorse and purple lavender. She started for the livery soon to cross paths with the new family of Fiona Farrell. Silé caught up with the two girls who carried a basket between them. Greetings were exchanged. "We are taking a luncheon to our friend Neil Howe and Malachy who we like as well," the older girl who was named Heather Anne factually stated. "Neil is my best friend Silé, he is teaching me to ride horses! He is so handsome." Heather Anne had just turned 11 and Silé recognized a childhood infatuation she hoped would not be detrimental to their friendship after she broke the news. "He is my friend as well Heather Anne, and Sissy you are so quiet today. Do you want to come to my wedding? Neil and I are getting married by the priest on Friday!" "I will come," were the first words from Sissy without a moment's hesitation. Heather Anne was silent. Silé s revelation was reflected in her facial torment. Her mind raced over why this event was so devastating to her comfort. "I will still like him,"

Heather Anne said, not looking at Silé who examined the girl's face for any hint of acceptance, rejection or jealousy. The face of Heather Anne was a blank canvas. Silé understood the courage the girl had to muster to make her statement. "I will take Sissy with me to your wedding. Where will it be?" She asked, finally squinting up to look at Silé, her hand shielding her eyes from the sun directly overhead. Silé remembered the conversation she had with Fiona Farrell who told her that both girls' lives were marred by recurring disappointments. She realized her wedding to the object of Heather Anne's childhood infatuation was just another frustration in her young life." "The wedding will be on the cathedral steps Heather Anne. You and Sissy will enjoy the cake and have a chance to find the ring in the bride's pie!" "That sounds like fun!" Sissy directed her comment to her sister who still retained a stoic look about her. Heather Anne said nothing but looked at her sister and nodded. Heather Anne's demeanor changed when they arrived at the livery to see a bare-chested Neil Howe watching them approach. He tossed away the hammer he held and walked toward them with his arms outstretched. Heather Anne's face lit up. "We brought you your luncheon, Neil. I made you an egg sandwich!" Her excitement was evident even to Malachy, his attention drawn to the little girl's exclamation. She left her sister holding on to the basket handle, her end falling to the ground as she raced toward Neil's outstretched arms. He stopped and backed up two steps recognizing the girls' intent. "Heather Anne no, you will soil your pretty dress! I am dirty and sweaty!" She skidded to a stop, then walked up to Neil grabbing his upper arm in both of her hands turning to look almost defiantly at her sister and the person who had won the affection of her childhood fancy. Neil was surprised and amused at Heather Anne's attention. Silé's thoughts returned to when she was growing up, thoughts of her father she tried to forget. He conspired with his brother to turn her into a prostitute. *"Forget them"* she thought, but the thoughts returned. She was forced to run, and she did. Heather Anne, who never knew her father, appeared to be trying to fill the void in her early life. Silé smiled choosing to kiss Neil on the cheek. A choice made to avoid a lingering greeting a jealous competitor would see as a serious interference in their relationship. "You will be my husband on Friday next," she said unfolding the handwritten letter. "Fiona's girls are going to come, isn't that right Sissy and Heather Anne?" There was a waiting period experienced just before hesitant words broke the tension. "Yes ma'am," the low conciliatory voice came from the mouth of Heather Anne who wandered away from the group, kicking pebbles with her foot. Sissy sat on the top rail of the corral swinging her feet, enjoying the present, or forgetting the past. Neil read the notice in its entirety before he reached for his future bride swinging her in a circle until she cried out. "Neil Howe, stop!" The sisters laughed. Silé Dooley laughed until tears started running down her cheeks. It parted the threatening clouds, and Heather Anne returned to her former self, an inquisitive happy child on the verge of moving from child to young woman. Adult considerations corrupted her thought process. For a moment Heather Anne forgot the basket and the egg sandwich, but she quickly recovered. "Neil, your luncheon, Mr. Brandon...come eat now!" Heather Anne shouted. She picked up the forgotten basket with two hands. Heavy, the basket bounced off her knees. Neil went to her rescue, grasping one end of the basket forcing her to run. She laughed and nearly fell, but Neil grabbed her around the waist, saving her from a puddle full of a revolting mixture of water, earth and animal. He pulled her and the basket to the table at the side of the livery. They stopped for a breath under the overhang where he and Malachy often sought shelter from an occasional cloudburst while they ate their lunch. The mid-day sun continued to shine. Heather Anne was ecstatic. Her eyes fixed on the man who made her heart pound. Malachy Brandon's eyes searched the contents of the basket. His nose caught delightful aromas. He was hungry. Neil Howe's eyes sensed movement at the corral fence. D'Arcy McGee motioned to him with a summoning finger. His eyes searched the street behind him. He was not followed.

SMUGGLERS TWO

Brendan Foley hated to handle the slimy denizens of the deep. He disliked even more the need to clean, filet and bury the remains of their catch. Instead, put a hammer or saw in his hands. Then, one would see his love of creating something out of wood with his hands. To rid himself of a distasteful part of his livelihood, he hired Flynn O'Connell to clean, chop and filet. A second wagon bed was complete. After his walk-around final inspection Donal was worried. Staining the wagon bed, a deep brown color would draw attention causing them angst, delaying completion of the storage compartment. "The stain is a preservative, brother!" Brendan's reasoning convinced Donal. They decided to go forward, and when completed the compartment allowed transport of at least a dozen long guns. Donal decided to test how secure the compartment was. Packed with thresh, no movement of the eight long guns could be heard. He directed the horse over rough rock-strewn terrain making up part of the winding path up from the shore. Brendan, happy about the test and proud of his carpentry skill, stood back admiring his work. He walked around to the other side of the wagon. He ran a hand over the wood. From every angle, from near and far, and then Donal did the same. Finally, they were satisfied, but still cringed at the thought of making the trip into Killarney. Once there, to be met again by the armed guard who inspected and questioned incoming travelers and freight wagons. Over tea in the afternoon they sat facing one another questioning themselves.

"We are not militant fighters for freedom. We are simple fishers of the lakes, one soon to take a wife, are we not Donal?" "It is my brother, George Washington or that Franklin fellow in America we are not, but what we recognize is the injustice directed to the common Irishman and the hidden desire we have to correct the injustice. 'Tis a small effort on our part and it puts us in mortal danger. "If our ruse is questioned or the height of the wagon bed becomes suspect, or the stain... How do we respond?" Brendan asked. "What do we say?" Donal thought for a moment, his fingers rubbing chin whiskers. "We transport heavy containers of water with live fish. The weight has weakened the original boards. Now, we have no fear and can transport much more weight," he said. "We can direct anyone's attention to the containers away from the stained wood. Hopefully, there will be more interest in salmon swimming." "I like your second solution," Brendan said, walking over to the wagon for further examination, "and with the addition of the side boards, 'tis hard to judge the thickness of the wagon bed. With each trip we make our return will allow us to collect stone and transport lumber for our new cottage." He leaned close with a hand on the side rail. "We are soon to need a friend for our faithful horse. A team would be better suited for heavy transport, and we need to enlist Flynn to collect stone." "Aye brother, if time allows, we should talk with the Howe Livery. Malachy does buy and sell, but until then I would ask Flynn to accompany us. He could distract the soldier with his knife throwing talent," Donal offered, making light of a serious mission. Brendan laughed, and then he abruptly stopped as if he were reconsidering the idea. Movement of Brendan's untrimmed eyebrows, and his facial contortions confirmed to Donal that his brother's mind was wrapped around his off-handed, frivolous comment. Brendan held out his cup for more tea water. He finished his bowl of toasted grains with cream supplied by Flynn through the efforts of Margaret O'Connell and the Guernsey. At the waters' edge he rinsed the tin and shook the water off. "When will we hear where to deliver? Would it be Killarney or Ennis?" Brendan asked. "Who will accept the weaponry?" Will it be someone we know and trust? 'Tis not a good idea to get involved in freedom fighting when we are living a simple but comfortable life, uninvolved, what say you brother?" Brendan was pacing back and forth after stuffing tobacco into his black bowled pipe. He puffed strongly, smoke trickled from his nose. He coughed. Bent over, he coughed again. Donal looked up as the aromatic scents reached his nostrils. "On the 'morrow we will hope to find out answers to all our concerns," Donal said. He stared at his brother. Brendan's face had turned red from the wracking cough.

BEST LAID PLANS

Sitting at a table across from each other, Rossa and McGee came up with a plan to aid the Clan O' Branigan, to disrupt the militia attempt to evict the hill people. Their plan initiative fell apart when several defectors in the ranks of the Irish volunteers read postings of what was likely to happen to suspect collaborators. Republican efforts to gain Irish independence from British rule made life miserable for English landlords. Irish descendants of the fathers and grandfathers who once owned the land taken away them gained a measure of revenge. Crops were burned, livestock were run off, barns were set afire. English landlords were given free-reign about what they could do as master of the property formerly owned by the Irishman who worked for him. The English forced true Irish to watch what they said, and never did they speak in Gaelic. It was forbidden. The postings depicted whippings and hangings, graphic illustrations meant to intimidate the poor Irish commoner. In addition, the untimely death of Patrick O'Brien was a devastating blow to Rossa and to D'Arcy McGee. Corky, O'Brien's dog lay in the corner of the back room of the Killarney Playhouse, one of several sites used for clandestine meetings out of the public eye. The dog emitted an occasional whine, lost without his master. Rossa brought the dog to Killarney at the request of Friar Jonathan who suggested Devon O'Connell, who earlier developed a close relationship with the dog, would take good care of him. Rossa paced, puffing furiously on his

Woodbine, his hands behind his back, lost in thought about what he could do, if he could do something. He shook his head declining a plan his mind deemed too dangerous. He stopped his pacing, gesturing with his hands, then, shaking his head again. "No! I can't do that," he shouted looking toward Muldoon, but not seeing him. The dog whined. Rossa flicked the Woodbine to the floor grinding it out with his boot. "Sorry Muldoon, I was thinking out loud." Muldoon and Danny Kissane, the "town clown" from Ennis stood by waiting for Rossa to break the silence with an alternative. Danny hoped to help deliver arms to militants in Ennis. Volunteers were disheartened when they heard the arms were without ammunition. Revolution without assets disheartened them at times, and when they learned the weapons had yet to be delivered caused sighs of disappointment. The cottiers who were able to read the notices depicting graphic illustrations of punishment posted alongside those of other political statements conveyed their message in the most convincing manner to those who could not read. "We will have musket balls! Today I will speak with the Foley brothers and Neil Howe," Rossa suddenly blurted. "That is all I can say for now. The less said the better for no one can be blamed but me if we are found out." He was worried. A match fired another Woodbine. Today was the day the Foley brothers would make a testing run to Killarney with the wagon empty of its future contents. Rossa hoped for a successful entry past the guard, some of whom were diligent. Others not so as they recognized regulars who traveled from town to town delivering merchandise. Rossa hoped luck was on the side of the brothers Foley. Danny Kissane reported that one of the guards charged freighters a fee to be allowed to make their deliveries. Checkpoints had yet to be installed outside of County Clare's capitol city, Ennis. D'Arcy McGee met with Neil Howe of the Howe Livery and Blacksmith Shop on more than one occasion. He agreed to witness his friend Neil's marriage to the Dooley woman. In addition, the forge and Malachy Brandon, the blacksmith operator of the livery, would be the supplier of ammunition for the rifle-muskets to be delivered to a nationalist supporter in Ennis, County Clare. Still there remained the pending militia march to the hills of the O' Branigan clan. *Could the remaining men of the clan be utilized to impede and disrupt the mission? Could they be taught in a few hours how to wage war?* Rossa wished for the help of Flynn O'Connell, the former French Foreign Legionnaire who appeared on the fringe of any nationalist effort to free Ireland.

+

Flynn had the palm of his hand on the half door when the Sessions clock bonged four times. In the dim light furnished by the whale oil lamp he looked first to the loft for signs of movement and then to the sleeping form on the canopy covered bed. Not the hint of a sound came to his ears, not even the rustle of a mouse making a home in the thatch above his head. In an hour or two the cottage would be alive with frantic movement to render relief to the Guernsey, feed the pigs, horses and hens before all could sit near the hearth for tea, scones with honey, and porridge with cream. Ewes and rams in the pasture would wait for his return. The half door swung shut behind him before his hands raised the collar of his coat. The same hands found warmth in the pockets where the pipe, matches and drawstring bag of tobacco offered comfort during his walk to the shore of the lake. The Foley brothers insisted he make this unscheduled trip to the village. It was to be a rehearsal for their entry into the Republican movement protesting political and religious injustice. Their reaction, a protest to the British inhumane unconcern for their own citizens. A small contribution it would be, but if discovered the charge would be treason and at best the sentence would be transportation to penal colony in a far-off land or a jail sentence. No need would there be to discuss the "at worst" sentence. Flynn's presence this day was to act as a distraction to the guard in the event he became suspicious of the wagon beds preservative stain. Donal asked him to wear the belt with the seven sheathed knives he used when he practiced his knife throwing. Ronan O'Neill, the Killarney Playhouse promoter and manager continued every week to intercept Flynn at some point in his visits to Killarney with the Foley brothers. Flynn continued to refuse O'Neill's attempts to schedule a performance of his talent at the playhouse even though the incentives to Flynn increased twice in the last six months. Flynn insisted he was not a showman. Margaret O'Connell left the decision entirely up to her husband. Minutes later Flynn was nearing the path that became a rutted grass free road leading to Killarney. He was half way to the shore, and it was still night. In the east he could see the tops of the hills. The sun was soon to wake to chase away the chill, the damp, and the fog obscuring the lake surface. Rarely did he encounter anyone on the road at this early hour. However, this morning was an exception. Two men crossed in front of him pulling a jaunting cart meant to be pulled by a horse. "Aye friend, do you have any food?" One of them asked stopping just beyond where Flynn was to cross. In the night brightened by the moon they saw the shoulder bag Flynn carried. "Not to share Irishman," Flynn replied. "Your hunger may be lessened for a time when you reach the trees sheltering the home of the vicar at the cathedral." "We have heard," was his reply. His two hands readied to again pull just before he looked at the man next to him. "Are you ready," he said. It was not a question but more of a command. There was a nod and the wheels of the cart began to turn. Flynn crossed the road and began the downward half of his morning sojourn. Whence they came Flynn had no idea, but to be pulling a cart loaded with whatever, appeared to mean the horse had died. Flynn remembered the tales his brothers told of how the poor and desperate salivated in anticipation of the demise of an animal, be it horse, dog or goat during their journey to wherever their ultimate destination might be. He couldn't believe. He was told how the Irish woman became adept at "bleeding" livestock, sneaking into the English landlord's estate in the middle of the night, using the blood to be cooked with nettles to keep her children alive. At the time he couldn't believe that either. The meandering route to the shore required Flynn's caution, a repeat of broken ribs he suffered two years ago still remembered. He stumbled when his eyes focused too long on the ghostly, swirling mist obscuring the surface of the lake. Marveling once again at the occupation of the Foley boys, undaunted by the night, and the fog, possessing an uncanny ability to navigate to their favorite fishing spot. Brendan always celebrated their return, standing, singing his arrival at the minute beach with a bountiful catch beneath his feet. Close enough now to the shore Flynn's nose captured the comforting scent of the turf fire promising warmth. Hot tea welcome, to offset the coolness of a new Kerry morning. Now, through the mist he could see only the bow of the unused watercraft beached. He caught the sound of the water end its rush to the sandy shore to retreat and come again. What he didn't want to encounter was another body washed up on the beach. Apprehensive, he might see what he didn't want to see, his eyes searched the tiny stretch of beach. Once again able to breathe, he reached for the tin cup on the bench with eyes on the lamps that remained lit. He thought it doubtful they could be seen from any distance out on the lake in the misty fog. *They will be here shortly.* Tired of searching through the mist he added turf to the fire and poured water for the tea. If the wind was right the aroma of the burning turf would act as a beacon to the brothers, but this morning the air was still with only sporadically, a hint of a breeze. A shivering foreboding came over Flynn when he looked up upon hearing the mournful call of the loon in the fog shrouded distance. The Irish were known to be forever superstitious! When Flynn checked the cottage, he saw Donal's culinary talents were on display when he lifted the lid of the cast pot ready to be placed over the fire. With butter, honey and some of the smoked salmon from the "black house" their hunger would easily be satisfied on their return. With the oven in his hands, he backed through the door heading for the fire. On his way he noticed the cleaned table, the knives he used embedded in the table top were used in the scaling and filleting of part of their nights' catch. His eyes tried to pierce the fog to no avail and his ears heard nothing but the sea birds warning of sunrise. The Meehan boat with the Foley brothers aboard should be returning soon. Flynn was ready for their arrival.

PADDY RINN

Paddy Rinn's boat was swallowed by the fog after his wrinkled hands pushed his skiff away from the side of the Foley brothers craft its lamps lit and Donal's turf furnace aglow. The dim light receded as his oars moved the boats apart. No one was at fault when the two boats came together in the dark, "more of a bump" was the way Brendan described the unscheduled meeting. Paddy Rinn, a lake fisherman for more years than most was evidenced by the lines on his face, the missing teeth and the yellowed fingers from the Woodbines. Stark evidence that Paddy Rinn was near, if not 70, the epitome of a gnarly, weathered and wrinkled old man of the lakes. When the fishing was good, he fished during the day, but when the fish "went away" in his words, he fished in the pre-dawn hours. He had little contact with the outside world, living on what he caught, selling his catch when he absolutely had to have the pound sterling. Paddy took full advantage of the opportunity to visit with the Foley boys questioning them on everything from politics to the escalating price of a pint, and why he brought up the subject mystified Donal because Paddy did not go to town or visit the pubs. He didn't drink, but he liked to visit, and the talk eventually focused on the effect the potato disease had on the Irish.

"May last, I towed seven poor souls to the shore near a wee village, so small nary a pub did it have," Paddy said. "The first day there was one, on the fourth day I snared two, and my memory fails me...." The women of the village demanded that the menfolk bury the wretches in a single grave, but not more than three feet below the sod they were laid." "Was the site covered with stone?" Brendan asked. "Nary, a chunk of granite was thrown down to cover. The gravediggers were so disgusted with the task, and their wives, they walked to the town of Rathmines and got drunk." "The men could have negotiated for favors," Brendan said with a huge smile on his face. "Aye, the lads paid the price of no favors for a time when they returned," Paddy said. "Ah, the poor lads...Paddy Rinn paid the price as well Foley boys. No longer will they buy my fish, only the women who sneak to the shore in the night to leave coin and take back my catch, more often now do they ask. Before, I visited not that often, only when I was short of the coin. Few do they leave now." "The women are your friend," Donal said, while he watched Paddy Rinn shake his head in obvious disagreement. "Sure it is, the men are not Donal Foley! Some weeks later, I was told that wild dogs dug into the grave and dragged the remains into the village. Children watched behind the half doors while the women tried to chase the dogs away. They were rebuffed, forced to back away from hungry dogs, snarling threats, and bared teeth. She cried tears Foley boys!" Paddy Rinn cupped his hands to warm them before he shook his fingers to restore the sense of touch. He leaned over the side of his craft to stare at Donal's furnace and the glow of the turf. "Aye, such warmth I would welcome Foley boy. Build me the

same for the last few times I fish these waters. 'Me
bones grow cold too quickly any more you know."

Donal and Brendan listened until the splash of his
oars cutting through the water faded away. The fog was
lifting, helped by a breeze prompting Donal to raise the
mast and unfurl the sail. Night would soon turn into
day, and Flynn had biscuits baking while he impatiently
paced looking into the white blanket covering the water
that lapped, and lapped, and then the wind that caused
the murky mist to swirl died, and a sail rendered
useless hung forlorn without its mate. Brendan shipped
the oars while the wind did its work, but now, out from
the sides of the vessel came the oars manned by the
beefy shoulders of the Foley brother who caught the
scent of the turf fire heating the pot and the tea water.
The boat leaped ahead with each strong stroke causing
Donal to grab the mast in fear he would be cast into the
sea. Flynn waited with his hands in the pockets of his
woolen sweater, his shoulders hunched, eyes straining,
and the pipe glowing red listening for the sound of the
oars piercing the water, and the grunts of the oarsman
who without a glance at the compass, knew the way.
Ahead of them, in the back recesses of three minds was
the mid-morning trip to Killarney town, a test of
Brendan's carpentry skill. What they didn't know or
notice in previous trips was the slowly increasing British
presence in and around the town. The guard on the
main road was now three, one of whom ministered to
the field gun pointed toward incoming traffic. Furtive

glances out sheer covered windows held aside saw British troops gathered in groups or strolling down boardwalks in the town not used to other than the demands of tourists and politicians. Children no longer played in the streets. Mothers took grumpy mischief makers inside preventing them from irritating the Brits who exhibited a sullen dislike for the Irish children's pranks.

"Flynn 'me boy, we are coming," the strong voice of Brendan shouted, a warning to the shore man to have butter and biscuits, black tea and honey ready when the bow of the boat hit the sand of the beach. "Hear you I do, but your whiskers I don't see," Flynn replied listening intently, and then the bow broke through the rising mist. Flynn ran into the water grabbing the bow, pulling mightily, to aid its security on the sand. "A fine, but cool morning we have Foley boys, you have work for your skilled apprentice to do?" Flynn grinned at Donal who had climbed out of the skiff and reached for the hook to remove the furnace from the boat. "The risk is ours friend Flynn," Donal said, not answering Flynn's humorous question. The thought of the upcoming scrutiny by a suspicious British soldier at the edge of town loomed fresh in Donal Foley's mind. He dumped the hot turf coals at the edge of the where the water meets the shore. Steam rose, like the fog rising to the heavens from the early mornings' dominance of the sun's promise for a reversal of the night's darkness. Like the moth drawn to the flame, and from different directions, three men found their way to the benches circling the turf fire's warmth countering the dawn's chill. In the eastern sky the blackness was turning to gray causing stars to wink out. Gracefully, one after another, they bowed to the sun about ready to make a dramatic resurrection, bursting forth to repeat its incarnation of the warmth being ushered by the wind gliding gently over the hills to the east.

"How did you know, Foley Boys, a timely return enables one to enjoy my baking skill!" It was Flynn who lifted the lid to reveal the brown topped contents emitting a wondrous, an irresistible assault on two senses of the three men who stared into the oven, ready to reach, to savor Donal's latest creation slathered with butter and honey. Knives of the brothers plunged into the biscuit of their choice followed by Flynn who waited to see the reaction of the brothers. Broken apart, Brendan's selection steamed and the butter he applied quickly melted. Three bites later he reached into the oven for an encore. His huge appetite won out over caution. Scorched hairs on his hands and arms forced a release of his prize. He yelped in pain tossing it skyward while he shook his hands and fingers to quell the result of his inadvertent quest. In a competitive moment Donal reached skyward with both hands hoping to intercept his brother's biscuit but pulled away when Brendan's fingers touched his. Falling, falling, to the sand the biscuit tumbled downward through the dark and then to the dawning light. Fingers of both reached trying to save it before it hit the sand, but the biscuit bounced off the small table eluding Brendan's fingers before he was able to rescue it with a well-timed swipe of his hand. He shot a disdainful look at his younger brother, who ended up face down on the sand of the beach. Brendan taunted, his ivories exposed while he shook his prize, showing Donal the now warm biscuit grasped securely. Flynn watched laughing at the comedic episode the brothers enacted after returning from hours on the water in the pre-dawn darkness. For just a moment, the challenge ahead of them was briefly forgotten.

Donal picked himself up from the sand with a smile on his face. His hands patted away sand from his pants and shirt. Brendan stood near the fire under the oven staring at Flynn who had speared a blackened biscuit from the oven overcooked, rendering it un-edible to anything but the fishes who swam in the lakes. With a practiced throw Flynn hurled the impaled piece of what was once bread dough toward the water. A splash was heard that appeared to return the Foley brothers to the business at hand. Donal returned from their cottage with the order list he handed to Flynn. Brendan lit the torches on either side of the cutting table at the side of the cottage. In an hour the torches could be extinguished.

THE TEST

Rossa waited impatiently at the depot for the arrival of the Foley brothers, and Flynn O'Connell. Striking a match, he lit his second Woodbine while he watched to see who and what arrived at the British checkpoint. Currently, a freighter driver directing a team of four horses was forced to uncover his load of sod cut from the bog lands. A Brit with a bayonet attached to his rifle-musket used it to probe the load of turf. A republican who was "on the run" could be hidden in the turf using a hollow reed to breathe. The followers of "Captain Rock" the "Rockites," were known to have used that method to smuggle arms. The practice of hiding fugitives was discontinued when one of them was killed by the thrust of a British bayonet. Rossa watched the probing and counted the number of attempts from one end of the wagon to the other, and up and down the sides. The probing ended at 13, and the driver was waved through. He didn't bother to recover the turf being near his destination. Quickly sold to merchants, publicans and residents, sod was the major source of fuel available. Next in line was a "jaunting cart" being pulled by a shirt sleeved young man with suspenders the color of the grass, his yellow hair was covered by an out of place hat Rossa knew was called a "bowler." His feet were bare, and a Woodbine hung from his lips. The lady, obviously a tourist dressed in her finery was seated and waved a fan in utter disgust at the smoke drifting her way. Rossa knowingly nodded to himself. "*The young man would*

have no luck in receiving a tip from that lady." The
young driver pulled his hat from his head in a sarcastic
and dangerous salute as he was quickly waved through.
His salute drew a look, his mockery nearly costly, saved
by three more conveyances that queued in front of a
soldier who extended his arms bringing the two wagons
and a cart to a stop. The second wagon belonged to the
Foley brothers. The trial run was at hand. A nervous
Rossa reached for a match wishing he was closer to the
checkpoint. With that thought he sprinted out the door
of the depot. Once outside, he nonchalantly walked
toward the checkpoint so desperate to examine the
faces of the British troops who inspected each transport
into the town. *A chance I take not to be recognized by
O'Connell or the Foley's,* he thought. Guilt by
association always concerned him when common
purpose friends were involved. *If anything happened...*
he walked toward the field piece, close enough to see
and hear the conversation and the faces of the
inspectors. The first wagon was waved ahead. The Brit
who stood by the cannon looked in his direction
deciding he posed no threat, just another Irish
commoner, he likely thought. The Foley wagon moved
forward between the two British guards who were more
interested in the contents of the containers than the
wagon itself. Rossa was pleased but hoped to hear soon
from a runner in Ennis on British activity around the
town. *Would the Foley brothers be faced with the
same scrutiny outside of Ennis?* Rossa watched Flynn
who stood next to the driver's seat pull one of the
knives from its sheath. His action drew a look from

one of the inspectors, but he said nothing at first, then, turned back to Flynn, his face full of questions. Rossa's presence was noted in the eyes of the Foley brothers.

"What is your purpose?" The inspector asked, pointing to Flynn's belted knives. "I am in the employ of the Foley fishmongers," Flynn answered, while his thumb tested the blades sharpness. "Proficient with knives as I am, I took up throwing as a pastime when free from preparing orders for the brothers. I have been asked to exhibit my ability at the playhouse." Suddenly, Flynn raised the knife behind his ear his eyes fixed on the wheel of the cannon several yards away. He threw, and the knife whistled through the air ending up in the hub of the wheel. The wheel had been Flynn's target, his throw a bull's eye. He walked to the field piece and worked the knife free of the axle hub. He turned toward the group as he replaced the knife. The lead inspector glanced up the road at the oncoming traffic, his attention shifting to Flynn, the knife thrower. "As a Legionnaire, I was told to aim for the 'oeil de boeuf,'" Flynn said, laughing at his impromptu use of the French surely to confuse the British soldiers. "Surely, my knife was not meant to disable your cannon," Flynn continued, a serious look, the opposite of the previous laughing comment, covered his face. "A Legionnaire he was, and the knives were our gift," a grinning Donal said, quickly responding, "he is a marksman with the knife as you saw, deadly accurate as we have seen, is not that a true statement brother Brendan?" Donal asked. "Aye brother, a true statement it is," Brendan responded. "Refrain from belting your knives in future visits, Legionnaire..., or they will be confiscated," the British officer advised. There was a stare down. Flynn nodded, and the Brit turned to look at the lineup on the road leading into Killarney.

While the conversation continued, carts, riders and wagons formed a line. Grumbling was heard causing the Brits to move with haste not previously shown. Rossa and the Foley brothers were pleased and relieved at the order to proceed. The British inspection, thought by some to be harassment, focused not on the refitted wagon or the contents of the Farrell Mercantile containers, but by the bone handled knives belted around the waist of the Foleys' talented employee. Tim O'Rourke, Killarney's magistrate, never had experienced a hint of revolutionary trouble in his years as Killarney's policeman. His past experiences involved the atrocities committed against the Irish by supporters of the Queen, vicious landlords and uncontrolled violence by armed British forces sent to suppress the activities of those who searched for something to eat. Irish merchants suffered when the troops wandered into town. Only the tourists enjoyed their presence.

Without a modicum of interest from the British contingent, Rossa wandered away, looking back, satisfied his conscripted fisherman and sheep herder were in no danger of being detained by the British. He would find them later at Clancy's, the favorite pub of

Brendan Foley. Reaching up, he found the Woodbine behind his ear, the one reserved. His Sulphur match flamed alive as he watched the Foley wagon pull away from the grasp of suspicion.

BRENDAN'S BETROTHED

Brendan Foley flicked the reins. The horse strained at the leather. Wagon wheels began to turn. Each of them looked at the other, and exhaled, a sigh of relief now that they were beyond the gauntlet. Donal chose to walk with Flynn who used a sharpening stone on one of his knives. Brendan looked to his rear more than once to assure himself the Brits had not changed their minds. The depot was ahead, bustling with activity at mid-morning. Carts, carriages and conveyances of all sorts gathered around the building. Coin and contents of wagons changed hands and locations. Loud protests from unhappy vendors or buyers were heard over the movement of wagons, snorts of horses and barks of dogs being chased by children allowed to roam freely amid the confusion. Brendan spotted the potato merchant Tom Steele in the groups of two or three bartering back and forth in animated negotiations. "Aye Tom Steele, late it is, but a fine day to peddle your potatoes. I have a lovely salmon for you," Brendan knew that Tom's diet consisted of potatoes and potatoes prepared in different ways when the food so many depended on was not destroyed by the fungus that spread uncontrolled over the last two years. "Later I will catch up with you Foley boys, you have smoked?" Steele had grown fond of smoked salmon. The former bodyguard of Daniel O'Connell was required to seek a new occupation since the death of his employer in Genoa. He was a regular visitor to the depot in Killarney and to the fields surrounding the town.

300

"Aye Tom Steele, I will put one aside for you. Midday will find us at Clancy's. Join us," Brendan shouted as they passed by. The Foley wagon rumbled into the edge of town where Flynn made his departure for the Howe Livery. "Oh, how I want to see my bride to be," Brendan mumbled a little ditty, suddenly sounding disconsolate, a reversal of his mood prior to jesting with Tom Steele. Brendan rarely revealed his true feelings, and Donal did not prod him about his plans after Sally, the barmaid became part of the Foley family. The horse appeared to sense what the driver was going to do when the street to their immediate left required a change in direction. A gentle tug was all the horse needed to turn down the street leading to the Farrell Mercantile. Today, the mercantile was the first of five deliveries, as requested by the owner, Fiona Farrell. Three days had elapsed since their last delivery, and the tank water needed to be changed. Fiona enlisted the two able bodied fishermen to help her change the tank water every two or three days to keep her swimming product alive. Her aquariums drew locals and tourists into the store to marvel at the salmon and trout and the small fish they fed on. Ms. Farrell now had three tanks, one of which was largest of the three, made of heavy glass to allow her to start a seascape inside the tank.

"Aye brother 'tis your turn to empty the tanks!" Brendan left for the rain barrel with two buckets. "No hurry there should be Brendan. The tanks need clearing before we add new water!" Donal knew his brother was thinking not of the job at hand but the meeting with his betrothed at Clancy's Pub. Just outside the mercantile doors Brendan paused and pushed his way back inside. Showing obvious impatience, grimly, he shook his head upset at his inattention to the current need for his assistance. The change of the water and the transfer of fish required the concerted efforts of all three involved and took over an hour. Fiona transferred fish from old tank water to new. She hoped very soon a method to pump air into the water would be discovered. The Foley brothers carried pail after pail of water, depleted of its life-giving oxygen, to the street to be added to muddy puddles already in existence due to the almost daily rains that came with little warning. When they finished, Fiona Farrell excused herself to freshen up when she had the honor of being the one to reach for slimy, slippery fish, to move them from one temporary home to another. Each time she ended up dripping and wet, not happy that young ladies who sought employment when told of the duty she undertook, would decline the opportunity to assist at the Farrell Mercantile. Jasmine O' Barsky was the exception. The young college student assisted when her classes allowed. She was willing to do anything Fiona Farrell asked of her. On this day she arrived as Donal and Brendan were ready to carry containers of live fish into the mercantile. She was ministering to the horse, scratching and rubbing, "Such a good girl you are," she whispered, receiving grateful huffs for the attention, but when Donal pulled a heavy container to the edge of the wagon, Jasmine grabbed the handle with both hands on the other end. Looking behind her, she backed up the steps spilling water, helping Donal carry it inside. Brendan followed with the larger container showing no signs of the effort, his massive arms and huge hands carried the lakes bounty up the steps without spilling a drop of water or losing a fish.

"You can have me for two hours Miss Farrell, if I can be of assistance?" Jasmine asked when she saw Fiona appear after refreshing herself from "being with the fishes" a term she used often. Fiona walked over to where Jasmine stood shaking her hands and reached for them, looking at the girl's palms.

"An hour later and you would not have had to acquaint yourself with the captives brought here by the Foley boys, my dear Jasmine," Fiona smiled and squeezed the girl's hands. She turned away allowing Jasmine to walk to a counter where she disappeared for a moment to search, successfully emerging with a hand sewn garment she held over her head, letting it fall to cover her clothing except for her bare forearms. She watched Donal drag first one container, then the second and third to near the tanks. Brendan stood at the window looking in the direction of Clancy's Pub. Jasmine took a deep breath, then walked purposefully toward her current assignment, regretting her untimely arrival to a class in marine life.

The end of the next hour found the Foley brothers exiting the Arbutus Hotel, their last delivery of the day.

All orders were filled and little remained alive or smoked. Donal set aside a smoked salmon for Tom Steele if he did visit at Clancy's. Brendan decided to walk while Donal would follow to secure the horse. Brendan's walk became a hurried pace and then a run-walk before Donal lost sight of him. In no hurry to join his brother, he poured water for the horse and passed a few minutes with the Magistrate, Tim O'Rourke who was on his way to lunch in the Arbutus dining room. He looked at the wagon, but Donal could not tell if there was any question forthcoming. 'Good days' were exchanged before Donal watched the magistrate push his way through the door of the hotel. Donal boarded and urged the horse forward. His own stomach gave a warning growl. He brought the horse to a stop when he saw Neil Howe leave the boardwalk, waving to attract his attention.

"A good day it is Donal Foley," Neil greeted. "Flynn O'Connell is stacking boards outside the byre at the livery. Your brother can use them. We have no use for the lumber, only the space." Neil's mother waited patiently on the boardwalk. "Brendan has the luck this fine day, Neil Howe. We will visit after our luncheon." Donal tipped his cap toward Martha Howe who waved and smiled. He watched her hand and arm drop to her side, her attention drawn to the sounds of activity behind her in the alley between the Arbutus and the hardware store. Donal's eyes followed as did Neil who saw men, women and children rummaging through discards and garbage cans yet to be moved away from the buildings. Hungry country folk had invaded the town searching for something to eat. Donal flicked the reins noticing up and down the boardwalk that storefront benches were occupied. People cupped their hands looking through windows into the interior of shops, knowing they would not be welcome inside. They had no coin. Or, if they did, they would not spare a single coin spent. Some of them knew not the value of the coin. Careless use of the coin might prevent passage on a ship bound for a better life.

In the middle of the next block a crowd gathered in front of Clancy's Pub. Donal heard angry shouts and cries of children. He recognized regular patrons of Clancy's, intermingled with country people in ragged clothing. Pushing and shoving took place while Donal approached, and who was in the middle of the fray but Brendan Foley, his arm around the waist of his bride to be. Sally Donaghy tried to escape his grasp while holding an iron skillet in her hand, shaking it in a threatening manner directed at a patron in front of her. The object of her ire wiped a streak of blood from his forehead as heads turned. Returning from a sumptuous lunch, Tim O'Rourke, the magistrate, came huffing and puffing his way arriving to get to the center of the disturbance. His entrance caused part of the crowd to quietly melt away. It was a confusing scenario. "He deserved worse," came the shout from a man who disappeared inside the pub. "She is nothing but a two pence whore anyway," another man said as he walked away. Mothers with babies in their arms knelt before

O'Rourke, all of them speaking the language he heard but didn't understand. Tearful mothers holding babies cried as the magistrate tried to make sense of what was going on. O'Rourke's arms were raised, his eyes fixed on one and then the next. All who remained were stoic, some turned away to leave assaulted by his accusing demeanor.

"What in God's name happened here?" He questioned those who still gathered. The hungry shook their heads and walked away, the others began the babble all at once, pointing fingers, gesturing and laughing among themselves. The publican was busy helping Sally Donaghy pass out crusts of bread and scrapings from plates into a tub like container that was surrounded by people on their knees scooping handfuls of whatever was uneaten. The scrapings were quickly devoured by all those desperately hungry, those who still had the ability to eat. Brendan Foley watched her for a moment then left for his corner table followed by Donal who had secured the horse behind the tavern. "The hungry ones came inside to steal food from the plates of patrons," one man said. Another man came forward. "They came inside to beg for food, not to steal. Sure! It didn't help when Mick Toon objected and pushed a woman to the floor," he said. "Sally yelled at him and picked the woman up, so weak from hunger she was, she couldn't get up on her own. He called her a two pence whore and that was when she bloodied his head with the pan." "She called him a 'fecking idgit' and told him that if he had a 100-pounds it would not be enough! I believe she was right," another man, a well-dressed tourist, said while he watched the activity on the boardwalk. It was obvious to others around him that he was stunned to see what was before his eyes. "How do they allow this travesty of inhumanity to continue?" The British rule over this land. England is the most powerful nation on this earth, why," he looked around, focusing on first one man who would shrug and turn away, and then another who would stare back without comment.

The bread was gone. Many hungry hands devoured the contents of the tub-like container. Nothing but a few well chewed bones remained allowing the publican and Sally Donaghy to resume their business inside the pub. Diners and drinkers who followed the altercation after it exited into the street returned to their seats inside the pub. Patrons were eager to debate the incident for hours over pints of Irish ale. The few country people left saw no reason to remain and started to shuffle away to continue their journey to wherever the ship may take them, or to seek another source of food. An impatient Brendan Foley was hungry. He hoped to spend more time with his beloved who returned following the pub man through the door. She hurried to his table where his muscular arms pulled her onto his lap. Her hands grabbed him behind the neck and her lips met his, but then she struggled from his grasp, gone like the morning mist over the moors. His eyes saw nothing but her back as she made her way between the tables to the kitchen. Minutes later she returned with a huge tray with plates of food she placed in front of diners working her way toward Brendan. Donal left his seat to visit with Tom Steele and Donovan Rossa who found a table on the other side of the pub dining room. Pleasantries were exchanged while all three glanced in the direction of Brendan who was being attended to by his 22 year "old maid" bride to be.

"I didn't know you were acquainted with Tom," Donal said to Rossa, who nodded in the affirmative a brief smile came as obviously he had other things on his mind. Tom Steele appeared confused as his eyes were on Brendan, shifting only to acknowledge the others at the table.

"When is your next trip to Ennis?" Rossa asked of Donal who shifted in his seat to glance again in Brendan's direction. "On the 'morrow we will arrive at mid-morning to deliver orders to four of our customers," Donal replied. Rossa reached to an inside pocket and slid a folded paper toward Donal's fingers. Tom Steele's concentration on Brendan relaxed. He watched the transfer with interest, his eyebrows moved, his eyes became slits. "You will have a new customer for a special delivery at the address on the paper," Rossa said. There is no checkpoint to enter Ennis. The memory of O'Connell remains strong enough to make the British cower and hide themselves."

"I knew Daniel's sons and your friend Flynn reminds me of them," Tom Steele remarked. He leaned on his chin inches from the table top quickly scanning the room. "Be assured my friends, what I have seen and heard today will remain with me," he whispered. Rossa and Donal Foley cast surreptitious glances around the dining room fearful someone would notice Tom Steele's whispered admission. Tom Steele's attention returned to Brendan Foley who sat alone at the table in the corner of the room. "'Tis difficult for Tom Steele to accept what has come over the elder of the Foley boys I must say. Donal...do you have an explanation?" Tom Steele waited for an answer that didn't come. Three men sat wordless, a stagnant moment of silence where even the murmuring of diners at adjoining tables was quelled like the closing of a vault door.

"Flynn does not claim Daniel as his father," Donal said, avoiding the question, his effort to change the subject with a shake of his head raising both hands to suggest total ignorance. Brendan Foley appeared to be content alone at the corner table, his eyes never leaving his bride to be. If she did disappear for a moment, he would turn his attention to the food on his plate. The usually raucous behavior of male diners in past visits was notably absent this day. The touchy-feely incidents Sally endured were substantially reduced having something to do with the burly fisherman in the corner whose demeanor, not to mention his accepted proposal of marriage, challenged anyone to make an improper advance toward the attractive young waitress. She went about her duties, occasionally passing by

Brendan's table where a few words were exchanged, and when she wound her way back to the kitchen through tables filled with admirers, she deftly avoided attempts at touching. Reaching hands came up empty, pulled back when the owner of those hands glanced guiltily to the corner where the muscular fisherman was about to rise from his chair. The mid-day lunch crowd was beginning to make their exit. Looks of disappointment were evident on the faces of disgruntled young and older who took lunch on a regular basis attracted by the charms of the comely waitperson Sally, who seemed to enjoy their fondling attention. What those young men didn't know they inevitably would learn as time passed. Sally's day was not over, and Brendan waited. She smiled and waved as they left the pub's dining room, removed their dishes, scraped the coin and an occasional pound they left into her apron pocket that was beginning to bulge, making the table ready for the afternoon and evening visitors. Donal knew that time passed quickly. No timepiece hung in the dining room, but Donal could see the clock in the kitchen when the door opened. His fingers tapped on the table top waiting for his brother and bride to be to finish their conversation.

"Promise me Brendan Foley! You will not take me away from this life I lead and enjoy each day. Your wife I will be, but part of me is married to Clancy's Pub in Killarney town. 'Tis not something to negotiate my love," she rose from her chair after a face to face discussion. The publican had caught her eye more than once with the silent request to get back to work. Brendan did not answer not having considered that Sally would not hesitate to leave her current situation in favor of a new life on the shore of the lake. He told her of his plans to build a roomy cottage with wood floors, a fireplace, a bedroom with a canopied bed, and a lavatory. She listened, she smiled and nodded and smiled again. "Will I be able to join you when you journey to the towns?" Fearful she was of being isolated away from the life she knew for years. Brendan took her hands in his with his promise that being away from her causes him to grieve.

Donovan Rossa leaned to Brendan Foley's ear before he left for Ennis that same afternoon to ready for the delivery the next day. Days passed by. Informants still had not heard when the march to the hills would begin. Rossa hoped for the sake of the Clan O' Branigan, the eviction would never take place. Donal and Tom Steele joined Brendan at the table in the corner after Sally Donaghy somewhat reluctantly, resumed her duties in the kitchen.

"Time it is for us to call on Malachy and Neil Howe at the livery my brother," an impatient Donal offered while attempting to have his brother recognize Tom Steele, Brendan's eyes moving from the kitchen door to the eyes of his brother. "Aye Tom Steele, truly you are a sight I have not laid eyes on since the planting of the early spuds began," Brendan finally acknowledged Tom's presence who held back appearing to be hesitant, unsure of the mental state of his fisherman friend. "Foley, I waited until your visit with your...was complete," Tom said. "When, tell me, did all of this come about, you have addled my brain Foley boy!" Brendan Foley merely shrugged his shoulders. Donal walked to the door with Tom Steele telling him of the years they spent having mid-day luncheons and his brother's infatuation with the girl that led to his proposal. Minutes later Tom Steele bid farewell to Donal Foley, more confused than ever about the upcoming marriage between Donal's older brother and the woman half his age. Back at the corner table, an ever impatient Donal watched his brother finish his lunch.

"I will meet Flynn at the livery to load lumber. When we finish, we will come by and pick you up. Is that agreeable?" Donal waited for an answer that finally came when Sally disappeared into the kitchen, lowering a curtain in front of his eyes breaking his fixation on the woman of his dreams. Donal turned on his heel and straight armed through the pub door nearly hitting a tourist who was reaching to the door. The patient horse watched Donal approach while noticing a man walking away hunched over with his hands in his pockets. He thought nothing of it until he remembered Tom Steele's request for smoked salmon, completely forgotten by both. While he poured water for the horse, he saw that the containers had been moved, the storage area under the seat was unclasped. The salmon was gone but the small tin box did not belong to Brendan or himself. *Hunger has no law,* Donal thought. He reached in to pull out a tin box that was heavier than it should be. When opened he found an oil-soaked cloth, but underneath were musket balls and a drawstring bag of gunpowder. *His hands were in his pockets.* He remembered the sight of the man walking away. *Did he take the salmon?* He pushed the box back inside the compartment and shut the door. Up on the wagon seat he released the brake and grabbed the reins.

+

Flynn finished moving and stacking the lumber from the byre to where it could be loaded into the wagon when Donal arrived. Neil Howe assisted when he was not tied up with a livery customer. While greetings were exchanged Neil ran his hands over the horse looking for signs of chafing, parasites and excretions from the horse's eyes and mouth. He examined four hooves and each ankle. Neil Howe, the former university student had paid close attention to the instruction of the farrier-blacksmith, Malachy Brandon. "Aye, Neil Howe what will your charge be for this examination?" Donal knew that Neil's love of horses led him to do what he did. "An apple smoked salmon would please my palate," Neil answered, "but if the lake fails you, I would not be one to worry, I will not tell my employer." Neil winked, and a wide grin covered his face. On a serious note he said, "you care well for your animal, Donal Foley." The loading began as raindrops started to fall. Flynn was at the fence enjoying a pipe but hurried back to the wagon as he cleared tobacco on the heel of his hand.

"Two trips will be needed," Flynn said while pulling on the leather gloves Margaret purchased from the town shoemaker. He and Donal loaded as much as they thought was the limit for the horse to pull and Neil helped pull the tarp over the load. All three ran for shelter as fast- moving clouds promised a quick end to the sudden shower. Minutes passed. They watched waiting, soon to be rewarded as the sun peeked through a popcorn filled sky. "Time it is to collect my lovesick brother," Donal said. "Two of us should walk to lighten the load don't you know. Neil Howe spoke of salmon and Tom Steele will have none this day Flynn. The salmon was missing but in its place was a tin with ammunition." "Musket balls and a pleasant day without rain on the way is a blessing," Flynn said as he raised a foot to board. Hearing no argument from Donal, he took his seat and the reins. The horse huffed and started forward, straining until the wheels turning made her job much easier. Donal walked alongside with a hand on the wagon box greeting people they met along the way. Martha Howe was on the boardwalk talking to Fiona Farrell as they passed by.

"You see! Don't you Fiona? The lout Brendan Foley is not with them. Not a doubt I have he's at Clancy's Pub with that Sally woman!"

"Excuse me please Martha. I have customers and we will talk later." Fiona turned away heading for her shop. Martha stood for a moment contemplating her irritation. She picked up her skirts and started to walk in the direction taken by the wagon driven by Flynn O'Connell. After several quick paced steps that slowed while she reconsidered, she stopped, and with an exasperated sigh turned and headed back to the house.

Flynn often supplied a two-fingered salute to those he recognized. He did the same when he saw the two women on the boardwalk. They did not return his greeting being too busy talking and listening, one in an animated outpouring of words, the other nodding and shaking her head seemingly impatient to return to whatever would free her from listening. Chattering children waved and ran alongside the wagon until they tired of the game. Free to roam the streets, they teased skittish horses and irritated drivers who tried to shoo them away when they dared to get too close to the wheels. Easily impressed by adult conversations, the children knew Flynn was the one their mother talked about with her friends. He was the one with the knives who hit the target while blindfolded. Children were in awe of the tall black-haired Irishman. British soldiers occupied benches on the boardwalk. Others were seen in groups of three or four smoking while they observed the activity on the street. Locals crossed the street to avoid contact with those on the boardwalk. Flynn tugged on the reins. The horse headed toward Clancy's Pub.

Rossa avoided the checkpoint on his way out of Killarney town catching a ride on a wagon headed in the right direction, but in a roundabout way he might have thought. He watched workmen in the cemetery they passed tend to the grounds surrounding the O'Dowd monument. The sun shone brightly on the tribute that rose purposefully above any other remembrance. The grounds surrounding the monument were dotted with smaller granite crosses and simple sandstone markers crudely carved with a name and a date of the deceased relative. His travel by foot resumed when the wagon changed direction but an hour later, he was fortunate to encounter Shamus "Skip" Dunigan on his way to Listowel. The stories he heard told were that Shamus ran away from home when he was ten and three, married an Irish girl when he was 17, and left six months later when he caught her in a compromising position with a delivery boy. Rossa heard that when Dunigan was asked how he came to be known as Skip, he would tell about his second marriage. "I was twenty and four and a year later I found that Millicent O' Maley was not at all like the Irish woman I thought I had married. A miserable, a lazy foul-mouthed drunkard she was, oh, how I was fooled for a time, but I recovered. I... be liken to the flat stone flung to the surface of the still water, to skip, skip, and skip again!"

Rossa spent the next hours absorbing the hazards encountered in the rocky, rutted pathway leading to Limerick and then to the river Fergus. Dunigan had few words to say during the trip but cautioned Rossa when he arrived at his destination. "Watch your back...hear me I say," as he nodded, unsmiling, not giving Rossa a chance to prod him for his reasons. Dunigan flicked the reins to urge his horse down the street past the monastery being renovated. Rossa watched him pull away before his attention was drawn to workmen restoring the crumbling walls of the monastery above him, and then to the street below where carts loaded with granite blocks were being unloaded. He knew when he neared the Shannon there would be more traffic on the road leading to a ride to Limerick and beyond. For a moment Rossa watched the activity before he resumed his objective to arrive in Ennis in the dead of night. He watched a nun pass out small bowls to a line of mothers holding babies, crying children and disheveled, poorly dressed men and women who waited for something better than the watery soup that likely consisted of their only meal the day before. *Killarney and Ennis are not the only towns where the hungry country people flock,* he thought. *If I am ever to be judged a traitor to the queen, I will use the lines of starving people I see as my defense,* he shifted his shoulder bag, and head down, for a reason he increased his pace. He hesitated to make eye contact with the travelers approaching from the other direction. To them, his shoulder bag might contain rations of some sort, and hungry starving people might resort to malicious attempts to relieve him of the burden of the bag if their pleas for food went unanswered. Hearing the clip-clop of horses, and the squeak and rattle of a wagon behind him Rossa moved toward the side of the road. The driver slowed the wagon alongside.

"Climb aboard lad," a friendly voice ordered. Rossa was quick to deposit the bag in the wagon bed grabbing the side board with both hands he swung himself up and over the side. "Come up here, next to me," the driver pounded the seat with his hand. "I need your company to take me' mind away from the sadness I witnessed behind. To where do you walk this lovely day? Tommy O'Toole has the reins lad." *Luck is with me this day,* Rossa thought, getting seated next to the driver. "'Tis an Irishman with a foreign name who sits next to you, Tommy O'Toole. I am Rossa on my way to Ennis town, and I hope to spend a few hours on this seat with you," he said grinning at his talkative seatmate. "Aye Rossa lad, beyond the Shannon we will go this fine day, a fine day it is for us, but not for them," he motioned with his head to what both had passed. Rossa nodded in agreement as a ragged group of six approached. One of the six, an older woman was bent over leaning on a stick to help make her way. The only man in the group walked back to her, took her by the elbow to assist. Her eyes raised briefly to glance toward the wagon to reveal a face wrinkled and gray, only to return her eyes to the ground in front of her as she made slow and deliberate steps. Rossa flinched when a step caused her knee to nearly touch the ground. He could tell that each movement brought pain to her joints. Both watched the six, a man, two women and three children shuffle their way until they were behind the wagon. "Three years it has been, and years before that they faced the same and change did not come to them. Now they have lost heart and desert the land they love. Soon, there will be no Irish left," O'Toole said, turning his head to look so seriously at his passenger that it caused Rossa a bit of discomfort. "What will be the next sorrowful encounter we will witness this day?" O'Toole asked, turning his head away from the questioning stare at Rossa to flick the reins, urging the horse along at a faster pace. Along the way they met a man with a staff herding sheep who nodded his thanks when O'Toole moved the horse and wagon to the side of the road to let them pass. A four-horse team pulling a wagon loaded with barrels appeared shortly after. Ahead of them the road narrowed and curved around the base of an outcropping of tall granite the high tip pointed as if it came from the bowels of the earth shot from the bow of a subterranean archer. Now they were on a slightly downward slope where they approached two young men who were singing and laughing as they walked toward O'Toole and Rossa approaching in the wagon.

"A lovely day it is wagon man, for Michael and I head to the coast and then to America!" Both raised their arms fists pumping in a moment of jovial celebration, jumping around, smiling and laughing. One of them lost his cap in the process. O'Toole's wagon passed them by, but they continued to walk backwards for a time waving, pushing and shoving at each other, to disappear out of sight when they entered the curve at the base of the granite. "Two healthy young Irishmen lost to this island, 'tis America's gain and Ireland's loss, I say Rossa." "Aye, they carry nothing with them and the distance to the coast at Tralee is a long walk, and then the passage...I hope they make it," Rossa said. "As do I, a truly free country awaits their footsteps," O'Toole said nodding to reinforce his belief. "Impulsive youth is often fraught with unwise decisions," O'Toole blurted, looking too directly at the smooth skin of a face free of signs of maturity. Rossa said nothing, but the hint of a smile came, and he nodded his acceptance of the driver's warning meant, he assumed, for youth in general, not just to the two young men or for his own consideration. Left behind them was the rocky, detritus strewn section of road. Ahead of them a panorama emerged, a treeless, grassy boreen where wagon tracks marred the beauty of the green. In the far distance the lines came to a point to disappear on the other side of the rising landscape. O'Toole brought the wagon to a halt to let the horse graze while he poured water into a cup, and a second was quickly emptied by the horse that huffed in appreciation. O'Toole poured more water offering it to Rossa who, without any hesitation reached for the cup. The lanes of Limerick lay ahead.

CONFRONTATION

Donal's presence on one side of the wagon was enough to deter any thoughts the children had of mischief making on his side. The unguarded free side of the wagon in the center of the street tempted little ruffians who dared each other to grab the wagon box, lift their feet and ride until caught by the driver. Dry streets brought more pedestrian traffic, but only one child in weeks past was run over by a freight wagon suffering a broken leg. Flynn directed the horse into the vacant lot next to the pub and set the brake while Donal poured grain into the feed bag. That accomplished, Donal slapped his hands together. "To rescue me' brother we go!" Flynn and Donal both laughed. On the boardwalk several local business people were gathered outside the pub door. Heads turned as Donal greeted the group, some of them his own customers. "Aye lads, we come to fetch me' dear brother Brendan who you all know." "He needs to be fetched away from the Brits," Finbar Roach, the undertaker, who seldom took lunch at Clancy's, said. Turning away, he secured his top hat with both hands, leaving the group without another word. Donal made his way through the group asking, "What did he mean by that?" He turned with his hand on the pub door seeking an answer, but no response came. Donal pushed through the door followed by Flynn. Their eyes adjusted to the dimness inside to see Brendan Foley in a sitting position against the bar being attended to by his betrothed who held a cloth to his forehead. He was groggy, barely conscious, the left eye swelled, a mere slit.

"What in God's name happened to my brother Brendan?" Donal asked, his question directed at Sally Donaghy while his eyes flew around the room to land on a table of four uniformed Brits. A series of scraping sounds were heard as all four, one after another, rose from their chairs. Donal's attention returned to his brother as he knelt and pulled away the cloth Sally held to his forehead. An ugly bruise and an open cut from his eyebrow to his hairline were revealed. "Who did this?" Donal shouted. Sally Donaghy turned and pointed to the departing troops. Flynn had walked to the door standing as the four who were leaving were blocked. "Before you leave please tell what happened here," Flynn said, "you are the only patrons here besides the man who lies unconscious on the floor with a wound that could only come from the butt of a musket." No response came.

"It was him!" The barman who had been polishing glasses walked around the bar pointing to the perpetrator who tried to move through the door being blocked by Flynn. Flynn's hand was on the chest of the guilty one his other pulled the musket from his grasp. "What right do they have to bring their weapons into my business place? They come in and my regular customers leave before they can order!" An angry barman stood, red faced with clenched fists. "Sally, please us to bring the magistrate Tim here. He takes lunch at the Arbutus," Flynn instructed. She looked at the barman for approval before she rose to her feet and hurried to the kitchen and out the back door. Donal had joined Flynn at the door. The barrel of the musket now rested on the floor the stock in Flynn's hands. Congealed blood glued hair to the butt of the weapon. Flynn and Donal looked at each other and then at the four complacent soldiers very evident to Flynn at least that no one was in charge or wanted to assume the title of spokesperson to offer any defense of their action. Movement at the bar drew their attention. Brendan Foley struggled to his feet. His left eye was shut. He stood, unsteady with a hand on the bar before straightening up and walking purposefully between the tables and chairs toward the group gathered at the door. Donal sensed his brother's purpose. He took four steps to meet him but was pushed aside. The owner of the contaminated weapon was his retaliatory objective. The British soldier cowered backing his way behind his comrades.

"Wait Brendan, for the arrival of O'Rourke." Donal grabbed the arm of his brother who had his fist clenched. Donal's grip was shrugged away. Brendan's facial expression was enough to render the strongest of men a cowering imitation of manhood, on his knees, pleading for his life. Voices were heard from outside as the pub door opened to the entry of Sally Donaghy followed by the magistrate. Tim O'Rourke took immediate charge. Tim O'Rourke was an honest man in a difficult position, loyal to the Crown, yet sympathetic to the Irish and their cause. A crowd of local people had gathered outside the pub, curious, hesitant to enter. Faces peered through the glass in the pub door. Those who were inside taking lunch knew the brawny fisherman who they saw brutally attacked. They had no kind words for the barely out of their teens, British soldiers. O'Rourke's loud voice was heard by all who stood on the boardwalk.

"What I see here is a total injustice, **give me that!**" he demanded as he relieved the first of three British soldiers of their weapons stacking them against the wall. His loud, but controlled voice received everyone's attention. "Your messenger Sally told me what happened here, and sure it is... **it will not happen again!**" While he talked, he walked to each Brit. His menacing stare reinforced his words. His next stop was to face Brendan Foley with Donal at his side to prevent any ill-advised response to the one who was the torment of his future bride. O'Rourke's eyes examined the damage. His fingers reached up but did not touch. Sally Donaghy followed behind and stood close to Brendan. She groped for his hand. Her dress was torn, the bodice ripped to expose had she not covered herself with her hand. Tears had been wiped away, but evidence remained. O'Rourke, a head shorter than the black-haired Irishman O'Connell who held the evidence, leaned down to examine the butt of the musket held by Flynn. He straightened up, to glance first at Brendan Foley and then at his assailant who squirmed under the gaze of the magistrate. "Tell me soldier, just because you wear the uniform of your country does not give you the authority. Were you trying to kill the man? You will be confined in my jail until your Commandant receives my report and comes to get you, and I hope he takes his time. As for the three of you...you are just as guilty and don't deserve to wear the uniform. Your names will be part of my report and I hope your punishment is severe!"

O'Rourke was thorough in his investigation interviewing everyone, obtaining signed statements, names and ranks of the soldiers before he allowed anyone to leave. He recommended that Brendan look for the services of a doctor and if one was not available which was likely, to seek something to help heal from the apothecary. He was last seen marching the detained soldier out the door as the crowds parted to let them through. Donal and Flynn knelt on either side of Brendan who found a chair while Sally Donaghy used a wet cloth on the wound. "You are going to have a scar, sewn shut or not," Donal predicted. "It will be a mark on your handsome face," he teased. Sally Donaghy put her hands to Brendan's face and kissed him on the nose. "Handsome you are to me, love," she said. "Wise it would be to stitch it up," Flynn said, "had I the needle, the thread, an ample supply of whiskey, and a short stick, I could do it. In the legion we were all taught. I closed legs and arms in Vera Cruz, but the kit at our cottage." "To include the stick?" Donal asked. "And what use would be made of the stick? On our way back, a stop to see Prescott is advised," Donal said. "To save Brendan's tongue to taste again," Flynn said, partly in jest. "To bite down helps to endure the needle," he continued. "How steady are you Brendan? Can Donal and I help get you to the wagon?"

Not a problem did he have when he tried to confront his attacker and administer punishment, but now the adrenalin was missing. With both hands on the chair seat he slowly rose to his feet, bent over while hands reached out ready to assist. A proud man, he straightened up, his height matched that of Flynn O'Connell, but his weight ten stone or more. "Back to our cottage Donal, I have only one eye, someone else should take the reins." His left eye was closed. He reached out a hand because he could not find his brother. Sally Donaghy ran out of the room removing her apron she threw into a basket at the entrance to the kitchen. Loud voices were heard causing all to stop at the front door. Sally Donaghy pushed through the kitchen door. "I am going with you Brendan, to take care of you until you are healed," she said. The bar man came out of the kitchen shaking his head, obviously in disagreement with the decision made by the one that drew regular customers to enjoy her service and attention. Her decision stunned Flynn and the Foley brothers, the implications awkward and confusing.

+

"We are near the town Rossa. The poorest of the poor who come in from the country take up residence here in the lanes. Squalor and filth hide behind the brick streets and boardwalks that front many prosperous shops. Two worlds exist in Limerick Rossa, English merchants and Irish poor." The crest in a rise in the landscape was reached and ahead of them was the town. Off to their left a crowd had gathered surrounding a large tree. A man was standing in front of two horses with riders aboard. He was reading from a book he held in his hands. O'Toole brought the wagon to a halt.

"We are going to witness a hanging Rossa. Their hands are tied behind them. Can you see?" At that point two other men with coiled rope attempted to throw the rope over the limb above the horses. The first attempt failed, the second was successful. Rossa and O'Toole watched the men tie off the rope to the base of the tree. The man with the book walked to first one and then the other. A moment later he appeared satisfied and turned his back walking several steps away before he turned and raised his hand. It was obviously a signal as a lash was applied to the hindquarters of each horse. Four feet reached for the ground that wasn't there. O'Toole had seen enough, shaking the reins to continue their journey.

"Two more Irishmen knock on St. Peter's door," Rossa said.

FUGITIVES COME CALLING

Each time the on-shore wind over the mountains brought the sound, Margaret cringed. The vocal noise she heard, unrecognizable words that originated as shouts from afar became faint voices from the valley. Sporadic wind currents carried the beat of drums imperceptible one moment, strong the next. When the wind carried the sound to her ears it made her pause to lean on the tool she used in the garden. Mary Margaret heard them and marched up and down the rows beating on the toy drum Flynn found in the shop of the Frenchman LaVigne. Much to his dismay, Devon was sentenced to at least three hours of reading, spelling, geography and mathematics at the table inside the cottage. After two days of intermittent showers that limited outside activity, the sun cast warming rays, but not on Devon. He would not neglect his lessons again. Margaret was fearful the British drills in the valley would lead to the discovery of the O'Connell cottage above them. Every day when Flynn was away in the evening, Devon and Mary Margaret visited the sheep pasture with her. This evening was no exception. When Devon finished with the count and none of the ewes had endangered themselves, they took the time to look down on the activity below them. Margaret and her daughter walked while watching Devon run to the low stone fence, a barrier that served as a deterrent to the sheep from leaving the pasture. It didn't always work. The stone fence also was an indicator of where the property ended. Mary Margaret carried the drum with her on those occasions to imitate the miniature drummers she watched stomping their feet. Nightfall? The summer moon made an appearance to forecast the night. Sol was ready to pay homage to the gods of darkness when without warning turmoil erupted down in the valley. Puffs of smoke rose into the air followed by reports from weapons causing Margaret to gather her children behind the brambles she shoved aside to be able to watch the activity below. The musket fire continued and when a ricochet scarred a granite boulder near them Margaret decided it was time to return to the cottage. Margaret took one last look and saw several soldiers scrambling in their direction. If they continued, they would find the O'Connell cottage on the plateau. What they were chasing was unknown until she spotted movement off to her right. Two men crouching low were making their way up using any cover available to avoid being seen. They would reach the plateau but avoid the pasture at about the same time she and the children arrived at the cottage.

"Hurry children, in the middle of a war we should not be." He hands urged a curious son and daughter who were hesitant to leave. Another report was heard. Flynn had instructed Margaret on the use of the weapon he carried as a French Foreign Legionnaire. She wondered if this was going to be the first threat she would face, having to use it to defend her home and children. Into the garden they ran until Devon veered off toward the corral to scratch the nose of the back horse that watched their progress with his head over the top rail. Mary Margaret ran ahead to disappear through the half door just as the moon reappeared from behind the clouds to brighten the grayness of dusk. Inside the cottage, Margaret turned up the whale oil lamp and lit another before she went to window on the right side of the door to look for Devon at the corral. What she saw made her gasp. Two men were standing near Devon, gesturing wildly, pointing in the direction of the valley. Three steps took her to the half door where she paused to look up at the musket over the door. She decided against it, picking up her skirts and running out toward Devon who ran several steps toward her before he stopped. "Mother, they are on the run, they are being chased. The soldiers will find them if they come here. We must hide them, Flynn said so." Margaret was speechless. One of the men was not. "We escaped their custody. We were identified as taking part in a raid by the Mollies. A traitor to our cause, a neighbor as well will receive favors from the Brits, damn him and them," he said. "Three of them continued to follow us. Is there a place to hide?" The second man, who identified himself as Mick O'Malley looked in all four directions. "They will search the cottage, the loft, the byre and the corral shelter," Margaret said. An excited Devon was pointing. "Mother, the privy, will they look there?" Years ago, Flynn had constructed the building. A stone path led to it, away from the cottage. Partially hidden from casual view, the pathway could be lighted with four oil lamps Flynn mounted on poles, but the lamps were seldom used. The privy Flynn called the toilet could serve two guests and each user had a bucket of lime nearby with a handy scoop. Never having to face a dilemma such as was presented Margaret was unsure of what she should do even though both had agreed to harbor those patriots who were "on the run."

"They may or may not, and we will chance that they may not," O' Malley said. "We will hide in the privy. If they decide to search it or put you and your family in danger we will leave," the second fugitive, Trevor O' Fallon said in parting. With haste they both hurried in the direction of the privy. Margaret ushered Devon and his sister toward the cottage. Devon went to the window framing the far end of the corral. Margaret lifted the musket from the pegs over the door trying to recall everything Flynn had told her. Confused thoughts flooded her mind. *There are three of them. Only one musket ball do I have.* She replaced the weapon to the pegs.

"Mother, they are here," Devon shouted. He saw the first soldier at the corral admiring the black horse. Margaret decided on a plan of action. She pushed through the half door determined to take the offensive. With a purpose, she strode without hesitation toward the soldier standing near the corral shelter. "What brings you to our humble farm, I ask you?" Margaret looked him in the eye and stood not a foot away. Mary Margaret, prone to disobeying orders, ran out of the cottage to her Mother's side. For the benefit of the soldier, she held her skirts and curtsied. His attention was immediately drawn away from Margaret's question.

"A pretty child! What be your name pretty one?" he asked. Mary Margaret chose this time to act shy, clinging to her Mother's skirts. "Her name is Mary Margaret, and I ask again your purpose here is what may I ask?" "No doubt you would have seen two dangerous fugitives who escaped from our detention earlier today. Have you seen them moving through the area?" Before she answered her eyes swept by the birthing shed, the pig pen and the small byre that held the Guernsey. One of the two other soldiers inspected the byre. The other was at the pig pen holding his nose. "Had they stopped for a visit I would have had them in for tea and a bite, however, they must have been in a hurry to reach the Killarney road not that far from here," Margaret sarcastically told him, pointing in the direction that would take them past Devon's favorite climbing tree. That suggestion did not work as the soldier stepped around Margaret to face the cottage. "No harm will come to you, but we will need to inspect your cottage just to assure you will be safe once we leave," the Brit said. "Will you allow us to enter?" His eyes scoured the landscape to the left and right of the cottage. He motioned to the two who apparently were satisfied with their inspection, standing and talking to each other. His motion was to the privy partially hidden. "You will see nothing of fugitives in our cottage, just my son who should be attending to his studies before the sandman calls," Margaret answered. "We must insist," he replied as he started toward the cottage. Margaret caught up to him just as the half door opened to Devon who carried the musket in both hands. Margaret screamed, the British soldier held up his free hand, the other held his weapon upright in a non-threatening manner. "We mean no harm young lad, but we need entry as your mother has granted to me. Only a moment we will take. "Devon..., please me to stand the musket at the wall...**now!**" she said. Devon complied, and the soldier pushed his way through the half door. He was greeted by the cheerful warmth of the turf fire in the hearth, and the lingering smells of baked bread.

"Please use the ladder to inspect the sleeping loft for the children so you can be on your way," Margaret prompted. Four steps and two rungs later the inspection was complete and without a word the Brit left the cottage. Midway between the corral and the cottage the other two soldiers stood waiting in the advent of night. As if to answer an unasked question, one of them shrugged, the other shook his head. The O'Connell family watched as they left in the direction that would take them to the path leading to the Killarney road. It wasn't long before night, aided by the brambles and blackberries, swallowed them into its darkness. Margaret breathed a sigh of relief then she glared at her son who cringed. "Bring the musket inside and replace it on the pegs," she ordered, her face a stormy thunderhead. Mary Margaret was quiet hoping to avoid punishment for disobeying her mother.

"Both of you stay here! I am going to the privy." *How did they escape capture?* she thought as she turned up the flame on the lantern. Once outside she realized the moon above was bright enough to light her way. At the door of the privy she pulled on the handle to find it unlatched. She stepped inside the still night air insufficient to chase away the unpleasantness. "Godspeed to them wherever they were headed," she said and turned to exit. "Oh missy, we are here" a muffled voice came from an unbelievable location, and at the same time the seating platform was raised by four hands to reveal in the lamplight the two heads of the fugitive Mollies. Margaret stepped back as first one then the other climbed out of the most disgusting place to hide that she could ever imagine. Later, when she related the story to Flynn, he told her that he purposely left the heavy seat unattached to allow for cleaning.

HOUSEGUEST

While he endured excruciating pain from a viscous blow delivered by the stock of a musket, Brendan Foley still took charge, allowing time for Sally Donaghy to change into a dress not ripped apart, and more suitable for travel. The footsteps, frantic activity and shouted expletives heard from her room above Clancy's caused laughter many times from Donal and Flynn. Brendan, dealing with immeasurable hurt only offered a weak smile when the sound of breaking glass followed by a shouted curse caused the floorboards above them to shake according to Donal Foley. Dust did in fact drift down from between the floorboards. Late diners did not miss the service of Sally, entertained as they were by her hurried attempts to ready herself for a trip to a place she had never been asked to visit. This time the initiative was her demand. Above them a door slammed shut. The sound of footsteps pounding down the stairs followed. Sally appeared with a belted bag with a handle, so heavily overstuffed that it bulged and required both her hands to carry it. Evidently, she intended to stay awhile. Taking a deep breath, she dropped the bag to the floor. Flynn recognized her plight going to her aid, relieving her of the bag. Her eyes smiled, and with a hand on his chest she whispered softly, "thank you, kind sir, who I have not seen at Clancy's." Turning away she went to Brendan who was in the process of standing. She offered her hands to help pull him up from the chair. No easy task for a slight woman who weighed just over seven stone. On tiptoes, she kissed him on the cheek, before she leaned close whispering something in his ear. His eyes widened. A nod confirmed acceptance of whatever she had told him.

"Let's be on our way," Donal said, heading for the front door. He was the first to the horse and wagon, relieving the horse of the empty feed bag and pouring water before Brendan and Sally Donaghy boarded. Donal took the reins while Flynn walked alongside the wagon nearest a still groggy Brendan, his head wound uglier than it was an hour ago. "We will see what the apothecary, Mr. Pigg has to say about the welt on your thick skull," Flynn said, using his fist to push gently again his employer's shoulder. Brendan turned his head and winked at Flynn. Their route would take them past the Farrell Mercantile and farther down the street, the Peter Howe House, newly named by Martha Howe who settled a debt to the livery by having an ornate wooden plaque carved and hung from the porch roof. Hammered copper shamrocks were affixed to the top corners and would eventually turn green according to the debtor turned craftsman who was recently evicted from his 10-acre farm. The former cottier now had a problem satisfying orders for his craft from merchants because he had to wait for lumber to be delivered from England. Patrick Kincade, the vicar at St. Mary's cathedral, was heard to have said that England would cut down and export the wood from all but one tree in the forest to save it for future hangings.

+

Prescott Piggerman, the apothecary, known to the village citizens as Mr. Pigg, did what he could for the damaged fisherman. He applied a medicinal powder to the wound, advising sutures to close the wound. He produced a sewing kit cautioning to all the necessity for cleanliness and sterile needles. His words caused Brendan to flinch. All were surprised when Mr. Pigg volunteered to close the wound. "Do you use the stick?" Donal asked. A puzzled look covered the face of the pseudo surgeon. "Lacking what I use, it would be the last resort," he said, after quickly understanding Donal's question. "After a glass of this elixir," he removed a bottle from the shelf, "you will feel little or no pain," he said. "Laudanum as a pain killer is well known. I have used it many times, as do dentists. My fee for the service will include costs for the materials and the suturing. In less than an hour you can be on your way" "'Tis Brendan's decision to make," Donal said, looking at his brother who had to turn his head to find Donal with his good eye. There was quiet in the room until a foot scraped the floor. It was Brendan's. "I trust you provide the finest Irish?" Brendan said after finding the apothecary near the shelving. Sally received that question to the apothecary as his decision to proceed. "Your fee I will pay," she said, holding up a small drawstring bag. "Two bottles of the 'finest Irish' you may need," Donal said, laughing at his injured brother's comical question. Flynn's hands squeezed the shoulders of his burly employer. "A brave fisherman 'tis my fortune to know," Flynn said.

Three hours later Flynn left the Foley brothers and the new addition to the family. A mildly sedated Brendan allowed the apothecary to clean and prepare the wound to be sutured, but an unsteady hand forced him to withdraw from the process of sewing the skin together. Flynn O'Connell took over after a brief discussion. A neat thin line marked the wound when he finished. Flynn made a comment Donal promised to relay to his brother when the drug wore off. "If I cause you pain, I would no longer be employed by the Foley boys..., then, who would perform the duties I saved you from?" His humorous statement meant for Brendan was likely heard from afar, a jumble of unrecognizable words that might have caught the ears of a heavily sedated man. "Have no fear friend O'Connell, your employment is secured," Donal assured him, going to Flynn. "Our delivery to Ennis will be short one man. Will you go in Brendan's place?" The delivery had been shoved to the dark recesses of the mind for everyone. Flynn thought for a second or two then nodded his acceptance. Brendan would be well cared for by his nurse/bride-to-be. Brendan's bride-to-be finished wrapping a length of clean white cloth around her future husband's head. The trip back to the lake began with Brendan's head lying in Sally's lap.

Night was fast approaching when Flynn left the lake and the Foley brothers. He hoped all would bode well for Donal. He faced a daunting task to help care for his brother, and to help Sally Donaghy settle into her new home for the next few days. Delayed in his return by the events of the day, he ran. When the footing was hazardous, he walked, and when thorny brambles blocked his path, he raised his arms to avoid scarred hands. The path leading to the Killarney road was just ahead when he heard labored breathing and movement through the brush covered screen that hid the O'Connell cottage. He reached the path. To his right and yards away on the Killarney side, two men burst through the bushes onto the path where they paused, bent over to catch their breath. One of them with his hands on his knees looked in Flynn's direction. "You, Irishman 'tis not wise to call on the missy with the children. The Brits are there, but they didn't find us. How far to the town?" He stood up and walked toward Flynn who was stunned, his face incredulous at the man's revelation. "Three quarters of an hour. And please me to explain yourselves. The 'missy' is my wife," Flynn said. "We escaped custody in the valley. Your latrine served us well don't you know. We hid ourselves since we were followed. We heard the kind lady when she came looking. The kind lady, your wife you say? A gracious lady she is, take care," and with that he turned away and both started on their way. Flynn didn't linger. He scrambled up the slope and ran with reckless abandon through and around thorns and blackberries, messages of guilt pounding into his brain. His steps slowed. He stopped. Flynn remembered what he said; "we were followed," but he had nothing to fear, no reason to be under suspicion other than being an Irishman in the darkness surrounded by British hunters. Instinct prevailed. With caution he advanced looking left and right not knowing how many or how far behind the pursuers were from their quarry. Flynn did not want to be detained. He knew the Brits would not hesitate to fire if they spotted him working his way toward the cottage through the brambles. He looked to the heavens thankful the moon had hidden itself for the time it took for him to move closer to home. He took one step, another and another, and a twig snapped underfoot like a rifle report in the silence of a mausoleum at midnight. Movement off to his left caused him to hold his breath as he crouched down. Muffled voices from at least two of them were too close. He moved forward to put the sounds of voices behind him. He was fearful the snap of the twig would attract them to that location. Bent over he chose his steps carefully until he counted 12. At that point he paused, listening, hearing nothing but the night, the wind, the rustle of leaves and the insects in the grass. All were loud and covered what he hoped to hear, the voices behind him growing faint. The moon fought through the clouds turning night into a semblance of day. He crouched even further down trying to make himself as inconspicuous as possible.

"Click!" Flynn heard the ominous sound of a musket hammer being engaged before the words came. "Stand up Irishman!" The order came from the uniform not more than 10 feet away. Flynn stood. "You are not one of the two. Who are you Irishman and why are you out here tonight?" He asked, as the other two hunters joined him. "I am O'Connell. My wife and children live in the cottage you recently searched. "How is it you know that we searched your cottage." "On my way here from the lakeshore I came upon two men who asked the way to Killarney," Flynn replied. "I am employed by the Foley brothers to clean, filet and smoke fish. They are your fugitives?" "Aye, they are, and the Foley fishmongers, I know of them. The smoked salmon they sell is a favorite. Brendan Foley is a jolly good fellow for an Irishman," he said. "That he is, I will pass on your thought and I smoke the salmon, you know. I did not want to be detained and knew I would be if discovered. Most Irish do their best to avoid the Brits, as do I. Fearful I am for the safety of my family should your fugitives return to my cottage." "That is understood, O'Connell," he said as he looked Flynn over from head to foot. "One of your own laid a musket stock to the head of Brendan this very day. He required stitches to close the wound. Hurt severely he is. O'Rourke, the magistrate holds the attacker in custody. May I go? My family waits," Flynn was impatient, but did not want to irritate the soldiers. "Sorry to hear of Foley's misfortune. We will send our doctor. Hurry yourself to your cottage, O'Connell. We have heard of your prowess with the knives belted around your waist." The other silent two mumbled something in agreement with the speaker. They nodded. Flynn turned away to leave. "A moment O'Connell, all of us are not as you might think. Keep that in mind and thank your wife for her consideration." Flynn gave him the two-fingered salute.

Swallowed up by the dark of night, the sole of his boot
the last image seen by the three hunters.

ROSSA'S FAILURE

Two hours after sunset in a pelting rain, Rossa arrived at the outskirts of Ennis. Hunched over, his collar turned up, and with his hands stuffed into sweater pockets, he could not avoid being soaked to the skin. Water dripped from the bill of his cap to his nose. Earlier he bid farewell and Godspeed to his driver O'Toole who he recruited into the network of freedom seeking Irishmen. Ahead of him a large tree with a massive trunk offered a little protection. It was night. He could afford to wait in hopes the rain would move on to Athenry, and beyond. His mind pictured the fire in the hearth, the warmth, in the cottage of Vincent Muldoon on the banks of the idyllic river Fergus where the quiet water pooled. Inis Fergus in the center of Ennis became a glassy surfaced pond before downstream returning to a fast-moving torrent. Muldoon's cottage was a safe-haven where he could dry off for the remainder of the night. He stood, plastered against the tree using his hands to scrape water away and wring his cap to dampness. *Not too smart, Rossa! Your clothing scattered around the town, some of it in Killarney. The oilskin hung on a peg in the Friary, shirts and boots in Muldoon's care, not too smart,* he thought, silently chastising himself. Water squished between his toes when he stepped out from behind the tree. He looked up through the canopy to see racing clouds reveal the moon after being hidden for three hours. *My good fortune to have the night breeze warm,* he thought as he sloshed his way through the grass to the wagon tracks that marked the road to Ennis. *Sorry I am to forget so easily after two sunny days*, he thought as he splashed his way through an unseen puddle.

An hour later he stepped away from the path to the grassy slope leading to Muldoon's place of business and his cottage. Anxious to get dry and sip a mug of hot tea he was encouraged to hurry as a light shone through a window helping to show him the way through rows of canoes turned upside down on stanchion supports. He ran the last few steps and reached for the door but it opened and framed Muldoon in his nightdress. He puffed on a curved stem pipe, the bowl carved into the face of a bearded man. "Aye lad, come into the warm, soaked to the skin you must be," as he stepped aside to let Rossa enter. "I am, as you say, 'soaked to the skin,' waterlogged from the liquid gold falling from the heavens," Rossa said in the Irish way of finding some good in an undesirable situation. Dripping water, he stood at the front of the hearth hands extended to catch the heat radiating into the room. "Tea and the caddy are ready on the table. Your boots and clothing are in the cabinet," Muldoon pointed. "Tend to yourself first. Later, we will sit for a time to discuss the coming days." Torn between two options, Rossa moved to the wooden bench near the cabinet and began to unlace his boots. Wool stockings to near his knees were laid in front of the hearth along with his boots to dry. Muldoon moved a rack near the hearth for his wet clothes. "Some of the clothing in the cabinet belonged to 'me brother. Look them over, they may fit you being as tall, but he was heavier than you," Muldoon offered. Rossa found the shirt he left and pants that belonged to the brother. Rossa was happy to be dry. Muldoon poured two mugs of tea while Rossa dried his hair with a towel, combing it into place with his fingers before sitting down opposite the owner and operator of the boat livery. "Oh Lord, my feet doth hurt," Rossa feinted pain. "What news do you have friend Muldoon," Rossa asked as he reached for the mug. "Well it is that you are here lad. The militia is in disarray, desertions have occurred. The 'Mollies have been active warning militia volunteers the folly of participating in a forced eviction. Some of them are spies from the North who get in the ear of the local volunteers, by that I mean desperate country men from Clare and Cork."

+

Paddy Gleason, an evicted cottier from South of Athenry had volunteered for the militia 6 months ago. When news was published of the need for volunteers for militia "activities" near Ennis, he was one of the first to sign up. In the past, his elderly Uncle Albert expressed many times how sorry he was that Paddy did not visit more often. His door was always open, and an invitation to stay with him was extended. Three days after his arrival at the home of his uncle, the Molly Maguires paid a visit in the dead of night. Excrement was thrown on Uncle Albert's front door. Printed sheets of paper blew around the streets. The rescued printing press that once belonged to Hugh Harrell was being put to good use in the catacombs of the Friary. The printed word told how Paddy Gleason and the militia planned to destroy the homes and farms of the O' Branigan clan. Paddy Gleason left Ennis two days later. In the interim no one would speak to him. The Irish turned their backs to him. Uncle Albert's stature as an elder statesman in the community suffered for months after Paddy left town. Other Irish volunteers suffered similar ridicule. They could not show their faces in pubs for fear accidents would occur. Spilled beer ended up on clothing. Chairs were pulled away as attempts to be seated ended up with a bruised rear end and no one appeared to notice, the perpetrator could have been one of several who stood nearby with pints in hand. Former friends, acquaintances, and neighbors did not smile or offer a hand.

Muldoon's examples of counter-intelligence along with the dark of night escapades of the Molly Maguires aimed at suspected collaborators led Rossa to consider recruiting those former militia volunteers. Those Irish just might want to redeem themselves to their neighbors and friends. "Do you have names?" Rossa asked. "Food and shelter we can provide to them for a short time. Well it is, if the march to the clan O' Branigan would be delayed if desertions continue, wouldn't you think? And if harassment by the Mollies is extended, the eviction plan could be cancelled altogether!" "No one should have to resort to living under a lean-to in a ditch," Muldoon said, handing Rossa a paper. "Four who are still here in Ennis, their names, Paddy Gleason returned to Loughrea, south of Athenry. "The poor lad was humiliated by friends of his uncle." Rossa's fingers tapped the table top. He stood up, so suddenly the bench wobbled. With hands in his pockets he paced, four steps, four steps back to the bench.

"On the 'morrow the weapons will be delivered by the fishmongers. O'Connell looked them over, but they have not been tested. Time it is...on the 'morrow a trip to the clan hillside will determine if the men are willing to defend what they have."

+

Flynn woke in the darkness, his hand searched for the brass knob on the lamp. A quarter turn allowed enough light to see Devon in his nightshirt on the loft ladder. *What noise did I make?* Flynn thought as he watched his yawning son rub the sleep out of his eyes. A sleeping Margaret remained curled up, her arms closed around a feather pillow. "Can I go with you Father?" Often, Flynn left before the morning chores leaving Devon to complete the morning routine. This day's journey to the lake would not begin until the sun rose over the eastern hills. "First our daily duties to attend, the Guernsey, pigs and chickens, after chores your mother and I will talk about it." "Mary Margaret can gather eggs and feed the chickens, father." Flynn stared at his pouting son. There was not a chance Devon's request would be honored. A hazardous mission was in store for Flynn and Donal Foley. If, by chance Margaret would let him go, Flynn would overrule her. She was not been told of the primary reason for Flynn's trip to Ennis. Devon's face mirrored disappointment. "Mother will not let me go, my lessons can wait, can't they Father?" Devon's pleading question and the anguished, wide eyed look on his face made Flynn hesitate for just a heartbeat. Devon was still a child mature for his age still three or four from the young man Flynn envisioned him to be, a man in the image of Neil Howe who Devon looked at as an older brother. Today was Neil Howe's wedding day.

"You know better Devon," Flynn said with a look that admonished his son. "You are charged with the safety of your mother and sister when you travel to the town for the wedding."

PREPARATIONS

Kneeling in the damp grass Neil Howe wiped the drops of sweat from his forehead. He had no need to hurry as his future was to change in the mid-afternoon hours. It was morning and two hours remained before the sun reached its zenith. The soon to be bridegroom paused to rest while watching his wife to be tying colorful ribbons together, a festive addition to the scene. Hours away from a life changing event Neil Howe stretched the rope taunt with one hand while the other removed the peg from between his teeth. His fingers searched for the hammer to drive the stake to secure the fourth corner of the tent. Tonight, there would be no need to tiptoe down the hall to his love Silé, and likewise she would not fear being caught for doing the same. After he combed his hair and changed his shirt to satisfy his Mother's demand, they both would be transported to the cathedral in Peter Howe's elegant carriage. Frantic activity surrounded him as preparations raced to completion. Mother Martha was in her glory. She walked from site to site, hands on her hips, pointing, shouting instructions, happy to finally realize her dream of a union and eventual grandchildren. Unknown to her, that event was already decided and would occur much sooner than expected. She was in charge and her future daughter-in-law could do nothing but nod and smile, and if Silé was asked for her opinion, or her approval, her answer did not matter. Her future Mother-In-Law would smile apologetically and follow up with "I thought it best" her reason for disregarding Silé' s wish which was of little concern to the soon to be bride. She was amused at the fuss and bother taken by Neil's mother not having been a witness to any wedding other than a union conducted by a Dooley clan leader. Travelers had little time for religious activities. Silé busied herself tying colorful ribbons to the top of tent stakes. Earlier, Neil helped to erect three of them on the lawn in the front of the cathedral steps. When Father Tom met with Neil and Silé, he indicated his wedding theme would be *One Step at a Time.* Guests could escape inclement weather and still be witness to the ceremony as one end of each tent was open to the cathedral entrance, closed to the wedding party. A table was placed in the center of the tents to serve as a buffet for foodstuffs for 25 guests who were invited to witness the event. A small table covered with oil cloth was reserved for the bride's pie, a traditional addition mainly for eligible young women. Young girls were often included dependent on what trinkets were to be found. Martha Howe had provided the baker with trinkets, rings, thimbles and coins to be baked inside the pie. Each item had a special meaning, and when found by eligible young ladies, emotions would range from happiness to sadness, and for some good fortune and long life. All in jest, laughter was usually the result when each item was found. The young priest who arrived in Killarney two days earlier was ministering to the sick inside the future house of worship. He arrived by carriage directly to the Arbutus hotel where, after securing a room, sought directions from the desk clerk. Father Tommy Mullally knocked on the door of the Howe residence to introduce himself, however briefly before he left to walk to the cathedral. Within a few hours after his arrival he expressed disbelief at the appalling condition of several of the children who had reached the state where no amount of food would prevent the inevitable journey from this horrible existence to the next. When Neil and his bride to be arrived after walking hand in hand to where another world existed, a world of soup kettles, sickness and sorrow, their conversation ended. Silé squeezed his hand. Their eyes found Kincade with the new priest at his side who was busy cutting up additions to the next batch of soup. The vicar Kincade, leaned on a blackthorn cane, bent over with his other gnarled and calloused hand holding a ladle. Neil's purpose was to let Kincade know that excess food left after the ceremony was his to be used to feed the hungry, and to reinforce their original invitation. The vicar saw them approach.

"Patrick, please come to the wedding, I would, and Neil would be pleased," Silé said, her hand went to his holding the knobby stick for support. "We have a seat reserved for you Patrick," Neil added. "The line at the kettle will be shorter. Your presence won't be missed for a short time. You will see what food is left for your use." "Bless you young Neil, 'me good leg and 'me gimpy one will take me to my seat. Bless you Silé Dooley, a brave young woman you are without fear to mingle with the sick and dying. Pleased I am to honor your kind request."

Neil and his future wife returned to the front of the building. Deliveries were arriving, and a wagon driven by Margaret O'Connell stopped under one of the large oaks on the grounds. Martha Howe started to run to the wagon but stopped when she saw her son returning.

"I have been looking for you Neil, the O'Connell's are here, and time it is for you and Silé to prepare. Margaret, will you come with us back to the house?" Greeting and best wishes were quickly exchanged. Silé picked up her skirts turning with a shrug toward Neil before following behind Martha and the O'Connell wagon.

"I will be along shortly mother," Neil shouted. He turned away quickly to avoid any further requests. Relieved, he stopped to adjust his cap over unruly locks while he surveyed the stage before him. His eyes swept from left to right, suddenly caught by the lone figure standing midway up the cathedral steps. He groaned, recognizing the person as the new daughter of Fiona Farrell. It was eleven-year old Heather Anne. Neil's work at the livery was often interrupted by the appearance of Fiona Farrell's adopted daughter who followed him around, infatuated as only a girl of her age could be. Irish boys and girls too soon became a shadowy likeness of Irish men and women often to marry in their mid-teens. His hint to Fiona was recognized, but as a business woman not always could she assure compliance with the cautions she directed to her older daughter. Heather Anne grew up an orphan with survival skills and stealth she retained to escape from time to time to resurrect her fantasy. Heather Anne would often employ those skills to leave the Farrell Mercantile. Neil Howe started to teach her to ride. Her heart would flip-flop every time Neil put his hands around her waist to help her mount the older mare. She learned quickly, but his time was limited causing her a foot stomping pout when a lesson had to be cancelled. Her instructor taught her well, but Neil declined her request to ride the spirited stallion he recently purchased for the livery. Her eyes followed Neil's approach, unblinking and as Neil recognized, somewhat defiant. He was at a loss for words but decided to be forceful and parental in his choice.

"My dear Heather Anne you are alone! I hoped to see you and your sister and Miss Farrell who would help to seat our guests. 'Tis an important duty and I would be pleased if you would relay my wish to Fiona. She disregarded his unconvincing greeting. "Neil Howe...I missed you today... and yesterday. Could we go riding together? I enjoy it so much and we have never gone riding together don't you know." Neil had a solution. "We will go riding together with your sister and Miss Farrell. Sissy is old enough to learn so riding together to the countryside will be a lot of fun! Don't you think?" "But I wanted..." Neil interrupted. "I know what you want Heather Anne, but what I want is the company of you, Sissy and Fiona as soon as they can get here for the wedding! Neil's patience was being tested more so when Heather Anne started to shake her head, pouting before she left the steps in a rush without a glance in Neil's direction.

+

Mist still clung to the green and clouds obscured the sun trying to fight its way to prominence. Flynn pushed his way inside the cottage to be met by Margaret who held out a cup of tea.

"'Tis hot my husband," she warned as Flynn reached for the cup yanking his fingers away when he made contact. "Wise you are to use the cloth Margaret, our son tends to his black friend, and you are free for the day." Flynn took the cup surrounded by the cloth. Mary Margaret entered with her basket. "How many eggs this fine morn daughter of mine?" Margaret asked. Mary Margaret peered into the basket moving eggs aside to count. "We have 20 chickens and 14 eggs mother, chicken soup, chicken soup, cluck, cluck, cluck," she replied. Her head bounced up and down to imitate a hen, pecking grain from the ground. Smiles came, and Mary Margaret got a hug from her father. She knew what happened to hens that failed to lay eggs. Flynn told her; "Be patient my daughter, an egg may arrive on the 'morrow." Flynn smeared a hot biscuit with butter before he dripped a liberal amount of honey that began to run. Bacon sizzled in the pan as Devon entered hanging his cap on the peg next to the door. Margaret cracked two eggs alongside the bacon. "The smell came to my nose," Devon said using a fork to turn over the slices.

"A helpful son I have Flynn," Margaret said while disposing of the egg shells. "Will you be back here by nightfall Flynn?" Margaret asked while moving eggs and bacon to a plate. "We will be back here in time to relieve the Guernsey," she said. "I will be late in returning sometime after sunset. It will be dark so leave a lamp in the window, Margaret." And with that, and after a satisfying breakfast, Flynn exited the cottage with the shoulder bag containing water, biscuits and a thick slice of smoked ham. His thoughts may have centered on Margaret's trip into Killarney and the wedding to take place on the cathedral grounds. He likely would rather have attended the wedding, than to journey to Ennis as a weapons smuggler alongside a less than political activist as was Donal Foley. He would wish the newlywed couple well at his first opportunity.

WEDDING

Relieved to be free of the confines of Peter Howe's house, and the constant attention paid to them by a demanding mother, Neil and the future Mrs. Howe tried their best to converse between themselves while on their way to the ceremony in the elegant Peter Howe carriage. Back at the house his mother insisted that his shirt be buttoned to the neck. They didn't escape her instructions. Already the shirt's stiff collar chafed each time he turned his head to either his expectant wife or his mother who attended to Silé to the point of being overbearing. Neil could do nothing right but sit with his nervous hands folded on his lap. Martha Howe repeatedly interrupted their conversation when she saw need for a correction in hair or on the powdered nose of her future daughter-in-law. The wedding dress was a constant source of irritation for her. The multi-layered strips of pastel cloth would not stay in one place to her satisfaction. Shades of purple, pink, green and white over solid silk blew around with each small gust of wind. Silé' s only concern was quelled when she went to the mirror and stood sideways to judge the progress of her recent stealthy trip down the hall to Neil's bedroom. She found that her condition was safe from whispered comments by a few of Martha's acquaintances who were invited. Their arrival was welcomed by shouts of greeting, the rasp of a toe-tapping fiddle and the beat of the bodhran. Hands met hands as the couple raced toward the steps of the cathedral through a cheering gauntlet of well-wishers. To his chagrin Neil noticed someone who was silent. The pouty lips belonged to Heather Anne standing in front of Fiona Farrell. Her excited little sister radiating the opposite emotion smiled and waved as the bride and groom passed by. Neil and his new bride were finally able to smile and stopped to kiss to raucous cheers before they reached the padded step where they knelt to hear the beginning of the ceremony. Raised hands of the young priest quieted the gathering as Father Tommy Mullally welcomed everyone and gave a lengthy blessing. Heads bowed as they squirmed impatiently, but they listened, and then the voice of the priest, in the middle of a final prayer, slowed as if he was confused, and suddenly, after "give us this day" was heard, his strong voice suddenly grew silent. Murmurs began and when heads were raised, people left their seats. Martha Howe stood on her tip toes to see what was going on before she collapsed into a chair, waving a folding fan imprinted with pastel peacocks to cool the heat created by a disastrous event. All eyes shocked to see three, there were four counting the woman who sat on the ground holding a suckling infant to her bare breast while she raised something to her mouth from the table of refreshments. Neil and Silé 's eyes focused first on the wide eyed and speechless Father Mullally, then to the activity at the table. Being discovered, the three men and the woman decided to leave when Malachy Brandon left a tent to enforce their return to the rear of the cathedral. The woman with the infant child struggled to her feet staggering her way behind the three men. Their exit was met by the vicar. Patrick Kincade moved as fast as he could, using his cane to admonish the four hungry peasants, one with child, who decided to invade the wedding ceremony in the middle of a perfectly lovely summer afternoon. Neil and a wide-eyed Silé with her hand covering her mouth, was aghast at what she watched. Four hunger-crazed refugees from the countryside helped themselves before the invaders began their escape in the face of Malachy's urging. At that moment a message was conveyed to the soon to be married couple who turned to look at each other. Without a word they left the step and walked to the area where a butcher's helper stood turning the spit that held the roasting pig. Wrapped in cloth, the end of the spit was warm to Silé' s hand as she and Neil carried it around the steps in front of the tents full of wedding guests toward the rear of the cathedral. Stunned by what had just occurred, Malachy Brandon, the muscular blacksmith and forger of musket balls, along with his part time assistant, realized the need to hurry after the two who carried the roasted pig. Malachy's glance caught Fiona Farrell tending to Martha Howe who with help, regained her feet, stretching on her tip-toes to see what was going on. The disruption proved too much for her, as the sight of the bride and groom moving the roasted pig away caused her to collapse.

+

One by one, oil lamps flickered on as the purple shades of night enveloped the town. Too tired to read

Punch, an exhausted Martha Howe molded herself to the rocker built for her by her late husband Peter. Her lap was covered by her favorite quilt while she watched the activity on the street. Good intentions brought a recent edition of the English newspaper to the table next to her, but it lay untouched. The ornate whale oil lamp burned its light without any purpose. She watched as a rain free day and evening encouraged residents and visitors alike to stroll past her window up and down the boardwalks. Lovers sat on benches across the street gazing at the brilliance of the moon and into each other's eyes. She likely remembered her youth when she and Peter Howe enjoyed the light of the moon on a bench near the park entrance. Occasionally a carriage passed by the opened window with the lace curtain pulled aside. Her son and his new wife had excused themselves earlier, and the faint sounds she heard from above brought the hint of a smile to her lips. Noise from the nearby taverns caught her ears as revelers exited smoke filled pub rooms to the freedom and fresh air afforded by a mild rain free evening. Sight and sound, the feel of the knitting needle she rolled in her fingers, was comfort for her as her eyes grew heavy and her chin began to fall.

+

Miles away, at about the same time, Flynn O'Connell returned to his cottage after his initial foray as an arms smuggler for the cause of Irish freedom.

SUSPICION

Their conversation ceased. In the distance the bridge entrance they hoped not to be guarded was seen to be free of red uniforms holding rifle-muskets with fixed bayonets. A bit of comfort came to Donal Foley. However, diligence remained their first-priority as two sets of eyes searched the landscape beyond the bridge. To cross the river Fergus unimpeded was the first obstacle to overcome. Ahead of them was the rendezvous hidden away in the back streets and alleyways of County Clare's republican stronghold. Hoping not to recognize anyone for he himself would be recognized, a familiar face caught Donal's eye. The man stood watching their wagon with his hands in his pockets until recognition came to him. A hand was withdrawn to wave as Donal and Flynn passed on the other side of the street. A weak smile crossed Donal's lips and his hesitant wave was returned in recognition of a recently acquired buyer and his greeting. His hope not to be seen by anyone on this unusual day in Ennis was dashed. Flynn glanced at Donal when he saw the furtive wave he offered to the man on the boardwalk. "A friend, a foe, you appear troubled friend Donal," Flynn reasoned. Donal's attention shifted away from Flynn to behind them and then back again. "Aye Flynn, he follows behind on the other side of the boardwalk. Not well do I know the man. He buys our labors, but only twice have we met. Not wise it is to have him follow." Quickly, Flynn cast an eye to find the man who hurried his way.

"Rein in the horse Flynn. I know the way. Continue to our meeting place. I will secure new business for us." Donal grinned as he stepped down from the wagon seat. Flynn jumped down to tend to the horse and check the condition of the wagon and contents without being too obvious in his inspection of the wagon bed. The container of live fish was an addition at the last moment to provide more evidence of their purpose should they be stopped and questioned. All the while he watched Donal Foley's exit that would eventually result in a suspiciously chance meeting on the boardwalk with a man he barely knew.

Never had Donal Foley been placed in the unusual circumstance he was currently afforded. He accepted the challenge when he grinned at Flynn O'Connell as he stepped down from the wagon seat, pausing to use his forearm to wipe away the consternation that accumulated on his brow. At some point he would encounter his new customer and not be stopped by a uniform that exited a doorway or crossed the street from the other side. It seemed to him that Brit's were everywhere. In Donal's mind, every citizen was suspect to reveal his purpose. All of them would point fingers! "It's him, it's him," they would accuse when they pointed him out to the soldier. If the fellow really followed them his questions and Donal's answers were sure to become the subject of bar-room speculation should his answers not be forthright. If it were not just coincidence Donal was ready to supply a reasonable explanation for his visit, but would it be acceptable to an English informant? Out of his comfort, the lake shore fog in the morning, the smell of the lake and the cry of the loons, Donal entered a different world, a world of fear, suspicion and hope. He stepped up to a crowded boardwalk where he had to move quickly to avoid school children who dodged in and out between adults. They reveled in the short freedom given them from tedious studies. A break for lunch did not appear to be main purpose of most of the young students who chased each other in between the carts and carriages on the busy street. Others on their knees bounced a rubber ball in the middle of the boardwalk. In awe, they would move when a red coated uniform approached. The wagon with Flynn directing the horse through the mayhem on the street became lost from Donal's view. He watched but no one appeared to follow.

"Aye Foley it is! Sure! It was you I saw. A fine day don't you know," the cheerful voice came from the next storefront as the owner of the voice with his finger held aloft, made his way, sidestepping young people, toward the recipient of his identifying shout. His welcoming demeanor caused Donal to relax just a bit. He smiled in return to the man's greeting. "Aye, we are blessed with a lovely day," Donal responded with a glance to the heavens. The man followed his glance skyward. "Sing his praises. I am Thomas Tillson, Foley. You have product to sell today?" He stepped down to the street. Donal thought for a moment before he answered, considering whether Tillson's "sing his praises" comment was an indication of his political or his religious persuasion, or both. Donal lied when he said his driver was to deliver the catch and that he was marketing his wares. Side by side they walked choosing relative safety of a busy street over the inattention of young students who burned accumulated energy on the boardwalk, often to the chagrin of matronly ladies. "No fear should you have, Foley. In this republican village the Irish who collaborate with the Crown are well known and I am not one of them!" Silence followed, the only sound being the "click, click," bouncing of a cobble being kicked by the toe of a boot. Tillson stopped in mid-stride, his hand grasped the forearm of Donal. "Go about your business Foley," an evident dismissal of his attempt to learn more about the unscheduled visit of the fishmonger. "Will you be calling again on our fair town?" "On our regular day Tillson, as early as possible, and our thanks to you for your business," Donal replied. Tillson departed, returning to the boardwalk now a safer place as the children had suddenly disappeared. Donal watched him depart, retracing his steps to the location of their first encounter. When he was out of sight Donal headed for the rendezvous where Flynn waited.

Four storefronts were ahead, three of them brightly painted, the last the drab unpainted building, the business place of the grain merchant who was to receive the smuggled weapons. Flynn brought the wagon to a stop and jumped from the seat. He surveyed the area for a moment while tending to the horse before resuming a tentative move ahead. Directing the horse to the back of the building a large door on an iron track started to grind its way, pulled open by two hands. Fully open now, one of the hands motioned Flynn to come forward. Flynn flicked the reins and entered the dimness of the interior flanked on either side by large bins most of which appeared to be empty. The darkness increased as the owner of the hands became a silent shadow that pushed the rusty tracked door closed. The silent shadow approached Flynn with an arm outstretched.

Donal's hurried steps took him to the back street where ahead of him was his rendezvous. Not seeing Flynn or the wagon, he cautiously approached, his eyes wary of those eyes that would sound an alarm, but those suspicious eyes were only in his mind. The wide wooden door on the back of the building was closed. Donal walked around to the front and entered through the front door with the sign above reading, **GRAINS, HAY, STRAW,** Peter Michael Quinlan, Prop. "Flynn, I am here," he shouted into the void while he walked to another door. Pushing through, he saw several young men and Flynn who were discussing the merits of the weapons removed from the hidden compartment in the Foley wagon. Flynn hurried toward Donal with his hand on the back of a big-bellied man who turned out to be the proprietor Quinlan. "Friend Quinlan pleased to introduce you to the wagon's owner Donal Foley," Flynn said. Hand met hand as eyes examined the face in front. "I am a merchant of the lakes Quinlan, wary of the deed..." Donal said, as his eyes left the face of his host to see that the young men seen earlier were suddenly and quietly gone along with the muskets they held.

"There are many others like you, and your friend with the name," Quinlan said. "I am a receptacle, a point of distribution. 'Tis done quickly as you see," he motioned to the area behind where minutes ago men had stood with weapons in their grasp. He walked to the wagon leaning with both hands on the wagon bed. "You will be asked again you know, an ingenious way to hide the contents," his palm slapped the wagon bed. "Your young friend Rossa is another who should not lose the step that keeps him ahead of those who wish harm to their own citizens." Flynn left Donal's side to walk to the massive door. He used both hands to pull, before pushing the door open to allow sunlight to brighten the interior. He looked to the sky. "Sol bends to the west horizon Donal. We should return."

+

After much pacing back and forth, and after many remnants of Woodbines littered the floor, he made the decision. D'Arcy McGee would meet with Neil Howe and the Foley brothers. "Godspeed!" Their whispered word was heard by Rossa as he adjusted his shoulder bag. With his back to them he raised a clenched fist in the air, pumping up and down. His trek to the village of the hill people began with a sendoff seen only by Vincent Mulcahy, Danny Kissane and D'Arcy McGee.

WEDDING NIGHT

"Your mother is sleeping in her chair Neil Howe, and what we do here on this night has been her dream, months away from being satisfied. Neil my love, you will be a father!" He knew what was to be, but Neil's attention was elsewhere. "Again! I heard, the sound, I did hear it Silé, didn't you?"" Neil said glancing to the window, the breeze moving the sheer ever so slightly. "Clink," Silé left his arms as Neil Howe raised himself on an elbow his eyes fixed on the window with the sheer curtain. "Clink," the sound came again causing Neil to throw the covers aside and leap from the bed. He hurried to the window propped open a few inches to allow the breeze to enter. Pulling the curtain aside not remembering his nakedness he scanned the street below. As he pulled aside the curtain a shadowy form caught his vision, the whiteness of an arm raised, apparently ready to heave another pebble. Suddenly, movement ceased, and the hand dropped the pebble. The hand went to her mouth, her eyes wide in shock or guilt. Neil saw the hands grab skirts and a hasty exit was made by the girl Neil recognized as Heather Anne, the adopted daughter of Fiona Farrell. Neil released the curtain but realized it was not in time for the girl to capture his aroused image in the dimly lit room above her.

"What do you see my love?" Silé asked, moving from under the covers to sit on the side of the bed ready to follow her new husband to the window. Neil turned and walked back the few steps to sit by her side.

"We have a young person who disagrees with our union," Neil said. "It was Heather Anne who I saw below, and who saw me in the window I'm sure of it." Silé pulled a light blanket around her shoulders. "Shut the window Neil, Heather Anne is a mischievous little girl on the edge of young womanhood. I remember the time myself and had no one to help me." Neil did her bidding while he listened removing the polished piece of blackthorn that served as a prop, his eyes looking for movement on the street. "Hurry back to me love. She is fortunate to have Miss Farrell to guide her, but now I have to cope with a younger female who has seen what only I have had the seldom pleasure...to see," she said, grabbing Neil around the neck and pulling, pulling him to a prone position on the bed, giggling as she struggled. Her lips and teeth found his ear lobe. "Ouch, a vicious woman you are Silé Dooley," he said while enjoying her struggle. "Silé Howe it is to you, Sir Neil my knight, or Silé Dooley-Howe, or should I change the Gaelic to the English and become Sheila Howe? We should have a talk with Fiona Farrell my love or is it you desire the attraction of an infatuated young girl to your charms," she whispered before raising a leg to straddle her husband who pulled her down to him. Both hands were behind her head when he kissed her on the lips. "My dear Silé, in three or four years our little Heather Anne will have grown-up. Should the desire between us wane..." Startled by his tomfoolery her tongue found his cheek and then his ear.

"You will NOT have the opportunity to explore a new relationship with an in-experienced woman my Neil," she said as she raised herself above him.

THE TREK

It appeared to Rossa that the entire population of Ireland was leaving for destinations known only to them. Carts, wagons, ragtag people on foot passed him by. Rossa was the only one headed inland, the others seen on hilltops in the distance all headed west, and Rossa could only assume the shores of the Atlantic was their destination. Ireland was bleeding its people. "Rossa, 'me boyo are ye' daft?" The voice came from the driver of an approaching wagon loaded with crates, chests and furniture. Next to the driver sat his wife and walking alongside were three children, the oldest appeared to be in his early teens. The leather in his hand was attached to the neck of the cow that grazed when the wagon's driver stopped alongside Rossa. "You should come with us lad. Three years of torture have made the decision for the Brennan's. All we have is aboard. We will sell the animal for passage when we arrive. Our cottage is gone." Jimmy Brennan, a cottager known to Rossa lamented, as a tear made its way down the cheek of a 32 year- old wrinkled face. Rossa walked to the side of the wagon and grabbed the forearm of his friend Brennan. "Godspeed and fare thee well to you and the fair Colleen," Rossa said, tipping his cap in her direction, "I have years ahead before such a decision faces this Paddy friend Jimmy." Rossa stepped away as the wagon wheels began to roll. He watched for a moment before he resumed his trek to the village of the hill people.

While Rossa watched the wagon grow small in the distance, George Brewster waited for the arrival of the last of his army of peasant hating enforcers from the north. He had run out of patience with the commander of the militia who he felt was foot dragging, not interested in helping enforce the eviction process wanted by this unscrupulous landlord. Some of those northern hooligans took no pay from Brewster, taking pleasure in exercising their hatred of those who pledged their allegiance to the Pope in Rome. They did not care or know the hill people had no religious persuasion to the Methodists, Presbyterians, or Catholics. Few of the eviction gang had weapons other than clubs made from blackthorn, the end of which was a burl or knot beneath of which was decorated with orange ribbon. They milled about the cavernous barn, twirling their sticks, playing cards and drawing pints from the barrel Brewster had brought in. Wallace Stroud, one of Brewster's army of thugs pointed with pride at the hair embedded in the knot of his club used to bash in the head of a poor cottier farmer. He was an expert at fashioning a noose to tighten around the neck of an unfortunate Irishman. A Scotch-Irish brute of a man, Stroud bragged he was named after William Wallace. As truth is to fiction, the history of Wallace Stroud was a contradiction, a misnomer of the honored name of the Scottish hero William Wallace.

The Ennis road led Rossa to the settlement of Tulla, half way between Ennis and Clonie in an area the English called the Baronry of Bunratty. In the dark village, Rossa saw two candles or lamps that illuminated the windows of two of the five buildings that made up the tiny village. The darkness enabled him to commandeer a bench outside an unidentified building with no light evident on the inside, however the scent of a turf fire caught his nose and the heat from the fire he could not see radiated through the thin outer walls. His shoulder bag furnished a flaky biscuit with slivers of smoked salmon tucked inside. He curled up in the blanket that was rolled and tied around his waist, thankful to be dry and out of the night breeze. Using the shoulder bag and its contents as a pillow, he soon was asleep with half his mission of mercy yet to go. Rossa's eyes opened to the sound of clicking steps on the boardwalk and a grunting sound that caused him to turn his head to see the snout of a pig, staring at him only inches away, grunting its irritation that food was not in sight of its eyes. A stare down lasted for only the time necessary to take a breath, and with a toss of a head the black and white sow lost interest, leaving the boardwalk for the dirt street. A rooster crowed. The inhabitants of Tulla would soon be awake. Rossa worried that today or the next day would be the one the militia captain chose to march on to the O' Branigan village. He gathered the blanket together, tied it around his waist and adjusted the shoulder bag. Oh, for a cup of tea he must have thought. He walked into daybreak out of the east, and away from the unbending hospitality of an empty wooden bench in a sleepy village, a blemish on the carpet of majestic green pasture fields, a blemish as would be the intrusion of a

40- year old Dublin whore seating herself in the front pew at Mass celebrated by the archbishop.

The blue gray of dawn was broken, but the maddening sun teased, yet to appear over the crest of the hills behind the woman named Noreen. Her day always began at the first hint of sunlight. She would have an hour before her children, exhausted from the previous days' activities would stir, awake and hungry. There was very little food in her hut, but for her, leftover porridge heated, with berries she picked the day before would have to try to satisfy her three children. A crust of bread..., she retained the ability to bake bread, and tea made from the bark of a tall bush on the upper slope would do little to quell the rumbling in her empty stomach. While the water heated, and the children slept, she pulled aside the curtain shielding all but a ray of sun finding its way inside the hut. She looked at the back of her hand on the curtain. The hand was wrinkled, the veins stood out, her nails were rough and in need of a trim. She raised her left hand. It bore the same evidence. Bowing her head, she stepped outside into the beginning of another day. Her husband, he was called "Danny O" by most of the clansmen, had left the hillside, his wife and children in search of work and food. He was one of three other O' Branigans' who were desperate to find work to purchase the grain they would need until the potato harvest could begin. Rare earth meant that every available spot of grass covered ground between the rocks on the hillside was planted with potatoes.

The women of the clan inspected the plantings daily. Today would be no exception. Noreen lifted her skirts and started up the hillside being careful to avoid a nasty fall. A few of the rocks were flat enough to serve as stepping stones, allowing her to pause to turn around and look back down at the line of huts with threads of smoke emanating from the hole in each roof. She saw no movement. This morning she was the first to venture out into the cool early air. Her purpose resumed as she stepped from rock to rock, and soon she was surrounded by the plants. Comprehension came seconds later. Hands that covered her mouth did little to stifle her scream of agony that echoed down the hillside. The early potato planting had wilted overnight, covered with black spots, the same symptoms that befell the crop in the previous two years. Noreen O' Branigan collapsed to the ground in agonized disbelief. Her wails resulted in an eruption of movement from the cottages and huts below her. Curtains were pulled aside, heads poked out. Half doors on two of the cottages swung back and forth as her screams continued unabated. Clansmen and women scrambled up the hillside toward her, and when they reached near enough to see they stopped in shocked disbelief at what some thought as the devil's work. Keiran O'Boyle, who lived in a nearby hut, helped the sobbing woman Noreen to her feet.

"Hold to my arm wife of Danny O," he said as he steadied her on her feet. "Danny O is back you know. In my hut he sleeps, fearing your wrath should you see him in his unworthy condition." O'Boyle struggled to walk down the path with her weight pressing on an arm that had lost strength. He had not eaten since the previous day when a clan woman who practiced the art of alchemy offered them edible roots and greens picked from the valley. Her gnarled hands and wrinkled fingers clutched a ladle of her fare from a steaming pot enticing watchers to sample. A hungry Keiran O'Boyle was the only observer who stepped forward.

"Surely, you do not jest," she said. "Danny O is back?" Her face turned to his for an indication of the truth. Keiran shook his head. His eyes met hers. "What you and I have seen is enough. The clan must leave this village for I fear the scourge will be followed by another." Wiping her tears away with the sleeve of his shirt, he helped her passage back down the hill. He knew what the return of the scourge meant. Very little food was left. Few coins stretched his drawstring bag. He was one year in arrears on rent on his rocky acre of land, and it did not matter how unjust was the language of the lease agreement he signed. He did not know. They did not care. They did whatever they wanted to do. He knew that eviction was imminent. He remembered the loose papers that tumbled down the lane in the breeze, enticing children to chase, giving notice to the villagers who already knew.

"Gather your children. Take with you what you can carry, I will do the same." Not until they reached the lane at one end of the settlement, did they notice the gathering at the far end of the village. Donovan Rossa had arrived. He stood on a potato crate talking quietly to several villagers who stopped to hear what the stranger had to say. He waited for more to arrive silently thanking the sun for its warming brilliance on a cloudless morning. The women of the village gathered around while the skeptics, the men, stood at the back. Rossa held one of the eviction notices in his hand. "There is no need for you to know my name. I am here to provide a warning to you. You are in grave danger if you stay here. But if you want to stay here you must fight for your right to stay." Keiran O'Boyle and Noreen arrived and heard his statement. "Fight with what, young lad? We have little left to fight for, little energy. We just came from the hillside where the potatoes were planted." He turned toward the hill and pointed. Heads nodded, sobbing was heard. "The blight has returned. I have no food and no money to pay the rent. I will leave this hillside. I have no reason to fight. There is nothing left for me, or for us."

"Save yourself!" shouted the clan woman who practiced alchemy and other mysterious rites that kept children away from her hut on the crest of the hillside. Rossa heard the murmurs of agreement among the women who stood only an arms-length from him. Rossa quickly realized how futile his effort was. The women outnumbered the men who had either deserted their wives or were off to the cities looking for work. The men who remained were not the type Rossa hoped to find. Out of the corner of his eye sudden movement turned his attention to the man who emerged from a hut, coughing, leaning over with his hands on his knees in obvious distress. Noreen O' Branigan saw her husband for the first time in weeks. A decision was made. Rossa realized an attempt to coerce and cajole the men of the clan to disrupt and discourage a group of Militia by throwing rocks was not going to work. The Militia was comprised of English supporters and indigent Irish who joined for survival which meant at least one decent meal. They paid the price for their action against neighbors and friends. They were shunned, ignored, and ridiculed in earshot of others. Altercations between friends and neighbors brewed animated political discussions in pub rooms, and on pulpits of churches no matter the religious preference. Rossa, of course, was not aware of the decision made by George Brewster to take the eviction into his own hands, to march to the beehive huts and cottages of the clan O' Branigan. The eviction party was on the way. "Where should we go?" A man in the back of the group asked. "For those of you who wish to follow me I will take you to Ennis by way of the villages along the way." In the back of his mind he considered the possibility of meeting the Militia on the way, if, by chance, they chose this very day. Meaning he would need to leave the Ennis road for the route likely taken by the debt collectors, a route that would provide a perfect spot for an ambush. A few pints and a set of loose lips belonging to a militia member revealed the route the evictors would take. *A foolhardy thought* Rossa immediately discarded as he watched hill people hurry back to their huts. A few did not. Rossa approached the four women he noticed who were in arm waving whispered conversation occasionally ending with a vehement exhortation. The woman named Siobhan removed herself from the group to face Rossa.

"We have...their weapon," she said pointing toward her hut. All heads turned as the husband of Siobhan emerged carrying a musket in two hands, the barrel pointed at the sky above. "We could make the Irish run back to their wife," Siobhan said. "We have their powder and round, but not one O' Branigan knows the way to fire the weapon," Liam O' Branigan said, with resignation evident in his voice.

DEFENSIVE MEASURE

Unknown to Rossa, a meeting was held in the lamp lit rear room of the friary. One by one they came, and a knock on the massive door resulted in the creak of rusty hinges. Supporters of Irish freedom were greeted by a hooded figure who pointed the way with a nod of his head. Cautious they were, fearful of discovery, but were unseen from the street by suspicious eyes. Danny Kissane was the Ennis informant who overheard the one with the loose lips who revealed the route and the day the march to the hill people would begin, Friday next. McGee and his recruit Tom Steele, quickly dispatched runners to notify the young men who had visited the grain merchant Quinlin days before. One of the runners was 13-year-old Sean Killmorgan. Those contacted came together from different directions on that Friday to meet out of sight of the town. Four of the 13 carried muskets. 15 were contacted by the runners. The missing two were in jail, suspected of being members of the Rockites. Their march, hours ahead of Bingham's minions, took them to the entrance of a granite canyon. A wide ditch, created by time and rain, allowed a shallow stream to fill a depression. Torches carried by three of the volunteers lit the rocky walls of the wide ravine. Eerie shadows were cast by the flickering flame of the torches causing superstitious Irish eyes to search for the demon lurking in their mind. McGee stopped the march, waiting until their attention refocused on him. The quiet was deafening until the sound of granite bouncing down the ravine wall attracted his eyes. Out of the darkness walked Flynn O'Connell, his rifle musket strapped over his shoulder. With Flynn O'Connell at his side, McGee's arm waved them forward. He relayed his plan to intercept the Bingham militia. Flynn offered his military experience gained in the French Foreign legion.

"A welcome addition you are, O'Connell. McGee thanked him for his suggestions to their strategy to counter Bingham's eviction havoc on the clan O' Branigan. Bingham's route would take his collection of hired thugs and murderers through the very ravine, the site to be used by McGee to conduct a clandestine counter move a mile away from the Ennis road. Minutes later they emerged from the trap and disbursed to either side of the rocky granite behind them. McGee sent Paddy Rinn to act as a lookout to warn them of the approach of the Bingham militia. Paddy accepted a much safer assignment often saying he would rather wait awhile before meeting St. Peter. He saw enough death floating in the waters of the loch where he cast his lines. The sun peaked over the horizon, and the wait began.

McGee's strong hands gripped the shoulders of Tommy Fealey. His thumbs found collar bones under the skin. "Tommy Fealey! You are to keep your stick at the ready if our objective decides to test our strength and resolve! Ready yourself to assist if one of ours is under duress. 'Wack' him with the knobby end of your stick!" The sod cutter was known to Flynn O'Connell who knew Tommy's allegiance was not to the crown. He was recruited, as were the two sons of Conor Kennedy, who had participated in the firing of Lord Biltmore's cattle barn. A reunion of sorts took place when the Kennedy brothers realized Flynn O'Connell, the former French Foreign Legionnaire, had joined them. McGee walked the length of the ravine, up one side and down the other, issuing instructions to his ragtag group of volunteers, most of whom carried the venerable shillelagh. The four with weapons were instructed by Tom Steele, who was the former bodyguard of Daniel O'Connell. Tom was proficient with the "Brown Bess" a name given to a dependable rifle-musket. Tom Steele sat on a stone surrounded by his student revolutionaries who ranged in age from 17 to 43.

"Aye, Tom Steele, not a military strategist am I, but what you say about placing our musket men at the far end of the ravine, two in front, and two behind? The first two fire at the line approaching and reload, the second two fire while the first are reloading?" McGee's face was a question mark waiting for an answer. "Accuracy is a challenge for our boys, firing at a line of our enemy has a greater chance of hitting a target, more effective than firing at one man from the side," McGee continued. Steele's forehead wrinkled in thought while he processed what McGee offered. "But our boys will be above and firing downward, and sure we don't know their strength in weapons, do we?" Steele asked. "Aye, a good stratagem you have offered, but I suspect they have as many weapons as we do," McGee speculated. "We should concentrate on the militia with the weapons first," Steele interjected before McGee had a chance to finish. As their conversation continued, the lack of experience in conducting a military ambush with young men barely old enough to shave, farmers who had more experience with a pitchfork or a plowshare became frightfully evident. *Why have I chosen this path,* Rossa thought as he looked at the willing faces ready to do his bidding. Flynn listened and offered a strategy both Steele and McGee brought to the attention of the volunteers who carried the muskets. "After you have taken a shot, move to a new protected location. Their confusion is to our advantage. They will be reloading, but you will not be where you once were! While they reload, we can attack them with our sticks and chunks of granite!" While the instructions continued, Flynn followed up with a weapons inspection resulting in one less musket available. Hours later they continued to wait. The sun moved too quickly from the protection of stormy gray clouds to its rendezvous with the western horizon.

DEPARTURE

Rossa carefully examined the musket while villagers stood around watching. His fingers touched searching for imperfections. Eyes and ears were part of his scrutiny of every working part, tested and approved until his attention shifted. When he asked for the powder and shot, O' Branigan hurried back to his hut and emerged holding a drawstring bag and a curved object that resembled a ram's horn. Onlookers gathered around to witness what Rossa prepared to do, anticipating what they assumed would be the power they, the hill people, might hold in their favor. Watching his every move while conversing with one another. Rossa recognized their interest, and the interest of the woman Siobhan, the wife of Liam. Rossa paused after each important movement of his hands. Excited conversations among the watchers began again, soon to stop as they watched him continue. Rossa replaced the wooden rod under the barrel and rose to his feet. The clan parted to allow the man with the gun to walk to the center of the lane between their cone shaped huts and stone walled cottages. He held the weapon in both hands with the barrel pointed upright until he reached a spot in the center of the lane. Nothing but a palate of blue sky dotted with fluffy popcorn shaped clouds appeared in front of him as far as the eye could see. A dog raced toward him ready to attack his ankle but veered off barking with his muzzle in the air. Rossa raised the musket fitting it tightly to his shoulder. The barrel did not waiver. Villagers clenched fists holding their breath in anticipation as his finger tightened on the trigger. Some of the women turned their backs. Others covered their ears. Rossa squeezed the trigger. "Click" came the disappointing sound as the weapon failed to fire. The hill people who had gathered around exhaled and looked at one another. Not to be denied after his thorough but unprofessional examination, he again raised the weapon to his shoulder, and with an explosion of powder and the resonating sound, the musket released its captive. The people of the knocks were in awe. Rossa stood before them watching their reaction. His hands gripped the musket barrel, the stock resting on the ground. The weapon provided a means of support as his eyes moved from one face to another until his eyes me those of the woman Siobhan who stepped forward. Her hand reached out and closed around the musket, her eyes seriously solemn. "Teach me," she said, pulling the musket toward her forcing Rossa to release his grip. Thoughts raced through Rossa's mind. *The weapon did belong to the woman and her husband.*

"Teach me," she repeated, lifting the weapon to her shoulder imitating Rossa as she squinted down the barrel her thumb pulling back on the hammer. She looked at Rossa, her eyes questioning, waiting for an answer while placing the stock on the ground. Her husband Liam watched the proceedings from the door of their hut before he disappeared inside. He emerged laboring, with a small trunk in both hands. Rossa was positive Siobhan O' Branigan would not have the opportunity to ever need to fire the musket in anger. He knelt in front of her to relay to her his limited knowledge of the firing procedure. She watched, listened and asked questions. Rossa repeated his instructions then watched her prepare the musket for firing. Satisfied, he saw her replace the rod under the barrel. He rose to his feet. "You must hold the stock tightly against your shoulder," Rossa advised as they both walked to the center of the lane where Rossa had stood before. He took the musket from her to demonstrate. At that very moment Liam pushed his way through the cloth covered entrance to the hut. He stopped to watch his wife working with the musket. With obvious intent, he started toward them, his demeanor exhibited displeasure at her interest in the workings of the firearm. When he reached them, he took her aside speaking softly in the Gaelic dialect used by most of the clan people. Rossa did not understand, but easily recognized his unhappiness as the two walked toward their hut. She held the weapon in her left hand, the stock bouncing up and down as they walked. Suddenly, Rossa realized the musket had been readied to fire. He ran after the two, hands extended to reach for the weapon before a jolt triggered a tragic accident.

"Siobhan! Stop!" Rossa shouted, and as he did, she turned with the musket now in both hands, its barrel pointed in Rossa's direction. Suddenly, smoke erupted, the sound reaching the ears of astonished hill people. The weapon discharged. The weapons recoil tore the musket out of her hands. Siobhan O' Branigan saw Rossa flinch from the whiz of a musket ball needing only a few inches to reach an unintended target. Out of breath when he reached the wide-eyed woman, he grabbed her shoulders shaking her gently. Liam O' Branigan stood in shocked silence.

"'Tis me' own fault, so sorry I am, are you well now?" Rossa asked, peering into her eyes that blinked recognition. And then came the release of breath held for what must have seemed to her, an infinite amount of time. Her husband recovered to place his arm around her shoulders relieving Rossa the need to reassure someone who just experienced a stunning emotional trauma. Both her husband and Rossa were rewarded with the hint of a smile and a nod. "I am well...what was the cause?" "The weapon has seen years of use. The mechanisms became worn from the effects of metal on metal. Care should be taken. Again, sorry I am to both of you." Rossa picked up the musket handing it to Liam his hand reluctant to accept. "Had I not..." Liam began, only to be interrupted by Rossa. "No need is there to worry yourself, 'tis well no one was hurt, and a lesson was learned by all," Rossa said. "I fear they are coming. Gather your possessions. To stay could mean death."

THE FISHERWOMAN

On the sand she waited. Warm raindrops slowed and then stopped prompting Sally to move to where the lake met the beach. Her eyes pierced the lightening dark of dawn as water lapped over her toes. She took a step backwards while her ears listened for the sound of oars cutting through the quiet surface of Neptune's domain. For Sally, sight and sound dominated an awakening of a new day, its birth heralded by the distant celebration of the sea birds coming awake. The tea water was hot, and the biscuits awaited a slathering of honey or butter by two fishermen, one who had promised himself to her in their future union. Three days had passed since her arrival at the shore cottage of Donal and her love Brendan Foley. She quickly found it to be an awkward arrangement. Her second day found her attempting to create order out of the disorder two brothers allowed to accumulate in the cottage. Now, after the third day the brothers and Sally Donaghy were becoming more comfortable with her intrusion. She attended to his injury each day thankful for the skilled hands of Flynn O'Connell who sewed the wound shut. They promised to make her a fisherwoman. About to turn away from the day's awakening, the sound of voices reached her ears. The brothers Foley were in a jovial mood singing a song about the sea that brought laughter to those who heard Brendan sing the song after his third pint at Clancy's pub. The seaman's song ended abruptly when Brendan stood to alert his future bride. His elbow was hooked around the mast. His huge hands were cupped around his mouth.

"We are coming, Sally love," he shouted through the gray dawning air. "Biscuits and bacon and a mug of hot tea I hurry to find waiting," he threatened, and then came his laugh. Sally could hear the oars as the boat drew closer. She stepped into the water ready to grab the bow of the boat. "Anxious for your return I have been, Mr. Foley..., the bacon is crisp" she said as the bow of the boat made its appearance. "Does a brawny fisherman love the loch more than me?" She asked while standing in the water with her hands on her hips, her face bore the ruse of her displeasure. All her strength did little to beach the boat as Brendan splashed into the water. He paid no attention to her question, but said, "Aye Sally love, the smells draw me to the fire and the tea, our harvest can wait!" With one arm surrounding her he gave a massive tug that made Donal lose his balance falling over the side into a foot of water. A whispered comment to her ear made her smile while a dripping Donal walked past, stoic, without comment.

Donal Foley reluctantly learned to accept his older brother's decision to wed a 22-year old bar maid. Before her decision to join the brothers at their cottage, he and Brendan had many near arguments over what Donal considered a mere infatuation, and that given time, Brendan would come to his senses. Some of the brother to brother discussions were held in Clancy's pub. Donal knew Sally recognized the reason for more than one vigorous nose to nose discussion, and she likely overheard at least some of his objections. Her knowing smile told Donal his overheard objections had not the priest's whisper of the penance required being followed by sinner or saint. In Donal's mind that little curtain covered door had closed. However, during the fourth day with a woman in their midst swayed Donal's opinion of her. Three days of observing her willingness to do whatever she could gained Donal a new respect for Sally Donaghy who didn't shy away from the labor of building the stone walls for the expansion of the Foley cottage.

MARCH TO ENNIS

Rossa hurried from one hut to another helping the women who were without a man gather meager belongings. A well to do clan member who lived in a stone cottage loaded furniture into a wagon. Neighbors sought him out asking if he had the room for a prized possession they could not carry. Children played as they did before, oblivious to the activity of their parent or parents when both were present. Sweat dotted Rossa's brow, and he often paused to listen and to watch for activity in the knocks below them. At the end of the lane a thin plume of white smoke drifted skyward. Smoke emanated from a crumbling thatched roof cottage, the habitat of an old woman, her face, her scrawny neck a mass of leathery wrinkles, sat on a bench talking with Liam O' Branigan. Her arthritic hands grasped a blackthorn stick a third again taller than the top of her head. She struggled to her feet and stood bent over, tiptoe to tiptoe with her visitor. Her hand moved wisps of gray hair falling from her bonnet as their conversation became animated. Seeing Rossa approach, O' Branigan turned shrugging his shoulders, hand gestures gave Rossa the impression of his being at a loss for what to do. He walked toward Rossa looking back at the woman who resumed her seat on the bench.

"She will not leave friend Rossa," he said. "She is alone and old, no family does she have...she said, 'I will trust in that God in heaven some talk about.' "If her heart tells her to stay, wise it would be for her to hide herself when the evictors arrive," Rossa replied. "She said death would be welcome if they arrive, the potato has gone away and she has no need for the plates in the cupboard," O' Branigan said, in an elegiac tone of voice. "Sure it is! I will tell her to hide herself in the brambles when the evictors arrive." Head down, he walked back to the cottage in need of thatch and stone, and the old woman on the bench. Rossa turned to look up the lane at the hill people who had gathered outside their huts. Women cried, children sniffled not knowing why their mother shed tears. Turf fires were left to burn to adhere to the centuries-old orders of the elders, a superstition to not let the home fire go out. Rossa balanced himself on a tree stump axed down years before for fuel or building material, he could only guess. Now, he watched them gather together with whatever possessions they could take with them. A cow was tied to the rear of a wagon, chickens poked heads out of crates, but a few of them had only a bundle tied to the end of a stick to carry over their shoulder. They were leaving. Siobhan O' Branigan fashioned a strap to carry the musket over her shoulder. Liam tied a rope to a trunk full of belongings. With the rope over his chest and under his arms he planned to drag the trunk to Ennis. As Rossa watched him test his means of transport, he immediately discarded the thought of using him to bring up the rear to assist any stragglers. After dropping the harness to the ground, O' Branigan looked toward Rossa with clouds of doubt covering his face.

"I hoped you might be able to help those who would find the journey difficult," Rossa said. "Your strength will wane quickly enough." "Aye, I will be at the rear soon enough," Liam admitted. Siobhan's attention turned from her husband to Rossa. "'Tis I who can assist any folk in need," Siobhan said as she appeared to be searching the crowd of villagers for a certain person. "I will find Mairead Mc Sween, and her sister, sure I know they would help. "I see them," she said adjusting the strap of the firearm as she made her way into the throng.

Finally realizing the life-threatening truth hill people had to make, they continued to run back inside their huts and cottages to retrieve a forgotten treasure.

BRIGANDS

While the people of the knocks were about to begin their exodus from a life they had always known, the brigands under the command of the ruthless landlord George Bingham were leaving behind the now half empty barrel of stout. A new purpose awaited them. They reveled in the enhanced lies and the horrible truths told from the lips of fellow boastful miscreants. There was no law this cabal of like-minded outlaws would follow as those who could author and enforce a law did not want to interfere with the power of the landlords. Whigs and Tories alike looked away allowing injustice after injustice. The drink enhanced their courage, the courage necessary to beat in the skull of a poor Irish peasant. Irish haters became angered when they could not find a tree from which to hang a man or woman while children watched. When a tree was found, they laughed and placed bets on how long it would take for the victims to die, when feet ceased reaching for the ground that was not there. An impatient Wallace Stroud could not wait for the march to begin. He had to be restrained by two men after an argument during a card game resulted in his opponent receiving a split lip and a broken front tooth.

"Save your aggression, Stroud," Bingham shouted while setting the overturned table back on its legs. "In due time you will have your pleasure." "Ready I am," Stroud shouted, raising his burled cudgel above his head. "Aye Wallace, we are with you," a militiaman responded, knowing the importance of being on the good side of Wallace Stroud. Shouts of support came as glasses were raised. Stroud's eyes scanned the occupied tables looking for anyone who didn't believe in the punishment he could inflict, and since the barrel still held almost half of its original content they would stay if Stroud was able to convince Bingham. Almost an hour passed before Bingham's chair legs left marks on the floor. He had no need to speak as ever so slowly his band of evictors left their seats. Bingham's enlisted force milled around outside until the driver moved the trap to the front. With a wave of his hand the march to the O' Branigan clan began, his mission to collect their delinquent rent. Obvious it was, George Bingham would not walk. His trap was ready with an ample supply of fine Irish whiskey, dried beef, and a wedge of Irish cheese.

"Pony and trap," one of them mumbled. He has a driver and a ride while we walk! Utter rubbish, I say," "'Tis crap, the trap," another responded. His attempt at humor was not well received as the other man pushed him, not gently, causing him to end up on the seat of his pants. He bounced up, his face a storm cloud, ready with clenched fists until Bingham ended the altercation. "Here, here you louts! Get along or leave I say." Evident was a twisted resemblance of camaraderie, even among thugs as two by two a grim-faced band of Irish haters followed the trap.

NEVER THE TWAIN SHALL MEET

Separated from Ennis by 15 miles of knocks and vale, the clan of the O' Branigan looked back with sorrow at the chimneys. White smoke rose to the heavens, before the huts and cottages of their former village left their sight. Grim faced and silent, their heads turned away having seen their hovel for the last time. The women cried. When tears were wiped away idle talk between neighbors and friends resumed in their language, at times interspersed with the English words they knew, verified by the nodding of heads or smiles as though something important had been understood. The downward slope was overgrown with lush grasses where whitewashed cottages built so close together it reminded Rossa of the mother leading her ducklings to the river. Cattle and sheep grazed within a stones' throw of limestone barriers marking the boundaries of a half-acre or a full acre parcel. Rossa viewed other cottages built from sod and thatch. Many had a potato garden within several feet of the front half door. *How could they... Rossa's* thoughts centered on how those cottagers could scratch out a living on such a small parcel of conacre land. Ahead, their journey would take them over a gurgling stream at the vale of the knock where a taxing effort would begin to traverse their next challenge. At the front of the que a small narrow bridge was just wide enough to allow a wagon to cross. Water rushed under the bridge between clumps of what once consisted of tall lush dark green grasses now faded, color lost from the constant rush of rainwater from above. Beyond their next challenge level grassland waited for them. Many minutes later Rossa was passed by a small cart being pushed by a bearded man and two young men aged 11 or 12 Rossa estimated. When asked, they said the horse had died on the way leaving them no alternative but to push. They were the last except for Siobhan O' Branigan who held the firearm in both hands in a white knuckled grip. She would often shoulder the weapon and sight down the barrel as she walked.

"What is it you see Siobhan O' Branigan? Is it a red deer or a mad dog you would kill?" "I have been told there are mad dogs and devils in red that I could kill," she said as she slung the musket over her shoulder. "Should it not fire, I would run them through with the knife (bayonet) on the end," she said as she removed the firearm from her shoulder, thrusting it forward to demonstrate. Rossa had to move a step but would not have been impaled. The expression on her face told him her statement was made with no lack of reserve. Rossa grinned at her, somewhat astonished by her show of militancy. "Be it a blessing the Brits will not cross your path" Rossa said. She turned away seeing her husband gesturing for her to catch up. Rossa watched her leave, and as if to reinforce her surprising show of animosity, her head snapped back toward him, her unsmiling face projecting not a hint of facetious jest.

Ahead of them lay the village of Clonie, the main street being better described as a rutted path captured on each side by three or four buildings painted in bright colors of red, yellow and blue. Rossa led the refugees on a route that would take them through the very ravine now occupied by D'Arcy McGee and his volunteers.

FLYNN'S EMERGENCE

"I will send Paddy Rinn back to you," Flynn said while adjusting the leather strap holding his rifle. "I leave to do a "reconnaissance," he said, using the French word causing Tom Steele to react not understanding the meaning. "Well it would be to have a second rifle with me McGee. I have powder and rounds for both." Tom Steele and McGee exchanged glances. "A strategy I have formed. It will do well for you and the hill folk," Flynn said. Tom Steele handed Flynn the second weapon. "Be wary in your travel and proceed with stealth and caution," McGee responded. Flynn departed much too quickly in the mind of McGee who thought *would he want to single-handedly insure safe passage for the clan?* They watched him leave with two rifles slung over his shoulder, his shoulder bag resting on his hip, the bottom tied with a leather strap around his thigh. "I see the sheathed knives he has strapped to himself," Tom Steele remarked. "Witness I have been to his proficiency with the knife," McGee answered. "He appears to be more than a fishmonger, more than a shepherd, and more than an entertainer or a showman on this day. He is a Legionnaire who walks away from us. 'Tis a memory he needs to erase. His past life so far distant from his life today, a herder of sheep, one who cleans salmon and herring for the love of his wife and children...a life of seclusion and calm." McGee mused, almost to himself. He considered if he was a little jealous of not having a life free of political activism that had little effect on the changes sought by Gavan Duffy and Daniel O'Connell.

A mile into his journey Flynn thought of ridding himself of the boots, remembering how Margaret in an earlier time, ridiculed him for being a typical hard-headed Irishman who disregarded the safety of heavy leather footwear. "Hard it would be to love a man with ugly bruises and bleeding cuts on his feet," she said. Flynn remembered her words. Her sarcasm was always followed by her coming to him, her arms around his neck, her body pressing into him. She finally convinced him when his route to the Foley cottage on the lakeshore hid jagged rock in the tall grasses. He avoided most of them with one remembered exception that convinced him to wear the boots. Margaret knowingly smiled. Today he was older and somewhat wiser. He dismissed the thought to be replaced by the one that continued to haunt him though not as often now. His hands went to his temples trying to block the pain that would come remembering the docks at Vera Cruz where he lay injured and helpless agonizing over the flames, and the screams he heard from the children trapped. The doors had been locked and the building set afire. Two men in his company had been killed. French trade interests were being disrupted by gangs of ruthless pirates. His head throbbed. Bent over, his hands on his knees he tried to focus and finally he could see the tousled gray head of Paddy Rinn seated with his arm and elbow resting on a chunk of granite that resembled a square box. Flynn's mind conjured a fog enshrouded tabletop holding plates, cups and saucers. The plate held steaming Colcannon with crispy bacon. His stomach could 'waken the dead. His shoulder begged for relief from the unfamiliar leather straps that chaffed skin under his wool shirt. Years before he had shouldered a weapon, but never two. Paddy Rinn concentrated on what might be approaching, unaware of Flynn behind him. Flynn stopped, watching the back of Rinn's head move from one sight line to another. He kicked a chunk of stone in his direction. Rinn's reaction was one of startled surprise. "Back to McGee I was going to send you," Flynn said. "However, I could use a man who can reload a weapon. Will you accompany me? We may intercept the brigands of the march to the O' Branigan hillside." "Should they see us, we two would be at their mercy, and they have none I hear," Rinn said. "I would show no mercy to them," Flynn immediately responded, his unsmiling face inches from the nose of Paddy Rinn who took a wide-eyed step back in response to Flynn's passionate statement. "Our route would take us through the hills and rocks near the cliff." Flynn argued. "The village of Clonie lies beyond the rough terrain. The hills will hide us, and then we will wait. I have a suspicion the brigands will invade the town, and when they do..."

Flynn's unfinished statement might have resurrected the same memory he coped with earlier when his mind took him unwillingly back to Vera Cruz where he lay wounded. Tormented for years by what he could not forget, he now had the opportunity to right an unforgivable episode in a former life.

"Sure as the Pope is in Rome you want me to leave this land of green to visit St. Peter at the pearly gates? Not many years do I have left O'Connell. Twenty years past, I would go with you but not this day...and you should be wary yourself," Paddy Rinn said, nodding his head emphatically. He ran fingers through uncombed hair before turning away to return to the ambush party who waited.

CLONIE

The grumbling continued. Darkness of night came and went hours ago, and the sun shone brightly, exceedingly warm on the faces of George Bingham's Irish haters who often had to pause in the march to relieve themselves of massive amounts of stout consumed earlier. To their left was the little village of Clonie, population 106 not including cats and dogs. Neat cottages flanked the business places on the main street. Heads focused on the town knowing every little village, no matter how small, had a public house where thirst could be quenched. The temptation was quite near to Wallace Stroud. Being at the front of the marchers he stepped to the side finding a rock to stand on facing Bingham's band of enforcers. His abrupt exit from the line caused the march to halt. The exception being the cart of George Bingham. Not knowing the march behind them had stopped, the driver and Bingham continued the journey until Bingham heard Stroud's voice. He grabbed the driver's shoulder, shouting "Stop I say, stop!" The driver who may have been half asleep pulled on the reins. Stroud looked to the sound as if it were an interruption, interference with an issue of monumental importance.

"Aye lads hear me! Who is with me to call on the good publican in the village?" Bingham stood up in the cart on hearing Stroud's request to see four of his militia leave the line to join Stroud. "I hear you Stroud, a mighty thirst I have in this hot sun" Mick Bradley, an

Irish militiaman said. Mick had no allegiances or religion. He learned to accept what he participated in as being the "status quo." If there was coin to be made to fill his pockets, he would quickly offer his services to whoever would furnish him the price of a pint or two or three. Bingham stood, leaning on a cane watching the proceedings.

"All of you, an hour you have in the town, that is all. Our mission will not be thwarted by your need for a pint!" He watched his minions scramble their way towards Clonie, the residents unaware of what was to come from the intrusion of a band of thugs. Resuming his seat, Bingham urged the driver to follow his enforcers into the peaceful village of Clonie. When the trap arrived outside the Clonie pub he glanced up at the sign over the doors. The carved lettering spelled the name HEAVEN IS LOST, M. McQuillan, Prop. Scratched letters under the name issued a warning. The advice read; *For all those who enter here.* The warning dared those whose thirst overcame their fear of God or the unknown. Under the protection of the trap's roof Bingham made his bulky body comfortable while the drive tended to the horse. Bingham sipped on a crystal glass containing a bit of the liquid he favored while away from the company of the Queen's politicians.

An apron clad Martin McQuillan, Marty to the locals, was behind the bar when the front doors burst open to admit a mixture of boisterous revelers. Four or five others who staggered in were identified by McQuillan as obviously hung over from previous imbibing. Chair legs scraped the floor as seats in the bar soon were filled by the invaders. Across the room, three normally friendly outgoing locals watched the strangers enter while they exchanged nervous glances. They leaned toward each other, whispering their fear of this group of strangers who emitted a sense of foreboding the moment they pushed their way into the quiet tavern.

+

Paddy Rinn regretted his decision to join the mission. He had too many aches and pains recently. At 52 years old his feet hurt, and he walked favoring his left leg. *O'Connell is addled. To venture alone into a den of vipers is not the action of a rational Irishman.* A half mile ahead the sun caught the metal of a musket barrel. *Surprise would be lost if weapons were not protected from detection,* he thought. "What did you see?" The sentry's question drew only the negative shake of Paddy Rinn's gray head as he passed by. "Why is O'Connell not with you?" McGee asked, while walking quickly toward Rinn. "Not of sound mind he is," Rinn uttered. "I suspect he will go to Clonie. He is of the mind the evictors thirst will take them into the town. He asked me, Paddy Rinn to go with him to reload!" He spoke indignantly while pounding his chest with his fist. "You, without a doubt thought better of it and returned to the safety of numbers," McGee said, his forehead wrinkled in thought. Rinn walked away finding a rock where he sat bending over to loosen the laces on his boots. Tom Steele left his position approaching McGee, his eyes questioned. "The legionnaire mind of friend O'Connell concerns me Tom Steele. Paddy Rinn is convinced Flynn will travel into Clonie where he thinks the evictors will stop to quench their thirst. I am nearly convinced we should not linger here a moment longer and follow Flynn to Clonie. "If Flynn's instincts prove right, he will walk himself into a den of murderers," Tom Steele responded. "Even if we wait here, we do nothing! A confrontation may not occur. We should abandon this site and go in support of the man with the premonition," he continued. "We must be active, the aggressor," Tom Steele shook his fist. Steele's reaction startled McGee. "Gather the men around me Tom. They should know of our change in plans and be given the opportunity to withdraw their support," McGee ordered.

+

At the same time McGee outlined his change in plans to the volunteers, miles away Flynn O'Connell climbed to the top of a granite outcropping. Lying prone, he watched for movement in the far distance. Satisfied that he could proceed on a route that provided a little cover of his movements, he made his way down tearing a shirt sleeve in the process.

+

"We have come this far. We remain with you McGee," Liam Kennedy stood with his brother, nodding their support. "As do I, Paddy Rinn said, and shouts of support came. Those who had muskets raised them in the air. Those who had a shillelagh raised them up with both hands. "Ready yourselves," McGee told them as he turned to sweep the horizon from his vantage point in one last assurance that his leadership would not be compromised by an unforeseen disruption. He stopped, squinting when he caught movement heading in their direction. Across the plain he saw carts, wagons, animals and people headed for the rocky ravine they were about to vacate. Tom Steele climbed up to see what attracted McGee's attention. "Aye McGee, I see them," he said while shading his eyes. Two people led the way toward them, and as they came closer McGee identified Rossa who was next to a woman who shouldered a rifle musket. "Without a doubt it is. Rossa leads the hill people," McGee said. "They have abandoned their homes to escape the horror of being evicted."

MEETING

Flynn was alone in his, some would say foolhardy objective. He was soon to arrive at a possible conflict, but unknown to him McGee, with his volunteers had changed plans that brought them less than a mile behind Flynn. Not wanting to be delayed, Flynn paused when sad faced people crossed in front of him with nary a glance in his direction on their way to a destination only, they knew. Babies cried, their way of telling all their bellies were empty. Flynn recalled the trips with Devon to the route used by poor Irish who appreciated the food Flynn and Devon provided. Tall grasses and brambles made Flynn's walk in a straight line impossible. With the sun over his shoulder, he would arrive at the outskirts of Clonie. A line of poorly clothed peasants passed, the last, a young man directing a brown and white cow ahead of him. Flynn used the stoppage to turn to face the direction he had vacated two hours before. Specks moved causing Flynn to squint not quite believing what he saw. He waited, not sure if he was witnessing another march to freedom from oppression. *Was McGee and his cadre changing plans? Have they given up their plan to ambush the eviction mob? Not better described other than with the term "horde."*

AN HOUR OF TERROR

Sweat began to dot the brow of Marty McQuillan as he tried to satisfy the requests of so many impatient strangers. To draw a pint of the stout properly was not worth the wait to some who changed their demand. A fist pounded the bar. Whiskey, the "water of life" to some, was demanded by a scowling invader. "Provide me a wee bit of patience lads?" McQuillan stared down the three strangers who continued to grumble at the end of the bar. Colum Daniel, one of the locals, left his friends at the table to offer his assistance. McQuillan pointed to the tap where the three men waited, insisting on a pint of stout no matter how long it took. That mere second of inattention caused him to tip over a half full glass. He wiped his forehead as a disgruntled customer slammed down coin on the bar, payment for his second glass. "Well worth the wait it will be," Colum Daniel said sliding the first mug toward a waiting hand, "and what brings you to our fair town?" "Enlisted we are to do a great service," one of the three said. "And what might that great service be, if you don't mind my interest?" Colum Daniel asked as he slid the next pint to another outstretched hand. "We head to the knocks! On a sun filled afternoon where freckled faces fear our arrival," a grinning evictor shouted as he looked around for support raising his glass as he did. His attention returned to Colum Daniel. The evictor's face inches and unsmiling from that of the man who had drawn his pint. Colum Daniel's eyes did not blink. The man turned away raising his glass. "To the knocks," he

407

shouted. A chorus of "ayes" erupted from the invaders. All had been served allowing Marty McQuillan to take a deep breath, to wipe his brow again, and to serve a third whiskey to a fellow who thought "the hair of the dog" was the best remedy for excessive imbibing the previous evening. Colum Daniel returned to rejoin his friends at the table in the corner. With forearms on the table, and hands and fingers intertwined he leaned forward to whisper. "I fear for the villagers, the O' Branigans, the hill people. Not far away from us they are. These rogues, his eyes moved around the room as he talked, are on their way to do harm." Heads leaning forward, furtive glances, and whispering among the locals attracted the attention of several of the invaders who had grown tired of their harassment of Marty McQuillan, under assault by a force of unfriendly and menacing strangers. Wallace Stroud grew tired of his constant complaints and harassment of the barkeep. When Marty's back was turned a mug would fall to the floor, or an unguarded glass would suddenly spill its contents. Several witnesses laughed. His torment was seen by the locals who were not party to abusive conduct. They didn't say a word. Stroud's attention was now focused on the tables occupied by Clonie citizens and, the table occupied by Colum Daniel and two others. He strolled toward the table then stopped behind the chair of Colum Daniel rocking back and forth while twirling his stick, whistling a tune only he knew.

"What say you Irishman?" He poked the back of Colum with his stick. A hush suddenly permeated the barroom, as if a summer breeze had suddenly died to be replaced by the ominous formation of billowing black clouds in the western sky. Chair legs groaned and screeched as Colum Daniel slid his chair back. He rose to face Stroud, his nose the length of a hand from the stick wielding Wallace Stroud. "A cowardly excuse for a man you must be to brandish a blackthorn in the face of another man...Sir!" Colum Daniel was not cowed. "What are you sir...without your crutch?" The silence in the public house was interrupted by a muffled giggle from one of Bingham's volunteers.

"He called Stroud sir," whispered the one who giggled while he tried to stifle another laugh. Stroud's head whipped around at the sound searching for the culprit. Eyes turned away from his steely eyed accusation. Holding his stick in a threatening manner, Stroud returned his attention to Colum Daniel. His face was a storm cloud, billowing, darkening, and then he swung the stick. With and agility and speed unknown to Stroud, Colum Daniel intercepted the stick he now held in his hands. Colum Daniel's possession of the stick that seconds before had been on its way to spill the brains of another Irishman brought a look of incredulous surprise to Stroud's face. His mouth dropped open watching the stick's new owner place it on the table. As he attempted to reach for it, the fist of Colum Daniel found the midsection of the bully who bent over in agony and in time to receive a bare-knuckled blow to his jaw. Another fist followed the second sending Stroud stumbling backwards where he landed on a table vacated by two associates who scattered just in time. The table collapsed on top of the bully who groaned from underneath the table top. He had just been introduced to Ireland's reigning bare-knuckled boxing champion in seven southern counties. Colum Daniel stood with fists clenched held in front of his face, the classic stance of an experienced boxer ready for all comers.

Marty McQuillan had seen enough! "Not all of you ruffians have paid, and you know who you are and what you owe! Leave your coin on the bar and please me to leave my once peaceful house!" To emphasize his demand he mounted a chair, climbed up to the bar with a long-barreled pistol in his hand. Grumbling commenced, but chairs slid back as two of the brigands searched pockets for coin. Chairs were tipped over in their haste after they saw the pistol. All but one had now paid, and he headed for the door where George Bingham stood stopping each man with his outstretched arm. "Have you paid the man?" He asked the man who had not paid. With a defiant look and a surly tone, he said, "Grog it was! I would not pay for grog." "You are here because I did not get paid. I expect to get paid, and when I do not, I will collect the debt! See the pistol he holds! Others drank what you say is the grog. Pay him now!" Bingham concluded while pushing the man away. He watched him head toward the bar before turning on his heel leaving to return to his seat while the driver waited for instructions.

+

Hidden by tall grasses, Flynn watched for any movement or sign the eviction force had reached Clonie. Absorbed in his surveillance he didn't notice what was taking place behind him until he felt a hand on his shoulder.

"Come back with me," McGee said. "Stay low lest we be discovered." He shouldered one of the weapons Flynn carried. Many minutes later both arrived out of breath to rejoin the encampment of the volunteer rescue party. McGee and the volunteers waited to allow Rossa and the O' Branigan clan to catch up before resuming their march toward Ennis. Hundreds of yards ahead lay the town and the main street of Clonie. McGee walked with Flynn and Rossa far ahead of a staggered line of carts and wagons, a cow or two or three, one with a calf, pigs, dogs and grim-faced people with confused children who could be seen sniffling most with tear streaked faces. Often the three stopped to look back at the refugees in a line stretching for hundreds of yards.

"Nothing is left for them. They have nothing to return to. No need is there for blood to be shed! Bingham is welcome to what remains on the hillside," Flynn said. "We have sufficient strength to allow our march through the center of town. No sign of Bingham

411

did I see, but they are headed our way. If we encounter them, they will see who follows and will have no reason to engage us in any aggressive action." "We have a militant firebrand among us," Rossa said, his head motioned to his left where Siobhan O' Branigan walked with a stride that displayed her determined purpose, the rifle musket strapped to her back. "I will speak to her, Flynn said. "Consumed with anger and hatred she is, and I fear she will cause blood to be shed. However, not a waste it would be, if she were to send one of those brigands to hell," Rossa said. Heads nodded in agreement.

"Let us caution her now, I should accompany you," Rossa said. "Wrong I was to show her how to shoot. I should have taken possession of the weapon!" The crest of a rise in the landscape was reached as he spoke. Ahead of them lay the little village of Clonie. McGee's hand was raised to signal a stop. He pointed to the stragglers at the rear. "Wait we will to allow them to close ranks before we proceed." Carts and wagons groaned and rattled toward McGee. Flynn and Rossa, who were standing out of sight of the village often were attracted to the sounds emanating from the procession of people and animals. The snort of always hungry pigs caged seemed forever tormented by dogs allowed to run loose overwhelmed the sound of ungreased wheels. *Should they be in Clonie they will hear us coming.* McGee's thoughts were distracted as he watched hungry children clutching skirts followed by the elderly who always were at the rear of a clan family. A clan woman with skirts raised hastened away from her group speaking in Gaelic to explain she had to find a sheltered spot to relieve herself "before she burst." Her explanation brought brief laughter. They watched her disappear behind tall grass and shrubbery before watchers were drawn to see a young pig being attacked by hungry dogs. The pig escaped its confinement, but now the pig regretted his escape, failing to outrun a dog that had his jaws clamped on a leg causing squeals of pain. The pig's owner used his staff to jab at the dog that released its grip on the pig in favor of the staff inflicting pain to his ribs. The pig ran off followed by two barking dogs that nipped repeatedly at the pig's legs. Younger clan children were able to distract the dogs after an exhausted pig stopped likely wishing he had never been tempted to leave the safety of his makeshift pen.

Meanwhile, a heavily loaded wagon became lodged in a muddy, water filled hole. One wheel was submerged to the hub, the other rear wheel was lifted off the ground and the wagon tipped precariously. The old mare was not strong enough to pull it free as the wagon's owner decided to unload the cargo to help free the wagon with the help of two O' Branigan clan villagers. Distracted by the frantic activity, it was not until Liam O' Branigan hurried to Rossa's side, pointing toward Clonie that Rossa knew another problem had surfaced. "Siobhan is gone," he exclaimed, wide eyed and pointing. McGee shook his head. "Go after her we must before she causes trouble and gets killed in the process," he said. "Stay here with the clan, Liam. We will find her and bring her back."

Pleased by her ability to free herself from the main body, Siobhan stopped to rest hidden behind a Blackthorn shrub out of sight of her husband, and eyes in Clonie that would discover her only 300 yards away. She watched as men exited a building to stand around waiting with hands in pockets, kicking dirt on each other's boots. *I will kill the fat one next to the trap.* Now rested, she decided to crawl to the protection of a solitary, misshapen beech tree not more than 50 yards from the nearest building in the town. She crawled but soon became exhausted from the effort. Little food had passed her lips the last two days. She rose to her feet, bent over she hurried to the shelter of the beech. The tree bore remnants of prior use bringing shivers to the clan woman. Tattered remains of a noose hung, swaying gently in a light afternoon breeze.

Yet to be noticed by the eviction party, Flynn, McGee and Rossa spotted Siobhan crawling toward a tree that offered the only cover available before arriving at the main street leading into Clonie. Bending low, they crept forward just as Siobhan shouldered the rifle musket, ready to fire. Dispensing with caution, McGee leaped ahead to grab the barrel just as the trigger was pulled. The sound reverberated alerting the mob milling around in the street. Three of the evictors ran back inside the "Heaven is Lost Pub." "You may have started a small war Siobhan O' Branigan." McGee wrested the weapon from her hands as a round scarred the gray bark spraying splinters, and then came the sound. All three dropped to the ground. "How many weapons do you see Flynn?" Flynn raised his head to see the one who fired in the process of reloading his weapon. A second muzzle poked out from behind the trap hiding Bingham and the armed evictor. "I see two and we have four," Flynn replied. Lying prone he shouldered the rifle remembering after many years what the French Foreign Legion taught him. He squeezed the trigger. The sound came to them of the round hitting metal, causing the evictor to scream an expletive dropping the weapon to the ground. "Now there is one," Flynn said, moving to align himself toward the second gunman. Two men ran to their comrade who had fired dragging him behind the trap. The weapon was retrieved and examined before the evictor threw it to the ground. Flynn's shot had rendered it useless. "Your aim was true, friend Flynn," Rossa said, reaching his arm around to pat O'Connell on the back. "Time it is for us to resume our journey. We should summon the clan to come forward. The evictor horde is in disarray. Another volley or two from us shall scatter the brigands for sure." Flynn expressed his confidence as he finished reloading. His second attempt was intentional. The shot scattered dirt frightening the trap horse that reared up and ran several steps exposing the trap's rider and the gunman to Flynn's marksmanship. They ran for the safety inside the only pub in Clonie. The pub door slammed shut behind Bingham, his driver and three evictors. Seconds became minutes before the door re-opened. Through the door stepped Bingham unarmed with his hands raised above his head. His driver followed holding a musket in two hands resting it against his thighs. He walked not hesitantly toward the beech tree "He wants to negotiate," Flynn said. "Who will step out among our three?" Flynn asked. McGee scrambled to his feet. "If you see the weapon pointed at me, you know what to do," he said as he pointed toward the musket carrier. Flynn nodded, "Aye McGee, we want no more blood spilled," Rossa added. McGee stepped away from the tree advancing to within earshot of the man who appeared to be acting as the leader of the eviction party. His eyes searched for activity at the pub ready to drop if he saw a rifle barrel. "We are leading the hill people, the O' Branigan clan to Ennis. They are behind us, all of them with one exception. The woman is old and unable to travel she is. She has put herself in the hands of the merciful one. If you come upon her please show her the same consideration. The potato is diseased. They have no money for the rent so there is no reason for them to stay and subject themselves to cruel eviction proceedings. We have an armed force behind us, and I see you have only one weapon. Please us and bring the weapon to me. Once we pass it will be returned to you. We have three rifles at the tree. One of them is an excellent marksman. We are going to pass through Clonie. Do not give us a reason to kill you." Bingham turned on his heel then stopped. With his hands in his pockets he turned back.

"You have the advantage. We will not interfere." Bingham turned away heading back to the Heaven Is Lost public house. McGee watched him leave as a shadow passed by him in full flight. He stopped, unbelieving at what he witnessed. The O' Branigan woman ran at red deer speed toward George Bingham. Her hand, raised above her head, held a long knife. Hearing her scream of rage, Bingham turned to see a poorly dressed woman intent on making him the target of the long blade she held above her head. He turned and ran as fast as his rotund body would allow for the safety of the pub. Her focus was so intent, her exposed breast caused her no concern. The man with the weapon brought it to his shoulder, but hurried by the need for haste, he had trouble with the mechanism and could not fire the weapon. The pub door opened too late for the absentee landlord who collapsed across the threshold with the handle of a long knife protruding from his shoulder. Consumed with rage, Siobhan O' Branigan used both hands to pull the knife free. Removal of the knife brought a painful groan from Bingham who tried to raise himself with his right hand. Two of his evictors inside pulled him across the threshold causing a scream of pain from the injured landlord. The knife wielding peasant woman turned her attention to the driver who assumed he had fixed the problem with the musket. He raised the weapon as she ran toward him waving the knife. Later, all would learn she had tied the knife to her thigh. His musket discharged harmlessly just prior to his face meeting damp earth from Flynn O'Connell's intervention. He was knocked to the ground sending his weapon flying to be retrieved by Rossa. The driver, hands raised, and eyes wide stumbled his way toward the door. Very cautiously, not knowing what to expect, McGee approached the clan woman who appeared overcome with emotion. Bent over, her hands on her knees, raspy sobs came as tears dripped to the ground from eyes and then cheeks creased by years older than what should have been. The knife lay in the dirt of the street, its variety of uses yet to be fully realized. McGee kicked it away.

"Siobhan, Siobhan..." McGee shook her, his hands lifted her to stand, "Go back to your husband. Find Tom Steele. Tell him to lead your people to us. Safe it is to proceed to Clonie. Bring everyone back, we will wait," Rossa instructed, watching a dejected Siobhan who only wanted to kill an Englishman, wipe her tears away. She glared at McGee, and he noticed. "Luck it is you missed the target Siobhan. He is still alive." She continued to glare, but turned, shuffling her way back to her husband and the refugees from the hillside.

Tom Steele and Liam O' Branigan lay at the apex of the slight rise in the terrain watching what transpired just outside of the town. Siobhan O' Branigan came into view among the blackthorn and the high grass. Liam rose to his feet, his facial features changed with the emotions that conflicted within him. Relief, happiness, irritation, and anger all came in one moment to be replaced by another until the reigning emotion controlled his thought process. His arms opened to receive her. For a moment no words came, but then a sudden cloud burst of emotion erupted. Soft words, lyrical in the sound of their language, were accompanied by the unspoken word conveyed by the silent language of the body, hands reaching, heads shaking, bowing, shoulders shrugging all told of a quiet reconciliation. Her tears came again, but flowed for only an instant, a star's winking, for there was no time for her or them. Reluctantly, she released from him to relay the message she carried.

Tom Steele hurried back along the line of carts, wagons, and occasional cow or ewe to advise the march to Ennis was to resume. "To travel on the main road through Clonie is better than fighting our way through bramble and blackthorn, rocks and pools of water hidden by grass," he remarked more than once on his way to the end of the caravan. Many of the hill people who heard his word didn't understand. They would turn to one another in hopes someone understood what he was saying. A few did, and Tom Steele saw in the bi-lingual ones a fervent desire to continue their journey, no matter the outcome. If seated, they stood ready talking their language while Tom Steele continued to point, to windmill his arms providing more understanding than his English words spoken in a heavy Irish brogue. McGee's volunteers gathered around an out of breath Tom Steele for instructions.

"You Kennedy boys," Steele jabbed a finger, "take the lead with your weapon held at the ready." All others should spread out on either side of the wagons and carts. If you have a cudgel or ax handle or any weapon, display it prominently." The caravan was ready to move as Steele raised his arm, then wind-milled the message to renew the march through Clone and then to Ennis. Liam O' Branigan, free of the trunk thanks to a neighbor who made space on his cart, joined the Kennedy's and his wife at the front of the column. Resumption of the march did not agree with some of the village people or the animals. After walking for hours, children and their mothers were tired from herding animals, avoiding thorns, retrieving goods that had fallen off carts. The all too brief respite from the march was not enough time to regain enough strength to continue for many of the elderly.

Mayhem erupted when the old mare, pulling the overloaded wagon, collapsed in its harness and died. An argument ensued when it was suggested the mare be butchered for the meat. Both distractions allowed a cow to wander off, and a woman's scream came when her 5-year old daughter was nowhere to be found. A search party was quickly formed. Many minutes later bawls of the Guernsey trapped in the brambles were heard. She was found and returned to the owner, but the search continued for the little girl. While searchers tramped through tall grass, blackberry and bramble, the vocal fellow who argued for butchering the horse watched as two clan men with experience did their best with sharpened knives. While they worked, they were forced to listen to the vocal fellow pontificate on the best way to carve the meat away from the bone. "Cut closer, with a wee bit of patience," he would say. He departed when one of the butchers, tired of the diatribe, rose to his feet waving the bloody butcher knife in his direction. Aoife Mallow, the lost little girl was found near massive granite outcroppings wrapped in her blanket with one of the clan dogs at her side. She was fast asleep. Attracted by the activity behind them, bringing the march to a stop, Paddy and Liam Kennedy looked to Tom Steele for approval of the need to investigate. "Go" was his answer.

Leaving their weapons, the brothers hurried back to see what had happened, and to offer their assistance. It was at that moment they heard the woman scream, shouting in Gaelic, "My baby, my baby, gone she is." Her cry received no response from able bodies who conferred around the wagon with the dead horse. They argued on what should be done as the Kennedy's passed by. *Do they not care about a lost child?" Liam thought.* Paddy Kennedy tried to reassure her with his English words she, of course did not understand, but she recognized his sincere demeanor, and was calmed. Other clan members gathered around speaking to her in Gaelic. Her nod and the hint of a smile gave her confidence in their message, "We will look for her and bring her back to you." Searchers moved away, 3 on one side of the caravan, Liam and his brother on the other. No one remembered to ask the child's name, but their shouts would attract the little girl's attention. Searchers fought their way through thorny brambles reaching out to tear at unprotected hands. "Aowee." A yell of sudden pain came from Liam Kennedy. Following the sound, Paddy Kennedy found his brother wrapping his wrist with cloth torn from his shirt. "Soon it is I hope to find the wandering little one," Liam said clutching his wrist with his other hand. "Hard to avoid are the blackberries taller than a man." "Better a hillside strewn with rocks and blackened potatoes," Paddy replied. "Sure it is, the O' Branigan clan would admire you for your wit and jest," Liam said after tying a knot on the bandage with his teeth and a free hand bleeding red from scratches of its own. Paddy examined the repair. Looking away, he pointed to the rocks, "You go that way, I will search to the left. She can't far away." More careful now Liam headed toward the granite taking a route that wandered because he had to stop at times to judge which path between which pair of brambles would take him to the rocks. *'Tis like an endless maze without an escape*, he thought. Tempted, he stopped again to pick fat blackberries, the branch drooping from the weight of the fruit.

The wayward Guernsey was found, swishing her tail and chewing contentedly. The dead horse was relieved of palatable meat to be salt cured or eaten before spoilage came. Aoife Mallow, the little girl lost was found by Liam Kennedy and returned to her mother. Chaos was avoided, and calm came over the caravan as Tom Steele urged the hill people at the front to resume their trek. The slight slope downward toward Clonie was not as overgrown and made for easier movement to the main street. Rossa and McGee met the caravan half way while Flynn O'Connell kept watch for movement at the Heaven Is Lost public house.

Rossa handed his musket to Tom Steele. "I must prepare in Ennis with the Friars. We have three hundred men, women, and children under our watchful eye. I will arrive ahead of you to have time to prepare for your arrival. Liam O' Branigan and his wayward wife joined McGee, O'Connell and Tom Steele at what was known as the water wagon. Barrels were attached to each side of the wagon. Liam O' Branigan, now ever watchful of his wife who lifted the ladle filled to the brim water spilling out when McGee met her gaze with his. "Darkness will cover us when we arrive," McGee said. She offered the tin to McGee and then to Rossa before refilling to offer Flynn and Tom Steele. *A peace offering?* McGee considered. Flynn refilled the ladle, offering it to the woman and her husband. Still, she did not smile. With his glance to the sky, Rossa saw the grayness of the early afternoon provide a background for the white clouds moving in from the west. Adjusting his shoulder bag, he made eye contact with each of them before he turned to look toward Clonie. Nothing was said. His walk became a trot. Two hours at his current pace would find him in Ennis.

The march resumed and stretched the length of a football field even after attempts to close ranks were made. McGee had positioned himself between the clan marchers and the tavern. He held the captured musket in both hands watching as members of the eviction party stood or sat on the stoop of the tavern. They hooted and howled, offering insulting comments laced with profanity meant to be heard by all as they passed by. Flynn O'Connell joined McGee just as a young girl wrestled herself away from another's attempt at restraint to rush toward the tavern where she stopped to scoop a handful of mud from a convenient puddle. She hurled the handful toward her target not watching to see the result, frantically retracing her steps, fearful of retaliation. Drippy mud splattered the boots of one of the brigands who feigned a three-step chase after the foolish little girl. Doors were opened by shop owners and town residents who watched silently as men, women, and children walked head down through the town with nary a glance at those who watched the procession splash through puddles down the main street still wet and muddy from an early shower. An eerie silence was broken only by the snort of a pig, and the creaking of wagon wheels as marchers made their way through the town. Even the taunting derisive comments from the eviction party ceased as they watched raggedly clothed hill people walk dejectedly, some with tears tracking down wrinkled cheeks.

+

Rossa's trot became a walk as his mind fought emotions ranging from sadness and despair to elation, then to hope when he thought of the circumstances surrounding the plight of the clan O' Branigan. *Forced to leave the only home they had ever known, what must be going through their minds, sadness for leaving but what were they leaving behind...nothing was back there on that hillside. The potato was diseased, no work was there to be had...the rent had not been paid, and for some, for the last two seasons.* He hoped most of them would look forward to a new beginning, especially the younger men and women and the poor children, *the children,* he increased his pace.

What Rossa didn't know was preparations for their arrival in Ennis was started by the monks. Building materials collected included stone for the walls to become modest cottages. Ennis volunteers, men and women with gnarled hands, and split nails completed the walls of the first cottage. Reed from the river was collected by young children for the cottage roof. Contests began as children soon filled a rack of reed to cover several cottages under construction. A resettlement agreement was negotiated with a compassionate landlord who recognized the value of the industrious Irish. Their work would make him a wealthy man. Women and children would be housed temporarily until the healthy men and women of the clan could complete new cottages already begun by the dedicated, brown robed devotees to their God. Sod was being turned for gardens. A new community would soon be born. Rossa's mind raced, but his pace slowed to a walk...and then when his feet demanded relief, he kneeled next to a welcome invitation in a grassy depression promising waters many uses. Eyes of a frog peered at him as he leaned down swishing the still water with his fingertips. Cupping his hands, he drank his fill. Reluctantly, the frog decided to leave its comfort. Rossa splashed a little to remove the sweat. At times, his effort dripped from the bridge of his nose causing him to shake his head. Thankful for the brief respite, for the moment off his feet, his search of the surroundings revealed only a red deer, its nose raised in alarm catching scent of him. Tightening the lacing on his boots, his journey resumed. One foot preceded the other, slowly at first, and soon it was, he ran.

MONTHS LATER

Flowers grew in a sunny spot in the cathedral cemetery, the gravesite of Martha Howe. Too young at age 48, she had passed away in her sleep. She was found by son Neil that morning when she, for the first time, was not the first to make her way down the stairs. Neil remembered her smile when he often paused at the last step watching silently while she heated the water and stoked the coals, always glancing at the stairs waiting for her family and any guests to arrive.

"She missed my Father," Neil explained to his grieving wife Silé, who visited the gravesite each week to weed and tend to the flowers. "But Neil, she so found happiness to think she would have our first born to tend?" He held her as tight as he could, but there were no words. Under Neil's direction, carpenters were busy building an addition to the Howe residence. In the future, the home would be transformed into a bed and breakfast with four additional rooms to greet the increasing tourist traffic each summer.

Expansion of Brendan's cottage was completed but was not as elaborate as what was a near palace he previously boasted to his new bride. He continued to reassure her but said the completion of a cottage for brother Donal was his priority. He boasted of the slate roof and the canopied bed with the overstuffed down mattress. Sally pouted for a time but understood privacy was lacking for all three with two of them married to each other. Sally returned to Clancy's Pub two days a week to resume her wait duties while Brendan and Donal delivered and took orders for the following week. Business increased dramatically during those two days much to the delight of the Publican and the male diners.

Flynn O'Connell returned to his simpler life. The life of a flax farmer, shepherd, and pork producer after Margaret threatened to have the hogs butchered if he didn't move the pig's pen farther away from the cottage. Margaret was pregnant again. She was shocked when Fiona Farrell told her she had put the mercantile up for sale. Fiona's second revelation was even more discouraging for Margaret. Fiona would be leaving for Dublin with Heather Anne, Sissy, and her new husband to be, the Englishman Doyle Wentworth. Devon O'Connell was upset to learn his friends Heather Anne and Sissy would be leaving. He moped, kicked dirt, and wandered around with his hands in pockets, head down looking totally lost. In addition to teaching Mary Margaret to ride, he was teaching Heather Anne and Sissy to ride the black horse named Jumper. Margaret was sure he had a special interest in Heather Anne who was older, more mature for her age than the younger Devon, who matured quickly in his own right, and was soon to inherit the symbol of Irish manhood, the shillelagh.

Still a young man, D'Arcy McGee solidified his stature as a writer and lecturer using his experience in America as a contributor, and later editor of the *Pilot* a newspaper aimed at the Irish population in Boston. On his return to Ireland he contributed to Gavan Duffy's and Young Ireland's journal, the *Nation.* He moved away from prior pursuits he considered dangerous to an equally dangerous profession of speaking out publicly and politically for Irish freedom and Catholic emancipation while keeping company with Mary Theresa Caffrey.

A new vicar had been appointed to oversee St. Mary's cathedral due to the death of Patrick Kincade who courageously fought against the disease that ravaged his once muscular body. Hundreds visited the cathedral before he was laid to rest under a huge oak. Flowers covered his gravesite, a tribute that may have evolved after Michael Collins was assassinated. Although Michael Collins was a Free-Stater, never a day passed since then when flowers covered his tomb in the Republican plot at Glasnevin Cemetery. He wanted freedom for the Irish people, even though that freedom would be indicated by an asterisk after the word.

Other novels by Rob Collins

A Cold Rain in Killarney, 1845

Cold Reign, 1846

CPSIA information can be obtained
at www.ICGtesting.com
Printed in the USA
BVHW031330310519
549793BV00001B/19/P